AF515527

Gems from World Literature

Gems from World Literature

The Greatest Italian Classics

Edited by

J.A. Hammerton

CRUST PUBLISHING HOUSE
G-2, 16 Ansari Road,
Darya Ganj, New Delhi-110 002

Published by Crest Publishing House
G-2, 16 Ansari Road
Darya Ganj, New Delhi - 110 002

The Greatest Italian Classics
ISBN 81-242-0479-9

First Crest Impression : 2004

Printed by Saurabh Printers Pvt Ltd
A-16, Sector IV, NOIDA 201 301

Editorial Board

Editorial Note

A SHORT story may be a mere anecdote of three hundred words or a work of ten or fifteen thousand. In content it may be anything from a glimpse of character, an incident, to a highly finished picture of life. But it should be a complete work of imagination, its effect achieved with a minimum of personages and events.

To select the best thousand examples was a task that could be achieved only on arbitrary lines. As to length, three thousand words was the ideal average, but this excluded some of the finest stories, so exceptions had to be allowed. National characteristics also had consideration. Another test was the value of a story as illustrating the development of the art.

PROBLEMS of arrangement were not entirely solved by classification according to the country of each writer's origin. This puts Richard Steele into the lrish volume and separates those ideal literary partners Agnes and Egerton Castle. But it is the best possible arrangement for the work, and the index makes reference easy. The inclusion of a series of stories of the War became possible when the War itself ruled out all modern German work.

A WORD as to the method of selection. The general editor prepared a trial list of titles, which was submitted to all the members of the Editorial Board, who rejected and added according to their individual tastes and knowledge, These individual lists were then collated and the final list evolved. The thousand stories selected are therefore representative of the combined opinion of the whole group of editors. A very few modifications of the final list were made necessary by difficulties of copyright and considerations of Anglo-Saxon taste in certain translations from foreign literatures.

MOST of the foreign stories have been specially translated, and all copyrights, in both stories and translations, the use of which authors and publishers have courteously permitted, are duly credited at the end of each volume.

J.A. HAMMERTON

Contents

CONTENTS

The Italian Story-Tellers

OF all writers of short stories, the Italians were the most fertile, the most sustained in creative impulse, and, from many points of view, the most interesting. For three and a half centuries their work was the image of the life around them, of its virtues and perversities, its stately splendours, its sombre tragedies, and its loose gaieties. No other school of writers in modern Europe has used the art of the short story for so long a period or with so varied a point of view. Every change in the manners and character of the Italian people, from the age of Dante to the age of the Medici Popes, is vividly mirrored in the little novels of Italy.

At the present time, the Italians scarcely rank among the supreme novelists of Europe. In both the novel and the short story their modern writers are surpassed by those of the French, the Anglo-Saxon, and the Germanic peoples. This is part of the price the Italians have to pay for that marvellous early flowering of their national genius which made their forefathers for three hundred years the leaders in nearly every field of civilisation. There are many signs that the creative spirit of the Italian race is again alert and preparing for high achievements. A few veritable masterpieces of the art of the story-teller in the latter part of this volume show what the modern Italian can do when he resumes the old traditions of his nation and breathes into them the new life of his own era. But on the whole, the work of the Italians of the Renaissance is more important at the present time than the work of the later men. For the older writers have both a high historic interest and an absolute intrinsic literary value, and on these grounds they rank above Poe and Merimée, Maupassant and Kipling, as well as above Verga and D'Annunzio.

MUCH has been added to the art of the short story since the old Italians practised it. Its structure has become clearer, its style has been refined, the dramatic movement has been quickened by skilful foreshortenings of the plot, and the more dexterous use of dialogue. But these improvements of detail are apt to be overvalued by the modern writer. By their grasp of the large essentials of their art, men like Boccaccio and Masuccio, Bandello and Giraldi, are assured of immortality. They are great story-tellers because they tell great stories—things that rank among the most moving creations in the literature of the world. They relate these things in a simple, conversational tone, their minds bent on the deep human interest of the story, just as the mind of a man would be who had seen some strangely comical or fiercely tragical scene that he wished to describe to a circle of friends. There is little art of preparing surprises or making telling points, and none of the tricks that every clever magazine-story writer now employs. The tale is the thing, and the Italian novelist is eager to pour it out and let it make its own impression. His is a natural way of telling a story, and it has special qualities which may bring it again into favour. Its freedom from all artifice more than compensates for the leisureliness of its manner.

And though the manner of the Italian novelists undergoes but little change for three centuries, there is a deep variety in the spirit of their stories. We have seen in the first volume the lovely qualities of the work of Boccaccio: a delightful old-world air of courtesy and grace comes into his tales from the fine chivalric life of Florence in the days of her freedom and power. Very little of the traditions of chivalry persists in the work of the story-tellers of the later Renaissance. The old republican spirit, with its restraint that made for intensity, and its orderliness of life that made for general strength, gave way to the frenzied ambitions, the greed and the selfishness of an age of tyranny. The townspeople were usually too self-seeking to maintain any form of democratic government, and too fond of money-making to undertake military service: in so many places they fell under the despotic power of some freebooter or some rich nobleman who invested his money in a most profitable manner in the hiring of large troops of mercenaries.

A FIERCER, wilder, and more cruel strain of feeling arose. The result was that the tales of Italy, which mirrored this change in the national life, became either very licentious or full of murders, treacheries, and savage atrocities. Masuccio, born about 1415 at Salerno, is the first great writer of this new school. He depicts the manners of the court of Naples, which was one of the most luxurious in the world. He was a Secretary of State, and his tales were written as a pastime, after having been told by word of mouth to the great lords and high ladies of Naples and Milan. The common people furnish only matter of laughter to the court chronicler, and even in the amusing tale of "Giacomo Pinto and the Conjurer" some young noble gentlemen of Salerno play the principal part. In "Friends in Love" he recaptures somewhat of the fine spirit of chivalry. Masuccio is a very original writer. He sees life with his own eyes, and instead of trying to imitate the diction of Boccaccio, he uses his native forms of speech with its popular idioms. From a purely literary point of view he is most famous as the creator of the first form of the story of Romeo and Juliet. In his tale the

Masuccio of Salerno

names are different, and the scene is placed at Siena instead of Verona : but the main action of the story is found in his work.

Gio Sabadino

MANY of the story-tellers of this period were courtiers who wrote simply for the amusement of their circle of princes, ladies, and friends. Story-telling was one of the chief pleasures of the age. Everybody took a hand in it, and those who pleased most were warmly encouraged, and often received some government position with a view to attaching them more closely to the ruling families. Gio Sabadino of the Arienti, the successor to Masuccio, was born in Bologna about 1450, and at the age of twenty-seven he accompanied one of the lords of his city to the baths of Porretta. There, in the pleasant society of fine ladies and brilliant courtiers, he related a bunch of tales in the manner of Boccaccio. No doubt as a reward for his success in entertaining his noble companions, he was made next year one of the magistrates of Bologna. He afterwards became a favourite at the splendid court of the Duke of Ferrara, and acted as his diplomatic agent. Thus, indirectly, a gift for story-telling was as profitable a talent then as it is now. Most of the tales of Sabadino are light in tone, like his merry study of university life, "Maestro Niccolo and the Pig." He was on a holiday when he composed them.

Giovanni Brevio

GIOVANNI BREVIO of Venice wrote with more seriousness. He was a priest of humble birth, who won his way to the front by great learning as a professor of canonical law, and his biographer states he was made a bishop. He has only left six tales, but one of them, "Belphagor," is a jewel of literature. There is some doubt whether Brevio or Machiavelli is the original author of this famous satire against women ; but the probability is that the priest was entitled to include it among his works. His other stories are not so distinguished for their invention. They are studies of actual life, in which a characteristically dubious view is taken of feminine character.

Matteo Bandello

TO another ecclesiastic, Bishop Bandello, our Elizabethan playwrights are deeply indebted. The worthy bishop was one of the full-blooded children of the Italian Renaissance, with a keen zest for life. His vivid sketches of the free, passionate energies of the Italians of the sixteenth century stirred the more sluggish temperament of our writers, and by opening out to them the vast and terrible possibilities of human existence, stimulated their imaginations in a powerful way. His most characteristic works, such as the tales of "Hamlet," the "Countess of Celant," and "The Duchess of Malfi," are novels rather than short stories. So we must turn to his lighter, briefer tales—like "King Mansor and the Fisherman" and "The Mischievous Ape"—to get examples of his art suitable for our purpose. Born at Castelnuovo in Lombardy, and made bishop of Agen in France by Francis I., Bandello ranks second only to Boccaccio as a master of the art of narration ; as an explorer of the dark recesses of the human heart, he is equal to the Florentine.

Bandello was not, however, always original, and one of the finest of his tales is only a paraphrase of the work of a soldier, Luigi da Porto.

Luigi da Porto

Da Porto was a captain of light horse in the service of Venice, and being seriously wounded in the neck in one of the battles of the republic, he was compelled to retire from his military career. A gallant example of the gentleman adventurer of the Renaissance, he was intimate with the chief wits and scholars of his day, and rivalled them in his classical studies. He is said to have written several tales, but they are all lost except one. This, however, is sufficient to make him for ever famous. It is so simple in style, so sober in details, so happy in its moving turns, so original in subject! It is the greatest of all love stories—"Romeo e Giulietta!" Da Porto says he heard it from one of his archers—"a man of fifty years, a companionable fellow and a great talker, like all the people of Verona." We have seen that Masuccio had a similar story to tell in a more popular manner, but he attributed it to a family in Siena, dating the event about 1476. It is hard to say if there is any historic fact in the later tale of the lovers of Verona, though it is remarkable that even in the days of Shakespeare the tomb of Romeo and Juliet was shown to strangers who visited the town.

A MONK of Vallombrosa is the next figure in the motley, glittering pageant of Italian fiction. But as a man of religious life, Agnolo Firenzuolo is much less estimable than as a wit and a classical scholar. He was a graceless, brilliant scamp who won rich abbeys by

Agnolo Firenzuolo

the most profane of arts. One of his chief admirers, the second Medici Pope, was compelled to annul his religious vows because of his scandalous misconduct. But in spite of his defects of character, Firenzuolo was an excellent writer. A Florentine by race, he had a pure, exquisite style, often applied to subjects that were neither pure nor exquisite. His distinctive merit as a novelist resides in his talent for observation, especially in regard to the life of the working classes of Florence. In "The Surprising Adventures of Messer Niccolo" he touches on romance, and outlines an interesting plot that has been developed by many modern novelists.

One of Firenzuolo's stories is taken from Pietro Fortini, an officer of the republican government of Siena, who, retiring into the country

Pietro Fortini

when his city lost its freedom, took to composing tales. Most of them are extremely light, but the old republican is finely inspired in his story of "The Heroism of Fiordespina." His portrait of the savage, unjust tyrant is done with passion, and his heroine shines like the Lucretia of ancient Rome. Gentile

Gentile Sermini

Sermini is another novelist of Siena in the sixteenth century, but he had the strange ambition to live two hundred years before he was born. He dated his work back to the age of Boccaccio, and forged a correspondence with that writer, in which he pretended he was contemporary with him, and he filled his tales with historic allusions to show they had been written about 1349. He was content to forego fame in his lifetime, in the hope of ranking after death with the early Florentines. But the critics have discovered his tricks, and his pleasant tale of "The Fortunes of Gallio and Cardina" is now regarded as a late variation of an old theme.

ANTON-FRANCESCO GRAZZINI, born in Florence in 1503, was a son of the Athens of Italy, in the hour of its sunset splendour. He was an apothecary with a passion for literature, and all his writings are marked by the lively grace and charming ease seen in his amusing account of "Why Gabriello Re-married his Wife." Florentine writers in the tragic days of their republic felt nothing of the agony of their great artists like Michelangelo. It was from northern Italy that the dramas of high passion came, and a professor of philosophy at Ferrara, Giovambattista Giraldi, surnamed by his admirers Cinthio, was one of the novelists who handed on the torch to Shakespeare. His "Story of Desdemona" is a magnificent piece of work, though written in rather a heavy style. He also provided Shakespeare with the plot of "Measure for Measure," and Beaumont and Fletcher and Dryden found in his stories the subject-matter for some notable tragedies.

Grazzini and Giraldi Cinthio

Girolamo Parabosco was another writer of the northern school, with a somewhat heavy style but a lively imagination. He was a very versatile man—organist at Saint Mark at Venice, musical composer, playwright, poet and novelist. Most of his tales are in a humorous vein, like "Faustino and the Meddlesome Tradesman." Humour is also the quality of Anton-Francesco Doni, an unfrocked priest and wandering musician, who settled at Venice and lived by his wits. He has a happy verve and a vivacious turn for satire. Francesco Sansovino is, as his "Discomfited Fops" shows, a writer with a similar gift for comedy. The son of a famous sculptor, he was born at Rome, and after trying to make a living at the law, he too settled at Venice and became a voluminous writer. Then comes a grave senator of Venice, Sebastiano Erizzo, with a dignified way of writing that he sometimes applied to discourses on government and sometimes to historical romances, of which "Timocrates and Arsinoe" is a good example.

Parabosco and Doni

Sansovino and Erizzo

BY the middle of the sixteenth century the Italian short story entered on its decline. Novelists were as numerous as ever, and their works were very popular; but their power of invention and their freshness of vision were sadly impaired. They drew largely on their predecessors for their plots, and even turned to mediaeval France for the matter of their stories. Ortensio Lando, for instance, had one eye on the life of his time and another on the story-books of the past. His "Astrologer and the Ass" is an amusing sketch of the superstitions of his countrymen: but his shortest and most famous story, "Evil for Evil," is taken from an old French poet and dressed up in Tuscan speech. But it deserves a place in our collection, for it is certainly one of the most famous stories in the world, and Lando tells it even better than the Frenchman.

Ortensio Lando

Celio Malespini, a Venetian nobleman of brilliant personality and revengeful character, gets more life and passion into his work than most of his contemporaries. His tale of "The Love Affairs of the Grand Duchess" is really a scandalous thing; it attacks a lady who was very kind to him, but the truth and vigour of this portrait of the most famous of the Grand Duchesses of Tuscany make it a piece of vivid art. "The Transformation" is another study from the life with a fine comic turn in it. Scipione Bargagli of Siena and Giovan-Francesco Straparola form, with Malespini, the last of the great Italian novelists. Bargagli, some of his admirers say, deserves to be placed beside Boccaccio. His curious and delicate qualities of style, however, are necessarily lost in translation; and though his story of "Ippolito and Gangenova" is an admirable piece of narrative, it scarcely ranks with the finest works of the earlier master. To English readers he has the special interest of having excited the admiration of Keats. Straparola, however, has won greater attention from Molière and other French writers. He wrote some of the most popular of our current fairy-tales, and in his tale of "Andrigetto the Impenitent" he gives an unforgettable study of a typical neo-pagan of the Renaissance at the point of death. The sombre courage of the villain is magnificent: he was a true son of his wild age.

Malespini and Bargagli

Straparola

It was men of this sort who exhausted the energies of the Italian race, and reduced Italy for some centuries to a mere geographical expression. During the seventeenth and eighteenth centuries the Italians contributed very little of importance to the art of fiction. They became largely dependent on France and England for literary ideas, and it was not until the influence of Sir Walter Scott told on Manzoni in the nineteenth century that the art of prose narrative revived in Italy. In the meantime the good Bishop Giovanni Bottari, in the seventeenth century, tried to be a religious Boccaccio, and wrote that gem of humour, conscious or unconscious, which we have here entitled "The Monk and the Woman." In the next generation we have a little comedy of "The Grape Stealers" from Count Carlo Gozzi—a brilliant improviser of pantomimes and fairy plays. The last flicker of the old Italian tale is the "Friar Timothy and the Woodman" by an obscure eighteenth-century writer, Michele Colombo. This was good enough for a French wit, Piron, to borrow; and slight though it is, it marks the end of a great creative period in the Italian art of story-telling.

Bottari and Gozzi

Michele Colombo

THERE is a break of more than a hundred years between Colombo, the last of the old school, and Luigi Capuana, the first of the modern school of Italian novelists. Capuana is a Sicilian, born at Mineo in 1839. He is a realist, inspired by the example of Zola, but his Italian sense of beauty preserves him from the gross faults of the French writer, and in "Quacquarà" and "The Rival Earthquakes" he shows a keen sense of humour as well as a faculty of minute observation that discovers new

Luigi Capuana

Enrico Castelnuovo

things in the commonplaces of life. His contemporary, Enrico Castelnuovo, was born in Florence in 1839, and has rather more lightness and grace of style, as becomes a native of the most artistic province of Italy. The study of life's little ironies attracts him, and his three tales, "It Snows," "The Lost Letter" and "The Theorem of Pythagoras," have somewhat of the strength of Thomas Hardy and the charm of Daudet.

Giovanni Verga

Antonio Fogazzaro

But the modern master of the Italian *conte* is the Sicilian, Giovanni Verga, born at Catania in 1840. His "Cavalleria Rusticana" is probably the best-known short story in the modern world. And this is not merely due to its success in operatic form: the original tale of Sicilian peasant life, with its strange mingling of the savage and the chivalric spirit, is one of the high things in modern literature. And quite as fine in a different way is the sombre, ghastly "She-Wolf." Maupassant never touched so tragic a depth in the human soul. Then we have the peculiar inimitable humour of "The War of the Saints," a remarkable study of the ways and thoughts of the Italian peasant. Some critics are inclined to place the northern Italian, Antonio Fogazzaro, by the side of Verga as a short-story writer. Certainly the fine suggestive art of the moving tale of "The Silver Crucifix" shows that Fogazzaro is as good at miniatures of literature as at large frescoes. But on the whole he might be described as the best modern novelist in Italy, while Verga is the best short-story writer.

Mario Pratesi

MARIO PRATESI is a Tuscan writer, born in 1842, and as his ironic sketch of "Doctor Phœbus" indicates, he takes a middle way between the fierce realism of Verga and the sympathetic interpretation of life of Fogazzaro. He has one of the best-balanced minds of his age, with an intensity of vision and force of emotion that make him the most sympathetic of ironists.

Edmondo de Amicis

There is less depth in the brilliant soldier-writer, Edmondo de Amicis, who, born in 1846 on the Genoa coast, spent the early part of his life in fighting the Austrians and in editing a military periodical. Amicis writes like a first-rate cavalry officer, with dash and brilliance and fervour. His "Little Sardinian Drummer" is an exciting battle-piece—all movement, smoke, stabbing flame, and high-hearted courage. And in "A Great Day" he gives a striking study of the frame of mind of some Italians of the better class during the heroic struggle for national independence. He died in 1908.

Gabriele d'Annunzio

WITH Gabriele d'Annunzio, born eighteen years after gallant Amicis, we come to the most problematic figure in modern literature. Our representative selection of his shorter works consists of "San Pantaleone," that reminds one of Verga's story of the rival Saints; and "Mastro Peppe's Magic," that seems to be an amusing variation on one of the favourite comic themes of the old Italian novelists. Then "The End of Candia" has clearly been suggested by Maupassant's "A Piece of String." It is the same with many of d'Annunzio's long novels: the theme, the treatment, and even the phrases used, can at times be traced to other writers. What is original in d'Annunzio is his rhetoric: he uses words as a musician uses sounds, and expresses his individuality by an iridescent torrent of language at high pressure.

Farina

Salvatore Farina, who was born in the same year as Amicis, is not so well known a writer, but as his charming tale of "Separation" proves, he has at least a personal way of looking at life, and a quiet humorous turn of mind. Humour is a great antiseptic, and if d'Annunzio had a little of it he would not be so strangely troubled by his maladies of the soul.

Matilde Serao

MATILDE SERAO was the first woman novelist to rise into fame in Italy. She was born in Greece in 1856, and though she is an Italian on her father's side, she never seems to have mastered completely the Italian language. But she has a sort of slovenly strength of expression that carries her through all difficulties, and as is seen in her tale, "An Intervention," she writes with great spirit and with a large knowledge of human nature. She has been deeply influenced by Fogazzaro.

Grazia Deledda

Grazia Deledda, born in Sardinia in 1872, is a woman novelist of a higher order than Signora Serao. She has the great classic qualities—simplicity, freshness, and that fine restraint that leads the small mind into aridity, and the great mind into intensity of effects. Her "Two Men and a Woman" is an excellent example of her genius. Her strong, simple islanders, with their impressionable passionate nature, are drawn by her with a woman's insight and the firm touch of an original artist.

Roberto Bracco

Roberto Bracco likes more complexity of character. He belongs to the ironic school, and his vivid little tale, "For the Saving of Souls," must not be taken too seriously. The dying poet will not die, and the pretty little nun will not run away with him. It is a charming comedy of make-believe.

Giulio de Frenzi

In Giulio de Frenzi's "A Survivor" we have another amusing study of the type of the young Italian who died about ten years ago. He was a healthy, vigorous fellow who fancied that he and his race were in a sad state of decline. He tried to look interestingly ill, and sometimes drank absinthe with the idea of tasting the fatal joys of decadence. But this French fashion of thought has been blown away by the new school of the Futurists, and "A Survivor" is now probably eating beefsteaks in the English style, and practising some system of physical culture.

Luciano Zùccoli

So we end in "Merry Company" with Luciano Zùccoli, who guides us through the slums of Milan. It is scarcely a merry tale, this study of the low life of a modern Italian city, but the art with which it is written is extraordinary. There is more life rammed into this short story than is found in most long novels.

E. W.

MASUCCIO OF SALERNO
1415

FRIENDS IN LOVE

THIS incident occurred during the late campaign in Romagna, at a time when both parties were compelled to abandon military operations, and retire into winter quarters, owing to the severity of the season. One of the celebrated commanders, Alfonso, Duke of Calabria, found it requisite to occupy the Pisanese territories, whither he led his fine Arragonese army, and cantoned it among the towns and castles in the vicinity. According to the rules of war, as well as to further the interests of the League, he then proceeded to a personal inspection of several of the noblest cities and fortifications of Italy. Being everywhere received with marks of triumph and distinction, it happened that, in passing through one of these cities, he was so much pleased with its appearance and the acclamations of the inhabitants, that he resolved to sojourn there for some time.

In the tournaments and festivals which distinguished this period, one of the Duke's favourite friends, of high birth and rare endowments, whose name was Marino Caracciuolo, bore no insignificant share. Gallantly riding at the head of his companions through the city, he chanced, among the beautiful faces that looked forth that day, to cast his eyes on one whose youthful charms captivated his attention far beyond all the others. As he passed on, her ideas still occupied his fancy, insomuch that he scarcely knew which road to take in order to find his way back. Frequently repairing, however, to the same spot, he so earnestly watched and followed her, that he attracted her attention, and at length prevailed upon her to return his favourable regards.

Marino was overjoyed when he discovered that she began to reward his passion. Resolved to avail himself of every occasion to promote his suit, among other means he announced a grand ball to be given in honour of his distinguished chief. Nearly all the ladies of the place were invited, and among these he had the delight of beholding the fascinating maiden, in honour of whose attractions the entertainment was really given.

Nor was the Duke himself less struck with her ; and, quite unconscious of his friend's attachment, he soon became so far enslaved by the surpassing beauty of her person and her manners, as to resolve upon obtaining her love at any price. The young lady, who had never before beheld him, though she had more than once heard him highly commended for all the best and noblest qualities befitting a Prince, was surprised to find that in magnanimity, courtesy, and heroic beauty, the reality so far outstripped the good report. She gazed upon him as the model of grace and noble manners; and, mingled with the highest admiration, she offered up vows in her secret heart for his happiness and good fortune.

Nor was it long before the Duke perceived the impression he had made, and employed the evening so well, that before he took leave of her they became perfectly aware of the feelings which they mutually entertained. After particular inquiries into her rank and character, these feelings soon ripened on both sides into the warmest passion, and, being introduced into her society by means of the richest bribes and presents, the Prince proceeded in his designs, scarcely doubting of ultimate success. In the meanwhile, the lady not only discountenanced Marino's visits, but everywhere treated him with the utmost indifference and scorn, which, contrasted with her previous kindness, threw the unfortunate lover into such a fit of jealousy and despair, that, giving rein to his passion, he abandoned his military duties and refused the society of his friends.

Struck with this sudden change, the Duke frequently questioned him as to its cause, but could obtain no satisfactory answer, until, imagining that he had now the object of his pursuit in his power, he, as usual on such occasions, ordered his friend Marino into his presence, observing,

"Though I find you are still unwilling to acquaint me with the real cause of your unhappiness, I shall nevertheless continue, as before, to confide to you every secret of my breast. As a proof of which, learn that I am at this time engaged, within a few hours, to a beautiful young lady whom I trust I may then call my own. I entreat you, therefore, no less from affection than from duty, to wear a less lugubrious face, and either inform me what is the matter with you, or show a little more of your former cheerfulness. I shall not half enjoy my triumph if you do not accompany me; so come, my friend, and protect me in this perilous enterprise, on which I should be unwilling to enter without your assistance."

Quite overpowered with these words, Marino, regretting that he had so long and so ungratefully concealed his passion from his best friend and master, related the whole affair, not without great emotion pronouncing the lady's name. The Duke listened to him with equal surprise and pain, considering within himself the strength of his friend's attachment, who stood before him overpowered with remorse and grief. Then, consulting his own duties and his dignity, and conceiving that his more exalted station demanded the exertion of a superior degree of generosity, he determined without the least hesitation to prefer a lover's happiness to his own unbridled will.

" I doubt not you will do me the justice to believe, my dear Marino," said the Duke, " that I never took so much real pleasure in anything as in sharing my fortune with my friends. At least you shall now be convinced of it ; for though I declare to you that I am passionately attached to this very lady, whom this evening I had prevailed upon to receive me to her arms, I shall not swerve from the line of conduct I have hitherto observed. I withdraw my claim, however much I may feel, for I cannot behold your affliction ; so cheer up, my dear friend, and prepare to come along with me. Nay, no resistance ; for I am resolved that before long you shall call our beloved girl your own. I have been much to blame, but you must forgive me, Marino, since I did not know that you loved her first. She is virtuous ; we have only to get a priest, and she shall make you happy."

On hearing this generous offer, Marino expressed the utmost gratitude, declaring at the same time that he had rather die than think of interfering with any engagements which his Highness had thought it advisable to make.

" No apologies are necessary," replied the Duke, smiling ; " and as I have said it, so it shall be " ; and, taking his friend's arm, the Duke led him to the lady's house.

Leaving a few of their followers, for further security, near, they were introduced into the presence of the woman they loved, who received the Duke, advancing first, with unfeigned delight. Although she recognised her former admirer, she bestowed no further notice upon him than if he had been a stranger accompanying his master to receive his orders. But the noble Duke, introducing him to her with a smile, and taking her hand in the most affectionate manner, thus addressed her :

" I entreat you, my dear lady, by the true love I bear you, not to be offended with what I am about to say, because I would only have you so far listen to my request as it is honest and of good report. Nor can you give me a stronger proof of your high regard for me than by acceding to it.

" In my last interview with my royal father, before setting out on the present campaign, among other wise precepts, he most particularly insisted on the necessity of prudence in regard to my allowing myself to be surprised or taken captive in the ambush of a lady's eyes, citing many famous examples of the bad effects of worshipping so tyrannical a deity as Love. And though I am inexpressibly grateful, and passionately attached to you, yet when I consider the late advice and injunctions of the King, the sorrow my love would entail upon you, and the sufferings of this my faithful friend and servant, whom nearest of all my followers I regard, it becomes my duty to inform you that he is deeply and desperately in love with you, and every way most deserving of your hand. But we are both yours ; it is for you to decide ; deal with us as you please " : and drawing his breath after this painful effort, the Prince remained silent.

Great indeed was the surprise and shock to the feelings of the lady, but, being discreet and virtuous, although in this instance she had been somewhat carried away, she resolved to emulate the generosity of the noble Duke, and making a virtue of necessity, and stifling her feelings, with a serene and cheerful countenance she thus replied :

" I shall not venture, my lord, to insist, as my excuse, upon the many noble and amiable qualities which, I confess with tears of shame, have brought me into this condition ; yet indeed you may believe me when I say that ambition was not my motive. I knew the distinction, the impassable barrier between us ; but I saw you loved me ; you addressed me, you followed me ; and I could not help loving you again. But as it is your wish—and I cannot but the more admire you for it, who, being the son of a powerful Monarch, and graced with beauty, power, and glory, resign voluntarily your wishes to another—I am ready to yield to your entreaties, my lord (I had rather you would call them commands), in behalf of the friend whom you so much love. And if he can forgive me, if studying his will and happiness can at all atone for my past weakness " (her sweet face was covered with tears and blushes), " here, my lord, is my hand."

And he placed it in that of his friend Marino.

GIACOMO PINTO AND THE CONJURER

Masuccio of Salerno

NOT many years ago there resided in Salerno a youth whose name was Giacomo Pinto, who, though of noble descent, and dwelling in the vicinity of Porta Nuova, where the academy of sense belonging to our city was commonly supposed to hold its sittings, would have found a much more suitable habitation in the heights of our mountain district, where nearly all of our ancient families are said first to have drawn their breath.

Now, though overburdened with neither wealth nor discretion, our hero was not wanting in a certain noble ambition, which spurred him on to lay siege to the affections of a young and pretty widow related to our fellow-citizen Stradico. This, his first love, he contrived to conceal in such a manner that not a child in all Salerno failed to perceive it, furnishing the most agreeable scandal to every party in the place. In fact, he became the butt of all his acquaintance ; but their darts were less keen than those of love, and, heedless of their point, he pursued his enterprise with a fervour and perseverance worthy of his ancestors.

Among others residing near him who most amused themselves with observing the daily proofs of his folly during the progress of the siege, was a gentleman of the name of Loisi Pagano, whose great penetration and pleasing manners winning poor Giacomo's entire confidence, the latter often entertained him with the history of this his cruel passion.

Perceiving the extravagant turn it had taken, Loisi began to think how he might employ the enamoured wight's folly to some useful purpose in chastising the conceit of a certain upstart in Salerno who took the name of Messer Angelo, and who, though only a farrier, had assumed the profession of a physician, trafficking in different parts of Italy, whence he returned home with the spoil of his dead patients. Conversing one day with Giacomo on the same eternal subject, he addressed the lover as follows :

" You must surely, my dear friend, care very little about the sufferings you talk of, when you might so easily put an end to them. You know Messer Angelo is one of the greatest conjurers in the world, and

I can give you a proof of it, inasmuch as I have happily consulted him on many occasions, and never been deceived. He is, moreover, your relation on the mother's side. Why not hasten to him, and prevail upon him with a little pleasing flattery to exercise his art in your favour, by which you will infallibly arrive at the object of your wishes? Or if he should think of imposing upon you, as he has most probably done upon many others, you can give him such a lesson in return as will teach him how to behave to gentlemen in future, and remember you ever after."

Great was the joy and gratitude evinced by Giacomo on hearing these words, and flattering himself with the happiest results, he promised to do everything required of him. His friend Loisi, then excusing himself, lost no time in finding Messer Angelo, to whom he communicated his plan with no slight pleasure, thinking of the sport they were about to have. Little did Messer Angelo suppose, as he stood laughing, with what satisfaction Loisi was anticipating his chastisement, while he made poor Giacomo his dupe, and arranged measures before parting for executing their roguish scheme.

Not long afterwards the lover despatched a messenger for Messer Angelo, and told him in a lamentable voice his grand secret, already known to everybody in the place, how sadly he pined in love, concluding, with many sighs:

"You know, my good uncle, a friend in need is a friend indeed; and I have been informed that you are a great magician, whose infinite skill, if you please, can easily deliver me from all my pains; and so I beseech you, in the name of Heaven, that you will take pity on me, that I may obtain the dear object of my wishes, and owe my life and everything I have to you alone."

With a cheerful countenance, Messer Angelo replied he should be happy to do anything in his power to serve him, and, among other things, at last addressed him thus:

"But, my dear Giacomo, I am somewhat fearful of the result, as my plan would require, on your part, the utmost resolution and courage."

"Only tell me what it is," cried the lover, "for I declare I am ready to descend into the infernal regions if necessary; such is the strength of my love."

"Nay," answered he, "it is worse than that; for the truth is, you will have to hold a dialogue, face to face, with a ferocious demon called

Barabas, the only one whom I have it at present in my power to summon for my commands."

"Well," continued Giacomo, "I will, if you please, speak to Satan himself, who is greater, you know; that is, if it be necessary."

"Heaven grant you courage!" cried the conjurer; "but how are we to get the proper implements for the work? We must have a sword that has despatched a man, in the first place."

"Oh, I can get one of my brother's that has killed ten in its time," cried Giacomo.

"Well, that is the most important," replied Messer Angelo; "we can easily provide the rest. However, let there be in readiness when I ask for them a black and well-fed wether lamb and four fat capons, and check your impatience till the moon is in her wane. Leave the rest to me, for I promise you, you shall have the lady in your own hands, for better or worse, whichever you please."

Overjoyed with such an offer, Giacomo vowed to have everything in readiness as the necromancer had pointed out; who then repaired to Loisi, informing him of what had been fixed upon, in order to obviate any mistake that might arise. Often did they amuse themselves, before proceeding to work, with the simplicity of Giacomo, who hardly ever ceased for three days to tease the conjurer to commence the ceremonies.

"Well, for my part, I am quite ready now," exclaimed Angelo, "but have you prepared what I enjoined you?"

"To be sure I have," returned Giacomo, "and think myself very lucky too, for I have got the finest capons you ever saw from my lady cousin; and, better still, I can show you a young wether as fat as a bull, jet black, with four great horns, enough to frighten you to look at."

Quite delighted, Messer Angelo observed, "Indeed, cousin, I hardly know you; love has so sharpened all your faculties at once. No one else could possibly have got together all the things requisite so very soon; but to-night shall reward you: I will put everything in order, and call for you when I set out."

Angelo then returned to Loisi, to tell him where he was to expect them, as all was fixed. It was no sooner night than the conjurer adjourned to the house of the lover, saying:

"Would you like to come? It is quite time."

He was answered in the affirmative; and seizing the homicidal sword, and placing the fat lamb on his shoulder, and a capon under each arm, he conducted the devoted lover into the midst of some awful ruins, where Loisi lay concealed accompanied by several friends, in order not to engross the whole scene to himself. Here Messer Angelo, turning towards Giacomo, said:

" Take notice, my friend, we are now advanced too far to think of retreating without the most imminent risk; so look you do not flinch, and above all, beware how you call on the Lord or the Virgin: aye, or confess yourself either, for we should all sink down together into the bottomless pit. But if you should feel some qualms of fear (and how can you help it ?), address yourself to the Redeemer, for you will want one, and we may perhaps escape the wiles of the Wicked One."

This our hero promised to do if possible, and the great necromancer then proceeded:

" You must repeat after me exactly what I say; and when we have conjured him up, Barabas will give a loud cry, saying, 'Now, give me my supper,' and then throw the capons at him to stop his mouth, and send the wether after them when the great horned beast roars out."

This the lover promised manfully to perform, and the order being given, out sprung the murderous sword, drawing a vast circle on the ground, and strange hieroglyphics within, while strong sulphurous fumes rose on all sides, and incantations dire, and contortions of hands and eyes were seen.

" Put your left leg into the circle this moment, Giacomo, and tell me whether you would rather see him in all his horrors face to face, or hear him speak from the old castle window yonder."

The poor lover, whose simplicity had brought him with such vast courage into the dilemma, hearing such an awful commencement, began to tremble, saying:

" It would perhaps be enough at first to hear him speak "; advancing his foot at the same time into the circle, and, against the agreement, recommending himself to every saint in heaven.

His master, perceiving that he already thought himself transported into the other world, ordered him three times to pronounce the name of Barabas: the first only of which he effectually did. Loisi, in the disguise of the wicked one, then threw up a blaze of fire with a noise like thunder, enough to frighten the stoutest heart. Whether Giacomo wished himself at home again there is little need to inquire; but, encouraged by the conjurer, he called out a second time, when a greater conflagration than before met his view.

Though his master failed not to observe the poor lover half dead with fear, he still urged him on, saying, " Fear nothing ; the monster is well bound ; he can do you no harm ; so call him lustily for the third time," which, with the utmost exertion, he did ; but in so faint a voice that it was scarcely heard.

Loisi, on this, having sent up a third fiery signal, uttered a terrible yell, that nearly put an end to the poor lover's life. But the master, reminding him that the demon was bound, bade Giacomo stand firm and repeat the invocation exactly as he told him. When he tried to speak, his heart beat so violently that he could scarcely support himself ; and Messer Angelo, fearing lest he had already carried things too far, began to lecture Barabas for being so very outrageous. But Loisi and his companions, almost dead with laughter, perceiving that the conjurer did not proceed. fearful of losing their sport, called out fiercely for the fat lamb and everything they had.

Then Messer Angelo, turning to the trembling lover, cried,

" Throw him everything you have, and fly for your life, without ever looking behind you."

No sooner did Giacomo, who truly felt as if he were got into the wrong world, hear these joyous words, than flinging capons, lamb, and everything else into the demon's den, he took to his legs at a speed that defied all pursuit.

After he had arrived with some difficulty at home, Messer Angelo soon joined him, saying,

" Well, what think you of my necromantic art ? Come, speak ; be of good cheer ; we shall finish the business next time."

" Say no more about it," cried Giacomo faintly ; " I would not go back with you for worlds ; so find some other way of conjuring the lady for me, and I shall be eternally obliged to you."

" Well, be it so," returned Angelo ; " I am determined you shall succeed, and will do everything in my power to serve you."

On which he left him to repose. Loisi, in the meanwhile, having taken the animals offered to him by way of oblation, dismissed his companions and betook himself to rest. The next day he resolved to give a splendid feast, with the help of these and other good things, in honour of Giacomo and the friends who had witnessed the preceding scene. The dinner-hour being arrived, not a guest could refrain from laughter when Giacomo with great solemnity entered the room. Whispers, peals of laughter, and cries of "Barabas, Barabas! make way for Barabas!" were echoed from side to side.

Giacomo soon found he was the sole object of their merriment; on which Loisi, who had laid the whole scheme, saw that the time was come to execute his design of turning the tables upon the conjurer himself, and correcting him for many of his old faults. With this view, taking Giacomo aside after dinner, he acquainted him in a friendly way with everything that Angelo had done to make him ridiculous in their eyes. Giacomo, bearing in mind Loisi's words, set off with the most deadly intentions to find the hated necromancer. Without saying a word, he seized him by the hair of his head, and throwing him down, began to punish him with a degree of severity which it was extremely difficult for the conjurer to bear. Leaving him for some moments senseless upon the ground, our hero in his passion seized upon a huge stone near him, which would for ever have terminated the conjurer's career, had not his friends approached to deliver him out of the lover's hands.

Recovering him from his rage, and aware of all the follies of which he had been guilty, Giacomo, overcome with shame, retired to his own house, which he only left again to depart also from the city. Having disposed of his little property, he purchased for himself a steed and arms, and setting out for the seat of war, had the good fortune, aided by prudence and valour, to arrive at wealth and honour, esteemed by his comrades and commanders. For the whole of which he may be said to have been indebted to love and Messer Angelo; the latter of whom having received his just deserts at the hands of Giacomo, it only remains for us to admire the very mysterious and miraculous powers of the blind archer-boy, who, with a little assistance from Fortune, can confer so much happiness on those who enjoy his smiles.

GIO SABADINO
B. 1450

MAESTRO NICCOLO AND THE PIG

NOT very long ago there were four noble, though somewhat humorous, students residing at our University of Sienna, whose names were Messer Antonio da Clerico, a canonist; Messer Giovanni da Santo Geminiano, a young jurist; Maestro Antonio di Paulo di Val d'Arno d'Arezzo; and Maestro Michel di Cosimo Aretino delli Conti di Palazzolo, who, when young, was surnamed Bacica, now a distinguished civilian in the University of Bologna, full of years and virtue, beloved by the whole people for his kind and charitable actions. But, waiving these last considerations, I proceed to inform you that, while remaining in the house of the Master of the Academy of Arts, the youthful pupils became acquainted with a certain disciple of Galen, who, though a mere quack, imagined he was possessed of more learning than Avicenna himself. His name was Niccolo da Massa, to which had been added that of *Portantino*, from the peculiarity of his ambling gait; and as his residence lay opposite to that of the governor, his singularities attracted the particular attention of the pupils.

Now it happened that in the month of February, during the salting season, the doctor had purchased a fine pig, which he subsequently had killed and hung up, as is usual, previous to the operation of salting, for four or five days in his kitchen. The merry scholars, aware of this stage of the proceedings, set their heads to contrive how they might feast at the doctor's charge. It so fell out that a fellow-student named Messer Pietro di Leri Martini, had lately left the academy, and afterwards died of a fever, and on this fact they resolved to ground the success of their exploit. Introducing themselves secretly into the doctor's premises, and watching their opportunity, they laid hands upon the pork, a fact which struck the doctor with equal horror and surprise when he beheld his kitchen the next morning emptied of its treasure. After indulging in a variety of imprecations and suspicions, his doubts at last fell upon his young neighbours, the scholars, who had indeed already acquired some little reputation for similar exploits.

Believing that he had now discovered the authors of the diabolical theft, he waited on Messer Amadio da Citta di Castello, the presiding magistrate in Sienna, who, having heard his evidence, despatched three several messengers commanding an immediate restoration of the pork to the right owner, unless the young gentlemen wished to be proceeded against criminally.

The answer which the magistrate received was, that the scholars were greatly surprised at such a message, and were sorry that they had not so fine a pig in their possession, happening to know nothing about it. But being still persecuted with the complaints of the doctor, the magistrate resolved to investigate the affair thoroughly, sending a warrant to search the scholars' chambers, and to bring them all before him should the pork be discovered in their possession.

Expecting such a visit, the students were not a little puzzled how to proceed, when Messer Antonio da Clerico, who by his singular ingenuity and facetiousness had always shown himself equal to every emergency, encouraged the flagging spirits of his companions, saying: "Fear not, my brave boys; fear not the Podesta and his myrmidons: we will be a match for them yet. We will extract a little amusement out of them, too, if you mind what I say. Let us get up a sick couch in the chamber opposite the entrance hall, and fill it with all kinds of the most sickly preparations that can disgust the human nose. And when the officers come, you must all stand at the entrance, buried in profound grief; and when they ask you what is the matter, shake your heads and point to the inner chamber, saying, 'Poor fellow! he is dying of the plague.' Now this sick gentleman shall be no other than the pig, and trust me, whoever ventures within sight of him shall wish himself away again as speedily as possible. For you know the whole city is disturbed about the death of our fellow-student, who died only the other day of the plague."

His companions immediately set up a loud laugh, in token of their approbation, crying, "Come, let us go to work, then; we cannot be hanged for it, after all."

Then preparing a table spread with cushions, they laid the pig upon it at full length, with a nightcap over his head, and stuck out his fore feet with white sleeves, so as to resemble the arms of a human being; while his hind ones were decorated with a pair of slippers. Soon after completing their arrangements appeared the officers of the police, who, on requiring entrance, were readily admitted by the scholars, some of whom, on advancing farther, they found overwhelmed with sorrow, wringing their hands, and crying out most piteously, " Oh, my dear, dear brother ! " at which the officers, apprehending some fatal accident, inquired into the cause of their complaint.

The shrewd Maestro Michel on this stepped forward : " It is my brother, my poor brother, who is here dying, we are afraid."

" Dying ! what is the matter with him ? "

" They say it is the plague ; but I will never desert him ! "

On this one of the officers opened the chamber door with some caution, and stumbling on the shocking object which presented itself, drew back in great alarm ; for on the left hand was seen Messer Antonio as the priest, administering spiritual consolation, with book and crucifix in hand, and wax-lights burning, to the poor scholar, falling apparently a victim to the plague. At this overpowering sight, without saying a word, he ran out of the house, followed by his companions. Returning to the magistrate, he with difficulty made himself understood, expressing the utmost horror of the business on which he had been sent.

" How," cried the magistrate, " can it be true ? "

" True ! " returned the officer ; " I saw the poor wretch stretched out, dying of the plague, and his brother and all his companions buried in the deepest grief."

" And did you go into the room ? Did you touch the body ? " inquired the magistrate.

" To be sure I did."

" Then why do you come here ? Away with you, you wretches ; we shall have the whole city infected " ; and the magistrate drove them away, forbidding them, as they valued their lives, again to enter into his presence.

The wily Messer Antonio, called the priest in the meanwhile, observing the rout of these myrmidons of the law, hastily dressed himself amidst the triumph and applauses of his companions, and set out for the house of the Podesta, in order to obviate any disagreeable consequences that might attend the tidings which had just gone forth. He arrived just in time to catch the magistrate as he was proceeding to the grand council to acquaint the members with the fact which had just transpired, and propose means for the safety of the city. To him, then, Messer Antonio related the whole of the affair on the part of the scholars as it had occurred from the beginning.

It was a great relief to the magistrate to hear that there was really no pestilential disorder abroad ; and he laughed outright at the humorous way in which Messer Antonio related to him the incidents of the story. "Oh you collegians !" he cried, "you are true children of perdition ! There is nothing of which you are not capable ; and woe to the unfortunate wretch that falls into your hands !"

As they were now approaching the Palazzo delli Signori, the Podesta resolved, instead of alarming them with tidings of the plague, to amuse them with one of the best stories which he had for some time heard. Such was the pleasure which it afforded, that they obliged its ingenious author to repeat the whole to them again, mingling their mirth with a little seasonable advice, and commanding him to make immediate restitution of the doctor's pig. But to this, with one voice, the scholars all demurred, beseeching their lordships that they would not please to insist on such hard conditions, inasmuch as it would be throwing a sort of discredit on real learning were they to refuse to permit the scholars to punish so much absurd quackery and ignorance as were manifested by this disciple of Galen ; and they trusted that their lordships would not interfere to interrupt the joke in the happiest stage, but would permit them to eat the pig since they had caught it. Grateful for the entertainment afforded them, the council could scarcely prevail upon themselves to treat the ingenious author of the plot with the rigour of the law, although they strongly advised restitution of the pig. But the humorous Antonio conducted his defence in so happy and eloquent a manner that the pork was allowed to remain in the hands of the scholars, and the court adjourned. They immediately proceeded to regale themselves with the spoils they had won. Frequently that night did they drink to the health of Dr. Portantino, who had presented them with a portion of the feast ; nor were the wines less relished after they had partaken of roasted pig.

GIOVANNI BREVIO
1480–1562

BELPHAGOR

WE read in the ancient archives of Florence the following account, as it was received from the lips of a very holy man, greatly respected by every one for the sanctity of his manners at the period in which he lived. Happening once to be deeply absorbed in his prayers, such was their efficacy, that he saw an infinite number of condemned souls, belonging to those miserable mortals who had died in their sins, undergoing the punishment due to their offences in the regions below. He remarked that the greater part of them lamented nothing so bitterly as their folly in having taken wives, attributing to them the whole of their misfortunes.

Much surprised at this, Minos and Rhadamanthus, with the rest of the infernal judges, unwilling to credit all the abuse heaped upon the female sex, and wearied from day to day with its repetition, agreed to bring the matter before Pluto. It was then resolved that the conclave of infernal princes should form a committee of inquiry, and should adopt such measures as might be deemed most advisable by the court in order to discover the truth or falsehood of the calumnies which they heard. All being assembled in council, Pluto addressed them as follows:

" Dearly beloved demons! though by celestial dispensation and the irreversible decree of fate this kingdom fell to my share, and I might strictly dispense with any kind of celestial or earthly responsibility, yet, as it is more prudent and respectful to consult the laws and to hear the opinion of others, I have resolved to be guided by your advice, particularly in a case that may chance to cast some imputation upon our government. For the souls of all men daily arriving in our kingdom still continue to lay the whole blame upon their wives, and as this appears to us impossible, we must be careful how we decide in such a business, lest we also should come in for a share of their abuse on account of our too great severity; and yet judgment must be pronounced, lest we be taxed with negligence and with indifference to the interests of justice. Now, as the latter is the fault of a careless, and the former of an unjust judge, we, wishing to avoid the trouble and the blame that might attach to both, yet hardly seeing how to get clear of it, naturally enough apply to you for assistance, in order that you may look to it, and contrive in some way that, as we have hitherto reigned without the slightest imputation upon our character, we may continue to do so for the future."

The affair appearing to be of the utmost importance to all the princes present, they first resolved that it was necessary to ascertain the truth, though they differed as to the best means of accomplishing this object. Some were of opinion that they ought to choose one or more from among themselves, who should be commissioned to pay a visit to the world, and in a human shape endeavour personally to ascertain how far such reports were grounded in truth. To many others it appeared that this might be done without so much trouble merely by compelling some of the wretched souls to confess the truth by the application of a variety of tortures. But the majority being in favour of a journey to the world, they abided by the former proposal.

No one, however, being ambitious of undertaking such a task, it was resolved to leave the affair to chance.

The lot fell upon the arch-devil Belphagor, who previous to the Fall had enjoyed the rank of archangel in a higher world. Though he received his commission with a very ill grace, he nevertheless felt himself constrained by Pluto's imperial mandate, and prepared to execute whatever had been determined upon in council. At the same time he took an oath to observe the tenor of his instructions, as they had been drawn up with all due solemnity and ceremony for the purpose of his mission. These were to the following effect:

Imprimis, that the better to promote the object in view, he should be furnished with a hundred thousand gold ducats; secondly, that he should make use of the utmost expedition in getting into the world; thirdly, that after assuming the human form he should enter into the marriage state; and lastly, that he should live with his wife for the space of ten years.

At the expiration of this period he was to feign death and return home, in order to acquaint his employers, by the fruits of experience, what really were the respective conveniences and inconveniences of matrimony. The conditions further ran, that during the said ten years he should be subject to all kinds of miseries and disasters, like the rest of mankind, such as poverty, prisons, and diseases into which men are apt to fall, unless, indeed, he could contrive by his own skill and ingenuity to avoid them.

Poor Belphagor having signed these conditions and received the money, forthwith came into the world, and having set up his equipage, with a numerous train of servants, he made a very splendid entrance into Florence. He selected this city in preference to all others as being most favourable for obtaining an usurious interest of his money; and having assumed the name of Roderigo, a native of Castile, he took a house in the suburbs of Ognissanti. And because he was unable to explain the instructions under which he acted, he gave out that he was a merchant who, having had poor prospects in Spain, had gone to Syria, and succeeded in acquiring his fortune at Aleppo, whence he had lastly set out for Italy with the intention of marrying and settling there, as one of the most polished and agreeable countries he knew.

Roderigo was certainly a very handsome man, apparently about thirty years of age, and he lived in a style of life that showed he was in pretty easy circumstances, if not possessed of immense wealth. Being, moreover, extremely affable and liberal, he soon attracted the notice of many noble citizens blessed with large families of daughters and small incomes. The former of these were soon offered to him, from among whom Roderigo chose a very beautiful girl of the name of Onesta, a daughter of Amerigo Donati, who had also three sons, all grown up, and three more daughters, also nearly marriageable. Though of a noble family and enjoying a good reputation in Florence, his father-in-law was extremely poor, and maintained as poor an establishment.

Roderigo, therefore, made very splendid nuptials, and omitted nothing that might tend to confer honour upon such a festival, being liable, under the law which he received on leaving his infernal abode, to feel all kinds of vain and earthly passions. He therefore soon began to enter into all the pomps and vanities of the world, and to aim at reputation and consideration among mankind, which put him to no little expense. But more than this, he had not long enjoyed the society of his beloved Onesta, before he became tenderly attached to her, and was unable to behold her suffer the slightest inquietude or vexation.

Now, along with her other gifts of beauty and nobility, the lady had brought into the house of Roderigo such an insufferable portion of pride that in this respect Lucifer himself could not equal her; for her husband, who had experienced the effects of both, was at no loss to decide which was the most intolerable of the two. Yet it became infinitely worse when she discovered the extent of Roderigo's attachment to her, of which she availed herself to obtain an ascendancy over him and rule him with a rod of iron. Not content with this, when she found he would bear it she continued to annoy him with all kinds of insults and taunts, in such a way as to give him the most indescribable pain and uneasiness.

For what with the influence of her father, her brothers, her friends, and relatives, the duty of the matrimonial yoke, and the love he bore her, he suffered all for some time with the patience of a saint. It would be useless to recount the follies and extravagances into which he ran in order to gratify her taste for dress, and every article of the newest fashion in which our city, ever so variable in its nature, according to its usual habits, so much abounds. Yet, to live upon easy terms with her, he was obliged to do more than this; he had to assist his father-in-law in portioning off his other daughters; and she next asked him to furnish one of her brothers with goods to sail for the Levant, another with silks for the West, while a third was to be set up in a gold-beater's establishment at Florence. In such objects the greatest part of his fortune was soon consumed.

At length the Carnival season was at hand; the festival of St. John was to be celebrated, and the whole city, as usual, was in a ferment. Numbers of the noblest families were about to vie with each other in the splendour of their parties, and the Lady Onesta, being resolved not to be outshone by her acquaintance, insisted that Roderigo should exceed them all in the richness of their feasts. For the reasons above stated, he submitted to her will; nor, indeed, would he have scrupled at doing much more, however difficult it might have been, could he have flattered himself with a hope of preserving the peace and comfort of his household, and of awaiting quietly the consummation of his ruin.

But this was not the case, inasmuch as the arrogant temper of his wife had grown to such a height of asperity by long indulgence, that he was at a loss in what way to act. His domestics, male and female, would no longer remain in the house, being unable to support for any length of time the intolerable life they led. The inconvenience which he suffered in consequence of having no one to whom he could intrust his affairs it is impossible to express. Even his own familiar devils, whom he had brought along with him, had already deserted him, choosing to return below rather than longer submit to the tyranny of his wife.

Left, then, to himself, amidst this turbulent and unhappy life, and having dissipated all the ready money he possessed, he was compelled to live upon the hopes of the returns expected from his ventures in the East and the West. Being still in good credit, in order to support his rank he resorted to bills of exchange; nor was it long before, accounts running against him, he found himself in the same situation as many other unhappy speculators in that market.

Just as his case became extremely delicate, there arrived sudden tidings both from East and West that one of his wife's brothers had dissipated the whole of Roderigo's profits in play, and that while the other was returning with a rich cargo uninsured, his ship had the misfortune to be wrecked, and he himself was lost. No sooner did this affair transpire than his creditors assembled, and supposing it must be all over with him, though their bills had not yet become due, they resolved to keep a strict watch over him in fear that he might abscond.

Roderigo, on his part, thinking that there was no other remedy, and feeling how deeply he was bound by the Stygian law, determined at all hazards to make his escape. So taking horse one morning early, as he luckily lived near the Prato gate, in that direction he went off. His departure was soon known; the creditors were all in a bustle; the magistrates were applied to, and the officers of justice, along with a great part of the populace, were despatched in pursuit. Roderigo had hardly proceeded a mile before he heard this hue-and-cry, and the pursuers were soon so close at his heels that the only resource he had left was to abandon the high road and take to the open country, with the hope of concealing himself in the fields.

But finding himself unable to make way over the hedges and ditches, he left his horse and took to his heels, traversing fields of vines and canes, until he reached Peretola, where he entered the house of Matteo del Bricca, a labourer of Giovanna del Bene. Finding him at home, for he was busily providing fodder for his cattle, our hero earnestly entreated him to save him from the hands of his adversaries close behind, who would infallibly starve him to death in a dungeon, engaging that if Matteo would give him refuge he would make him one of the richest men alive, and afford him such proofs of it before he took his leave as would convince him of the truth of what he said; and if he failed to do this, he was quite content that Matteo himself should deliver him into the hands of his enemies.

Now Matteo, although a rustic, was a man of courage, and concluding that he could not lose anything by the speculation, he gave him his hand and agreed to save him. He then thrust our hero under a heap of rubbish, completely enveloping him in weeds; so that when his pursuers arrived they found themselves quite at a loss, nor could they extract from Matteo the least information as to his appearance. In this dilemma there was nothing left for them but to proceed in the pursuit, which they continued for two days, and then returned, jaded and disappointed, to Florence. In the meanwhile, Matteo drew our hero from his hiding-place, and begged him to fulfil his engagement.

To this his friend Roderigo replied:

"I confess, brother, that I am under great obligations to you, and I mean to return them. To leave no doubt upon your mind, I will inform you who I am"; and he proceeded to acquaint him with all the particulars of the affair, how he had come into the world, and married, and run away.

He next described to his preserver the way in which he might become rich, which was briefly as follows: As soon as Matteo should hear of some lady in the neighbourhood being said to be possessed, he was to conclude that it was Roderigo himself who had taken possession of her; and he gave him his word, at the same time, that he would never leave her until Matteo should come and conjure him to depart. In this way he might obtain what sum he pleased from the lady's friends for the price of exorcising her; and having mutually agreed upon this plan, Roderigo disappeared.

Not many days elapsed before it was reported in Florence that the daughter of Messer Ambrogio Amedei, a lady married to Buonajuto Tebalducci, was possessed by the devil. Her relations did not fail to apply every means usual on such occasions to expel him, such as making her wear upon her head St. Zanobi's cap, and the cloak of St. John of Gualberto; but these had only the effect of making Roderigo laugh. And to convince them that it was really a spirit that possessed her, and that it was no flight of the imagination, he made the young lady talk Latin, hold a philosophical dispute, and reveal the frailties of many of her acquaintance. He particularly accused a certain friar of having introduced a lady into his monastery in male attire, to the no small scandal of all who heard it, and the astonishment of the brotherhood.

Messer Ambrogio found it impossible to silence him, and began to despair of his daughter's cure. But the news reaching Matteo, he lost no time in waiting upon Ambrogio, assuring him of his daughter's recovery on condition of his paying him five hundred florins, with which to purchase a farm at Peretola. To this Messer Ambrogio consented; and Matteo immediately ordered a number of masses to be said, after which he proceeded with some unmeaning ceremonies calculated to give solemnity to his task. Then approaching the young lady, he whispered in her ear:

" Roderigo, it is Matteo that is come. So do as we agreed upon, and get out."

Roderigo replied: ' It is all well; but you have not asked enough to make you a rich man. So when I depart I will take possession of the daughter of Charles, King of Naples, and I will not leave her till you come. You may then demand whatever you please for your reward; and mind that you never trouble me again."

And when he had said this, he went out of the lady, to the no small delight and amazement of the whole city of Florence.

It was not long again before the accident that had happened to the daughter of the King of Naples began to be buzzed about the country, and all the monkish remedies having been found to fail, the King, hearing of Matteo, sent for him from Florence. On arriving at Naples, Matteo, after a few ceremonies, performed the cure. Before leaving the Princess, however, Roderigo said:

" You see, Matteo, I have kept my promise and made a rich man of you, and I owe you nothing now. So, henceforward you will take care to keep out of my way, lest, as I have hitherto done you some good, just the contrary should happen to you in future."

Upon this Matteo thought it best to return to Florence, after receiving fifty thousand ducats from His Majesty, in order to enjoy his riches in peace, and never once imagined that Roderigo would come in his way again.

But in this he was deceived; for he soon heard that a daughter of Louis, King of France, was possessed by an evil spirit, which disturbed our friend Matteo not a little, thinking of His Majesty's great authority and of what Roderigo had said. Hearing of Matteo's great skill, and finding no other remedy, the King despatched a messenger for him, whom Matteo contrived to send back with a variety of excuses.

But this did not long avail him; the King applied to the Florentine council, and our hero was compelled to attend. Arriving with no very pleasant sensations at Paris, he was introduced into the royal presence, when he assured His Majesty that though it was true he had acquired some fame in the course of his demoniac practice, he could by no means always boast of success, and that some devils were of such a desperate character as not to pay the least attention to threats, enchantments, or even the exorcisms of religion itself. He would, nevertheless, do His Majesty's pleasure, entreating at the same time to be held excused if it should happen to prove an obstinate case.

To this the King made answer, that be the case what it might, he would certainly hang him if he did not succeed. It is impossible to describe poor Matteo's terror and perplexity on hearing these words; but at length mustering courage, he ordered the possessed Princess to be brought into his presence. Approaching as usual close to her ear, he conjured Roderigo in the most humble terms, by all he had ever done for him, not to abandon him in such a dilemma, but to show some sense of gratitude for past services and to leave the Princess.

"Ah! thou traitorous villain!" cried Roderigo, "hast thou, indeed, ventured to meddle in this business? Dost thou boast thyself a rich man at my expense? I will now convince the world and thee of the extent of my power, both to give and to take away. I shall have the pleasure of seeing thee hanged before thou leavest this place."

Poor Matteo finding there was no remedy, said nothing more, but, like a wise man, set his head to work in order to discover some other means of expelling the spirit; for which purpose he said to the King:

"Sire, it is as I feared: there are certain spirits of so malignant a character that there is no keeping any terms with them, and this is one of them. However, I will make a last attempt, and I trust that it will succeed according to our wishes. If not, I am in your Majesty's power, and I hope you will take compassion on my innocence. In the first place, I have to entreat that your Majesty will order a large stage to be erected in the centre of the great square, such as will admit the nobility and clergy of the whole city. The stage ought to be adorned with all kinds of silks and with cloth of gold, and with an altar raised in the middle. To-morrow morning I would have your Majesty, with your full train of lords and ecclesiastics in attendance, seated in order and in magnificent array, as spectators of the scene at the said place. There, after having celebrated solemn mass, the possessed Princess must appear; but I have in particular to entreat that on one side of the square may be stationed a band of men with drums, trumpets, horns, tambours, bagpipes, cymbals, and kettle-drums, and all other kinds of instruments that make the most infernal noise. Now, when I take my hat off, let the whole band strike up, and approach with the most horrid uproar towards the stage. This, along with a few other secret remedies which I shall apply, will surely compel the spirit to depart."

These preparations were accordingly made by the royal command; and when the day, being Sunday morning, arrived, the stage was seen crowded with people of rank and the square with the people. Mass was celebrated, and the possessed Princess conducted between two bishops, with a train of nobles, to the spot.

Now, when Roderigo beheld so vast a concourse of people, together with all this awful preparation, he was almost struck dumb with astonishment, and said to himself:

"I wonder what that cowardly wretch is thinking of doing now? Does he imagine I have never seen finer things than these in the regions above—ay! and more horrid things below? However, I will soon make him repent it, at all events."

Matteo then approaching him, besought him to come out; but Roderigo replied:

"Oh, you think you have done a fine thing now! What do you mean to do with all this trumpery? Can you escape my power, think you, in this way, or elude the vengeance of the King? Thou poltroon villain, I will have thee hanged for this!"

And as Matteo continued the more to entreat him, his adversary still vilified him in the same strain. So Matteo, believing there was no time to be lost, made the sign with his hat, when all the musicians who had been stationed there for the purpose suddenly struck up a hideous din, and ringing a thousand peals, approached the spot.

Roderigo pricked up his ears at the sound, quite at a loss what to think, and rather in a perturbed tone of voice he asked Matteo what it meant.

To this the latter returned, apparently much alarmed:

"Alas! dear Roderigo, it is your wife; she is coming for you!"

It is impossible to give an idea of the anguish of Roderigo's mind and the strange alteration which his feelings underwent at that name. The moment the name of "wife" was pronounced, he had not longer presence of mind to consider whether it were probable, or even possible, that it could be her. Without replying a single word, he leaped out and fled in the utmost terror, leaving the lady to herself, and preferring rather to return to his infernal abode and render an account of his adventures, than run the risk of any further sufferings and vexations under the matrimonial yoke.

And thus Belphagor again made his appearance in the infernal domains, bearing ample testimony to the evils introduced into a household by a wife ; while Matteo, on his part, who knew more of the matter than the devil, returned triumphantly home, not a little proud of the victory he had achieved.

MATTEO BANDELLO
1480–1562

KING MANSOR AND THE FISHERMAN

KING MANSOR of Morocco, among other amusements, was immoderately fond of the chase; and it one day so happened that, being on a hunting excursion, he was surprised by a terrific storm, which, with irresistible fury laying waste both corn and woodlands, soon dispersed his courtiers on all sides in search of shelter. Mistaking his way in the confusion which ensued, King Mansor, separated at length from his companions, wandered through the forests until nightfall, and such was the tempestuous raging of the winds that, almost despairing of finding shelter, he checked his steed, doubtful which way he should venture to proceed. From the terrific darkness of the sky, relieved only by sheets of flashing light shooting across the far horizon, he was fearful of going farther, lest he should incur still greater danger, either by riding into pitfalls or the deep marshes bordering the forest grounds. As he thus stood, listening to the distant thunder and the raving of the storm, he stretched his view in vain to discover some signs of human existence; until, on proceeding a few more steps, a light suddenly appeared at only a short distance from him. It was from the window of a poo fisherman's hut, who earned his livelihood by catching eels in the adjacent pools and marshes. On hearing the voice of the King, who rushed forward with a shout of joy on beholding a human habitation, the fisherman hastened to the assistance of the bewildered traveller, whom he believed to have lost his way in the storm. Inquiring who called, King Mansor approached near, and entreated him, if he possessed the least charity, to direct him by the shortest path to the residence of the monarch.

"The King's court," replied the poor man, "is distant from this place above ten long miles."

"Yet I will make it worth your trouble, friend, to guide me thither; consent to oblige me, and you shall have no reason to complain," said the King.

"Though you were King Mansor himself," returned the fisherman, "who entreated as much, I would not venture upon it at this hour of the night, and such a night as this is ; for I should render myself guilty, perhaps, of leading our honoured Monarch into destruction. The night is dark, and the waters are out around us."

" But why should you, friend, be so very solicitous about the safety of the King ? "

" Oh," replied the good man, " because I honour him more than I do any one else, and love him more than myself."

" But what good has he ever done you," asked the King, " that you should hold him in such high esteem ? Methinks you would be rather more comfortably lodged and clothed were you any extraordinary favourite of his."

" Not so," answered the fisherman ; " for tell me, Sir Knight, what greater favour can I receive from my honoured King, in my humble sphere, than to be protected in the enjoyment of my house and goods, and the little earnings which I make ? All I have I owe to his kindness, to the wisdom and justice with which he rules over his subjects, preserving us in peace or protecting us in war from the inroads of the Arabs, as well as all other enemies. Even I, a poor fisherman, with a wife and little family, am not forgotten, and enjoy my poverty in peace. He permits me to fish for eels wherever I please, and take them afterwards to the best market I can find, in order to provide for my little ones. At any hour, night or day, I go out or I come in just as I like, to or fro, in my humble dwelling ; and there is not a single person in all these neighbouring woods and valleys who has ever dared to do me wrong. To whom am I indebted for all this but to him for whom I daily offer up my prayers to God and our holy prophet to watch over his preservation ? But why do I talk, when I see you, Sir Knight, before me, dripping from the pelting of this pitiless storm ? Deign to come within, and receive what shelter my poor cabin will afford ; to-morrow I will conduct you to the King, or wherever else you please."

Mansor now freely availed himself of the invitation, and, dismounting from his horse, sought refuge from the still raging storm. The poor steed likewise shared the accommodation prepared in a little outhouse for the good man's ass, partaking of the corn and hay. Seated by the side of a good fire, the King was employed in drying himself and recruiting his exhausted strength, while the wife was busily cooking the eels for his royal supper. When they were served, having a decided distaste for fish, he somewhat anxiously inquired whether there was no kind of meat for which he might exchange them. The fisherman very honestly declared that it was true he had a she-goat with a kid ; and perceiving that his guest was no unworthy personage, he directly offered to serve it up to table ; which having done, he presented the King with those parts generally esteemed the best and the most delicious. After supper the Monarch, retiring to his rustic couch, reposed his wearied limbs and slumbered until the sun was up.

At the appointed hour he once more mounted his steed, attended by his kind host, who now took upon himself the office of a guide. They had scarcely proceeded beyond the confines of the marshes when they encountered several of the King's party, calling aloud in the utmost anxiety and searching for their royal master in every direction. Unbounded was the joy and congratulation of the courtiers on thus meeting with him safe and uninjured. The King then, turning round to the poor fisherman, informed him that he was the Monarch whom he had so much praised, and whom he had so humanely and honourably received the foregoing evening, and that he might rely upon him that his singular courtesy and good-will should not go unrewarded.

Now, there were certain hunting-lodges which the King had erected in those parts for the convenience which they afforded in his excursions, and several of his nobles had likewise adorned the surrounding country with various seats and other dwellings, so as to give a pleasing relief to the prospect. With the view of bestowing a handsome remuneration upon the good fisherman, the grateful Monarch gave orders that the pools and marshes adjacent to these dwellings should be drained. He then circumscribed the limits of a noble city, comprehending the palaces and houses already erected, and after conferring upon it various rich immunities, by which it shortly became both very populous and powerful, he named the place Cesar Elcabir, or the Great Palace, and presented it as a token of his gratitude to the honest fisherman.

At the period when his sons succeeded to it, no city throughout the King's dominions was to be compared with it in point of splendour and beauty of appearance. The mosques were extremely grand, nor were the colleges and hospitals less worthy of admiration. The inhabitants were in general liberal and kind-hearted men, of simple manners, and neat and plain in their dress and appearance. The gardens were at once spacious and beautiful, abounding in all kinds of fruits, which supplied a weekly market, the emporium of all the surrounding country.

THE MISCHIEVOUS APE

Matteo Bandello

IN the time of Lodovico Sforza, the unfortunate Duke of Milan, there was kept, among other living curiosities, in the ducal palace, a large and beautiful ape, whose amusing yet harmless manners, full of practical jests and witticisms, had long obtained for him the liberty of going at large. Such, indeed, was his reputation for prudence and good conduct that he was not merely permitted the range of the whole palace, but frequently visited the outskirts, in the vicinity of Maine, of Cusano, and San Giovanni, and was not unfrequently seen conversing with some friend upon the walls. In fact, most people were eager to show their respect for him by presenting him with fruits and other dainties, no less from regard to his ducal patron than to his own intrinsic merits. The singular pleasure he afforded to all classes of society by his happy talents of various kinds was always a sufficient passport from place to place.

But his favourite resort, among many others, was the house of an ancient gentlewoman, situated in the parish of San Giovanni, upon the walls, where he cultivated the society of her two sons, one of whom in particular, though at the head of a family, invariably received his monkey guest in the most amiable manner, making him as much at home as if he had been the lady's favourite lapdog. These young men, perceiving their aged mother amused with the animal's unequalled exhibitions of his art, vied with each other in paying the most gratifying attentions to his monkeyship, and would certainly, had he not happened to have been ducal property, either have purchased or stolen him, merely out of regard to their mother. The whole household, likewise, received orders to treat him with the same invariable kindness and respect, studying what appeared most agreeable to his taste, so as to give him an affection for the old lady's house. This last motive weighed so greatly with his apeship that he almost deserted his other neighbours in order to enjoy more of the society of these very agreeable friends, although he was careful to return to his own ducal residence at the castle in the evening.

During this time the aged lady, becoming very infirm, no longer left her chamber, where she was affectionately attended by her whole family, who supplied her with every alleviation in the power of medical advice to bestow. Thither, occasionally, our facetious hero was also introduced for the purpose of awakening a smile on the wan features of the patient by his strange and amusing manners, receiving some delicate morsels in return from the poor lady's own hand. As he possessed a natural taste, in common with most of his race, for every kind of sweets, he was in the habit of besieging the old lady's room with great perseverance and assiduity, feasting upon the best confectionery with far higher zest than the poor patient herself. Worn out at length by long infirmities and age, she soon after departed this world, having first with becoming piety confessed herself and received the holy sacraments of our Church, with the communion and extreme unction at the final close.

While the funeral ceremonies were preparing, and the last offices rendered to the deceased, the monkey appeared to pay remarkable attention to all that was going forward. The corpse being dressed, and placed on the funeral bier, the holy sisterhood then attended with the usual ceremonies, offering up hymns and aves to the Virgin for the soul of the deceased. The body was afterwards borne to the parish church not far distant, not unobserved by the monkey, who watched the procession depart. But he soon turned his attention to the state of things around him ; and after feasting on the cake and wine, being a little elevated, he began to empty the boxes and drawers, and examine the contents. Having observed the deceased in her last habiliments, and the form of her headdress when she was laid out, the facetious ape immediately began to array himself in the cast-off garments, exactly in the manner he had witnessed ; and so perfect was the resemblance, that when he had covered himself up in bed, the physician himself would have been puzzled to detect the cheat. Here the false patient lay when the domestics entered the chamber, and suddenly perceiving the monkey thus dexterously laid out, they ran back in the utmost terror and surprise, believing that they had really seen either the corpse or the spirit of the deceased. After recovering sufficient presence of mind to speak, they declared, as they hoped to be saved, that they had seen their mistress reposing upon her sick-couch as usual.

On the return of the two brothers with their friends and relatives from church, they directly resolved to ascend in a body into the sick-chamber ; and night already approaching, they all felt, in spite of their affected indifference, an unpleasant sensation on entering the room. Drawing near the bedside, they not only fancied they saw and heard a person breathe, but observing the coverings move, as if the patient were about to spring from the couch, they retreated with the utmost precipitation and alarm. When they had recovered their spirits a little, the guests requested that a priest might be sent for, to whom, on his arrival, they proceeded to explain the case.

On hearing the nature of it, the good friar, being of a truly prudent and pious turn, despatched a person back for his clerk, with orders to bring with him the large ivory crucifix and the illuminated psalter. These, with the help of holy water, the wafer, and the priest's stole, were judged a sufficient match for the devices of the Evil One ; and thus armed, repeating the seven psalms, with due ejaculations to the Virgin, they once more ascended the stairs, the clerk, in obedience to the friar, bearing the huge ivory crucifix at their head. He had previously exhorted the brothers to have no fears for the final salvation of their parent, as the number and excellence of her confessions were an effectual preservative against the most diabolical efforts of the adversary. He maintained that there was not the least cause for alarm, for what the servants had beheld were merely Satanic illusions, which he had frequently been in the habit of dispelling with singular success ; and that having made use of his exorcisms, he would then bless the house, and, with the Lord's help, lay such a curse upon the bad spirits as would deprive them of the least inclination to return.

When they arrived at the chamber door, all the guests, in spite of these encouraging exhortations and the sprinkling of holy water, drew back, while the bold friar ordered his clerk to advance in the name of the Lord ; which he did, followed only by his superior. Approaching the sick-bed, they perceived Monna Bertuccia, our facetious ape, laid out, as we have said, in perfect personification of the deceased. After mumbling some prayers, and flourishing the cross in vain, for some time, they began to entertain doubts of their success, though at the same time they felt ashamed to retreat. So sprinkling the holy water with a more liberal hand, crying "*Asperges me domine* ; *asperges me*" ; they complimented the ape with a portion of it in his face. Expecting upon this to be next saluted with a blow of the huge cross, he suddenly began to grin and chatter in so horrible a manner, that the sacred vessel fell from the priest's hands, and the clerk at the same time dropping the crucifix, they both fled together. Such was their haste, that they stumbled one over the other down the stairs, the priest falling upon his clerk when they reached the bottom.

On hearing the sudden crash, and the terrified exclamations of the good friar, " *Jesus, Jesus, Domine, adjuva me,*" the brothers, followed by the rest of the party, rushed towards the spot, eagerly inquiring what dreadful accident had occurred. Both of the holy personages gazed on the guests without being able to utter a word, but their pallid looks spoke volumes sufficient to answer all demands. The poor clerk fainted away, no less from excess of fear than from the terrible fall he had just received. Having obliged both to partake of some restoratives, the priest at length summoned courage enough to say, " It is true, my dear children, I have indeed seen your poor departed mother in the form of a fierce demon " ; when just as he had finished these words, the cause of all their disturbance, desirous of securing the remnants of the feast, was heard approaching at a pretty brisk and clattering pace down the unlucky stairs.

Without giving any of the party time to discover a fresh place of refuge, or even to prepare their minds for his reception, he bounced suddenly into the room, armed *cap-à-pie,* in the fearful petticoats of the deceased. His head was dressed to a nicety exactly in the same manner as the old lady's, and his whole body very decently arrayed in her late habiliments. He placed himself in the midst of the company, all of whom stood rooted to the spot, silent and awe-stricken, awaiting the dreadful scene that might ensue. The wrinkles in his countenance certainly bore no small resemblance to those in the features of the deceased, to which his very serious demeanour added not a little. Yet, after a few secret ejaculations for divine protection on the part of the guests, the facetious visitor was soon recognised by one of the brothers, the only person who had possessed courage to look the monkey in the face on his sudden entrance into the room.

Momentary prayers and exclamations were then as suddenly converted into bursts of laughter, and in a few minutes the author of all their sufferings began to resume the usual hilarity of his disposition, to exhibit his best manœuvres in the saltic art, and with the greatest politeness severally to accost the company. He evinced, however, the utmost aversion to disrobing himself of his new honours, snapping at any one who ventured to approach him, while he performed his antics in the ablest and most whimsical manner. In full dress he thus set out on his return to the castle, meeting with reiterated plaudits as he passed along the streets. In this state he was welcomed home by the domestics of the castle, producing infinite diversion among the courtiers, and all those who witnessed his exploits. Nor did the two brothers punish him for his involuntary fault ; rather kindly permitting him to return to his old haunts, where he feasted and frolicked away his days, until he attained to a happy and respectable old age.

LUIGI DA PORTO
1485–1529

THE STORY OF ROMEO AND JULIET

AT the period when Bartolommeo della Scala, a gentle and accomplished prince, presided over the destinies of Verona, there flourished two noble but rival families, whose exasperation against each other was carried to the utmost extreme. The name of one of these was the Cappelletti, that of the other the Montecchi; and both families, we are told, were equally powerful and wealthy, abounding in friends and relatives, and highly favoured in Verona, under the above-mentioned prince.

Whether of a private or a public nature, the feud which arose between them was of a very ferocious and fatal character, various partisans on both sides falling victims to its rage. Nor was it until weary of mutual wrongs, and awed by the repeated commands and entreaties of their prince, that they were induced to enter into such terms as to meet or to address each other peaceably without apprehension of further violence and bloodshed. But daily becoming more reconciled, it happened that a festival was to be given by Messer Antonio, the head of the house of the Cappelletti, a man of gay and joyous character, who made the most magnificent preparations to receive all the chief families in the city.

At one of these assemblies there one evening appeared a youth of the Montecchi family, who followed thither some lady whom he was desirous, as lovers often are, of accompanying in person (no less than in mind) upon such occasions of general festivity. He had a noble and commanding person, with elegant and accomplished manners; and he had no sooner withdrawn his mask, screening himself in the character of a wood-nymph, than every eye was turned with admiration on his beauty, which appeared to surpass even that of the most beautiful ladies present. But he more especially attracted the attention of an only daughter of Messer Antonio, whose charms both of mind and person were unrivalled throughout the whole city.

Such was the impression she received at his appearance, that from the moment their eyes first met she found that she was no longer mistress of her own feelings. She saw him retire into a distant part of the assembly, seldom coming forward either in the dance or in converse with others, bearing himself like one who kept a jealous watch over some beloved object whom he would fain have held aloof from the joyous scene. Such a thought struck a chill to her heart, as she had heard he was a youth of warm and animated manners.

About the approach of midnight, towards the conclusion of the ball, was struck up the dance of the torch, or of the hat, whichever we choose to call it, usually proposed with us before the breaking up of the feast. While the company stand round in a circle, each dancer takes his lady, and the lady him, changing partners as they please. As it went round, the noble youth was led out by a lady who chanced to place him near the enamoured daughter of Messer Antonio. On the other side of her stood a youth named Marcuccio Guercio, whose hand, ever cold to the touch, happened to come in contact with the fair lady's palm ; and soon after Romeo Montecchi, being on her left hand, took it in his, as was customary. On which the lady, anxious to hear his voice, said :

" Welcome to my side, Messer Romeo."

And he, observing her eyes were fixed upon his, awaiting his reply, and delighted at the tone of her voice, returned :

" How ! am I indeed then welcome ? "

" Yes, and I ought to thank you," she returned, smiling, " since my left hand is warmed by your touch, whilst that of Marcuccio freezes my right."

Assuming a little more confidence, Romeo again replied :

" If your hand, lady, feels the warmth of mine, my heart no less has kindled warm at your eyes."

A short bright smile was the only answer to this, except that in a lower tone, as fearful of being seen or heard, she half whispered back :

" I vow, O Romeo, there is no lady here whom I think nearly so handsome as you seem to me."

Fascinated by her sweet address, Romeo, with still greater warmth, replied :

" Whatever I may be, I only wish you, sweet lady, to hold me ever at your service."

When the festival broke up, and Romeo had retired to his chamber, dwelling on the harsh usage of his former love, from whose eyes he had drunk softness mixed with too much scorn, he resolved to give his soul wholly, even to the fair foe of his father's house. She, on the other hand, had thought of little else since she left him than of the supreme felicity she should enjoy in obtaining so noble a youth for her lord. Yet when she reverted to the deadly enmity which had so long reigned between the two houses, her fears overpowered the gentler feelings of her soul, and unable wholly to subdue them, she inveighed against her own folly in the following words :

" Wretch that I am ! what enchantment thus drags me to my ruin ? Without hope or guide, O how shall I escape ? for Romeo loves me not. Alas ! he perhaps feels nothing but hatred against our house, and would perhaps only seek my shame. And were it possible he should think of taking me for his wedded wife, my father would never consent to bestow my hand."

Then, revolving other feelings in her mind, she flattered herself that their attachment might become the means of further reconciliation between the houses, even now wearied with their mutual feuds ; and, " Oh ! " she exclaimed, " what a blissful means of changing foes into relatives ! "

Fixed in this resolve, she again met Romeo with eyes of softness and regard. Mutually animated with equal ardour and admiration, the loved image was fixed so deeply in their imagination, that they could no longer refrain from seeing each other ; and sometimes at the windows and sometimes in the church, they sought with avidity every occasion to express their mutual passion through their eyes, and neither of them seemed to enjoy rest out of the presence of the beloved object. But chiefly Romeo, fired at the sight of her exquisite charms and manners, braved all risks for the pleasure of having her near him ; and he would frequently pass the greatest part of the night around her house, beneath her windows, or, scaling the walls, force his way to the balcony that commanded a view of her chamber, without the knowledge either of herself or others ; and there he would sit for hours, gazing and listening his soul away, enamoured of her looks and voice. He would afterwards throw himself listlessly to sleep, careless of returning home, in the woods or in the roads.

But one evening, as love would have it, the moon shining out more brightly than usual, the adventurous Romeo was discovered by his lady, as she opened the casement, on the balcony. Imagining that it might be some one else, he retreated, when, catching a glimpse of his figure, she gently called to him :

" Wherefore, O Romeo, come you hither ? "

" It is the will of love : therefore do I come," he replied.

" And if you should be found here, Romeo, know you it will be sudden death ? "

" Too well I do, dear lady ; and I doubt not it will happen so some night, if you refuse me your aid. But as I must at some time die, wherever I may be, I would rather yield my breath here as near you as I dare, with whom I would ever choose to live, did Heaven and you consent."

To which words the lady replied, " Believe me, Romeo, it is not I who would forbid thee to remain honourably at my side ; it is thou, and the enmity thou and thine bear us, that stand between us twain."

" Yet can I truly aver," replied the youth, " that the dearest hope I have long indulged has been to make you mine ; and if you had equal wishes, on you alone it would rest to make me for ever yours : no hand of man, believe me, love, should sunder us again."

On saying this, they agreed on further means to meet again, and converse much longer some future evening ; and they retired, full of each other, to rest.

The noble youth having frequently in this way held appointments with her, one winter's evening, while the snow fell thick and fast about him, he called to her from the usual spot :

" Ah, Juliet, Juliet ! how long will you see me thus languishing in vain ? Do you feel nothing for me, who through these cold nights, exposed to the stormy weather, wait on the cold ground to behold you ? "

" Alas ! alas ! I do indeed pity you," returned a sweet voice, " but what would you that I should do ? often have I besought you to go away."

" No, no," returned Romeo, " not away : and therefore, gentle lady, deign to give me refuge in your chamber from these bitter winds."

Turning towards him with a somewhat scornful voice, the lady reproached him :

" Romeo, I love you as much as it is possible for woman to love ; therefore it is that you ask me this ; your worth has led me farther than I ought to go. But, cruel as you are, if you dream that you can enjoy my love by long prevailing suit in the manner you imagine, lay such thoughts aside, for you deceive yourself, Montecchi. And as I will no longer see you nightly perilling your life for me, I frankly tell you, Romeo, that if you please to take me as I am, I will joyfully become your wife, giving myself up wholly to your will, ready to follow you over the world wherever you may think best."

" And this," replied the gentle youth, " is all I have so long wished ; now then let it be done ! "

" So let it be, even as you will," cried Juliet ; " only permit the Friar Lorenzo da San Francesco, my confessor, first to knit our hands, if you wish me wholly and happily to become yours."

" Am I to suppose, then, that Friar Lorenzo, my love, is acquainted with the secret of your breast ? "

" Yes, Romeo," returned Juliet, " and he will be ready to grant us what we request of him " ; and here, having fixed upon the proper measures, they again took leave of each other.

The friar, who belonged to the minor order of Osservanza, was a very learned man, well skilled no less in natural than in magical arts, and was extremely intimate with Romeo, in whom he had found it necessary to confide on an occasion in which he might otherwise have forfeited his reputation, which he was very desirous of maintaining with the vulgar. He had fixed upon Romeo in his emergency, as the most brave and prudent gentleman he knew to trust with the affair he had in hand. To him only he unbosomed his whole soul ; and Romeo, having now recourse to him in his turn, acquainted him with his resolution of making the lovely daughter of Messer Antonio as quickly as possible his wedded wife, and that they had together fixed upon him as the secret instrument and witness of their nuptials, and afterwards as the medium of their reconciliation with her father.

The friar immediately signified his consent, no less because he ventured not to oppose or disoblige the lover, than because he believed it might be attended with happy results ; in which case he would be likely to derive great honour from the heads of both houses, as the means of their reconciliation.

In the meanwhile, it being the season of Lent, the fair Juliet, under semblance of going to confession, sought the residence of Friar Francesco, and having entered into one of the confessionals made use of by the monks, she inquired for Lorenzo, who, hearing her voice, led her along after Romeo into the convent. Then, closing the doors of the confessional, he removed an iron grate which had hitherto separated her from her lover, saying :

" I have been always glad to see you, my daughter ; but you will now be far dearer to me than ever if you wish to receive Messer Romeo here as your husband."

To which Juliet answered that there was nothing she so much wished as that she might lawfully become his wife, and that she had therefore hastened thither, in order that before Heaven and him she might take those vows which love and honour required, and which the friar must witness, as her trust in him was great.

Then, in the presence of the priest, who performed the ceremony under the seal of confession, Romeo espoused the fair young Juliet; and having concluded how they were to meet each other again at night, exchanging a single kiss, they took leave of the friar, who remained in the confessional awaiting the arrival of penitents. Having thus secretly obtained the object of their wishes, the youthful Romeo and his bride for many days enjoyed the most unalloyed felicity, hoping at the same time for a favourable occasion to become reconciled to her father, in acquainting him with their marriage.

But Fortune, as if envious of their supreme happiness, just at this time revived the old deadly feud between the houses in such a way, that in a few days, neither of them wishing to yield to the other, the Montecchi and the Cappelletti meeting together, from words proceeded to blows. Desirous to avoid giving any mortal hurts to his sweet wife's relatives, Romeo had the sorrow of beholding his own party either wounded or driven from the streets, and incensed with passion against Tebaldo Cappelletti, the most formidable of his adversaries, he struck him dead at his feet with a single blow, and put his companions to flight, terrified at the loss of their chief. The homicide had been witnessed by too many to remain long a secret, and the complaint being brought before the Prince, the Cappelletti threw the blame exclusively on Romeo, who was sentenced by the council to perpetual banishment from Verona.

It is easier for those who truly love to imagine than it is here to describe the sensations of the young bride on receiving these tidings. She wept long and bitterly, refusing to hear any consolation; and her grief was deepened by the reflection that she could share it with no one. Romeo, on the other hand, regretted leaving his country on her account alone, and resolving to take a sorrowful farewell of the object of all his soul's wishes, he had again recourse to the assistance of the friar, who despatched a faithful follower of Romeo's father to apprise his wife of the time and place of meeting, and thither she eagerly repaired.

Retiring together into the confessional, they there wept bitterly over their misfortune. The young bride at length, checking her tears, exclaimed in an accent of despair :

" I cannot bear to live ! What will my life be without you ? Oh, let me fly with you ; wherever you go I will follow, a faithful and loving servant. I will cast these long tresses away, and by none shall you be served so well, so truly, as by me."

" No, never let it be said," replied Romeo, " that you accompanied me in other guise than in that of a cherished and honoured bride. Yet were it not that I feel assured that our affairs will soon improve, and that the strife between our two families will very shortly cease, indeed I could not bear, my love, to leave you. We shall not long be divided, and my thoughts, sweet Juliet, will be ever with you. And should we not be quickly restored to each other, it will then be time to fix how we are to meet again."

So, after having wept and embraced each other again and again, they tore themselves asunder, his wife entreating that he would remain as near her as possible, and by no means go so far as Rome or Florence.

After concealing himself for some time in the monastery of Friar Lorenzo, Romeo set out more dead than alive for Mantua, but not before he had agreed with the servant of the lady that he was to be informed, through the friar, of every particular that might occur during his absence ; and he further instructed the servant, as he valued his protection and rewards, to obey his wife in the minutest things which she might require of him. After her husband had departed, she gave herself up a prey to the deepest grief, a grief so incessant as to leave its traces on her beauty, and attract the attention of her mother. She tenderly loved her daughter, and affectionately inquiring into the cause of her affliction, she merely received vague excuses in reply.

" But you are always in tears, my daughter," she continued ; " what is it that can affect you thus ? Tell me, for you are dear to me as my own life, and if it depend upon me, you shall no longer weep."

Then, imagining that her daughter might probably wish to bestow her hand in marriage, yet be afraid of avowing her wishes, she determined to speak to her husband on the subject ; and thus, in the hope of promoting her health and happiness, she pursued the very means that led to her destruction.

She informed Messer Antonio that she had observed, for many

days past, that something was preying on their daughter's mind, that she was no longer like the same creature, and that although she had used every means to obtain her confidence as to the source of her affliction, it had been all in vain. She then urged her suspicions that Juliet perhaps wished to marry, but that, like a discreet girl as she certainly was, she was averse to declare her feelings.

" So I think, Messer Antonio, we had better without more delay make choice for our daughter of a noble husband. Juliet has already completed her eighteenth year, on St. Euphemia's Day; and when they have advanced much beyond this period, the beauty of women, so far from improving, is rather on the wane. Besides," continued her mother, " it is not well to keep girls too long at home, though our Juliet has always been an excellent child. I am aware you have already fixed upon her dower, and we have nothing to do but to select a proper object for her love."

Messer Antonio agreed with his lady, and highly commended the virtues and the prudence of his daughter. Not many days afterwards they proposed and entered into a treaty of marriage between the Count of Lodrone and their daughter. When it was on the point of being concluded, the lady, hoping to surprise her daughter with the agreeable tidings, bade her now rejoice, for that in a very few days she would be happily settled in marriage with a noble youth, and that she must no longer grieve, for it would take place with her father's consent and that of all her friends.

On hearing these words, Juliet burst into a flood of tears, while her mother endeavoured to console her with the hope of being happily settled in life within the course of eight days.

" You will then become the wife of Count Lodrone; nay, do not weep, for it is really true: will you not be happy, Juliet, then?"

" No, no, my dear mother, I shall never be happy."

" Then what can be the matter with you? What do you want? Only tell me; I will do anything you wish."

" Then I would wish to die, mother; nothing else is left me now."

Her mother then first became aware that she was the victim of some deep-seated passion, and saying little more, she left her. In the evening she related to her husband what had passed, at which he testified great displeasure, saying that it would be necessary to have the affair examined into before venturing to proceed further with the Count. And fearful lest any blame might attach to his family, he soon after sent for Juliet, with the intention of consulting her on the proposed marriage.

" It is my wish, my dear Juliet, to form an honourable connection for you in marriage. Will you be satisfied with it ? "

After remaining silent for some moments, his daughter replied :

" No, dear father, I cannot be satisfied."

" Am I to suppose, then, that you wish to take the veil, daughter ? "

" Indeed I know not what "——and with these words out gushed a flood of bitter tears.

" But this I know," returned her father, " you shall give your hand to Count Lodrone, and therefore trouble yourself no further."

" Never, never ! " cried Juliet, still weeping bitterly.

On this Messer Antonio threatened her with his heaviest displeasure did she again venture to dispute his will, commanding her immediately to reveal the cause of her unhappiness. And when he could obtain no other reply than sobs and tears, he quitted the apartment in a violent passion, unable to penetrate into her motives, leaving her with her mother alone. The wretched bride had already acquainted the servant intrusted with their secret, whose name was Pietro, with everything which had passed between herself and her parents, taking him to witness that she would sooner die than become the wife of any lord but Romeo. And this the good Pietro had carefully conveyed through the friar to the ears of the banished man, who had written to her, encouraging her to persevere, and by no means to betray the secret of their love, as he was then taking measures, within less than ten days, to bear her from her father's house.

Messer Antonio and his lady Giovanna being unable in the meanwhile, either by threats or kindness, to discover their daughter's objections to the marriage, or whether she was attached to another, determined to prosecute their design.

" Weep no more, girl," cried her mother, " for married you shall be, though you were to take one of the Montecchi by the hand, which I am sure you will never be compelled to do ! "

Fresh sobs and tears at these words burst from the poor girl, which only served to hasten her parents' preparations for her nuptials. Her despair was terrible when she heard the day named, and calling upon death to save her, she rushed out of her chamber, and repairing as fast as possible to the convent of the friar, in whom, next to Romeo, she trusted, and from whom she had received tidings of her husband, she revealed to him the cause of her anguish, often interrupted by her tears. She then conjured him, by the friendship and obligations which he owed to Romeo, to assist her in this her utter need.

" Alas ! of what use can I be," replied the friar, " when your two houses are even now so violently opposed to each other ? "

" But I know, father, that you are a learned and experienced man, and you can assist me in many ways if you please. If you should refuse me everything else, at least, however, grant me this. My nuptials are even now preparing in my father's palace ; he is now gone out of the city to give orders at the villa on the Mantuan road, whither they are about to carry me, that I may there be compelled to receive the Count, without a chance of opposition, as he is to meet me on my arrival at the place. Give me, therefore, poison, to free me at once from the grief and shame of exposing the wife of Romeo to such a scene. Give me poison, or I will myself plunge a dagger into my bosom ! "

The friar, on hearing these desperate intentions, and aware how deeply he was implicated with Romeo, who might become his worst enemy were he not in some way to obviate the danger, turning to Juliet, said:

" You know, my daughter, that I confess a great portion of the people here, and am respected by all, no testament, no reconciliation taking place without my mediation. I am therefore careful of giving rise to any suspicions which might affect me, and should especially wish to conceal my interference in an affair like the present. I would not incur such a scandal for all the treasure in the world. But, as I am attached both to yourself and Romeo, I will exert myself in your favour in such a way as I believe no one ever before did. You must first, however, take a vow that you will never betray to others the secret I now intrust you with."

" Speak, speak boldly, father," cried Juliet, " and give me the poison, for I will inform nobody."

" I will give you no poison," returned the friar ; " young and beautiful as you are, it would be too deep a sin. But if you possess courage to execute what I shall propose, I trust I may be able to deliver you safely into the hands of Romeo. You are aware that the family vault of the Cappelletti lies beyond this church in the cemetery of our convent. Now I will give you a certain powder, which, when you have taken it, will throw you into a deep slumber of eight and forty hours, and during that time you will be to all appearance dead, not even the most skilful physicians being able to detect a spark of life remaining.

In this state you will be interred in the vault of the Cappelletti, and at a fitting season I will be in readiness to take you away, and bring you to my own cell, where you can stay until I go, which will not be long, to the chapter ; after which, disguised in a monk's dress, I will bear you myself to your husband. But tell me, are you not afraid of being near the corpse of Tebaldo, your cousin, so recently interred in the same place ? "

With serene and joyful looks the young bride returned, " No, father ; for if by such means I can ever reach my Romeo, I would face not this alone, but the terrors of hell itself."

" This is well ; let it be done," cried the friar ; " but first write with your own hand an exact account of the whole affair to Romeo, lest by any mischance, supposing you dead, he may be impelled by his despair to do some desperate deed ; for I am sure he is passionately attached to you. There are always some of my brethren who have occasion to go to Mantua, where your husband resides : let me have your letter to him, and I will send it by a faithful messenger."

Having said this, the good monk, leaving the lady in the confessional, returned to his cell, but soon came back bringing a small vase with the powder in it, saying :

" Drink this, mixed with simple water, about midnight, and fear not. In two hours after it will begin to take effect, and I doubt not but our design will be crowned with success. But haste, and forget not to write the letter, as I have directed you, to Romeo, for it is of great importance."

Securing the powder, the fair bride hastened joyfully home to her mother, saying :

" Truly, dear mother, Friar Lorenzo is one of the best confessors in the world. He has so kindly advised me that I am quite recovered from my late unhappiness."

Overjoyed on perceiving her daughter's cheerfulness, the Lady Giovanna replied :

" And you shall return his kindness, my dear girl, with interest ; his poor brethren shall never be in want of alms."

Juliet's recovered spirits now banished every suspicion from the mind of her parents of her previous attachment to another, and they believed that some unhappy incident had given rise to the strange and melancholy disposition they had observed. They would now have been glad to withdraw their promise of bestowing her hand upon the

Count, but they had already proceeded so far that they could not, without much difficulty, retreat. Her lover was desirous that some one of his friends should see her; and her mother, Lady Giovanna, being somewhat delicate in her health, it was resolved that her daughter, accompanied by two of her aunts, should be carried to the villa at a short distance from the city—a step to which she made no opposition.

She accordingly went; and imagining that her father would immediately on her arrival insist upon the marriage, she took care to secure the powder given to her by the friar. At the approach of midnight, calling one of her favourite maids, brought up with her from her childhood, she requested her to bring her a glass of water, observing that she felt very thirsty; and as she drank it in the presence of the maid and one of her aunts, she exclaimed that her father should never bestow her hand upon the Count against her own consent. These simple women, though they had observed her throw the powder into the water, which she said was to refresh her, suspected nothing further and went to rest. When the servant had retired with the light, her young mistress rose from her bed, dressed herself, and again lay down, composing her limbs as if she were never more to rise, with her hands crossed upon her breast, awaiting the dreaded result.

In little more than two hours she lay to all appearance dead, and in this state she was discovered the next morning. The maid and her aunt, unable to awake her, feeling that she was already quite cold, and recollecting the powder, the strange expressions she had used, and, above all, seeing her dressed, began to scream aloud, supposing her to have poisoned herself. On this, the cries of her own maid, who loved her, were terrible.

"True, too true, dear lady: you said that your father should never marry you against your will. Alas! you asked me for the very water which was to occasion your death. Wretch that I am! And have you indeed left me, and left me thus? With my own hands I gave you the fatal cup, which, with yours, will have caused the death of your father, your mother, and us all. Ah! why did you not take me with you, who have always so dearly loved you in life?"

And saying this she threw herself by the side of her young mistress, embracing her cold form. Messer Antonio, hearing a violent uproar, hastened, trembling, to ascertain the cause, and the first object he beheld was his daughter stretched out in her chamber a corpse. Although he believed her gone beyond recovery, when he heard what she had drunk, he immediately sent to Verona for a very experienced physician, who having carefully observed and examined his daughter, declared that she had died of the effects of the poison more than six hours before.

The wretched father, on hearing his worst fears confirmed, was overwhelmed with grief; and the same tidings reaching the distracted mother, suddenly deprived her of all consciousness. When she was at length restored, she tore her hair, and calling upon her daughter's name, filled the air with her shrieks.

"She is gone! the only sweet solace of my aged days. Cruel, cruel! thou hast left me without even giving thy poor mother a last farewell! At least I might have drunk thy last words and sighs, and closed thine eyes in peace. Let my women come about me, let them assist me, that I may die! if they have any pity left, they will kill me; far better so to die than of a lingering death of grief. O God! in Thy infinite mercy take me away, for my life will be a burden to me now!"

Her women then came round her, and bore her to the couch, still weeping, and refusing all the consolation they could offer to her. The body of Juliet was in the meantime carried to Verona, and consigned with extraordinary ceremonies, amidst the lamentations of a numerous train of friends and relatives, to the vault in the cemetery of San Francesco, where the last rites to the dead were discharged.

The friar having occasion to be absent from the city, had, according to his promise, confided Juliet's letter to Romeo to the hands of one of his brethren going to Mantua. On arriving, he called several times at the house without having the good fortune to meet with Romeo, and, unwilling to trust such a letter to others, he retained it in his own hands, until Pietro, hearing of the death of Juliet, and not finding the friar in the city, resolved to bear the unhappy tidings to his master.

He arrived in Mantua the following night, and meeting with Romeo, who had not yet received the letter from the priest, he related to him, with tears in his eyes, the death of his young bride, whose burial he had himself witnessed. The hue of death stole over the features of Romeo as he proceeded with the sad story; and, drawing his sword, he was about to stab himself on the spot, had he not been prevented by force

"It is well," he cried, "but I shall not long survive the lady of my soul, whom I valued more than life! O Juliet, Juliet! it is thy husband who doomed thee to death! I came not, as I promised, to bear thee from thy cruel father, whilst thou, to preserve thy sweet faith unbroken, hast died for me ; and shall I, through fear of death, survive alone ? No, this shall never be ! "

Then, throwing a dark cloak which he wore over Pietro's shoulders, he cried, " Away, away ! leave me ! "

Romeo closed the doors after him, and preferring every other evil to that of life, only considered the best manner of getting rid of it. At last he assumed the dress of a peasant, and taking out a species of poison which he had always carried with him, to use in case of emergency, he placed it under the sleeve of his coat, and immediately set out on his return to Verona. Journeying on with wild and melancholy thoughts, he now defied his fate, hoping to fall by the hands of justice, or to lay himself down in the vault by the side of her he loved and die.

In this resolution, on the evening of the following day after her interment, he arrived at Verona without being discovered by any one. The same night, as soon as the city became hushed, he resorted to the convent of the Frati Minori, where the tombs of the Cappelletti lay. The church was situated in the Cittadella, where the monks at that time resided, although, for some reason, they have since left it for the suburb of San Zeno, now called Santo Bernardino, and the Cittadella was formerly, indeed, inhabited by San Francesco himself. Near the outer walls of this place there were then placed a number of large monuments such as we see round many churches, and beneath one of these was the ancient sepulchre of all the Cappelletti, in which the beautiful bride then lay.

Romeo approaching near not long after midnight, and possessing great strength, removed the heavy covering by force, and with some wooden stakes which he had brought with him, he propped it up to prevent it from closing again until he wished it ; and he then entered the tomb and replaced the covering. The lamp he carried cast a lurid light around, while his eyes wandered in search of the loved object, which, bursting open the living tomb, he quickly found. He beheld the features of the beautiful Juliet now mingled with a heap of lifeless dust and bones, on which a sudden tide of sorrow sprung into his eyes, and amidst bitter sobs he thus spoke :

" O eyes, which while our loves to Heaven were dear, shone sweetly upon mine ! O sweeter mouth, a thousand and a thousand times so fondly kissed by me alone, and rich in honeyed words ! O bosom, in which my whole heart lay treasured up, alas ! all closed and mute and cold I find ye now ! My hapless wife, what hath love done for thee, but led thee hither ? And why so soon two wretched lovers perish ? I had not looked for this when hope and passion first whispered of other things. But I have lived to witness even this ! " and he pressed his lips to her mouth and bosom, mingling his kisses with his tears.

" Walls of the dead ! " he cried, " why fall ye not around me and crush me into dust ? Yet, as death is in the power of all, it is a despicable thing to wish yet fear it too."

Then, taking out the poison from under his vest, he thus continued:

" By what strange fatality am I brought to die in the sepulchre of my enemies, some of whom this hand hath slain ? But as it is pleasant to die near those we love, now, my beloved, let me die ! "

Then, seizing the fatal vial, he poured its whole contents into his frame, and catching the fair body of Juliet in his arms in a wild embrace, " Still so sweet," he cried, " dear limbs, mine, only mine ! And if yet thy pure spirit live, my Juliet, let it look from its seat of bliss to witness and forgive my cruel death ; as I could not delighted live with thee, it is not forbidden me with thee to die " ; and winding his arms about her, he awaited his final doom.

The hour was now arrived when, the vital powers of the slumbering lady reviving, and subduing the icy coldness of the poison, she would awake. Thus straitly folded in the last embraces of Romeo, she suddenly recovered her senses, and uttering a deep sigh, she cried :

" Alas ! where am I ? in whose arms, whose kisses ? Oh, unbind me, wretch that I am ! Base friar, is it thus you keep your word to Romeo, thus lead me to his arms ? "

Great was her husband's surprise to feel Juliet alive in his embrace. Recalling the idea of Pygmalion,

" Do you know me, sweet wife ? " he cried. " It is your love, your Romeo, hither come to die with you. I came alone and secretly from Mantua to find your place of rest."

Finding herself within the sepulchre and in the arms of Romeo, Juliet would not at first give credit to her senses ; but, springing out of his arms, gazed a moment eagerly on his face, and the next fell on his neck with a torrent of tears and kisses.

" O Romeo, Romeo ! what madness brings you hither ? Were not my letters which I sent you by the friar enough to tell you of my feigned death, and that I should shortly be restored to you ? "

The wretched youth, aware of the whole calamity, then gave way to his despair.

" Beyond all other griefs that lovers ever bore, Romeo, thy lot has been ! My life, my soul, I never had thy letters ! "

And he told her the piteous tale which he had heard from the lips of her servant, and that, concluding she was dead, he had hastened to keep her company, and had already drunk the deadly draught. At these last words, his unhappy bride, uttering a wild scream, began to beat her breast and tear her hair, and then in a state of distraction she threw herself by the side of Romeo, already lying on the ground, and, pouring over him a deluge of tears, imprinted her last kisses on his lips. All pale and trembling, she cried :

" Oh, my Romeo ! will you die in my sight, and I too the occasion of your death ? Must I live even a moment after you ? Ah, would that I could give my life for yours ! Would that I alone might die ! "

In a faint and dying tone her husband replied :

" If my love and truth were ever dear to you, my Juliet, live, for my sake live ; for it is sweet to know that you will then be often thinking of him who now dies for you, with his eyes still fixed on yours."

" Die ! yes ! you die for the death which in me was only feigned ! What, therefore, should I do for this your real, cruel death ? I only grieve that I have no means of accompanying you, and hate myself that I must linger on earth till I obtain them. But it shall not be long before the wretch who caused your death shall follow you " ; and uttering these words with pain, she swooned away upon his body. On again reviving, she felt she was catching the last breath, which now came thick and fast, from the breast of her husband.

Friar Lorenzo, in the meanwhile, aware of the supposed death and of the interment of Juliet, and knowing that the termination of her slumber was near, proceeded with a faithful companion about an hour before sunrise to the monument. On approaching the place, he heard her sobs and cries, and saw the light of a lamp through an aperture in the sepulchre. Surprised at this, he imagined that Juliet must have secreted the light in the monument, and awaking and finding no one there, had thus begun to weep and bewail herself. But on opening the sepulchre with the help of his companion, he beheld the weeping and distracted Juliet holding her dying husband in her arms, on which he immediately said :

" What ! did you think, my daughter, I should leave you here to die ? "

To which she only answered with another burst of sorrow :

"No! away! I only fear lest I should be made to live. Away, and close our sepulchre over our heads; here let me die. Or, in the name of pity, lend me a dagger, that I may strike it into my bosom and escape from my woes. Ah, cruel father! well hast thou fulfilled thy promise, well delivered to Romeo his letters, and borne me safely to him! See, he is lying dead in my arms"; and she repeated the fatal tale.

Thunderstruck at these words, the friar gazed upon the dying Romeo, exclaiming with horror:

"My friend, my Romeo! alas! what chance hath torn thee from us? Thy Juliet calls thee, Romeo; look up and hope. Thou art lying in her beauteous bosom and wilt not speak."

On hearing her loved name, he raised his languid eyes, heavy with death, and fixing them on her for a short space, closed them again. The next moment, turning himself round upon his face in a last struggle, he expired.

Thus wretchedly fell the noble youth, long lamented over by his fair bride, till, on the approach of day, the friar tenderly inquired what she would wish to do.

"To be left to die where I am," was the reply.

"Do not, daughter, say this, but come with me; for though I scarcely know in what way to proceed, I can perhaps find means of obtaining a refuge for you in some convent, where you may address your prayers to Heaven for your own and for your husband's sake."

"I desire you to do nothing for me," replied Juliet, "except this one thing, which I trust, for the sake of his memory," pointing to the body of Romeo, "you will do. Never breathe a syllable to any one living of our unhappy death, that our bodies may rest here together for ever in peace. And should our sad loves come to light, I pray you will beseech both our parents to permit our remains to continue mingled together in this sepulchre, as in love and in death we were still one."

Then, turning again towards the body of Romeo, whose head she held sustained upon her lap, and whose eyes she had just closed, bathing his cold features with her tears, she addressed him as if he had been in life:

"What shall I now do, my dear lord, since you have deserted me? What can I do but follow you? for nothing else is left me: death itself shall not keep me from you."

Having said this, and feeling the full weight of her irreparable loss in the death of her noble husband, resolute to die, she drew in her breath, and retaining it for some time, suddenly uttered a loud shriek and fell dead by her lover's side. The friar, perceiving that she was indeed dead, was seized with such a degree of terror and surprise, that, unable to come to any resolution, he sat down with his companion in the sepulchre bewailing the destiny of the lovers. At this time some of the officers of the police, being in search of a notorious robber, arrived at the spot, and perceiving a light and the sound of voices, they straightway ran to the place, and seizing upon the priests, inquired into their business.

Friar Lorenzo, recognising some of these men, was overpowered with shame and fear; but assuming a lofty voice, exclaimed:

"Back, sirs, I am not the man you take me for. What you are in want of you must search for elsewhere."

Their conductor then came forward, saying:

"We wish to be informed why the monument of the Cappelletti is thus violated by night, when a young lady of the family has been so recently interred here. And were I not acquainted with your excellent character, Friar Lorenzo, I should say you had come hither to despoil the dead."

The priests, having extinguished the lamp, then replied, "We shall not render an account of our business to you; it is not your affair."

"That is true," replied the other; "but I must report it to the Prince."

The friar, with a feeling of despair, then cried out, "Say what you please"; and closing up the entrance into the tomb he went into the church with his companion.

The morning was somewhat advanced when the friars disengaged themselves from the officers, one of whom soon related to the Cappelletti the whole of this strange affair. They, knowing that Friar Lorenzo had been very intimate with Romeo, brought him before the Prince, entreating that, if there were no other means, he might be compelled by torture to confess his reason for opening the sepulchre of the Cappelletti.

The Prince, having placed him under a strict guard, proceeded to interrogate him wherefore he had visited the tomb of the Cappelletti, as he was resolved to discover the truth.

"I will confess everything very freely," exclaimed the friar. "I was the confessor of the daughter of Messer Antonio, lately deceased in so very strange a manner. I loved her for her worth, and being compelled to be absent at the time of her interment, I went to offer up certain prayers over her remains, which, when nine times repeated by my beads, have power to liberate her spirit from the pangs of purgatory. And because few appreciate or understand such matters, the wretches assert that I went there for the purpose of despoiling the body. But I trust I am better known. This poor gown and girdle are enough for me, and I would not take a mite from all the treasures of the earth, much less the shrouds of the departed. They do me great wrong to suspect me of this crime."

The Prince would have been satisfied with this explanation, had it not been for the interference of other monks, who, jealous of the friar, and hearing that he had been found in the monument, examined further, and found the dead body of Romeo, a fact which was immediately made known to the Prince while still speaking to the friar. This appeared incredible to every one present, and excited the utmost amazement through the city.

The friar, then aware that it would be in vain farther to conceal his knowledge of the affair, fell at the feet of His Excellency, crying:

"Pardon, oh pardon, most noble Prince! I have said what is not truth, yet neither for any evil purpose nor for love of gain have I said it, but to preserve my faith entire, which I promised to two deceased and unhappy lovers."

On this the friar was compelled to repeat the whole of the preceding tale. The Prince, moved almost to tears as he listened, set out with a vast train of people to the monument of the family, and having ordered the bodies of the lovers to be placed in the Church of San Francesco, he summoned their fathers and friends to attend. There was now a fresh burst of sorrow springing from a double source. Although the parties had been the bitterest enemies, they embraced one another in tears, and the scene before them suddenly wrought that change in their hearts and feelings which neither the threats of their Prince nor the prayers of their friends had been able to accomplish. Their hatred became extinguished in the mingled blood of their unhappy children. A noble monument was erected to their memory, on which was inscribed the occasion of their death, and their bodies were entombed together with great splendour and solemnity, and wept over no less by their friends and relatives than by the whole afflicted city. Such a fearful close had the loves of Romeo and Juliet, such as you have heard, and as it was related to me by Pellegrino da Verona.

AGNOLO FIRENZUOLA
1493–1548

THE SURPRISING ADVENTURES OF MESSER NICCOLO

IN ancient days, it is said, there flourished in Tuscany two noble citizens, both extremely wealthy, and both descended from good families. Not satisfied, however, like too many, with the reputation acquired by their ancestors, nor esteeming the works of others as any kind of ornament to themselves, they vied with each other in conferring distinction upon their nobility by their actions, rather than in assuming it from the dignity of their birth. Thus in their correspondence, their manners, and the whole tenor of their life and transactions, they procured for themselves a high reputation throughout Florence, which was not a little enhanced by the mutual esteem and more than fraternal kindness that was invariably observed to exist between them. They were generally seen in company together, their pursuits were nearly congenial, and their days appeared to flow at once in so noble and so pure a stream, that Fortune herself seemed to respect their virtues and their happiness.

Her smiles, however, as of old, were delusive; for Niccolo degli Albizi, one of these two friends, hearing of the decease of an uncle, his mother's brother, who died extremely rich in Valencia, leaving Niccolo, in default of children, his sole heir, was under the necessity of making a voyage into Spain. Mentioning his intention to his friend Coppo, the latter directly proposed, as he expected, to accompany him. Having made their arrangements, therefore, they were just upon the point of departure, when, unfortunately, Coppo's father was seized with a mortal distemper, which terminated his existence in a few days, a circumstance that left Niccolo no alternative but that of giving up his voyage or proceeding alone.

Adopting the latter resolution, after taking a sorrowful and affectionate leave, he bent his course towards Genoa, and there took his passage in a Genoese vessel upon the point of sailing for a Spanish port. It was now that his fortune first began to wear a different aspect; for the ship had hardly made fifty leagues from shore, when about sunset the sea was observed to become white and foamy, presenting at the same time various other signs of an approaching tempest. And before the master of the vessel had completed his orders, she was enveloped in a torrent of rain, while the fierce hurricane rendered her unmanageable, bearing her onwards in a shroud of mist and darkness that defied the eye of the oldest navigator.

This soon became, if possible, more horribly appalling by contrast with the lurid flashes of lightning that broke athwart the gloom, consigning them again to utter darkness. Images of the most terrific nature haunted the fancy of the crew, thus suddenly deprived of all external objects ; and it was piteous to think of the efforts of those who retained heart enough to struggle with the adverse elements, while they often adopted, in hope of rescue, measures that tended, perhaps, only to accelerate their own destruction. Even the stentorian voice of the master could no longer be heard through the storm, while the straining and rending of the masts and sails, intermingled with occasional cries, and the deep volleys of thunder rolling in the distance, formed altogether a union of appalling sounds that struck terror to the boldest spirit.

The danger still increased, and their remaining courage dying away in their last feeble efforts, soon wholly forsook them ; for they were now borne mountains high, now plunged, as it were, into the abysses of the deep, from which the ship would again emerge, to the surprise of all, like a sea-bird from the hollow caverns of the deep. So terrific indeed, before she yielded, did the scene appear, that the hair of the boldest sailor stood on end, as he felt rather than saw the furious commingling, the utter confusion, and the wild reverberation, of heaven, air, and sea. Alas ! how hastily did the most niggardly and grasping hands consign their treasure, their richest silks and stuffs, to the remorseless deep, with all the precious metals that were first thrown overboard ; though, when lightened of her load, she only seemed to drive more madly before the winds.

The affrighted passengers, who had before sought to shun the sight of their approaching doom below, at length rushed tumultuously upon deck.

" The cabin is filling with water ! " was the cry, while every sailor who before had stood to his post then fell on his knees, and embracing his nearest friend, and joining in the general cry of *Misericordia !* appeared to consign himself to his doom.

How many who wanted comfort themselves generously tried in that bitter moment to support others yet weaker and more appalled!

How many who had seldom or never prayed were heard muttering faint and incoherent appeals to Heaven!

Some called upon the Blessed Virgin, some upon San Niccolo di Bari, while others trusted to San Ermo; and pilgrimages to the holy sepulchre and religious vows were abundantly poured forth in the hope of being miraculously rescued, like Jonas, from the bowels of the deep.

The libertine was even heard to make a vow of marriage; dealers and usurers swore to make restitution; while such few as loved the world less uttered the most tender expressions to their absent fathers, mothers, children, and friends, at the same time mingling their pity for each other.

While thus employed, the mainmast with a terrific crash went into the sea, which was the signal for the vessel's parting, hardly affording time for a few of the most bold and active to seize the scattered pieces of the wreck. Niccolo, however, being among these last, supported himself with the aid of a small table, nor ever yielded his hold until he found himself thrown upon the coast of Barbary, a short way from Susa. Being there perceived by a party of fishermen, they took compassion upon him, and conducted him to a small hut belonging to them, where they restored him to animation over a large fire. Upon finding that he spoke in the Latin tongue, the fishermen, supposing him to be an infidel, and that they were not likely to catch any more valuable fish that morning, agreed to carry him instantly for sale to Tunis. There they sold him to a wealthy merchant of the name of Lagi Amet, who, liking his youthful and gentlemanlike appearance, resolved to retain him about his own person.

In this service the captive displayed so much discretion and fidelity as to merit the regard of the whole household, but, most unfortunately for his master, of one in particular, the lovely wife of Amet having been unable to behold the pleasing and handsome stranger with indifference. Possessed of the greatest beauty and accomplishments, she remarked the superiority of his manners and appearance to every other person around her, and at first taking an innocent delight in hearing the narration of his life and travels, she soon began to feel uneasy when out of his company. She would sit and hear him converse, and gaze upon him for hours, and yet so open and undisguised was her admiration, that Lagi Amet, entertaining no idea of the possibility of danger, made his beautiful lady a present of the amusing slave upon whom she bestowed so much attention. Overpowered with agitation and delight, she attempted to conceal the pleasure which such an offer gave her, and for some time succeeded in it, though she now began to be aware, when too late, of the real nature of her feelings.

In spite of her caution, she was often on the point of betraying them to the object of her regard, but the idea of the confidence reposed in her by Amet, and of bestowing her affections upon a slave, deprived her of the power of utterance. Besides the difficulties she would have to encounter, her life, her honour, everything which she valued, would be at stake; and frequent and long were the struggles she made against the growing passion that consumed her.

"Wretched creature that I am!" she would exclaim, "to be so deeply sensible of those superior merits and accomplishments that I must not love, nor hardly admire, and yet all these affections are bestowed upon a slave, an outcast, and a Christian, one who, upon the first glimpse of liberty, would leave thee to weep over thine own weakness in sorrow and despair! And how could he love me, indeed? Could a slave love me as he loves his own liberty? Oh, abandon the very thought! it is alike treason against my honour and my life! If I sacrifice myself, let it at least be for some nobler object; let it not be said that the wife of Amet died for a slave! But, alas! why did I not feel and act in this way before—before I became thus tortured, lost, abandoned to passion and despair? Besides, am I not wed—am I not already the property of another? Yes, it is madness to pursue the path I am in, and still I feel, I know, I have not strength to abandon it. If I yield not, if I tell him not all my love and sufferings to-day, should I continue still to see and to listen to him, I only prolong the period of my ruin until to-morrow. Let me hasten, then, and acquaint him while there is yet time; for though a foreigner and a slave, he has a noble spirit, and it is Fortune only that is to blame. She cannot rob him of those sweet and courteous manners, of that true nobility of soul that shines in every tone and look, and of all those virtues which seem to surround him with a radiant light that attracts my very soul, and which I feel sure he must possess beyond all the men I have ever seen. Can Fortune deprive him of these and of his noble birth? No; to be unfortunate is the common lot of all; and even were I the next moment to become a slave, should I not still be the same I now am? His ill fortune, therefore, ought not to make me love him the less; and who can say I may not be the happy means of bringing him over to the true faith, while at the same time he will on that account become more passionately attached to me ? And why should a weak and wretched creature like myself attempt to master a feeling that has enslaved thousands of the wisest men upon earth ? I must at least see and speak to him, though I refrain from giving him the most distant idea of my love ! "

With these weak and dangerous sentiments, the unhappy lady, half reconciled to her fate, sought the presence of her handsome slave ; nor was it long before this was followed by an explanation, that, almost inarticulate between tears and blushes, invested Niccolo rather with the character of her lord than of her slave. Still he was long in doubt whether he ought to credit the words he heard, whether it were reality or a dream, a snare laid for his honour or the proudest tribute that could be rendered to his worth. At first, then, he was about to check the torrent of her feelings, expressing equal surprise and alarm at what he heard ; but when he next reflected upon the many gentle tokens of her kindness and attention to him, and upon her superior sense and accomplishments beyond all the women he had ever seen, bethinking himself at the same time of the story of the Comte d'Anversa and the Queen of France, besides many others, he began to consider the whole as nothing less than actual truth.

Warmly expressing his deep gratitude for the distinction conferred upon him, and far from being insensible to her transcendent beauty and accomplishments, the enslaved Niccolo bent himself lowly at his fair mistress's feet. Yet, possessing high and honourable principles, he resolved to make her his upon no other condition than consenting to be baptized in the name of Jesus of Nazareth.

The lady, who had every inclination to become a believer on these terms, finding that she had no chance of adding him to the disciples of Mohammed, readily gave her consent, sealing it at the same time with a thousand Saracenic oaths : upon which Niccolo thought it incumbent upon him to explain a little more clearly the nature of the Christian religion and what it imposed upon her. Thinking the conditions at first a little hard, she made some slight demur, proposing that they should rather both embrace the doctrines of Mohammed, which were certainly more easy and much more likely to be fulfilled.

Niccolo, however, assured her that as a Christian she was bound to observe as many duties as possible, and to pray for grace to perform such as she felt an inclination to omit; that she must never be weary of her task; that she must be found always watching, and not like the foolish virgins, who forgot to trim their lamps, and whose lights went out. On hearing him utter these words, she would certainly have pronounced him mad had she not already been too deeply in love. As it was, she contented herself with saying, after revolving a variety of confused ideas in her mind, "Come, you shall make me what you please"; and accordingly she was the same day baptized, christened, confessed, received the communion, and married to Niccolo according to the rites of the Holy Church.

And so sweet in a short time did its new mysteries and duties appear to her, that being naturally possessed of superior intellect and endowments, she no longer regretted the faith of her ancestors, and began to take delight in nothing so much as having the Christian doctrines expounded to her by the voice of Niccolo.

While she thus continued making daily progress under the judicious instructions of Niccolo in a subject so important to her best interests, Niccolo's friend, Coppo, in the meanwhile had not been idle, inquiring in all directions wherever he conceived it probable that he might have been wrecked or captured. Not content with this, he himself set out in quest of him, and arrived at Tunis just as Niccolo happened to be passing with the lady close by the place where he was seen dismounting, so that they met and recognised each other in the streets.

Niccolo testified his gratitude to Coppo for so striking a proof of his fidelity, but at the same time requested him not to execute his intention of procuring his ransom until he should hear further from him; and then giving him his address, and shaking him cordially by the hand, he accompanied his lady home. A little surprised at this occurrence, the lady inquired, with a smile, who he was and what business he could have with her slave, being particularly jealous of everything that might interfere with her own views, questions which her Christian husband answered with his usual eloquence to her entire satisfaction.

Yet, as we may easily believe, Niccolo was still anxious to return to his native land, but he was aware that if the enamoured lady discovered his design, she would effect his utter destruction, or at least would counteract his plans. He was therefore uncertain how to act, and for this reason he had exhorted Coppo to secrecy as to the object of his arrival. Besides, he would have preferred, rather than basely desert her, to remain in the pleasing slavery to which his adored lady had consigned him. Fly, however, somewhere, they shortly must, as she had now become so extravagantly attached to him that he was fearful of the affair reaching the ears of Lagi Amet. With this view, he now determined to persuade her to accompany him, insisting that it was one of the duties of a Christian wife to share her husband's fortunes and follow him wherever he went. He therefore considered the arrival of Coppo as a very fortunate circumstance, and after consulting with him, and reflecting upon the best method that could be adopted, they determined to carry her along with them.

So Niccolo represented to his wife that there was no time to be lost, if they wished to avoid the fate of so many unfortunate lovers, who had fallen victims to the bowstring or the sack; and to this judicious opinion the lady, without any sort of hesitation, subscribed.

"Yes," she added, "I will see your beautiful Italy; there is no question of it at all: whatever sacrifices I make, whatever pleasures and honours I relinquish, they are for your sake, and I shall not regret them. And yet I tremble when I think upon the dreadful risks I am about to encounter, even if I escape alive out of the hands of the savage infidel who called me his consort, whom it would perhaps be the wisest way to strangle before we go."

Here Niccolo, grieved that she should have made so little progress in the duty of Christian charity, reminded her that she must no longer consider these things in the light she had been used to, adding that he felt inclined rather to pity the fate of Amet in being deprived of so much beauty and perfection, were it not that it was his paramount duty to convert infidels to the true faith. Then, advising her to collect the whole of her treasures, but to respect the property of Amet, he hastened to fix the time and method of his departure with his friend Coppo.

All at length being in readiness, they planned a little pleasure party, feigning it was entirely for the amusement of Amet, to which the foolish infidel, not a little proud of so delicate a compliment, gladly consented. Having conveyed everything on board a fast-sailing little pinnace, they said that they would just pay a visit to one of the Dey's large ships before they called for their master; and, hoisting all sail, they very wisely left the old merchant behind them.

They had proceeded about half a league from shore, when some of Lagi Amet's servants, observing them pass the vessel at full sail and boldly hold on their course, raised a hue-and-cry that very quickly reached the ears of their master. Tearing his hair, at least what little was left of it, the credulous old infidel, in a fit of rage and despair, despatched boats in pursuit without number, employing himself in the meantime with trying different bowstrings and other refined instruments of torture to welcome their return. And unluckily, as it happened, though they escaped pursuit and set foot in safety on the Sicilian shore, they took up their quarters at an hotel in Messina, where the following unpleasant circumstances occurred.

For the ambassador of the King of Tunis having that very day arrived at the same place to transact affairs of great importance at the court of Sicily, occupied apartments in the same house, and casting his eyes upon the disordered dress and dark complexion of the lady, he thought that he recognised in the fugitive one whom he had often seen at Tunis. At the same moment arrived letters advertising him of the lady's flight, and imposing upon him the duty of securing her person, with the leave of His Sicilian Majesty, with whom he was to use his utmost influence to have her sent back to her own husband. So immediately requesting an audience, the ambassador expounded his master's wishes on the subject ; and the King having verified the fact, expressed the greatest readiness to remand the fugitives, since it would afford pleasure to his ally, from whom at that time he was desirous of obtaining some essential favours.

What were the feelings, then, of the unhappy party, who, imagining that they had secured their escape, found they had rushed upon their own destruction, and were to be consigned into the hands of an offended and relentless enemy ! The heart of Coppo was torn with distraction for his friend, while the lovers uttered the most piteous cries and prayers, pleading also that they were united in faith and in marriage, both deserving of freedom, and both Christians. All, however, was of no avail, for the King, anxious to conciliate the Dey, commanded them to be re-embarked forthwith in the same vessel under the care of one of his own captains, who had orders to land them in Barbary, and deposit them safely, with the King's compliments, in the hands of their lawful sovereign. And already were they proceeding upon their wretched voyage with calm and favourable breezes, from which they turned in anguish to the shores that were receding from their view, when Fortune, as if weary at length of her continued persecutions, again raised a furious tempest before the vessel had time to make the port, and drove her back until she reached the Tyrrhene Sea, near Leghorn, where, broken and dismantled, she became the easy prey of some Pisan corsairs,

But noble ransom being offered them by the unfortunate captives, they were shortly afterwards put on shore, and at length arrived in safety, with some portion of their remaining treasures, at the city of Pisa. There, owing to the infinite dangers and sufferings to which she had been subjected, the hapless lady was seized with a fever that had nearly proved mortal, and it was the incessant care and affection of Niccolo alone that succeeded in restoring her.

Upon her recovery, they bent their way towards Florence, where, on their arrival, they were received with the utmost surprise and the warmest congratulations by all their friends, while feasts and revelry on all sides testified the joy that was felt for their return. When the health of his beloved proselyte and benefactress was a little recruited, Niccolo kindly proposed, for their more complete satisfaction, that his beloved wife should be again baptized in the Church of San Giovanni; and being christened by the name of Beatrice, she was once more solemnly espoused by him, with the utmost splendour and magnificence, according to the minutest rites and ceremonies of the Holy Church.

At the same time, in order to bind their interests in a still nearer union, Niccolo bestowed upon his friend Coppo the hand of his sister, who, in addition to the charms of beauty, boasted likewise all the virtues of her brother. Beatrice, delighted with everything she saw and heard, even beyond the picture held out to her by the happy Niccolo, soon made such rapid progress in every desirable virtue and accomplishment as to astonish the Florentine ladies by the richness and vivacity of her ideas, and the charms of her manners and conversation.

In a short time, also, she became so fondly attached to her new sister-in-law as to render it difficult to decide whether their friendship or that of their husbands was the most rare and exemplary. Certain it is that the two happy pairs passed their days in such entire amity and peace, that there never occurred the slightest cause of dissatisfaction or division, an instance of domestic happiness highly deserving of commemoration, and which attracted universal admiration and applause. Indeed, so far from becoming disagreeable to or weary of each other, they appeared daily to take more pleasure in one another's company, and more intent upon amusing, gratifying, and instructing themselves and their friends around them, in such a manner that, becoming extremely popular with all parties, they exercised the most happy and beneficial influence over the manners and feelings of the people of Florence.

GENTILE SERMINI
15TH CENTURY

THE FORTUNES OF GALLIO AND CARDINA

IN the province of Cabar, in Asia, there once flourished two noble and magnificent cities, situated within ten leagues of each other, called Soriana and Belfiore.

Jealous of their respective power and influence, they merely observed an external show of amity, and, though engaged in commercial intercourse, they never cordially united together. The people of Soriana being the more powerful of the two, frequently threatened the independence of those of Belfiore, and attempted by every means in their power to weaken and humiliate them. Well aware of their danger, the latter, rather than submit an inch of their dominions to the sovereignty of the Soriani, were prepared to throw themselves into the arms of the Christians or the Jews, and even to renounce the faith of their ancestors.

Now, in the city of Belfiore there was a noble youth of the name of Gallio, who happened to be deeply enamoured of a young girl named Cardina, daughter of the great Marmoreo, who, strongly opposing the attachment of the young people, took measures to have the lover falsely accused and declared a rebel to the state. Immediately after his banishment, Gallio set out for the city of Soriana, and there learning that Marmoreo himself had been the author of his disgrace, stung with a feeling of resentment, he adopted the most subtle plans of revenge (inveighing bitterly against the father), all of which he as suddenly abandoned when he reflected upon the unaltered passion which he felt for the daughter.

At such times he would exclaim:

" Oh, wretched, wretched Gallio! How dare I even imagine these means of revenge?—revenge at the expense of my beloved Cardina! To injure her father is to injure her—her whom I must ever worship and ever serve, though the daughter of my bitterest enemy! Oh, distraction! I am torn with contending duties; I am injured, and I burn for revenge; I love, and yet I am about to offend the object of my idolatry. For, alas ! I must do it, or remain for ever dishonoured ! Hath he not driven me forth as a rebel and a traitor from my native place ? Yet thou, my love, my Cardina, wert not here to blame, for I fondly trust thou hast shed tears over my lot. When shall I behold thee—when return to Belfiore again ? Oh, ye gods ! that I could cease to think, cease to exist, under the cruel thoughts that rack me ! For revenge ought to call louder than my love, and yet I know I can do nothing to displease her. Fester thy base heart, Marmoreo, that could conceive the foul and vindictive purpose of rendering me the veriest wretch that loads earth's weary bosom, weary of such monsters as thee ! "

Gallio having thus resolved to abandon all measures of vengeance, absence and hopelessness had soon the effect of weakening his love. In the course of a year or two the image of Cardina ceased to haunt his fancy, but feelings of revenge and hatred, on the other hand, seemed to have usurped its place. She no longer continued to stand, like a good genius, between him and her father ; and after revolving a thousand schemes of vengeance in his mind, he resolved, in order to deprive his enemy both of his authority and his life, to attempt the subjugation of his countrymen under the yoke of the Soriani.

With this view he made himself acquainted with a party whose secret object was to watch every opportunity of rendering themselves masters of Belfiore. The number appointed consisted of fifteen, and to these Gallio discovered his design of subjecting his native place, observing at the same time :

" I require of you nothing further than the power of disposing as I please of the persons of Marmoreo and Cardina : the one for the sake of vengeance ; the other, I trust, to be treated in a kinder way."

To this the confederates gave their ready consent, and the conspiracy was matured before the beginning of the ensuing year ; while a number of persons, amounting to sixty, of Sorian families which had long resided at Belfiore, united with them, in order better to betray the place.

Among these, Saladino, who had the command of the Porto Marina, was the most powerful, his family having enjoyed many lucrative offices of high trust in Belfiore during a period of nearly two hundred years. With him Gallio and his party arranged the manner in which they were to be admitted through the said gate ; and at the appointed hour the whole force of the Soriani was secretly marched by night into the province of Belfiore.

Gallio, having been intensely engaged during many days previous, allowing himself little time for sleep, devoted a few moments to repose before setting out on his final exploit, and tried to compose himself to rest. In this state of suspense the idea of Cardina naturally occurred to his mind ; and the goddess of love attempting, from compassion, to counteract the influence of Mars and Saturn that so greatly predominated in him, presented her image in his slumbers, arrayed in more than her usual beauty, and with an expression of sorrow and tenderness in her countenance, while she seemed to say that her everlasting love and gratitude should be the reward of his forbearance, if he would consent to abandon his cruel and sanguinary designs.

So vivid was the impression upon his mind, that, opening his arms as if to embrace her, he awoke, and found he had clasped only his sword that lay at his side. With a feeling of rage and disappointment, he felt inclined to turn it against his own bosom, so strongly had his dream affected him, and altered his previous resolution of persevering in his enterprise. His love for Cardina also seemed to acquire renewed strength ; and recollecting every word and action of the vision, his desire of vengeance and all his bitter hatred against her father were forgotten as he burst into a passionate flood of tears. Then the hope of mutual passion which she appeared to hold out to him in his dreams, and the expression of her grief and trouble, all combined to turn the tide of his feelings into a more loyal and patriotic course.

Suddenly acting under the impulse of this change, he summoned his fellow-conspirators, exiles, like himself, from Belfiore, to a secret meeting, and proceeded to address them in the following words :

" Fellow-citizens and brothers ! Can it be true that we are about to destroy the place that gave us birth and to betray the city of our ancestors into the hands of her deadliest foes ? Let us pause ere we produce irreparable evils, that may call down on us the execration of posterity, by turning our arms against our native land, that ought to be directed against its enemies. Alas ! how shall we bear to see the Soriani lords of us and of our countrymen, ourselves the worst of vassals ! For let us not flatter ourselves that we shall reap other than the traitor's reward. Honour and treachery are yet in our power to choose. Fellow-citizens, which shall we embrace ? "

" Honour and our country ! " exclaimed all with one voice.

"Stay, hear me further," cried Gallio, taking advantage of the enthusiasm he had produced; "a messenger is just arrived, bringing me such tidings that, if you have heart to join me, we will return to our own city, but not without the glory of having first vanquished its enemies!"

Inspired with the fervour of his patriotism, the whole of his companions promised to follow him whithersoever he would lead.

"Then," cried Gallio, "let one of you attend me," and he selected the man he wished, "and let the rest await us here!"

Having thus agreed upon the course they were to pursue, Gallio, along with his companion, affected to proceed with the scheme as before, and, under the pretence of an interview with Saladino, the governor of the Porta Marina, in order to fix upon the signals that were to be given for entering into the city of Belfiore, they proceeded forwards on horseback, until they reached Castel Fioralto, of which the governor, Parione, was one of the principal citizens, and strongly exasperated against the people of Soriana on account of their having cruelly slain his father; and with him they took further counsel about their plans. On his inquiring into the cause of their arrival, Gallio replied:

"We are come to inform you that it is in our power either to destroy or make our city twice as powerful as it is, and as we are quite aware of your wishes, we shall reveal everything to you just as it occurred."

On hearing the particulars, Parione expressed his entire concurrence, and united in their plans with the utmost joy. Having matured these and sworn fidelity to each other, Parione, speedily mounting horse, took his leave, and arrived before sunset at Belfiore, where, presenting himself before Patrioni, master of the palace where the seigniory held their sittings, he desired him to call a secret meeting of a hundred of the chief citizens of the place. This done, and the subject being proposed, it met with the general approbation of the whole assembly; and instantly closing all the gates and doubling the guards, they gave orders for the arrest of Saladino and the sixty conspirators, ready prepared for the undertaking.

Upon being subjected to the question and confronted with Gallio, they made confession and were placed in strict confinement. The whole city, in the meantime, was put under arms and prepared for the reception of the force of the Soriani led on by Gallio. About two hours before daylight, the tramp of horse was heard approaching; and

Saladino was compelled to open the gate, as had been agreed upon, at the appointed signals, betraying his party to destruction, on condition that his own and his children's lives should be spared ; the whole of his family, in case of his failure, being involved in one common ruin. When the time approached, therefore, though desirous of saving his own party, he opened the gates by command of Gallio, and the hostile force, led on by the chief citizens of Soriana, rushed forward into the city.

Many of the leaders were richly armed and caparisoned, vieing with each other in the splendour of their appearance, and shining with gold and precious gems, ornaments in which their country abounded. Add to these, the great variety of burnished shields, lances, bows, and quivers, with dark plumes nodding in the air, and the flash of arms glittering through the moonlight. Thus proudly decorated are the Soriani accustomed to march forth to meet their enemies in the open field, the chief lords and gentlemen eagerly pressing forward in the van, leaving the least considerable of the citizens to bring up the rear. Marshalled, accordingly, in their best array, the Soriani now arrived at the Porta Marina, where, received by Saladino, they believed themselves upon the point of becoming masters of the city.

By the advice of Gallio, they immediately marched forward and took possession of the cloister of Diana's temple, to the number of six thousand men, while three thousand were held in reserve in the temple of Mercury. Before daybreak, however, just as they imagined they were on the point of striking a decisive blow, they were startled by the loud clash of arms above them, and looking up, beheld crowds of armed men lining the walls of the great cloister of Diana, the chiefs of whom addressed the astonished Soriani with the cry of, " Yield, traitors, yield ; or death to our prisoners ! " at the same time showering down loads of burning combustibles upon their heads, so as to convince them they had not the least chance of escape.

After some threats of rage and despair, the Soriani, finding every means of opposition useless, were induced to surrender, and threw down their arms. The whole of their rich equipage and all their golden ornaments became the spoil of their adversaries, while they were themselves led away in ranks of ten to be consigned to the gloomy dungeons of Sabar. Their great commander, Rabooth, who guarded the temple of Mercury with his three thousand soldiers, shortly afterwards met with the same fate, appealing only to the mercy of his victorious enemy.

By the intercession of Gallio, he was pardoned on the following conditions: that he should make oath never again to enter into the city of Soriana or attempt anything against his victorious enemy. After making a solemn engagement to this effect, he was allowed to go free, and directly took his departure from the city, establishing his residence, with his companions, at Sarbonia, one hundred leagues from Soriana.

The Belfioresi then returning in triumphal procession to the grand cloister of Diana, collected the spoils of their adversaries, and carried them afterwards to their palace-master, who appropriated them to the benefit of the community. They next proceeded to witness the execution of the treacherous friends of Saladino, who had entered into terms with Gallio to betray their country, and who now were lead forth into the large square to the number of sixty-five, all of whom were quartered alive. Over the heads of the traitor and his sons, whose lives were spared, was written in large letters the result of the invasion in the following manner:

"We, the people of Belfiore, have revenged ourselves upon our enemies by turning their arms against themselves; let the traitor Saladino bear witness to this. We send him and his children to you, with his companions, all of whom may be known by the tickets appended to their necks; the rest of the soldiers, for good reasons, we, the people of Belfiore, think proper to retain. Moreover we decree that in future no native of Soriana shall become resident in our city, or dare to assume the name of a Belfiorese, that he may no longer enjoy the advantage of betraying us, and of turning our hospitality into our ruin."

Along with this fatal proclamation were sent four cartloads filled with the dead bodies of their enemies, which reached about nightfall the gates of Soriana, whose inhabitants were expecting the arrival of their countrymen with a very different escort. Upon the return of the party to Belfiore, a grand tournament, with festivals of every kind, was proclaimed for the people, to be continued during a series of many weeks.

Gallio, who had now greatly distinguished himself in the eyes of the Belfioresi, ordered a great feast in honour of the victory, and proceeded with a numerous party to wait upon Patrioni, grand-master of the palace, requesting an assemblage of the chief citizens, to which Marmoreo and his daughter Cardina should be invited. When met together, Gallio entered with a train of friends and nobles, and harangued them in the following words:

"My honoured fathers, senators, and chiefs of bands! When I contemplate the singular degree of prudence, fortitude, temperance, and valour with which you have hitherto conducted your affairs, I bow to the decree that rendered me an unhappy exile from my native land. Nor am I here come to question the justice of the proceeding instituted against me by your learned and distinguished citizen, Marmoreo, though I still remain in ignorance of his motives. Rather would I accuse myself in having been so unfortunate as to draw down upon myself the weight of your displeasure; for which I do here humbly entreat your forgiveness, more especially in consideration of my tender age, not presuming to make other defence or set up any better excuse. And so far am I sensible of your high wisdom and authority and of my own slight deserts, that I am here ready to deliver myself up to your judgment once more, as a traitor to my country, and the author of the hateful and sacrilegious plot just attempted by your enemies. True, it was I, and I alone, who brought the whole secret power of Soriana into the bosom of your homes, who induced Saladino, with his fellow traitors, on whom you had conferred your offices of trust and honour, to league with your foes in this nefarious design, and open to us your gates, that we might bring you under the yoke of Soriana, from which you are now fortunately for ever free. And let me caution you, before I yield my forfeit life, never in future to commit offices of trust or the command of gates to the Soriani, or to any other foreigners upon the face of the earth. It is enough to grant them passports through your dominions; but to make them governors over gates and citadels is the height of infatuation; for the love of country never becomes entirely obliterated from the human breast.

"Now, as the unhappy cause of the great evil that had so nearly befallen the state, I surrender my person into your hands, entreating only, with my dying prayers, that the glory and triumph of our last noble enterprise may be wholly attributed to the youthful and beauteous Cardina, whose many virtues have produced, by their influence over my soul, the present happy result. It was she who snatched the patricidal sword out of my hand, who, when I was bent on the irretrievable destruction of her father and her friends, stood between us, like a guardian angel of peace, and with her tender and sorrowful aspect, her passionate tears, and sweet appeals to my love and honour, restored me to higher and better thoughts, pointing out to me the path of patriotic duty that I have since pursued. If, then, death be due to me as a traitor, to her let triumphal arches and honours befitting a queen be afforded ; let her praises be sung over my obsequies ; let her be called the saviour of Belfiore, and soothe my wounded spirit ere it take its final flight ! "

Here Gallio became silent, and kneeling in the midst of the council, he raised his hands, as if in prayer, while his eyes were bent upon the ground, and awaited in this attitude his sentence. The chiefs and elders of the city, imagining that Gallio would have closed his harangue by soliciting honours and rewards for his great services, having risen by his last exploit high in the estimation of all ranks, were surprised at such proofs of unfeigned humility and contrition, and began to consider him in a still nobler point of view than before. Mingled tears, congratulations, and applause followed the conclusion of his address. But the emotions of Cardina and her father, the author of all Gallio's sufferings, far surpassed those of any others present : the lady's tears flowed dispassionately and uncontrolled ; her sobs drowned her voice when she attempted to intercede for him ; while the more silent but deep and painful struggles of her father, torn as he was by the sense of ingratitude and remorse, produced a sensation of awe and trouble throughout the assembly.

It was evident that the lovers had long been attached to each other ; that he must have opposed their union by the most cruel and unjustifiable measures, and a feeling of compassion for both soon communicated itself to the people, who, rushing forward with wild and tumultuous cries, demanded the head of Marmoreo, and declared Gallio their liege lord and prince. The chiefs and elders, yielding to the popular commotion, rose from their seats, and deputing one of their members to bear the ensigns of authority, they placed the gold staff in the hands of their new master.

After a due degree of modest refusal and deference to the superior claims of the aged senators, Gallio was induced to accept the government of the state, and mounting the sovereign tribunal, in an harangue to the people expressed his gratitude for the high trust reposed in him. The people then becoming acquainted with his attachment to the Lady Cardina, unanimously insisted upon her taking her place as his bride-elect at his side, the sole condition upon which they consented to spare the life of the treacherous and cruel Marmoreo.

The nuptials were accordingly soon after solemnised in the most splendid manner, followed by every variety of games and jousts, and such exhibitions as were best adapted to gratify the taste of the people. Wherever Gallio made his appearance he was welcomed with the most enthusiastic shouts of applause as the beloved sovereign of his people ; and he long continued lord of Belfiore, blest in the affections of the wise and beautiful Cardina, and esteemed for his equal administration of the laws.

The season of these joyous festivals being over, it was resolved in council that the dungeons of Sabar should be blocked up on all sides, with the six thousand Sorian soldiers enclosed within, all of whom thus miserably perished. A herald was next despatched to summon the city of Soriana, which was soon compelled to send in its submission to Gallio, and was annexed to his dominions.

ANTON-FRANCESCO GRAZZINI
1503–1585

WHY GABRIELLO RE-MARRIED HIS WIFE

SOON after Maestro Basilio, a wealthy doctor of Milan, came to live in Pisa, he had the pleasure of having it frequently hinted to him by several respectable Pisanese that the honour of his alliance would by no means be unacceptable to them, and many were the young beauties who passed in review before him.

At length he fixed his eyes upon a young lady, both of whose parents were deceased, and who, though not rich, was of a good family. She brought the doctor little more as her wedding portion than the house she lived in, though she afterwards presented him with a large family; and for many years, increasing in wealth, they lived extremely happily together. By this lady he had three sons and a daughter, the latter of whom, as well as one of her brothers, their parents very happily bestowed in marriage when they became old enough to settle in the world. The youngest boy had a decided taste for letters, while the second, who gave his parents great anxiety, was of an extremely dull and obstinate disposition, with a great aversion to learning and every species of improvement; morose, abstracted, and unamiable, when his negative was once pronounced, it was as unalterable as his own nature. The doctor at last finding that he could mould him into nothing, to get rid of him, sent him into the country, where he had purchased at least half a dozen different estates, and whither he was fond of retiring to escape the continued noise and turbulence of the city.

But about ten years after he had despatched his son Lazzaro—for this was the fool's name—into this retreat, there arose a dreadful malady in Pisa, which carried off numbers of people in a violent fever, which subsiding into a deep lethargy, they awakened no more, and it was, moreover, as infectious as the plague. The doctor, desirous of showing his skill, and taking the lead of the other physicians on this occasion, exposed himself so fearlessly for his fees, that he took the infection, which soon set at defiance every application of his most esteemed syrups and recipes, and in a few hours he retired from the profession for ever. Nor was this all, for he communicated the disease to his family, and one after another they all died, until there was only an old nurse left alive in the house.

It was indeed a dreadful visitation upon all Pisa, and the mortality would have been still greater had not the survivors fled in haste from the city. With the change of season, however, its severity seemed to mitigate, the persons attacked gradually recovered, the inhabitants returned to their houses, and the people resumed their usual occupations.

It was now that Lazzaro succeeded to all the property left by his deceased relations, though he merely added a single domestic to the reduced establishment of his father, consisting only of the old servant. His farms and the receipt of his rents were left in the care of an agent, as he bestowed no attention upon business.

Many families, notwithstanding, appeared anxious for the honour of his alliance, without making the slightest objection to his rusticity and folly; but the only answer that he uniformly returned to these proposals was, that he had made up his mind to wait for at least four years, and that he afterwards might perhaps be induced to think of it. As he was known never to have changed his mind, no one importuned him further upon the subject. Though he was fond of amusements in his own way, he admitted no one to his confidence, and started on beholding a card of invitation like a guilty spirit at the sign of the cross.

Opposite to his house there resided a man of the name of Gabriello, with his wife and two children, a boy about five years old and a little girl, whom he supported as well as he was able by his skill in bird-catching and fishing. Though his abode was humble, his nets and cages were of the very best construction, and he managed them so judiciously, that, with the assistance of his wife, Santa, who had the reputation of an excellent sempstress, he made a very pretty livelihood.

It happened that Gabriello was an exact counterpart in voice, countenance, and appearance of our foolish friend Lazzaro; their very complexion and their beards were of the same cut and quality. If they were not twin brothers, they ought to have been so, for they were not only of the same age and stature, but in their taste and manners they greatly resembled each other. It would have been impossible even for the fisherman's wife to have recognised Lazzaro disguised in the dress of her husband; the only distinction that could be made was that one was dressed as a labourer and the other like a gentleman.

Pleased with the happy resemblance which he could not but acknowledge between himself and the fisherman, and fancying it laid him under a sort of obligation for which he felt grateful, he began to solicit his acquaintance. This he did in the pleasantest manner possible, frequently sending him good things from his table and a bottle of old wine. The fisherman's gratitude was so pleasing that he soon also sent for him to dine and sup with him, passing the evenings in the most agreeable conversations imaginable ; the adventures of the good fisherman, and the prodigious lies he told, being a never-failing source of admiration and delight to Lazzaro. For the fisherman's skill extended far beyond his art, and the rogue contrived to insinuate himself into the good graces of his patron, until the latter was hardly ever easy out of his company.

Thus having one day treated his rustic friend to a noble feast, they began to talk, over their wine, of the various modes of fishing, all of which were explained greatly to the satisfaction of the host. None, however, seemed to take his fancy so much as the description of the diving net, on which the fisherman dwelt with uncommon enthusiasm, as the most useful and delightful invention in the world. It inspired Lazzaro with the ambition of immediately witnessing a specimen of this part of the piscatory art, in which great fish may be caught, not with nets and lines merely, but with the very mouth, a drag-net hanging round the neck of the diving fisherman !

" Oh, let us go now ! let us go now ! " exclaimed the happy Lazzaro, while the guest, as usual, expressed himself ready to attend his patron.

As it happened to be the middle of summer, nothing could be better ; and finishing their dessert, Gabriello took his drag-nets and they went out together. They bent their way through the Porta à Mare directly towards the Arno, along the fence of pales, above the great bank crowned with alder-trees, spreading a most delicious shade. There the fisherman begged his patron to sit down and refresh himself while he observed the manner in which he should proceed.

Having first stripped himself, he bound the nets round his arms and neck, and then, boldly plunging into the river, down he went. But being a complete adept at his business, he rose again very shortly to the surface, bringing up with him at one drag eight or ten great fish, all of the best kind. This was a real miracle in the eyes of Lazzaro, who could not divine how he could possibly see to catch them under water, and he resolved to ascertain the manner in which it was done. With this view, it being a hot July day, and thinking that a cold bath might refresh him, he prepared, with Gabriello's assistance, to step in. He was conducted by him to a shallow part, and when about up to his knees, Gabriello left him to his own discretion, only warning him that though the bottom shelved down very gradually, he had better go no farther than where a certain post rose above the rest ; and pointing it out to him once more, he pursued his business.

Lazzaro felt singular pleasure in being thus left to himself, and splashing about, performed all sorts of antics in the water. His eyes were often fixed in admiration upon his friend Gabriello, who every now and then rose from the bottom with a fish in his mouth, the better to please his patron, who at this sight could no longer restrain his applause. " It is very plain now," he cried, " that it must be light under water, or he could never have seen how to catch that fish in his mouth, besides all the others in his net. I wish I knew how."

So saying, the next time that he saw Gabriello dive, he imitated the motion by ducking his head, and at the same time losing his footing, slipped gently down, till he not only reached the post, but passed it with his head still under water. When he fairly got out of his depth, still trying whether he could see, it appeared a strange thing to him ; for he found he could no longer get his breath, and he endeavoured in vain to fight his way up again, the water pouring in at his mouth and ears, at his nose and eyes, in such a way that he could see nothing.

In short, the current at length catching him, bore him away in perfect amazement, and he was too far gone to cry out for help. Gabriello was in the meantime employed in diving down into a large hole he had discovered near the stakes, full of fish, which he was handing into his net with the greatest alacrity, while his poor friend and patron was already more than half dead, having now come up and gone down again for the third time, and at the fourth he rose no more.

Just at this moment, Gabriello, with a prodigious draught, again appeared, and turning round with a joyous face to look at Lazzaro, what was his surprise and terror when he found his master was gone! Gazing round with the hope of perceiving him somewhere, he only found his clothes, just as he had left them. In the utmost alarm he ran again to the water, and in a short time discovered his body thrown by the current on the opposite bank.

He swam to the place, and on perceiving that his good patron was quite cold and lifeless, he stood for some moments like a statue, overpowered with grief and terror, without knowing how to act. In the first place he was afraid, if he published the tidings of his death, of being accused of having drowned him to plunder him of his money, an idea which threw him into such alarm, that, covering his face with his hands, he stood buried in profound grief and reflection.

At length he suddenly uttered an exclamation of joy, as the thought rushed into his mind, " I am safe ! I am safe ! There are no witnesses of the accident, and I know what I will do : it is the hour when, luckily, everybody is asleep."

With these words he thrust the nets and the fish into his great basket, and taking the dead body of Lazzaro on his shoulders, heavy as it was, he placed it among some wet reeds hard by the shore. He then bound the nets round his poor friend's arms, and again bearing him to water, he contrived to fasten the strings in such a way round one of the deepest stakes, that they could with difficulty be withdrawn, giving the body the appearance of having been thus entangled while fishing.

He then assumed his patron's attire, and got even into his very shoes, and sat down quietly on the bank, resolved to try what fortune would do for him. His strong resemblance to his deceased friend, if successful, would now not only save his life, but make it ever after, as he believed, most happy and comfortable. As the hour seemed now arrived, with equal skill and courage, he entered upon the dangerous experiment, and began to call out lustily for help in the person of poor Lazzaro : " Help ! help, good people, or the poor fisherman will be drowned ! Oh, he comes up no more ! " and with this he roared out tremendously.

The miller was the first man who reached the spot, but numbers of people were gathering on all sides to learn what could possibly cause such an insufferable noise. Gabriello continued to bellow even for some time after they arrived, the better to counterfeit his patron, weeping the whole time as he told his tale—how the poor fisherman had dipped, and brought up fish so often ; but the last time he had stopped nearly an hour under water, and having waited for him in vain, he began to be afraid he was coming up no more.

The people inquiring, with a smile at his simplicity, whereabouts it was, he pointed out the spot, on which the miller, who was a great friend of Gabriello's, began to strip, and plunged into the river. And there, sure enough, as he believed, he found his friend Gabriello caught in his own net, and entangled fast by his neck and heels to the unlucky stake.

" Heaven have mercy on us ! " cried the miller ; " here he is, poor Gabriello, poor Gabriello ! quite drowned in his own entangled net " ; using his utmost efforts at the same time to loosen it from about the stake.

Such were the lamentations of Gabriello's friends on hearing this, that he could scarcely refrain from betraying himself. Two more threw themselves into the water to assist the miller, and at length, with some difficulty, they fished the body out. The arms and legs were all entangled in the net, and his relations in their indignation tore the unlucky cords to tatters.

The tidings of his death being spread abroad, a priest immediately attended, and the body was borne upon a bier to the nearest church, where it was laid out in order to be recognised by Gabriello's friends. His disconsolate widow, accompanied by other relations bewailing him and her children, now hastened to the spot. Believing the body to be his, a scene of tender affliction ensued. After beating her breast and tearing her hair, she sat down and wept with her little children, while every one around, and above all the real Gabriello, could not restrain their tears.

So overpowered indeed was he by his feelings, that pulling his poor patron's hat over his brows and hiding his face in his pocket-handkerchief, he addressed his wife before all the people in a hoarse and piteous voice :

" Come, good woman, do not despair, do not cry so. I will provide for you, and take care both of you and your children ; the poor man lost his life in trying to amuse me, and I shall not forget it. He was a clever fisherman ; but leave off crying—I tell you I will provide for you. So go home, and go in peace, for you shall want for nothing while I live, and when I die I will leave you what is handsome " ; and this he ended with a kind of growl, intended to express his concern both for her and the deceased fisherman.

For these words he was highly applauded by all the people present, while the imaginary widow, somewhat consoled by his promises, was conveyed back by her relations to her own dwelling. But Gabriello in his new character immediately marched and took possession of Lazzaro's house, walking in exactly as he had often observed his poor friend was wont to do, without noticing any one, He went into a richly furnished chamber overlooking some beautiful gardens, and taking the keys out of his deceased patron's pockets, he began to search the trunks and boxes, where he found other lesser keys, which admitted him to all the treasures and valuables in the place. It was a storehouse of wealth indeed, for it not only contained the fortunes of the deceased doctor and other relations of Lazzaro, to the amount of several thousand florins of gold, but was equally rich in jewels and plate.

At the sight of these Gabriello repressed with difficulty loud exclamations of rapture and surprise, and he sat down to devise fresh means of supporting his title to Lazzaro's estates. With this view, being perfectly acquainted with his late friend's character, he went down about supper-time uttering the most strange and wild exclamations of grief. The two servants of the house, who had heard of the fatal accident and the cause of it, ran hastily to his relief. But instead of listening to their consolation, he directly ordered six loaves and a portion of the supper, with two flasks of wine, to be carried to the disconsolate widow across the way.

On the return of the domestic with the poor widow's grateful thanks, Gabriello partook of a light supper set out in the handsomest style, and, without saying a word to any one, shut himself up in his chamber and went to bed. There he remained until the hour of nine the next morning, in order the better to indulge his reflections and his grief. Though the difference between his voice and language and those of their former master was perceptible to his domestics, they attributed it entirely to his violent sorrow for his deceased friend. And the poor widow, finding how well he seemed inclined to keep his word of supporting her and her children, very soon dismissed the condolences of her relations and retired as usual quietly to rest.

The next day Gabriello began to rise at his old friend's usual hour, and though he had now a variety of cares upon his hands, he never permitted the poor widow, Santa, to want for anything. He imitated his late patron's way of life very exactly, for he really seemed to have also succeeded to his indolence, which he adopted without an effort. He was still, however, extremely concerned to hear that his wife's grief for his death continued unabated, though he certainly felt flattered by it, and began to think in what way he could console her, and how he could contrive means to marry her again. Feeling not a little puzzled upon the subject, he resolved to go to her house, where he found her, accompanied by one of her cousins, it not being long since the period of his supposed death.

Having informed her that he wished to speak to her upon an affair of some importance, her kind relation immediately took his leave, aware of the numerous obligations which her rich neighbour had so charitably conferred upon her. When he had left them, Gabriello closed the door with the same air of familiarity and confidence as formerly, at which the poor woman could not help testifying some surprise, fearful lest he might presume too far upon the services he had rendered her. When Gabriello advanced, taking her little boy by the hand, she drew back timidly, at which action he could not help expressing his admiration of his wife's propriety in an audible voice and with a grin of delight.

Then, taking her by the hand, he spoke to her in his accustomed manner, and she gazed for a moment doubtfully in his face, while Gabriello, taking his little boy in his arms, tenderly caressed him, saying, "What, boy, is your mother weeping at our good fortune?" and shaking some money in his hand with a triumphant air, he gave it to him, and went on playing with him as usual.

But perceiving that his wife was overpowered with a variety of emotions which she could not control, unable longer to disguise the truth, he first fastened the door, and, fearful lest any one might overhear the strange story he had to reveal, he drew her into an inner chamber, and there related the whole affair just as it had passed. It is impossible to convey an idea of her surprise and joy as she hung weeping upon his neck. But they were delicious tears, and her husband kissed them away with far greater rapture than he had ever before felt, and they sank overpowered with emotion into each other's arms.

It was necessary, however, to use the utmost precaution in retaining the fortune they had so strangely won; and after explaining the plans he had in view, and engaging his wife's promise to keep the matter secret, Gabriello returned to his new house. His wife, still affecting to retain her grief for his loss, frequently took care, before all her neighbours, to recommend her poor children to the gentleman's notice, who uniformly treated them with kindness.

The ensuing night he lay broad awake devising how he might best put his future plans into execution. Having at length resolved, he rose early, and bent his way to the Church of Santa Catterina, where he knew a venerable and devout monk, almost worshipped by the good people of Pisa, whose name was Fra Anselmo. He here announced a very strange and important piece of business, respecting which he wished to consult the conscience of the learned friar. The good father carried him into his cell, where Gabriello introduced himself as Lazzaro di Maestro Basilio da Milano, relating at the same time his whole family genealogy, and how he had remained sole heir of the whole property owing to the late plague.

He at last came to the story of poor Gabriello, the fisherman, laying the sole blame of the accident upon himself in persuading the wretched man to accompany him in a fishing excursion along the Arno. He then proceeded to relate the deplorable circumstances in which he had left his family, and taking into serious consideration the cause of the calamity, he felt it weigh so heavily upon his conscience, that he was resolved at all risks to make every reparation in his power.

But what reparation could be made to a woman, who, however lowly her condition, had fondly loved her husband, except by consoling her for her loss by directing her affections towards another object.

" And the truth is," he continued, " I am willing to marry her, and become a father to her children, and then," he continued with the greatest simplicity, " perhaps God will forgive me for the great sin I committed in taking him out a-fishing with me."

Though the pious father here smiled, it appeared so conscientious a proposal that he did not venture to oppose it, saying that he would not fail in this way to obtain the mercy of Heaven upon many of his past sins. Hearing this comfortable doctrine, Gabriello opened his purse-strings and presented the friar with thirty pieces, observing that he wished the mass of San Gregorio to be sung for three Mondays together, to ensure peace to the soul of the deceased fisherman. The venerable monk's eyes brightened at the sight, and he promised mass should be sung the very next Monday. With respect to the projected alliance, he observed to Gabriello, that he rather praised him for his disregard to wealth and nobility in the proposed union.

" Make no account of it," he continued ; " you will be rich enough in the grace of Heaven : we all belong to the same father and the same mother, and virtue is the only true nobility. I know both her and her parents ; you could not do better, for she is born of a good family. So, go home, my good signor, and I will attend you when you please."

" Well, to-day, to-day, then ! " cried Gabriello, as he prepared to depart.

" Ah ! leave it to me," returned the friar, " and take my blessing with you, my son, and bring the ring in the meantime."

Gabriello hastened home, and purchased the ring accordingly, persuading himself there could be no harm in making sure that everything was quite correct in the difficult circumstances under which he laboured. So, with the consent of all the lady's friends and relations, the marriage was celebrated a second time. Gabriello, in the person of Lazzaro, then conducted his wife to her new house, where a splendid feast was prepared, and all their friends met to receive them.

Soon after, Gabriello gradually assuming the manners of a gentleman, dismissed the old maid- and man-servant with liberal gratuities, and set up a handsome equipage and noble establishment. He astonished all Lazzaro's friends with the striking improvement that had taken place in the simpleton's manners, while his wife, Santa, became exceedingly genteel in all her actions.

The twice-married pair spent together a tranquil and happy life, and had two sons subsequently born, who, assuming a new family surname, called themselves De' Fortunati, and from these children sprang a race of men renowned both in letters and in arms.

GIOVAMBATTISTA GIRALDI CINTHIO
1504–1573

THE STORY OF DESDEMONA

THERE was once in Venice a Moor of great merit, who for his personal courage and the proofs he had given of his conduct, as well as his vigorous genius in the affairs of war, was held in great esteem by those gentlemen who, in rewarding patriotic services, excel all the republics that ever existed.

It happened that a virtuous woman of great beauty, called Desdemona, not drawn by female appetite, but by the virtue of the Moor, fell in love with him ; and he, subdued by the charms and noble sentiments of the lady, became equally enamoured of her. Their passion was so successful that they were married, although her relations did all in their power to make her take another husband. They lived together in such peace and concord while they were at Venice, that there never passed between them either word or action that was not expressive of affection.

The Venetians resolving to change the garrison which they maintain in Cyprus, elected the Moor to the command of the troops which they destined for that island. Although he was extremely pleased with the honour proposed to him (as it is a dignity conferred only on those who are noble, brave, trusty, and of approved courage), yet was his joy diminished when he reflected on the length and inconvenience of the voyage, supposing that Desdemona must be very averse to undertaking it.

His wife, who valued nothing in the world but her husband, and rejoiced exceedingly in the testimony of approbation so lately shown him by a powerful and celebrated republic, was extremely impatient for the departure of the troops, that she might accompany him to a post of so much honour. But she was very much vexed at seeing the Moor disturbed, and, not knowing the reason, said to him one day at dinner :

" How can you be so melancholy after having received from the Senate so high and so honourable a distinction ? "

' My love for you, Desdemona," replied the Moor, " disturbs my enjoyment of the rank conferred upon me, since I am now exposed to this alternative—I must either endanger your life by sea or leave you at Venice. The first would be terrible, as I shall suffer extremely from every fatigue you undergo, from every danger that threatens you: the second would render me insupportable to myself, as parting from you would be parting from my life."

"Ah, husband," returned Desdemona, "why do you perplex yourself with such idle imaginations? I will follow you wherever you go, though it were necessary to pass through fire instead of only going by water in a safe and well-equipped vessel. If there are dangers in the way I will share them with you; and, indeed, your affection for me could not be great if you thought of leaving me at Venice to save me from a sea voyage, or believed that I would rather remain here in security than share with you both danger and fatigue. I insist, therefore, on your preparing for the voyage with all that cheerfulness which your dignity ought to inspire."

The Moor then tenderly embraced his wife, saying, "May Heaven long preserve us in this degree of reciprocal affection."

Soon afterwards, having settled his affairs and prepared the necessary stores, he went on board the galley with his wife and his company, and sailed for Cyprus with a favourable wind.

He had in his company an ensign of a very amiable outward appearance, but whose character was extremely treacherous and base. He had imposed on the Moor's simplicity so successfully that he gained his friendship; for although he was in fact a very great coward, yet his carriage and conversation were so haughty and full of pretension that you would have taken him for a Hector or an Achilles.

This rascal had also conducted his wife with him to Cyprus, who was a handsome and discreet woman; and, being an Italian, Desdemona was so fond of her that they passed the greatest part of their time together. In the same company was also a lieutenant to whom the Moor was much attached. The lieutenant went often to the Moor's house, and dined frequently with him and his wife. Desdemona, seeing that the Moor was so fond of him, showed him every mark of attention and civility, with which the Moor was much pleased.

The detestable ensign, forgetting his duty to his own wife, and violating all the laws of friendship, honour, and gratitude with which he was bound to the Moor, fell passionately in love with Desdemona, and thought only how he might enjoy her. He dare not, however, avow himself, for fear the Moor, if he discovered it, should instantly put him to death. He sought by all the private means in his power to make Desdemona conscious of his love. But she was so entirely taken up with the Moor that she thought neither of him nor of any one else ; and all that he did to engage her affections produced not the least effect. He then took it into his head that this neglect arose from her being pre-engaged in favour of the lieutenant ; and not only determined to get rid of him, but changed his affection for her into the most bitter hatred.

He studied, besides, how he might prevent in future the Moor from living happily with Desdemona, should his passion not be gratified after he had murdered the lieutenant. Revolving in his mind a variety of methods, all impious and abominable, he at last determined to accuse her to the Moor of adultery with the lieutenant. But knowing the Moor's great affection for Desdemona, and his friendship for the lieutenant, he plainly saw that unless his deceit was very artfully conducted, it would be impossible to make him think ill of either of them. For this reason he determined to wait till time and place afforded him a fit opportunity for entering on his wicked design ; and it was not long before the Moor degraded the lieutenant for having drawn his sword and wounded a soldier upon guard.

This accident was so painful to Desdemona, that she often tried to obtain for him her husband's pardon. In the meantime the Moor had observed to the ensign that his wife teased him so much in favour of the lieutenant that he feared he should be obliged at last to restore him to his commission. This appeared to that villain the proper moment for opening his scheme of treachery, which he began by saying :

" Perhaps Desdemona is fond of his company."

" And why ? " said the Moor.

" Nay," replied he, " I do not choose to meddle between man and wife ; but if you watch her properly, you will understand me."

Nor would he, to the earnest entreaties of the Moor, afford any further explanation. These words had stung the Moor so severely that he endeavoured perpetually to find out their meaning, and became exceedingly melancholy. Whereupon, when his wife some time afterwards repeated her solicitations that he would forgive the lieutenant, and not sacrifice the service and friendship of so many years to one slight fault, particularly as the lieutenant and the soldier were friends again. The Moor grew angry, and said to her :

"It is somewhat extraordinary, Desdemona, that you should take so much trouble about this fellow; he is neither your brother nor your relation, that he should claim so much of your affection."

His wife, with much sweetness and humility, replied:

"I have no other motive for speaking than the pain it gives me to see you deprived of so excellent a friend as you have always told me the lieutenant was to you. I hope you will not be angry with me; yet his fault does not merit so much of your hatred: but you Moors are of so warm a constitution that every trifle transports you with anger and revenge."

The Moor, still more irritated by these words, replied:

"Perhaps one who suspects it not may learn that by experience; I will be revenged for the injuries done to me, so thoroughly that I shall be satisfied."

His wife was much terrified by these expressions, and seeing him, for the first time, in a passion with her, submissively answered:

"I have none but the purest motives for speaking on the business: but, not to displease you in future, I promise never to speak of it again."

The Moor, on this new application made by his wife in favour of the lieutenant, imagined that the ensign's words meant that she was in love with him. He therefore went to that scoundrel in a state of great dejection, and endeavoured to make him speak more intelligibly. The ensign, bent on the ruin of this poor woman, after feigning an unwillingness to say anything to her disadvantage, and at last pretending to yield to the vehement entreaties of the Moor, said:

"I cannot conceal the pain I feel in being under the necessity of making a discovery which will be to you so very shocking; but since you insist on it, and the attention which I ought to pay to the honour of my commanding officer prompts me to speak, I will not now refuse to satisfy your demand and my own duty. You must know, then, that Desdemona is only displeased at seeing you angry with the lieutenant, because, when he comes to your house, she consoles herself with him for the disgust which your blackness now occasions her to feel."

These words penetrated to the very bottom of the Moor's heart; but to be better informed (although his previous suspicion made him give great credit to the ensign's information) he assumed a threatening countenance, and said:

"I know not what prevents me from cutting out that insolent

tongue of yours that has so impudently attacked the honour of my wife."

The ensign then replied:

"I expected no other reward for this friendly office of mine; but since my duty has made me go so far, and my regard for your honour still remains, I tell you again that the case is so; and if her feigned affection for you has blindfolded you to such a degree that you have not seen what is so very visible, that does not at all lessen the truth of my assertion. The lieutenant himself, who is one of those who are not content with their own enjoyments when some other is not made acquainted with them, told me so; and," added he, "if I had not feared your displeasure, I would have given him at the time that death he merited. But since the information I give you, which concerns you more than any one else, makes you treat me so very improperly, I am sorry I did not hold my tongue, that I might have avoided giving you offence."

The Moor then answered, in great agitation:

"If you do not make me to see with my own eyes the truth of what you tell me, be assured that I will make you wish you had been born dumb."

"This would have been easy enough," replied the villain, "when he came to your house: but now that you have driven him away for a much lighter reason than that which ought to have banished him thence, it will be difficult to prove it. For though I think yet that he continues to enjoy Desdemona whenever you give him an opportunity, he must necessarily proceed with greater caution now than he did before he had incurred your displeasure. But I do not despair of making you see that which upon my word you will not believe."

They then separated. The poor Moor went home with a barbed arrow in his side, waiting impatiently for the day when the ensign should show him what was to render him for ever miserable. But the known purity of Desdemona's conduct gave no less uneasiness to the villainous ensign, because he was afraid he should not be able to convince the Moor of what he had so falsely assured him. He applied himself therefore to the invention of new malice, and devised other expedients.

I have already said that Desdemona went frequently to the ensign's house, and passed great part of the day with his wife. The villain had observed that she often brought with her a handkerchief that the Moor had given her, and which, as it was very delicately worked in the Moorish taste, was very highly valued by them both ; he determined to steal it, and by its means complete her ruin. He had a little girl of three years old that was much caressed by Desdemona ; and one day, when that unhappy woman was on a visit to this villain, he took up the child in his arms and presented it to Desdemona, who received it and pressed it to her bosom. In the same instant this deceiver stole from her sash the handkerchief with such dexterity that she did not perceive him, and went away with it in very high spirits.

Desdemona turned home, and, taken up with other thoughts, never recollected her handkerchief till some days after ; when, not being able to find it, she began to fear that the Moor should ask her for it, as he often did. The infamous ensign, watching his opportunity, went to the lieutenant, and, to aid his wicked purpose, left the handkerchief on his bolster. The lieutenant did not find it till the next morning, when, getting up, he set his foot upon it as it had fallen to the floor. Not being able to imagine how it came there, and knowing it to be Desdemona's, he determined to carry it back to her ; and, waiting till the Moor was gone out, he went to the back-door and knocked.

Fortune, who seemed to have conspired along with the ensign the death of this poor woman, brought the Moor home in the same instant. Hearing some one knock he went to the window, and, much disturbed, asked:

" Who is there ? "

The lieutenant hearing his voice, and fearing that when he came down he should do him some mischief, ran away without answering. The Moor came down, and finding no one either at the door or in the street, returned full of suspicion to his wife, and asked if she knew who it was that had knocked. She answered with great truth that she knew not.

" But I think," said he, " it was the lieutenant."

" It might be he," said she, " or any one else."

The Moor checked himself at the time, though he was violently enraged, and determined to take no step without first consulting the ensign. To him he immediately went, and related what had just happened, begging him to learn from the lieutenant what he could on the subject. The ensign rejoiced much in this accident, and promised to do so.

He contrived to enter into discourse with him one day in a place where the Moor might see them. He talked with him on a very different subject, laughed much, and expressed by his motions and attitudes very great surprise. The Moor, as soon as he saw them separate, went to the ensign, and desired to know what had passed between them. The ensign, after many solicitations, at last told him that he had concealed nothing from him.

" He says he has enjoyed your wife every time that you have stayed long enough from home to give him an opportunity ; and that in their last interview she had made him a present of that handkerchief which you gave her."

The Moor thanked him, and thought that if his wife had no longer the handkerchief in her possession it would be a proof that the ensign had told him the truth. For which reason one day after dinner, among other subjects, he asked her for this handkerchief. The poor woman, who had long apprehended this, blushed exceedingly at the question, and, to hide her change of colour, which the Moor had very accurately observed, ran to her wardrobe and pretended to look for it. After having searched for some time :

" I cannot conceive," said she, " what is become of it ! Have not you taken it ? "

" Had I taken it," replied he, " I should not have asked you for it. But you may look for it another time more at your ease."

Leaving her then, he began to reflect what would be the best way of putting to death his wife and the lieutenant, and how he might avoid being prosecuted for the murder. Thinking night and day on this subject, he could not prevent Desdemona from perceiving that his behaviour to her was very different from what it had been formerly. She often asked him what it was that agitated him so violently.

" You, who were once the merriest man alive, are now the most melancholy."

The Moor answered and alleged a variety of reasons, but she was not satisfied with any of them ; and knowing that she had done nothing to justify so much agitation, she began to fear that he grew tired of her. She once in conversation with the ensign's wife expressed herself thus :

" I know not what to say of the Moor ; he used to treat me most affectionately ; and I begin to fear that my example will teach young women never to marry against their parents' consent, and the Italians in particular, not to connect themselves with men from whom they are separated by nature, climate, education, and complexion. But as I know him to be the confidential of your husband, whom he consults on all occasions, I entreat you, if you have heard anything that might explain this mystery and be of use to me, not to deny me your assistance." These words were accompanied with a flood of tears.

The ensign's wife, who knew all (as her husband had in vain endeavoured to prevail upon her to become an accomplice in the murder of Desdemona), but durst tell her nothing for fear of her husband, only said:

"Take care not to give the Moor any cause for suspicion, and do all in your power to convince him of your affection and fidelity."

"Why, so I do," said she, "but to no purpose."

The Moor, in the meantime, did all in his power to prove what he desired not to find true, and begged the ensign to make him see the handkerchief in possession of the lieutenant. Although this was a difficult undertaking, yet the villain promised to do all in his power to give him a satisfactory proof of this.

The lieutenant had a woman in the house, who was a notable embroiderer in muslin, and who, struck with the beauty of Desdemona's handkerchief, determined to copy it before it should be returned to her. She set about making one like it, and while she was at work the ensign discovered that she sat at a window where any one who passed in the street might see her. This he took care to point out to the Moor, who was then fully persuaded that his chaste and innocent wife was an adulteress. He agreed with the ensign to kill both her and the lieutenant; and, consulting together about the means, the Moor entreated him to undertake the assassination of the officer, promising never to forget so great an obligation. He refused, however, to attempt what was so very difficult and dangerous, as the lieutenant was equally brave and vigilant; but with much entreaty and considerable presents he was prevailed on to say that he would hazard the experiment.

One dark night, after taking this resolution, he observed the lieutenant coming out of the house of a female libertine where he usually passed his evenings, and assaulted him sword in hand. He struck at his legs with a view of bringing him to the ground, and with the first blow cut him quite through the right thigh. The poor man instantly fell, and the ensign ran to him to put him to death. But the lieutenant, who was courageous, and familiar with wounds and slaughter, having drawn his sword, notwithstanding his desperate situation, and raised himself for defence, cried out " Murder!" as loud as he could.

The ensign, perceiving that some people were coming, and that the soliders quartered thereabouts had taken the alarm, fled for fear of being caught, and, turning about again, pretended likewise that he had been brought there by the noise. Placing himself among the rest, and seeing that the leg was cut off, he concluded that though he was not dead, he must die of this wound; and although he was exceedingly rejoiced at all this, yet he condoled with the lieutenant as much as if he had been his brother.

The next morning this accident was spread all over the city, and came to the ears of Desdemona, who being very compassionate, and not suspecting that this could occasion mischief to herself, expressed the greatest concern for the lieutenant's misfortune. The Moor drew from hence the worst of inferences, and said to the ensign:

" You must know that my simpleton of a wife is almost mad with sorrow for the lieutenant's accident."

" How could it be otherwise," said he, " as he is her life and soul?"

" How," said the Moor, " her life and her soul! I will separate her soul from her body. I should disgrace my manhood if I killed her not."

And discoursing together if poison or the dagger would be best, and not liking either the one or the other, the ensign said:

" A method has occurred to me that would satisfy you without creating the least suspicion. The house where you live is very old, and the ceiling of your chamber is broken in many places. Desdemona might be beaten to death with a stocking full of sand, and no marks of this would remain on the body: when she is dead we will pull down a part of the ceiling, and bruise your wife's head; then give out that a beam in falling has done this, and killed her. If you follow this course you will avoid all suspicion, and every one will believe her death to have been accidental."

This savage advice pleased the Moor; and waiting for a convenient opportunity, he concealed the ensign one night in a closet that communicated with their chamber. When they were in bed, the ensign, according to his instruction, made a noise in the closet, and the Moor immediately asked his wife if she had heard it.

" Yes," she answered.

" Get up, then, and see what it is."

Poor Desdemona obeyed, and as soon as she was near the closet-door the ensign rushed out, and, with the stocking that he had prepared, gave her a violent blow on the small of the back. She fell down scarce able to breathe; but with what little force she had, she called the Moor to her assistance. He got out of bed and said to her:

"Most infamous woman, you are now to receive the just reward of your infidelity!—even so are those wives treated who, pretending to love their husbands, are untrue to their beds."

The poor woman hearing these words, and feeling that she was ready to expire from a second blow that the ensign had given her, said:

"Since the justice of this world is refused me, I invoke God's Justice in witness of my honour and my truth!"

And thus praying to God, she was finished by the impious ensign, who struck a third time. Afterwards they placed her in bed; and, after breaking her skull, they drew down, as they had determined beforehand, a part of the ceiling. The Moor then called out for help, as the house was falling. The neighbours on this alarm ran thither, and found Desdemona dead under the beams. Her life had been so virtuous that every one lamented her fate; and the following day she was buried, to the great sorrow of the whole island.

But God, who is a just observer of the hearts of men, suffered not so great a crime to pass without the punishment that was due to it. So that the Moor, who had loved Desdemona more than his eyes, finding himself deprived of her, began to regret her so extremely, that he almost lost his senses, and went about the house looking for her in every room. Reflecting besides that the ensign had been the cause of his losing along with her all the enjoyments of life, and even his own faculties, that villain became so insupportable to him, he could not bear the sight of him. Had he not feared the strict justice of the Venetians, he would have put him openly to death. But not being able to do this with safety to himself, he degraded him from his commission, and permitted him no longer to remain in the company.

Hence arose between them the most bitter enmity that can be conceived; and the ensign, the greatest of all villains, studied only how he might be revenged on the Moor. He went to the lieutenant, who was cured and walked about with his wooden leg, and said to him:

"The time is now come when you may be revenged for the loss of your leg; and if you will come with me to Venice, I will tell you who the assassin was. Here I dare not inform you for many reasons; but there I will be your witness in a court of justice."

The lieutenant, who felt violently angry against his unknown enemy, thanked the ensign, and came away with him to Venice. When they were arrived, the ensign told him that the Moor was the person who had cut off his leg, because he suspected him of adultery with his wife, and that for the same reason he had murdered her, and afterwards given out that she had been killed by the ceiling's falling in upon her.

The lieutenant, on hearing this, immediately accused the Moor before the Council of the injury done to himself, and the murder of Desdemona; and the ensign being called as a witness, asserted the truth of both these accusations. He added that the Moor had communicated to him the whole project with a view of persuading him to execute both these crimes; and when he had murdered his wife from the impulse of a furious jealousy, he had related to him the manner in which he had put her to death.

The Venetian magistrates, hearing that one of their fellow-citizens had been treated with so much cruelty by a barbarian, had the Moor arrested in Cyprus and brought to Venice, where, by means of the torture, they endeavoured to find out the truth. But the Moor possessed force and constancy of mind sufficient to undergo the torture without confessing anything; and though by his firmness he escaped death at this time, he was, after a long imprisonment, condemned to perpetual exile, in which he was afterwards killed, as he deserved to be, by his wife's relations.

The ensign returned to his country, where, still continuing his old practices, he accused one of his companions of having attempted to murder a nobleman who was his enemy. The man was taken up and put to the torture, and, denying firmly the crime laid to his charge, his accuser was also put to the torture; where he was racked so violently that his vitals were injured, and upon being conducted home he died in great agony. Thus was the divine vengeance executed against those who had murdered the innocent Desdemona.

The ensign's wife, who had been informed of the whole affair, after his death thus circumstantially related the story.

FILARGIRO THE MISER

Giovambattista Giraldi Cinthio

THERE was a Greek merchant from Corfu, who, having trafficked in various parts of Italy, at length settled in Mantua. His name was Filargiro, one of the most avaricious characters in the world; for though he had realised a handsome property, all his thoughts were bent upon amassing more and more, his avarice still increasing with the increase of his wealth.

It happened that on returning one day from a sale of some of his goods, with a purse of four hundred gold crowns, while engaged in transacting other business, he was unlucky enough to lose the whole sum, nor was he aware of his loss until he reached home. Arriving there, he opened an immense chest containing many thousand crowns, and on preparing to add the four hundred to the number, he was struck dumb with astonishment to find that they were gone. He uttered an exclamation of horror every time he put his hand into each of his pockets, till, convinced at last that his loss was but too true, he ran off in great consternation along the path he had come, inquiring of the very dogs he met on the way whether they had seen or seized upon his treasure. He was quite confounded when he reached the place where he had first received the money, without obtaining the least tidings of it.

Almost overwhelmed with despair, he suddenly bethought him, as a last resource, to apply to the Marquis, entreating that a public crier might be instantly sent forth, and offering the sum of forty crowns for the recovery of his treasure. With great courtesy the Marquis acceded to his request, expressing himself at the same time concerned to witness the excessive affliction under which the unfortunate Filargiro seemed to labour.

The reward was accordingly proclaimed, and the gold soon afterwards made its appearance in the hands of one of those aged old ladies, who, being great devotees, always walk with their eyes upon the ground as they come from church. In this way she discovered the lost treasure, and fearful lest her conscience should be loaded with such a weight of gold, though extremely poor, she would have been very greatly perplexed in what way to act, had she not luckily heard the crier announcing the reward of forty crowns, which she hoped she might receive with a safe conscience. Observing her destitute appearance, the Marquis very humanely inquired whether she had any means of procuring her subsistence, and whether she had no one to assist her.

"I have nothing," she replied, "but what I gain by the work of my hands and the help of one daughter; we weave and spin, signor, to earn as much as we want, living in the fear of the Lord in the best way we are able. My daughter, to be sure, I should wish to see married before I die, but I have nothing to give her for a portion."

The Marquis, on hearing the poor woman's account of herself, highly praised her integrity in thus restoring what she might so easily have reserved for herself and for a marriage-portion for her daughter; observing that it was an action of which he feared that few others, under the same temptation, would have been capable. He then summoned the merchant, informing him that the lost treasure was found, and requesting him at the same time to put into the poor woman's hands the stated reward.

The raptures of the miser were truly amusing when he beheld and seized upon the gold, even in the presence of the Marquis; but on hearing the demand of the stipulated sum, his countenance again fell, and he began to think how he could possibly withhold the promised reward. Having numbered the pieces once or twice exactly over, though he found them perfectly correct, he turned towards the old woman, saying:

"There are four-and-thirty ducats short of the sum which I put into this bag."

The old lady appeared extremely confused at this accusation, exclaiming in a distressed tone to the Marquis:

"Oh, signor, can that be possible? Is it likely I should have stolen thirty-four ducats, when I had it in my power to possess myself of the whole? No; believe me, noble signor, I swear, as I value my hope of heaven, that I have restored the exact sum which I found on my return from church; not a single farthing have I taken out."

But the miserly old wretch continuing to affirm most solemnly that the ducats were in the same bag with the crowns, and that she must consider them as a sufficient remuneration, the affair seemed to perplex the Marquis not a little. Yet when he reflected that the old miser had only mentioned the four hundred crowns in the first instance, he began to suspect his design of imposing upon the poor woman in order to save the paltry sum offered as a reward.

The Marquis felt the utmost indignation at the discovery of this deceit, believing no punishment to be too severe for this despicable breach of faith; but checking his rising passion for a moment, he reflected that the most effectual chastisement he could bestow upon the miser's attempt to impose upon the magistracy would be to make him fall into the very snare he had laid for another. With this view he thus addressed the merchant:

"And why did you not mention the full amount of your loss before proclaiming the reward?"

"I overlooked it; I quite forgot it," was the reply.

"But it seems somewhat strange that you, who appear so particular about trifles, should not have recollected the circumstance of the ducats. And as far as I can understand, you wish to recover what is not your own. I mean to say that this bag of gold could never have belonged to you at all, since the sum you first mentioned is not to be found in it. I imagine the real owner to be myself, since a servant of mine lost exactly the sum here contained on the very same day you pretend to have lost yours."

The Marquis then turned towards the old woman, observing:

"Since it is clear that the money is none of his, but mine, and you have had the good luck to find it, pray keep it: the whole is your own; present it as a wedding-gift to your daughter. If it should happen that you meet with another purse, containing the ducats as well as the crowns, belonging to this gentleman, I beg you will return it to him without demanding any reward."

The poor lady expressed her gratitude to the Marquis for this generous mark of his favour, and promised to observe his directions in everything.

The wretched merchant, finding that the Marquis had truly penetrated into his motives, and that there was not a chance of succeeding in his nefarious design, declared that he was now quite willing to pay the reward he had promised, if she restored the remaining money, which was indisputably his own.

But it was now too late. The Marquis, turning towards him with an angry air, threatened to punish him for such a disgraceful attempt to defraud another of so large a sum, since, from his own account, it could not possibly be his.

"Get out of my presence, and beware how you exasperate me further. If this good woman should be fortunate enough to meet with the purse, with the exact amount you mention, she has promised to restore it to you untouched. That I think is enough."

Without venturing to answer a single word, the unhappy Filargiro was compelled to leave the place, unaccompanied by his newly-recovered treasure, and filled with sorrow and regret at having refused to fulfil the conditions he had made. The poor old woman, on the other hand, went away overjoyed with her unexpected good fortune, and full of gratitude to the Marquis. She hastened to impart the happy tidings to her daughter, who, after having long indulged a vain attachment, had at length the pleasure of being united to the object of her choice, at the expense of the avaricious old merchant.

GIROLAMO PARABOSCO
1510–1557

FAUSTINO AND THE MEDDLESOME TRADESMAN

THERE formerly resided in the rich and beautiful city of Bologna a brave and intelligent youth of the name of Faustino, whose birth and accomplishments entitled him to rank among the noblest and proudest of the place. To these gifts of nature and of fortune was added a susceptible heart, and he soon became deeply enamoured of a young lady of exquisite beauty, whose name was Eugenia, and who in a short time seemed inclined to return his passion with equal tenderness and truth.

Such was her lover's extreme desire of beholding her, that he availed himself of every opportunity and encountered every risk to enjoy her society, frequently being in wait for hours to catch a mere glimpse of her, and employing numberless emissaries to instruct him as to her motions. Though the young lady's parents had been unable to extort any confession of her attachment from her own lips, they were at no loss to perceive it, and endeavoured to obviate the danger to be apprehended from its indulgence, believing that the young lover, on account of his superior rank and fortune, entertained no serious intentions of making her his wife. With this view they kept a very strict watch over their daughter, debarring her from the visits, and even from the sight of Faustino, as much as they possibly could.

Yet her mother, being of a religious turn of mind, was unwilling that she should relinquish her usual attendance on divine worship, and herself accompanied her daughter every morning to hear mass at a church near their own house, but at so very early an hour, that not even the artisans of the city, much less the young gentry of the place, were stirring. And there she heard service performed by a priest expressly on her own account, though several other persons might happen to be present who were in the habit of very early rising.

Now among these was a certain corn merchant, who had been established only for a short time in Bologna. His name was Ser Nastagio de' Rodiotti, a man who had driven many a hard bargain and thriven wonderfully in his trade, but of so devout a turn withal, that he would not for the world have made an usurious contract, or even speculated to any extent, without having first punctually attended mass, believing doubtless that so good an example more than counterbalanced, in the eye of Heaven, the evil consequences of his actions. And these were certainly very great, especially in the way of raising the price of bread by his vast monopoly of that necessary article of life.

Such, however, was his exemplary conduct in attending church, that he lost not a single opportunity of showing himself there among the earliest of the congregation, having afterwards the consolation to reflect that he had discharged all his religious duties and was ready for business before a great portion of his fellow-citizens were stirring.

Now in a short time it also reached the ears of Faustino, through the good offices, it is supposed, of the young lady, that mass was to be heard every morning at a certain church, with every particular relating to the devotees who attended and the nearest way thither.

Rejoiced at this news, her lover now resolved to rise somewhat earlier than he had been accustomed to do, that he might avail himself of the same advantage that the lady enjoyed in beginning the day with religious duties. For this purpose he assumed a different dress, the better to deceive the eyes of her careful mother, being perfectly aware that she merely made her appearance thus early with her daughter for the sake of concealing her from his sight.

In this way the young lady had the merit of bringing Faustino to church, where they had the pleasure of gazing at each other with the utmost devotion ; except indeed when the unlucky tradesman whom we have just mentioned happened to place himself, as was frequently the case, exactly in their way, so as to intercept the silent communion of souls. And this he did in so vexatious a manner, that they could scarcely observe each other for a moment without exposing themselves to his searching eye and keen observation.

Greatly displeased at this kind of inquisition into his looks and motions, the lover frequently wished the devout corn-dealer in purgatory, or that he would at least offer up his prayers in another church. Such an antipathy did he at length conceive to Ser Nastagio, that he resolved to employ his utmost efforts to prevail upon him to withdraw himself from that spot. Revolving in his mind a great variety of plans, he at last hit upon one which he believed could not fail to succeed, and in a manner equally safe and amusing. With this view he hastened without delay to the officiating priest, whom he addressed in the following pious and charitable strain :

" It has ever been esteemed, my good Messer Pastore, a most heavenly and laudable disposition to devote ourselves to the relief of our poorer brethren, and this you doubtless know far better than I can inform you, from the fact of our blessed Saviour having actually appeared on earth to redeem us from our sins. But though every species of charity is highly commendable, that which seeks out its objects without waiting to be solicited far transcends the rest. For there are many who, however destitute, feel ashamed to come forward for the purpose of begging alms. Now I think, my worthy pastor, that I have of late observed one of these deserving objects in a person who frequents your church. He was formerly a Jew, but through the mercy of Heaven, which never ceases, not long ago he became a Christian, and one whose exemplary life and conduct render him in all respects worthy of the name. Yet, on the other hand, there is not a more destitute being on the face of the earth, while such is his modesty that I assure you I have frequently had the utmost difficulty in persuading him to accept of alms. It would really be a very meritorious act, worthy of the excellent character I have heard of you, were you to touch some morning upon his cruel misfortunes, relating his conversion to our faith, and the singular modesty with which he attempts to conceal his wants. This would probably procure for him a handsome contribution ; and if you will only have the kindness to apprize me of the day, I will take care to bring a number of my friends along with me, and we shall be sure to find this poor fellow seated in your church, where I know he is often employed in listening gratefully to your spiritual advice and consolation."

Our kind-hearted priest, impelled only by pure zeal and charity, cheerfully complied with the wily lover's request. He proposed, then, as the most favourable occasion, the next Sunday morning, when a large assemblage of people would be present, regretting that he had not been sooner made acquainted with the affair.

Faustino next gave the priest an accurate description of the features, person, and dress of our unfortunate corn merchant, observing that the poor man always appeared neat and clean, so that he could not possibly mistake him. Then taking leave of the good friar, he hastened to communicate this piece of mischief to some of his youthful companions, all of whom now awaited with great impatience for the approaching Sunday. Punctually, on its arrival, were they found assembled at the church, even early enough to hear the first mass, and there Messer Nastagio was seen stationed at his usual post, surrounded by a crowd of people collected for the purpose of witnessing the consecration of the place. When the Gospel and the Creed were finished, the good priest paused and looked about him; then wiping his forehead and taking breath for a while, he again addressed the congregation, opening his subject as follows:

"Dearly beloved brethren, you must be aware, for our Saviour Himself has enlightened you on that head, and I have myself likewise insisted upon it as well as I could; you must be aware, I say, that the most pleasing thing you can do in the eyes of the Lord is to show your charity towards poorer Christians, loving and assisting them according to their wants, as far as lies in your power. I trust, therefore, I shall not have much difficulty in persuading you to show the fruits of this good seed of charity in the manner I desire. For as I know you are not wanting in charity, but rather abounding in good works, I am not afraid to inform you that there is a most deserving yet destitute object before you, who, though too modest to urge your compassion, is in every way worthy of it. Pray take pity upon him; I commend him to your kindness. Behold him," he cried, pointing full at Ser Nastagio; "lo! thou art the man. Yes," he continued, while the corn merchant stared at him in the utmost astonishment, "yes, thou art the man! Thy modesty shall no longer conceal thee from the eyes of the people, which are now fixed upon thee. For though thou wert once an Israelite, my friend, thou art now one of the lost sheep which are found, and if thou hast not much temporal, thou hast a hoard of eternal, wealth."

He addressed himself during the whole of this time, both by words and signs, to Ser Nastagio, yet the poor merchant could by no means persuade himself, against the evidence of his own reason, that he was the individual pointed out. Without stirring, therefore, from the spot, he somewhat reluctantly put his hand into his pocket, so far conquering his avarice as to prepare to bestow his alms in the same manner as the rest of the congregation. The first person to present his contribution was the author of the trick, who approaching the spot where the merchant stood, offered his alms, and, in spite of Ser Nastagio, dropped them into his hat, making a sign to the people expressive of his admiration at the poor man's modesty. And though the incensed tradesman exclaimed in an angry tone to the young lover, " I have a longer purse than thou hast ears, man ! " it availed him nothing.

The good priest pursued his theme without noticing Ser Nastagio's remark, except by saying :

" Give no credit to his words, good people, but give him alms—give him alms ; it is his modest merit which prevents him from accepting them." Then once more directing his attention to the confused and angry merchant, he exclaimed :

" Do not look thus ashamed, but take them—take them ! for believe me, good friend, many greater and better men have been reduced to the same piteous plight, yea, even worse than that you are now in. You should rather consider it as an honour than otherwise, inasmuch as your necessities have not been the consequence of your own misconduct, but solely arise from your embracing the light of truth, and becoming a disciple of our Lord."

The priest had no sooner ended than there was a general rush of the whole congregation towards the place where the astonished merchant stood, endeavouring who should be the first to deposit their donations in his hands, while he in vain attempted to resist the tide of charitable contributions which now poured in upon him on every side. He had likewise to struggle against his own avarice, no less than against the officious donors of alms, for he would willingly have received the money, though he did all in his power to repulse their offers.

When the tumult had at length a little subsided, the incensed merchant began to attack the priest in the most virulent terms, until the preacher was almost inclined to suspect that he must really in some way have been misinformed as to the proper object of his charity. He then began to make his excuses, as well as he could, for the error into which he had fallen ; but the lover's purpose was accomplished and the deed could not be recalled. For it was soon reported that Ser Nastagio, the corn merchant, had that very morning been recommended to the charitable notice of the congregation as an example of true conversion from the Jewish to the Christian creed. This story was quickly circulated throughout the whole city, to the infinite amusement of all its inhabitants, more especially of the young lovers, who had now full leisure once more to contemplate each other's perfections, free from the observation of Ser Nastagio, who was never known to enter that church again.

PIETRO FORTINI
D. 1562

THE HEROISM OF FIORDESPINA

IN the noble city of Spoleti, in Umbria, there resided, not many years ago, a young man of the name of Anton Luigi Migliorelli, nobly born, but of a strange and whimsical disposition. Being also of a sanguine temperament, combined with too little judgment, he had the misfortune to imagine himself in love with a very beautiful and accomplished young lady, sprung from one of the first families in Spoleti, whose name was Fiordespina.

What rendered the affair worse, she had already bestowed her hand in marriage upon another, a wealthy citizen of good descent, called Filolauro, from which his lady most generally went by the name of Fiordespina Lauri.

In point of manly beauty and accomplishments, Filolauro was in no way unworthy of possessing so charming a companion ; nor do I believe that throughout all Italy there was a similar instance of conjugal union, happiness, and fidelity. Such, indeed, were the mutual sacrifices, the devotion, and tenderness which they invariably displayed, as to afford a perfect pattern of the respective characters and the conduct to be observed in so intimate a union. Their happiness seemed as if it were too exquisite and unalloyed to last ; and the secret fiend that was about to invade the Eden of their love and repose was already at work, inspiring the soul of Anton Luigi with thoughts equally dangerous to their safety and their honour. Ardently bent upon the pursuit of every object in which he engaged, and having frequent opportunities of enjoying the society and observing the charms and accomplishments of the lovely Fiordespina, he grew so deeply enamoured of them, that in a short time he felt himself unable to control the expression of his feelings.

Yet, after having adopted every expedient in his power, all the arts and flatteries of which he was the master, he had the mortification to find that he not only made no progress in her good opinion, but that she did not even deign to notice his numerous efforts to conciliate and please her. Equally piqued and impassioned, he vowed to be revenged upon her supposed pride and indifference; while he was compelled at the same time to conceal his attentions as much as possible, as the manners of the people of Spoleti were far more strict in this respect than those of many other places, persons of both sexes being in the habit of revenging themselves upon very slight provocation, and even of bearing arms, when occasion required, in open field against their enemies. And there is no point upon which they are more eager to proceed to extremities than in regard to the honour of their women, so that they will scarcely permit the breath of heaven to play upon the faces of their married dames of rank, while the husbands, on the other hand, are not permitted to show the least regard for single ladies.

Thus our unfortunate lover found himself rather awkwardly situated, his feelings being about as unpleasant as those of a culprit preparing for his final journey, since his beloved Fiordespina paid no more attention to him than if there had been no such person in the world, a behaviour which he felt far more difficult to bear than if she had honoured him with her resentment, or even her aversion and contempt.

In this dilemma he believed the wisest as well as the shortest way would be to put a period to his existence; but always when he was on the point of executing his threat, the idea that he was for ever leaving the beautiful Fiordespina flashed across his mind, and he relinquished it. Still he conceived it quite incumbent upon him either to die like a true lover or win the lady's regard, and with this magnanimous resolution he watched his first opportunity of obtaining a final interview with the lady.

Happening to hear that Filolauro was about to accompany a party of young men on an excursion of pleasure into the country, he had no sooner watched the servant who followed him fairly out of sight, than he hastened to his house, but had the mortification to perceive the beloved object in company with two of her youthful companions. Upon this his exasperation was such as to mount to a degree of frenzy, and being in a most favourable mood for listening to the counsels of our great adversary, who is never known to neglect such happy opportunities of adding to the number of his subjects, he resolved in one way or other to bring the matter to a conclusion, whether it were by dagger, rope, or poison, that very evening.

With this view he continued to keep watch until after Filolauro's return, who, being accustomed to walk out with his friends, sometimes as far as the Borgo San Maffio, when the evening was fine, upon this occasion did not take leave of them until near midnight. His beautiful wife, whose thoughts were ever with him in his absence, anxious at the lateness of the hour, was now eagerly looking out for him, after having prepared what viands she imagined would prove most agreeable on his return. Filolauro had just reached the piazza near the fort, close to his own house, when he was met by Antonio Luigi full of the most desperate designs, who, drawing his sword, cried out in great fury: "At last, villain, thou art dead!" at the same moment wounding him severely.

"Ah! traitor," exclaimed the other, "this to me!" and rushing upon him, he closed with him before he could make his escape.

The noble lady, overhearing some disturbance, and recognising her consort's voice, with the courage that distinguished the ladies of Spoleti, instantly seized her husband's javelin that lay at hand, and rushed to the door. There she indeed beheld him struggling in the grasp of his assassin, while his blood stained the ground upon which they fought; and sufficiently distinguishing the combatants by the light of the moon, with the strength of an Amazon, she passed the weapon through the body of Anton Luigi at a single blow. He instantly fell dead at her feet, while she, crying out to her husband that he was only wounded, besought him to take refuge in the house.

By the time she had assisted him back and restored the javelin to its place, a numerous crowd was collecting upon the spot, some of whom, observing the way they took, followed them into the house, where they found the lady attempting to staunch her husband's wounds, at the same time trying to encourage him and calling out for assistance. Discovering no weapon but the sword lying by the side of the deceased, they were unable to account for what they saw; and having borne the body of Anton Luigi into an adjoining church and procured surgical aid for the wounded man, the people gradually dispersed.

On the following morning, the governor, hearing of the homicide, and no one being accused of it, thought it somewhat strange, and instituted a more strict inquiry. Being a native of Lucca, of severe character, and not very kindly disposed towards the ladies of Spoleti, he despatched his officers at once to the residence of the fair Fiordespina, with orders to seize her, together with her husband, the last of whom, wounded as he was, they threw into a dungeon.

His unhappy wife was next conducted bound into the hall allotted for the execution of assassins, where, the evidence of some persons in the crowd being taken, she was actually condemned by her merciless judge to suffer the torture of the question. But rather than accuse either her husband or herself of having committed such an act, which she had reasons for knowing that her inexorable judge would never admit to have been done in self-defence, she chose to submit, with the fortitude of a martyr, to everything that his cruelty could devise. Moved with pity at her sufferings, several of the spectators voluntarily came forward to prove that no weapon except that of the deceased had been found upon the spot, and that it was hardly likely that a single woman could have deprived a soldier of his own sword and of his life.

To this the savage tyrant only replied that such was more probably the case than that so noble a youth should have destroyed himself; and upon this he commanded the executioners to proceed. When, however, the populace, who believed her to be innocent, heard her renewed cries, there ran a confused murmur among the crowd, that, gradually assuming a louder and more angry tone, reminded the cruel governor that he had to deal with the proud and daring natives of Spoleti.

Finding his victim resolutely bent against confession, he began to take the alarm, and ordering her to be set free, he consoled himself with the hope of inflicting still heavier punishment upon her husband. For this purpose he had him brought forth, and condemned to suffer yet more terrific pains than had been inflicted upon his wife.

The moment, however, she beheld him in the presence of their ferocious tormentor, she was unable to bear the very idea, much less the sight, of the most beloved object on earth sharing with her the same fate. Although instant death became the penalty of her confession, yet, in order to spare him the suffering she had herself so nobly borne, she thus addressed the governor:

"Unbind that gentleman, signor. Never let it be said that a savage and remorseless tyrant, such as thou art, had it in his power to inflict his savage torments upon the limbs of my honoured lord. No, it was I who did the deed. Hear me, I say! I alone smote the assassin of my husband dead at my feet. Oh! ye just heavens, ye noble people of Spoleti, be near me; aid me in my utter woe; let him not deprive me of the only object that is dear to these eyes!"

At once surprised and grieved to hear her declare herself guilty of an act by a confession which the severest tortures had failed to wring from her, the spectators, as well as the governor himself, struck with the excessive proof of affection which it displayed, were inclined to consider it as little less than miraculous. What must have been the excess of tenderness and attachment that could excite the soul of a delicate woman to such an unexampled degree of heroism and magnanimity as to confess, out of pity and affection for her husband, what she would otherwise have concealed under the infliction of torture and of death itself!

To such an appeal even the heart of the governor, callous and ferocious as he was, could no longer be insensible. Taken by surprise, astonished at the grandeur and beauty of sentiment it displayed, and of which he had formed no previous idea, after remaining lost in doubt and wonder for some moments, his aspect assumed a perfectly opposite expression, and in milder tones than he had ever before perhaps uttered, he commanded the officers to unbind her husband. He next sent for the father of the deceased, requesting to know what course he wished to be pursued.

The poor old man, thus unhappily deprived of his son, yet aware that no cause of enmity had subsisted between the families, nobly came forward to state everything he knew relating to the unfortunate passion of his son, and boldly taxed the governor with the most culpable conduct in having omitted to receive his evidence until he had unjustly condemned the innocent to suffer. At the same time he tenderly embraced the unhappy prisoners, and weeping over the guilty conduct of his son, appealed to the feelings of the spectators, conjuring them to join in soliciting a free pardon, if pardon it could be called, where no offence had been committed, at the hands of the governor. The relenting feelings of the latter at length yielded to the energy and truth of the old man's appeal; for, having liberated the captives, he descended from his judgment-seat, and, struggling with contending emotions, turned away from the spectators, and soon disappeared.

ANTON–FRANCESCO DONI
1513–1574

SAN GIOVANNI THE YOUNGER

THERE has lately risen up, in a place on the confines of Lombardy, a new saint, now ready to be added to the calendar. Having abandoned the profession of curing bodies, in which his conscience began to reproach him with having despatched nearly the whole list of his patients to another world, he undertook the more harmless cure of souls, induced by the same motive of enriching himself at the expense of others. For his cloak of religion, then, he assumed a lion's skin, in which he came to Piacenza, entitling his order—The Apostolic Rule of the Four Evangelists, in the Habit of the First Hermit, St. Paul.

This new invention he supported by a thousand other spiritual fabrications of the same kind, studying the most successful impostures of his predecessors, and persuading the good people, like a rogue as he was, to erect him a convent for his new disorder of monks, quite worthy of their great superior, whose creed was principally to lighten the pockets of their congregation and of simple wayfaring travellers, by virtue of the miracles and relics which they exhibited to view.

Thus, in a short time, from a death-dealing doctor he became a little spiritual despot, reconciling it better to his conscience to tyrannise over the minds than to torture the bodies of his patients ; until Fortune, who can ill support the sight even of a good man in prosperity, lent him a few such smart kicks in the exercise of his new functions from one who had detected his imposture, as to lead him to conclude he had gone somewhat too far, though he found it too late to retrace his steps.

In short, after having shorn his flock as close as any shepherd well could, he was himself overreached, exposed, and compelled to take to flight, by some superior master in the same art, whose subtlety exceeded even his own. For though he fought hard to maintain his spiritual government and again to recover his lost ground, it was all in vain ; no new relics, no fresh miracles could avail him ; the charm of his reputation was flown, and a still more successful candidate was now elected to the throne.

In these circumstances he took to an ambulatory mode of warfare, proceeding from monastery to monastery, husbanding his relics and miracles in a most surprising manner, and exhibiting them only as necessity seemed to require. In the course of these his travels, the last and greatest of his impostures is well deserving of record, even among those preserved in the catalogue of San Ciappelletto.

It happened that, in journeying one day towards Nizza, he was taken seriously unwell; so much so as to be obliged to seek refuge in a neighbouring convent, belonging to the friars of I know not what disorder, where he was glad to be able to repose. Here, as long as he had money enough to make himself comfortable, his residence was highly agreeable to the holy fathers, although the fame of his wicked impostures had reached the place before him; but the moment his resources began to fail, there was a marked change for the worse in their conduct towards our San Giovanni.

Their whispers became louder, they began to consult the reputation of their monastery, and the patient could scarcely rest in his bed for their importunities to get rid of him and to send him to the hospital; for as to themselves, they declared that they were heartily tired of him. In this way they went on day after day, worse and worse, as well as the patient, who by his condition seemed resolved to have the benefit of dying in their hands. There was, indeed, only about another hour's life in him, when they came to the resolution of removing him; upon which, in order better to defeat their plan, he died in half an hour, congratulating himself that he had thus succeeded in laying his bones with them, like a pious monk, even against their will.

The whole fraternity, not a little perplexed how to act, and desirous of obviating the scandal which might attach to them of having received so notorious a delinquent under their protection, resolved to put the best face they could upon the matter, to give him all due funereal honours in a public and pompous display, to pronounce an oration, and clear his memory from the vile imputations cast upon it; and if all this proved not enough to absolve them in the eyes of the people, to canonise him by the name of "Saint Giovanni the Younger" without delay.

For this purpose, the most specious and oratorical monk of the brotherhood was fixed upon to deliver the oration, who went through the whole service with so much credit both to himself and to the deceased saint, that the people, not satisfied with giving mere empty applauses, immediately began a collection beyond expectation of the most sanguine of the order. Our hero, then, was unanimously made a saint in a style that would have excited the envy of his predecessor, San Ciappelletto, ana proceeded to work various miracles accordingly. But for my own part, I do not give the least faith to these saints who excite the wonder and applause of the vulgar, confining it only to such as are duly approved and beautified by the Holy Church of the faithful at Rome.

FRANCESCO SANSOVINO
1521–1586

THE DISCOMFITED FOPS

THERE were once two spruce young gentlemen who had more reason to pique themselves upon their good descent than upon the strength of their mental endowments. To use a familiar expression much applied by the good people of Milan, they both belonged to the parish of Saint Witless, and from a great similarity of disposition, they had contracted so strict an intimacy, that they were seldom to be seen asunder. When they happened to be in other company, they invariably aimed at leading the conversation to points of fashionable interest, in which alone they were calculated to shine, displaying their abilities in criticising the tastes of others and indirectly complimenting each other. Their continued repetition of the same fashionable nonsense, so impertinently introduced upon all occasions, had at length the effect of wearying and disgusting all parties where their presence was tolerated.

During fine summer weather they were in the habit of wearing the most costly white silk costumes; their vests were of white velvet, their ruffs of the whitest cambric, their pantaloons and stockings of white silk, and their hats of white velvet with white feathers in them.

And yet they had the assurance to appear thus accoutred in public, displaying their feathers with all the vanity of peacocks, as they turned arm in arm along the piazzas, full of their own perfections, and eager to attract the notice of spectators, who failed not indeed to smile as they passed; a circumstance which these young sparks placed entirely to their own credit. So pestiferous did they at length become to society by this display of their vain folly and presumption, that whenever they appeared in a perfectly new suit, their friends invariably avoided them, as they were certain to be regaled with a dissertation upon French tailors and the newest points and lacings then in mode.

"Observe these linings! how well they sit upon this waistcoat! how brilliant are these feathers! By Jove! how nobly they wave with the least breath of air. Yet they would not sit well upon any one, let me tell you; there is an art in a man's wearing a handsome dress by no means common."

And in this way they would run on by the hour together. Among others who had thus suffered under their intolerable rattle was a sensible and spirited young fellow, who had a particular enmity to the race of fops, and made a solemn vow, in a moment of irritation, to hit upon some species of revenge that might tend to remove such a nuisance from society, and perhaps put the authors of it on their good behaviour in future. With this view he conceived a plan which he thought could not fail to produce a happy effect, and only waited for a good opportunity of carrying it into execution.

This soon occurred during the summer season, when our cavaliers were in the habit, as we have said, of assuming their white array, and when they frequented the neighbourhood of our more sensible friend's residence, in order to make themselves agreeable to a party of ladies who were accustomed to walk near his house. One evening, therefore, he stationed himself at his garden gate, as if enjoying the coolness of the air, expecting these two giddy sparks, who in a short time came fluttering by, having displayed their plumes to the amusement of the ladies, who had now returned home. Stepping suddenly forwards and seizing a hand of each, their friend declared he would make them his prisoners for the rest of the evening; for he had just received some excellent wine, of which he wished to have their opinion.

They accepted his challenge, and, with a fashionable roll of their shoulders, accompanied him in, when, finding the servants busily clearing the dining-room, he invited the gentlemen to go and give him their opinion of his selection of wines as they lay in his vaults, where they might also taste it perfectly cool; observing that he often went there when he found every other place in the world too hot for him. Each of them, then, seizing his glass, mightily amused at the idea, they followed their friend into the vaults, a servant preceding them with a torch, while his fellows were laughing heartily at their master's humour in the room above, one of whom, being intrusted with the secret, had communicated it to all the rest.

Several guests in the drawing-room were likewise waiting the event, with no slight mirth exhibited in their countenances. While the glasses were filling, the two coxcombs were busily criticising the various sorts of wines submitted to their taste, and enjoying the coolness as they rambled about the vaults. Now there was a large vessel filled with water lying near for the purpose the host had in view. It was of such respectable dimensions as apparently to defy the exertions of a single person to remove it. Attracting the notice of his guests, the host, as if casually passing, observed:

"Large as you seem to think it, there is one of my fellows who can throw it upon his shoulders and carry it upstairs for me whenever I please."

One of our fashionables, who likewise piqued himself upon his bodily prowess, instantly laid hands upon it, but finding it resist his efforts even to stir it, he pretty roundly swore he would wager a dozen of champagne that their host was mistaken. But the fact was again as positively affirmed, till the dispute growing warm on both sides, the young gentleman declared that it would be the fairest way to put it to the proof.

"I have no objection," returned the wily host; "here is the very rascal we were just speaking of; he has shoulders broad enough to bear the world: so take up that huge tub, you rogue, and walk. Show the gentlemen the way upstairs, and take heed you do not let it fall."

Forthwith he pitched it upon his neck; and the master leading the way, the two disciples of San Simpliciano somewhat imprudently followed in his rear. The steps were tolerably steep, and the porter, feigning great difficulty, just as he had reached the top, suddenly tripped, and sent the contents of the vessel back again, flying all abroad on every side. Strange was the confusion, and the sputtering, and the exclamations which the two unfortunate fashionables now made; still more strange was the sprinkling and spoiling of their delicate new garments, which truly cut a woful figure. Instead of a pure white, they now exhibited all the colours in the rainbow, with the addition of black patches, which stuck to their fine ermine, while they sighed and sobbed with the effects of the cold bathing they had just received. The water had been deeply impregnated with ink and assafœtida, and with other nauseous drugs, to such a degree that neither of them was free from the taint for more than a twelvemonth.

The porter, however, had the humanity to prevent the tub itself from falling, which would otherwise have totally overwhelmed the dripping sparks, who were by no means made of such stout materials as to withstand the shock it might have occasioned, being of that brittle texture which, like glass, will bear no rough usage, though it can receive a polish. The rogue of a porter instantly took to his heels on viewing the awful ruin he had wrought, while his master, pretending to be in the highest degree offended at his negligence, hastened after him, leaving our poor heroes to digest the venom of his joke as they best could.

But not possessing wit enough to see into the jest, they shook hands before they left with the happy and triumphant host, who watched them, along with some of his guests, tripping homewards as fast as they well could, shivering as if in an ague fit, to the infinite amusement of all beholders.

SEBASTIANO ERIZZO
1525–1585

TIMOCRATES AND ARSINOE

AT the period when the tyrant Nicocles swayed the sceptre of Sicyon, alike feared and hated by its citizens, two only were found who, equally distinguished by their rank, their wealth, and their spirit, disdained longer to bear the intolerable weight of his oppression. Surpassing their fellow-citizens as well in courage as in rank, they were the first to conspire together how they might best achieve the freedom of their native place, though even by the death of its despotic ruler, aware that the seeds of liberty are best watered with the blood of its enemies.

With this view, having fixed upon a certain hour and spot, they waited with much anxiety for the period of its accomplishment, but, seized with a sudden panic when the moment arrived, one of the two conspirators refused to proceed any farther in the affair. Not satisfied with this, and afraid of being anticipated by his colleague, he went instantly to the palace of the tyrant, and the better to ingratiate himself, acquainted him with the whole transaction, affecting at the same time to have given ear to it only with a view of revealing the real author to the King, as was the duty of every loyal subject. Having in this manner been made acquainted with the full particulars of the conspiracy, Nicocles, giving entire credit to the account, despatched forthwith a company of his guards to the residence of Timocrates, with orders to level the gates with the ground and to bear the traitor alive into his presence.

The noble citizen was in this way seized and carried before the tyrant, who, having feasted his eyes with the sight of his victim, and thrown him into one of his most horrid dungeons, condemned him on the very same day to die. But as it was the custom of those times that such as were found guilty of capital crimes should be executed during the night within the walls of their dungeon, when their cries could not be heard, Timocrates was thus condemned to suffer on the following evening.

When tidings of this terrific punishment came to the ears of his poor consort, Arsinoe, who was most tenderly attached to her husband, so great was her surprise and terror as well-nigh to deprive her of existence. On recovering sufficiently to dwell upon the dreadful subject, she long revolved every means that her affection could suggest of averting so heavy and unexpected a calamity. She well knew how worse than unavailing it would be to pour her prayers and tears at the feet of the tyrant, a measure that might crown their sufferings by bringing along with it the dishonour as well as the death of her husband. She resolved, then, to think and to act only for herself ; and it was not long before her ingenuity supplied her with an idea, which with fearless breast she prepared to carry into speedy effect.

On the evening that her consort was to suffer, no sooner was it twilight, than, wrapping herself in a dark cloak and veiling her beauty in deep black crape, she took her fearful and solitary way, without acquainting a single friend with her purpose, towards the dungeon prepared for the tomb of all she held most dear. On her arrival, taking aside one of the guards, she besought him, bitterly weeping while she spoke, to permit her to see her husband for a few moments before he died, and to yield her the sad consolation of a last tear, a last embrace, without which they should neither of them die in peace. Touched at her deep and passionate distress, the rest of the guards gathered round her, and unable long to resist her entreaties, they all of them, catching the soft infection from each other, at length agreed to let her pass.

On beholding her husband, however, instead of longer giving way to womanly lamentations and tears, Arsinoe assumed all the fortitude of a heroine, boldly yet sweetly advising and consoling him, while she entreated him no longer to despair. Then, hastily acquainting him with her plan, she began to array him in her own dress, and having disguised his face in the thick veil, and thrown the cloak over his shoulders, she took one kiss, breathed a soft farewell, and quietly assumed his place.

The guards, believing that it was the lady returning apparently drowned in grief, offered no sort of opposition ; and in a little while Timocrates was beyond the limits of the tyrant's sway.

But the hour was come when the executioner proceeded with the guards to receive his victim from their hands, bearing along with him the infernal implements of his trade. What was their surprise, on approaching nearer, to lay their unhallowed hands upon a gentle and beauteous lady, who was immediately borne by the executioner into the tyrant's presence, to learn in what way he was to proceed. Here she was received with scowling and terrific looks, while she appeared wholly unable to answer the threats and inquiries of the incensed Prince. Vainly attempting to hide her terror, she again and again burst into tears whenever she prepared to speak, so as even to awaken some touch of compassion in the tyrant's obdurate breast.

"Be not so much alarmed, lady," he continued in an altered tone: "what is it you fear? Only reveal the real motives which led you to set my power at defiance, to rescue my prisoner, a traitor doomed to death, and to deceive my guards."

"It was not to defy you or deceive your guards I came," replied Arsinoe. "It was love, only love and pity for my unhappy husband that impelled me to it; and I would hazard much, much more, even more than life itself, did I possess it, for his sake. When the fearful tidings burst upon me, when I heard that he was condemned to suffer an ignominious death, and when I reflected upon his whole life and conduct, nor found the slightest cause for blame or for your princely displeasure, I was determined to peril everything for his rescue. This I have done, and succeeded; and I willingly yield me a victim, if such I must be, in his place. Yet I would still hope that you will not behold my affliction and my tears unmoved; but attribute all my error and my crime to the tender love I bore him, a love which grew up with our earliest years, and which is such that you must tear away my heart-strings before I can quietly see him perish. Surely, then, you cannot pretend to exercise any law against true and devoted affection: severe as you are esteemed to be, you would not punish me for feelings over which I have no control."

Such was the affecting appeal of the wretched Arsinoe, which produced so extraordinary an effect upon the mind of Nicocles that, cruel and unforgiving as he naturally was, and vehemently exasperated against Timocrates in particular, he yet felt his fury and indignation die away within him at the sound of her mournful words. He therefore admitted her conjugal affection to be a sufficient justification of her conduct, and dismissed her uninjured from his presence. But not so fortunate were the guards, whose humanity was deserving of a better fate. Against them his wrath burned with unmitigated fury.

"And now seize me those caitiff villains," cried the tyrant, "who, false to their trust, permitted access to my prisoner. Their blood be upon their own heads, for I will never consent to be thus wholly cheated out of my revenge"; and the unhappy guards were accordingly led to execution by the hired mercenaries of the tyrant.

In the course of a short time, Arsinoe, having obtained tidings of her husband, disguised herself in male attire, and, accompanied by a single faithful servant, fled secretly from her house, and joined the object of her love in a distant and secure retirement.

CELIO MALESPINI
1531–1611

THE LOVE AFFAIRS OF THE GRAND DUCHESS

THE bank of the Salviati was one of the numerous Florentine businesses established some years ago in the lovely town of Venice. In this bank there were many young men who wrote and kept the books, and among them was Pietro Buonaventura, a very handsome and courtly young Florentine.

Next to the bank, lived a Venetian gentleman of the house of the Capelli. He had a very numerous family, and one of his children, Bianca, was a pretty and gracious girl, and with her Buonaventura fell madly in love. Thanks to the closeness of the two houses and the convenient way in which they were built, Buonaventura was able to meet Bianca and tell her what love he bore her.

The girl thought he was one of the heads of the business, or at least a partner, and, liking his fine manners and handsome presence, she began to look on him with loving eyes. Their love increased day by day, and reached such a point that, under promise of marriage, they lived as husband and wife, without anybody knowing it, except an old nurse of Bianca.

The two lovers continued to see each other, and one evening, Bianca stayed with her lover in the neighbouring bank till dawn, having left open the door of her father's house that was only four steps away. The baker to the Capelli came to see if they wanted any bread. After he had whistled and knocked at the door, he was told to make the bread: and as he went away, noticing that the door was half open, and acting for the best, he shut it.

Hearing the baker's whistle, Bianca knew that it was time to depart. After sweetly kissing her betrothed husband, she rose up and went with him to the door to regain her father's house. There she found the entrance closed, and it so frightened her that she was beside herself and did not know what to do or say. Returning to Pietro, who usually waited until she had gone in, she told him she had found the door closed and could not understand how it had occurred. Then, trembling like a reed in a storm, she fell into the arms of the young man.

Pietro comforted her, and said there was nothing to be afraid of. Rushing at once into the street, he called and whistled to the nurse to open the door. But all his efforts were in vain, for he could not make himself heard by the old dame. Already the light of dawn began to shine. So the two lovers, fearful of being discovered, resolved to fly the country, being persuaded that if they were found in such a situation they would be put to death.

Having then collected all their courage and their energy, with the little money and the clothes they could hastily get together—the girl only had a serge dress over her shift, as it was the height of summer—the two young people hurried on a ship, and, as secretly as they could, made their way to Florence. There they found shelter in the house of the father of Buonaventura, above San Marco place, not far from the Church of the Annunziata.

Although the father of Buonaventura was a Florentine citizen, he had but little wealth; and, seeing that he had two more mouths to feed, he was obliged to dismiss his maidservant and get Bianca to do her work. For his own wife was too old to look after the house. The charming girl took charge of everything, and did it all lightly and gaily for several months.

At Venice, when the flight of the two lovers was discovered, the father and the relatives of the girl became furious, and their anger was increased by the fact that they were persons in a high position. They so managed the matter that an atrocious proclamation was published against the loving couple, sentencing them to be pursued and killed, even on foreign soil. When the fugitives heard of this ban they went cold to the bone with fright, and Bianca was so terrified that she never let herself be seen, and always worked indoors at her household affairs.

As the lovers were living in this perilous position, the Grand Duke Francesco, by a happy chance, passed in his carriage under the windows of the house. Bianca, who had never seen him, raised the blind a little to get a good look, and her glance met that of the Grand Duke. The Lord of Tuscany was so moved that he put his head out of the carriage and stared at the window in the hope of seeing the young lady again: but it was in vain. A simple glance had sufficed to give birth, in the soul of the Grand Duke, to such a passion that he was most anxious to know who the girl was, and learn everything about her.

When he was informed of her miserable situation, his heart was filled with pity for her misfortunes and his desire to see her again increased. It was easy for him to observe her at the window, either when he went morning and evening to one of his estates called the Casino where he remained till the dinner-hour, or when he went to mass at the Church of San Marco, close to the Buonaventura house, or to the Church of the Annunziata. Thus he found many occasions to steal another glance at Bianca.

But a great desire came to him to see her at closer range. He told this wish of his to a Spanish gentleman, whom, at an early age, the Grand Duke Cosimo had given him for governor and guardian. Mandragona, as the Spaniard was called, promised to bring the affair about. Going at once to his wife, he requested her to make friendly advances towards the mother of Pietro.

This was easily done. The two women, as is natural between persons of their sex, were not long in talking over their private affairs. La Mandragona, who knew how to conduct these operations, brought the talk round to Pietro and asked if he were married.

" Certainly, Signora," said the mother, " but in a very unfortunate way."

And she then told what had happened in Venice. The courtly dame feigned to feel a great compassion for Bianca, and said she would like to take her to the palace and see if she could help her.

" It would be a very difficult thing," said the other woman, " to get her to go out. She never leaves the house. She has no other dress but the one she wears, because we are so poor we could not buy anything for her. And she would be ashamed to appear before you in rags, seeing that she also is a beautiful lady of noble birth."

" We can easily remedy that," said La Mandragona, " by sending her some dresses, and then I shall be able to see her and get to know her."

" I do not know if she will agree to do so," said Pietro's mother, " without permission from her husband. I will do all I can to get her to come and see you, but I fear I shall not succeed. For she takes much pleasure in living in this humble retired manner without seeing anybody. My son has often asked her to go with me to mass at San Marco, but she has never cared to do so. Since the blessed hour when she entered our house, she has never stepped out of doors ! "

" Use every effort, I pray you, to bring her to me," said La Mandragona. " I will send a carriage in which she can come in safety, without being seen by anybody. And tell her that my friendship, far from injuring her, may perhaps be a great help and a great benefit."

" I will not fail to do all I can to please you," said Pietro's mother.

Returning home, she began to talk with her daughter-in-law and tell her, point by point, all that the great Court lady had said.

" Think of it," she said, " this lady is the wife of the first favourite of the Grand Duke. Her friendship is sure to be of help to you, and she may be able to obtain through her husband the safe conduct you so long for, to enable you to live in Florence. Then you will be protected from the power of your father who is so furious to get you in his hands."

When poor Bianca heard the talk about her safe conduct, though she still had no desire to leave the house and walk about Florence and become known to the townspeople, she was shaken from her first resolve, and promised to see the lady if her husband agreed.

Pietro was as anxious as his wife to obtain the safe conduct, and he thought it would be easy to obtain it through the wife of the favourite of the Grand Duke. So he gave his consent and word was sent to La Mandragona that she might despatch a carriage at a favourable opportunity.

A carriage soon came, and Bianca and her mother-in-law rode to the palace, where La Mandragona received them with much joy and many caresses. She led them into a splendid room and there they talked of a thousand things, and the lady again offered to get her husband to do all that was necessary to obtain the safe conduct. While they were talking, the favourite, Mandragona, entered the room, as though unaware of what was going on, and asked his wife to introduce him to her friends.

" They are," she answered, " two ladies who have need of our favour and our influence with the Grand Duke."

Then in a few words she told him the story of Bianca—a story he knew better than she did—and begged him to interest His Highness in the matter. The Grand Duke was in fact hidden in the room, and saw and heard everything. And he saw that, while Mandragona's wife was speaking, Bianca kept her eyes lowered, while such intensity of desire shone in them that, without her speaking, it was easy to see how passionately she longed for the safe conduct.

" All that you desire, Signora," said the favourite, when his wife had done, " is very little beside what I should like to do for you. I shall have little trouble in obtaining it, for the Grand Duke is so magnanimous and courteous that he is always quick to render justice to all who ask it of him, and especially to gracious ladies, whom he is bound to serve under the laws of chivalry. So take heart and be certain that all your wishes will be satisfied."

And saying this, he left the room. Bianca, gladdened by his offers and promises, began to talk with a happy heart, and her face shone with joy. Then La Mandragona took her by the hand.

" I should like, Signora," she said, " to show you our palace, and see if you find in it anything resembling the great and superb buildings of your town. In the meantime, Signora Buonaventura, who looks tired, can rest until our return."

" Yes," said the old lady, " I have not enough breath left to climb up and down so many stairs."

So arm-in-arm, with smiling faces, Bianca and La Mandragona strolled about the palace, the building of which was not then completed. Bianca was astonished at the costly ornaments that abounded in every room, and was loud in her praises. They came at last into a very beautiful chamber, in which was a fine bed and a magnificent chest, and La Mandragona opened a drawer and took out a large number of jewels of high beauty and gave them one by one to the young lady, who looked at them with great admiration.

" Now I would like to show you," said La Mandragona, " some dresses that seem to me of the Venetian mode. Please wait a little, while I look for the keys of the chest in which they are kept."

Scarcely had she gone than the Grand Duke came in. At his sudden appearance, Bianca shook with fear, for in a flash she at once saw why she had been brought to the palace. Falling on her knees in a humble suppliant attitude, she cried :

" Since by an evil fate I have lost my parents, my liberty and my native country, and only my honour remains to me, I pray you be my protector and help me ! "

" Fear nothing, Signora," said the Grand Duke, taking her by the arms and lifting her up, " I have not come here to do you wrong, but to console you and help you, for I know what misfortunes you have suffered. No ! You must rejoice that you have at last found a protector, and be sure that on no occasion will you receive from me anything but favour and courtesy."

And making a bow he went away, leaving the lovely lady all pale and confused until La Mandragona returned, and said to her with a laughing face :

" Don't be surprised at the unlooked-for visit of the Grand Duke. At any moment, when we have almost forgotten his existence, he will arrive unexpectedly, and amuse himself by playing some prank either on me or on my girls. It seems to me you have given him a talking to, if I can go by the way his face reddened. How glad I am! After such a reprimand, he will not be so bold in the future."

" I said nothing to him," said Bianca, " but that I wished to keep my honour, and I begged him to be the guardian and the defender of my good name."

" And I assure you," said La Mandragona, " that he will do it. For he is not the sort of man to waste his time over a good woman like you. But to come to the heart of things, I must tell you that you ought to feel happy that Heaven, in pity for your sufferings, brings such a strong arm to deliver you from your misfortunes. So hold tight to this arm and you will be happy and protected. There are very few women with a Grand Duke burning for love of them, and you can be sure of obtaining everything from him."

There was more talk of the same sort between the two ladies, and in the end the gentle Venetian lady consented to permit the amorous Grand Duke to sue for her favour. From day to day their love for each other increased, until the Grand Duke took Bianca for his wife and had her crowned Grand Duchess of Tuscany.

THE TRANSFORMATION

Celio Malespini

MANY years ago there dwelt in the city of Ainalto a certain merchant, who, among his other speculations, was unlucky enough to venture in the matrimonial lottery, and to draw a very bold and artful woman for his wife. Now, his business frequently leading him to a distance from home, the lady was at full liberty to indulge her love of pleasure and power, neglecting no opportunity of domineering over her household, and coquetting with the prettiest young fellows she could find.

One of these at length became so particular a favourite as to excite the notice of one of the merchant's neighbours, who often amused himself with counting the number of visits paid to her by her gentle cavalier during the husband's absence. He next resolved to add to his amusement by acquainting the poor gentleman with his suspicions, who, expressing all the surprise and concern possible upon the occasion, thanked his friend for his advice, observing that he would take care to provide a remedy. And in order to convince himself the more effectually of what he did not in the least wish to know, he fixed to return suddenly to his own house the very first night he should be supposed to be at a distance. So, to be as good as his word, he feigned a pretty long journey, but retracing his steps towards evening, he went straight to his friend's house, situated just opposite his own, whence he could easily descry the motions of his enemy, if such indeed were lurking about his premises that night.

His friend, who had stationed himself at his side, when he was just on the point of dropping to sleep, about midnight was suddenly roused by an exclamation of horror from the poor merchant, and looking out of the window beheld the lover standing at his usual station. The door not being immediately opened, the latter took a few turns before the house with an easy and confident air, by no means an auspicious sign in the eyes of our jealous spectator, who pronounced himself to be a very unhappy man.

With his friend's advice, therefore, he resolved to employ the following stratagem. After disguising himself as well as he could, he very quietly stepped downstairs, and joining the gentleman upon the terrace, he accosted him in a low tone as follows :

" My mistress, Signor, knows very well who it is, and has sent me to say, that, fearing her husband's return, she wishes me to introduce you some other way into the house, lest any one should observe you walking before the door."

Signor Drudo, believing him of course one of the lady's domestics, consented to accompany him, and upon approaching another entrance, the husband took a key from his pocket, and led the unsuspecting lover up a back staircase into a room where lay a huge chest.

" My mistress begs me to conceal you a few moments in this trunk, Signor, until my foolish master goes, when you may depend that she will not delay a moment in coming for you herself, and will give you the best entertainment that the house can afford. So jump in, Signor ; plenty of room and plenty of air ; and you will not have to wait many minutes."

Accordingly, with a becoming deference for the lady's orders, the bold youth stepped in, and the husband, locking him fast, put the key into his pocket and hastened back again to the house of his friend.

" He is caught ! " he cried ; " the rat is fast in the trap. What will be the best way, think you, of disposing of him ? "

This soon became a very general question, all his friends and relations being summoned to decide upon it, especially the female portion, who were quite delighted to hear the tidings, having long owed the merchant's wife a grudge for the haughtiness and intolerance of her manners. To add to the publicity of the affair, the lady's parents were roused from their beds in the middle of the night and requested to attend ; and even her brothers and sisters, and cousins from the country, were not spared upon the occasion : all being assembled in council to strike the souls of the guilty pair with tenfold awe, confusion, and despair.

With this charitable view the whole procession directed their steps towards the house of their victims, while in the meantime the unhappy lover had been rather anxiously awaiting the arrival of his beloved, who on her part was looking as anxiously out of the windows, wondering what could possibly delay him so long, as he was accustomed to anticipate the hour. Hearing footsteps passing in all directions but none approaching near, the poor lover, already half stifled, began to kick and cry out with all his strength, in which he was successful enough to attract the lady's ear in the next apartment, who inquired in a great fright what it was.

"It is I, my dear soul," returned a feeble voice; "I am just dead. I wonder you can be so cruel as to keep me here."

"Why, how did you get there, in the name of all the saints? It is none of my doing, I am sure."

"I do not know," said the voice, "but your servant put me here by your orders, lest your husband should see me."

"O Lord, help me, then!" she cried. "I see how it all is; it is my husband's doing. It is all discovered. What, in the name of Heaven, shall we do?"

"Let me out by all means," cried the voice, "unless you wish to see me perish."

"Oh dear! but my husband has got the key and it is impossible to break it open; besides, he would murder me if I did."

"Look for another key, then," said the voice.

"That is a good thought; so I will," said the lady; and directing her search very effectually, she hit upon the right key, and was happy enough to liberate her lover.

Once free, after drawing many deep sighs, not for love, but to recover his breathing, he was about to take his leave of the lady and secure his escape while there was yet time, when, seizing him half frantic in her arms, she conjured him not to abandon her alone to death and to dishonour.

"But what can be done?" cried he; "how can you contrive to escape?"

"Why," said she, "if we could put somebody else into the trunk, there might be some excuse for letting you out."

"True," said her lover; "but who can we find to take my place so that I may go, for it is quite time?"

"Now I think of it," returned the lady, "there is a young ass in the stable; if you would assist me to get it here, and shut it up in the box!"

"Certainly I will do that," replied the lover, though not much flattered at the idea of his successor; "I will do that; and let us go about it quickly."

So, having achieved this feat and kissed his fair deliverer tenderly, he ran out of the house; while the lady, having locked up the little donkey, very quietly went to rest. Ere long, however, she was roused by a tremendous noise at the door; all the relations she had in the world were arrived, and she went downstairs to welcome them herself.

"Now," cried the enraged husband, rushing in followed by the whole troop, "I will convince you of the truth of all I have said. Go in, go in! and you shall take this vile daughter of yours home with you after we have despatched her wretched paramour before her face!"

This they one and all promised him to do, proceeding with lighted torches and drawn swords to the scene of action, and followed at a convenient distance by the women, extremely curious to behold the termination of the tragedy. The lady expressing the utmost astonishment at these proceedings and the strange reception she met with on all hands, her husband, without deigning to reply, lent her a pretty severe box on the ear, a species of compliment which was as eagerly returned.

"Mind whom you have to deal with and what you say!" exclaimed the insulted fair one; "do you think I will be thus treated in the presence of my parents?"

"Oh, you vile, abandoned woman!" he returned; "what will you say when I show them your wicked paramour, whom we are going to kill before your face?"

And upon this a volley of abuse was launched on her from all sides, not a single one of her friends or relatives joining their voice to hers.

"Yes, go on, go on!" she cried; "call me by all the horrid names you please; for I have the satisfaction of knowing that you all lie in your throats; yes, you do, you do! or else you are all stark mad: my husband must have driven you out of your wits."

"Let us inquire of this chest," retorted he; "let us hear what that will say!"

"O villain!" cried his wife, "you know I never had the key in my life; and whoever you may have hidden there, I swear I have never had anything to say to him in all my life, and I trust that Heaven will help me, and make my innocence manifest to the world. Yes, and Heaven will interfere, for it is all a vile conspiracy to rob a poor inoffensive and injured woman of her chief crown and jewel, her innocence and honour!"

"Come, no whining!" cried her husband. "I have long known your practices; but I hardly thought that he could have made such a complete hypocrite of you: he seems to have taught you to some purpose indeed! Your time is at length come. I will give ample proof of your depravity! Come along, I am going to open the box. But first, my good friends, have your weapons ready, and draw closer round. Strike sure, and take good care he does not escape; for I can assure you he is a fierce and powerful fellow."

"Never fear," they all cried at once; "we will do his business; I think we are a match for him!" and wrapping their mantles around them, and brandishing their swords, they entreated him to proceed.

One of them even cried in an insulting tone:

"Have you confessed yourself, villain? for you are likely to have no other priests to officiate than ourselves."

As the jealous husband was unlocking the trunk, his mother and sisters turned their heads aside, as if desirous of shunning the horrid sight, even the shedding of a wicked man's blood.

With hands and eyes intent upon the approaching slaughter the men of vengeance stood; the box opened, and the ass, uneasy at having been so long confined, got upon his legs, and the better to take his breath, brayed a long and discordant welcome to his friends. Such was the sudden shock he gave them that some of the spectators fainted; the more fortunate ran away, and great was the terror and confusion before order could be restored. The more devout cried out that it was a miracle sent to prove the innocence of the lady and the wicked design of injuring her reputation; so that with one accord changing the object of their resentment, they began to revile the poor merchant, and accuse him of the most flagitious conduct in attempting to ruin the reputation of his own wife: indeed, had he not quickly sought refuge elsewhere, the lady's brothers would have consigned him to the fate they had prepared for her lover. It was some time before he was again received into favour by the lady and her friends, nor was he ever afterwards known to make the least complaint.

SCIPIONE BARGAGLI
1541–1612

IPPOLITO AND GANGENOVA

AMONG other families that in times gone by are known to have ornamented the city of Siena, one of the most noble was the Saracini, a house which still preserves unsullied its ancient worth and splendour. In the long list of names that constituted its different branches we find mention of one Ippolito, the sole surviving heir of a distinguished cavalier. At the period we are about to refer to, he numbered no more than eighteen years, was extremely graceful and handsome in his person, of elevated mind and intellect, and much esteemed by his friends and fellow-citizens for the vivacity and courtesy of his manners.

Now it fell out, as is most frequently the case with youths of a fine temperament, that he became deeply enamoured of one of the most beautiful and attractive girls in all the city, whose surpassing charms and accomplishments were celebrated wherever she had been seen. Her name was Gangenova, the youngest of three daughters left to the care of a widowed mother, the relict of Messer Reame Salimbeni, whose family ranked among the first in Siena for numerous services rendered to the republic in periods of the greatest peril, though now, along with its arms and palaces, become altogether extinct, nothing of its past grandeur remaining but the name. The delight of all her relations, as well as of the society in which she moved, it was no wonder, then, that the fair Gangenova should so far have enthralled the soul of young Ippolito, that, by frequent contemplation of her beauties and accomplishments, he resolved to run all hazards in order to win her love. Nor had he, in the few opportunities permitted him of conversing with her, any reason for despair, since he rightly interpreted the tones and looks with which she occasionally addressed him.

But in consequence of the very strict superintendence of her mother, which was exercised with greater severity over Gangenova than over her elder sisters, the interviews of the lovers were very rare ; a system of intolerance so little in accordance with the open and ardent character of Ippolito, that, despising the very particular forms and ceremonies which it exacted, he was apt to grow impatient for the enjoyment of a more unconstrained society with the object he adored. With this view he made known his wishes to the young lady's mother, leaving the terms of their future union, in the most liberal manner, wholly to her, and beseeching her only to grant him a little more of the society of her he loved. What was his surprise to receive a direct refusal, on the ground that it was the lady's duty as a mother to attend first to the disposal of her two elder sisters ! an answer that threw the young lover into a paroxysm of mingled rage and despair.

The grief of Gangenova was little less than his own, and her affection, gathering strength by opposition, was indulged with double freedom upon receiving the sanction of such an offer. Aware at the same time that her lover's conduct in attempting to obtain an interview added only to the jealous caution of her mother, she was at a loss in what way to proceed, being so closely watched as scarcely to be allowed to breathe the air, much less to partake of the innocent sports and amusements to which young persons of her age are attached. It was impossible, however, to preserve so strict a watch as to deprive them of all kind of mutual intelligence, and Ippolito became acquainted with her unhappy situation. She even entreated of him, in pity to her, that he would discontinue his assiduous attentions, and either absent himself, or feign absence, during a short period, from the city, as she grew fearful of the extremities to which her friends in their anger might proceed. At the same time, she besought him to consider this as a proof of regard, not of coldness or indifference, as she would ever endeavour to show herself grateful, and worthy of the high opinion that he had so kindly and nobly avowed for her.

These tidings served at once to increase the passion that Ippolito already entertained, and the unhappiness he felt in being the unwilling cause of the least portion of suffering to her he loved, when he felt as if he could gladly have sacrificed his life to her happiness and repose. Still he exulted in the idea that she returned his affection, and he tried to flatter himself with the prospect of brighter days to come. And in order to convince her of the purity and disinterestedness of his attachment, he resolved, however difficult the task, to obey her wishes, and to leave for awhile his native place, giving out that he was gone upon a pilgrimage to the shrine of San Jacomo of Galicia. He was, moreover, desirous of thus proving the sincerity of the affection of her he loved, and of ascertaining whether her regard was likely to increase or diminish by distance; and with this view, having arranged his affairs and bade adieu to all his friends, as if on the eve of a long voyage, he assumed his pilgrim's dress, and, to the surprise and grief of all his acquaintance, left the city.

When the unhappy maiden heard of his departure, she shed many tears, regretting that she had ever proposed so harsh and trying an alternative, and upbraided herself as the sole cause of every sinister event that might chance to follow, never having imagined it possible that he would venture upon so painful and hazardous a journey. And in this she reasoned well, for when Ippolito had pursued his way until about sunset, he abandoned the great road, and, striking into one of the thickest woods near at hand, he there deposited his pilgrim's mantle, cowl, and staff; then retracing his steps in another dress, he entered, about the hour when the gates were closed, without observation into Siena. Proceeding direct to the abode of an old nurse, the only person whom he had admitted into his secret counsel, he there provided himself with everything requisite for his purpose.

Now, near the Church of San Lorenzo was a little country-seat, with a small orchard attached, belonging to Ippolito, both of which he had presented to his aged nurse, who, on her side, had always felt the same affection for him as for an only child. Next to this little tenement lay a spacious and beautiful garden, the property of the mother of the fair Gangenova, Ippolito's beloved mistress; and here with her daughters she was often accustomed to take the air and enjoy the fragrance of the new-blown flowers. "Surely," thought the gentle and enamoured boy, "here at least we shall hardly be suspected; nobody will believe me bold enough to seek her under her mother's very wing; let us only find an opportunity of conversing with each other, and I cannot fail to discover some means of bringing our difficulties to a happy termination."

And solely for this object did he keep himself concealed, like a bird that shuns the eye of day, within the bounds of his little cottage ground, never venturing forth except late in the evening, when, scaling a lofty wall, he descended into the garden of his beloved Gangenova, and approached close under her chamber window. Up the side of these there chanced to flourish a lofty and lovely mulberry tree, one of whose spacious branches overshadowed the apartment in which she lay, and where her mother kept her, as being the youngest of her charges, constant company by night. Under its shade likewise Ippolito was wont to take his evening station, eager to avail himself of any opportunity of beholding or discovering himself to the object of his attachment.

In this way he was soon convinced that the sole chance he had of profiting by his situation was about the hour of sunrise, when he observed the fair girl appear on the balcony overlooking the garden, on which were placed a number of beautiful plants, interspersed with lilies and violets, from which she would cull some of the sweetest to deck her lovely breast and hair. There, too, he observed her amuse herself with a pretty linnet which had nested itself in the noble tree, and which, won by her sweet encouragement, would hop in by the window and nestle in her bosom ; and it was then his delight to watch her thousand gentle looks and motions, and to imagine how delicious it would be to appropriate to himself the whole of those kisses and caresses. Often had he been on the point of accosting her, however great the risk, when her mother, her sisters, or some one in attendance, suddenly appearing, would dash all his hopes, and compel him to be doubly cautious, lest a discovery should be the cause of fresh restraints over his beloved.

He next resolved to avail himself of the assistance of his kind old nurse, who, under a variety of pretences, obtained admission into the mother's house, of which she took advantage to gain the ear of the young lady, and inform her of all that her lover had done for her sake ; of his passionate attachment and devotion, so well worthy a return, and his extreme desire of beholding her once more. Finding her equally delighted and surprised with what she had already heard, the nurse ventured to reveal to Gangenova the place of her Ippolito's concealment ; and the pleasure she experienced on finding that he was so near became almost too much for her to support.

" Has he not, indeed, deserted me then ? is he not really journeying far away, over seas, and in a foreign land, on my account ? Oh, dear nurse ! tell him that his image is engraven on my soul ; that I am too blest, too happy, and never more will give him reason to complain ! "

Upon hearing these words, the good old dame, thinking that she had happily succeeded in her mission, returned as fast as she could, in order not to forget the least portion of the message, which she well knew would carry such joy to the soul of the young lover.

Ippolito preserved the utmost caution in his proceedings, and it was not long before Fortune seemed to favour his wishes ; for keeping watch one evening very assiduously, he saw the arrival of a messenger bearing tidings that the wife of one of the old lady's brothers was taken suddenly ill, and entreated to see the mother of Gangenova without a moment's delay.

She was thus compelled to set out and leave her precious charge for one night, at least, to her own discretion ; and Ippolito believed that he had at length an opportunity of convincing himself of the reality of his beloved girl's affection for him, by inducing her to embrace the long-wished occasion, and to secure their happiness by flying together and uniting their fate in one. Fired with the hope, he hastened to his usual station underneath the mulberry tree that overspread her chamber window, and in order better to attract her attention, he shook some of its boughs, imagining that her beloved bird if nestling there would fly to her, and by its little cries and flutterings lead her to appear on the balcony. Not succeeding, however, in this, he hastily ascended the tree, when soon the affrighted bird, flying with timid cries into some neighbouring shrubs, uttered such loud and sorrowful tones as to startle the gentle girl out of her slumber, who, fearing some sad accident had befallen it, hastily ran to the window. With a simple veil thrown over her neck and bosom, and her fine bright tresses carelessly yet gracefully arranged, she appeared in the eyes of her enchanted lover rather like a vision than a creature of mortal beauty, while a mingled look of anxiety and tenderness was impressed upon her countenance. Solicitous for the fate of her little companion, she cast her eyes eagerly on all sides, when, instead of her pretty linnet, the accents of Ippolito, eager to dissipate her alarm, met her ears.

The next moment she beheld him nearly at her side, and he succeeded almost in reaching her chamber window, while he attempted to prevent her crying out by addressing her in the lowest and sweetest tone:

"Fear not, my gentle Gangenova ; it is your Ippolito who speaks ; fear not, either for yourself or your little favourite, for soon he will resume his blithesome notes, secure and happy as before. But mine, alas ! how different a fate, though far more fond, a thousand times more passionately devoted to you, serving you so long and faithfully ! Had you the heart, then, my sweetest, to think I was now taking my woeful pilgrimage far from thee, through remote and strange parts, perhaps gone upon my everlasting journey? Oh, no, no ! I knew you had not, and I have been near you day and night ever since the period when I left my friends to go upon my feigned pilgrimage. For, alas! when I cannot turn my thoughts from you for a moment, how could I wilfully bend my steps another way? How could I find a moment's repose till I had laid my wearied limbs and my burdened heart as near you as I could possibly venture without quite breaking upon your hallowed rest? Hath not our poor nurse told you all I have done and suffered for your sake; my lonely days and sorrowing yet delicious nights, passed amidst the scenes you have loved, among the very trees, and fruits, and flowers, where you have wandered; nay, in these lofty and verdant branches that so richly and beauteously overshadow the sanctuary of my love? Often have I seen you at the glimpse of dawn gathering flowers or caressing your bird, yet venturing not to intrude, afraid of calling down still further anger from your jealous guardians upon your innocent head. But my fond and unceasing vows have wearied Heaven at last: your mother is gone, and the hour arrived that is to repay us for a world of anxiety and dread, the fear of losing thee, and all that promised to make life sweet to me. Yet our time is precious, and I came to gather from thine own lips that thou dost indeed honour me with thy love; that thou wilt deign to receive my plighted vows and loyalty unto death. And this I would entreat in the name of all my anguish, all my fears for thee, by the horror of a rival's arms, and by thine own surpassing beauties, that amidst all our city's charms have alone succeeded in riveting my enchanted sight. Yet I know how all unworthy I am; how much better and longer thou deservest to be sought ere won. Still thou knowest my whole life and bearing, though thou canst not form an idea of the sighs and tears I have poured for thee. Pity me, then; and with pity let love and reason, let all the heavenly gifts you possess, plead in my favour, and induce you to receive me as your favoured and honoured lord."

Here he ceased, waiting with eager and trembling looks for a reply: while the beautiful Gangenova, overpowered on her side by a thousand wild and sweet emotions, was almost unable to articulate a word. Having descended into the balcony, on her sudden alarm, to recover her favourite bird, she had attempted on first hearing Ippolito's voice to fly; yet surprise and terror chained her to the spot; for having read the fabled metamorphoses of plants into mortals, and human beings into plants, on hearing a voice from the mulberry tree, her blood began to run cold, and her attempt to call out died away ere it passed her lips. Yet there was something in the tone that convinced her she need not fear, and gradually recovering her confidence, her heart seemed actually to swim in a tide of rapture before her noble lover had concluded his passionate appeal.

" Dear Ippolito," she at length replied, " it grieves me that we are so situated that it would be dangerous to tell all I have thought and felt since last we met and parted, much less the delight I have at finding you safe and near me once more. But, alas ! this is no place for you ; speed away, I beseech you, and think me neither hasty nor unkind, as indeed I esteem all your love and goodness to me as tenderly as I ought. But I fear for you, my kind Ippolito, and I entreat you to bid me one adieu, and let me see you safely depart."

At this moment, hearing a noise in the antechamber, and fearful lest her sisters should approach, Gangenova hastily drew back, while Ippolito, imagining that it proceeded from her room, and hearing a rustling noise continue for some time, was seized with sudden suspicions of some rival being harboured there, either by her sisters or the fair Gangenova herself. Maddened by this idea, he no longer remained master of himself, and in his attempt to reach her window from the tree so as to obtain a view of what was passing, such was the hurry of his spirits, that, missing his footing, he fell to the ground.

Startled at the terrific sound, the fair girl again rushed forward, bending as far as possible over the balcony, and calling on the name of Ippolito in a subdued and gentle tone ; but no longer did the sound reach his enraptured ear where he lay deprived of sense upon the cold earth. Suspense and terror seized upon the heart of the tender girl when she received no answer ; love urged her to afford him her immediate assistance, while fear of discovery restrained her steps. Unable, however, longer to control her fears for his safety, she hastily descended into the garden by a back staircase rarely made use of, having remained from ancient times as a retreat in seasons of trouble, and having its outlet at the extreme part of the garden. And there, alas ! she found him stretched under the mulberry tree, lying cold and pallid, apparently deprived not only of sense but of life itself.

Almost as insensible as he, she threw herself at his side. Upon recovering her consciousness, showers of tears expressed the intensity of her sufferings ; her cries would have moved rocks and beasts of prey to pity, such were the piteous tones in which these words were uttered :

" Sweet Heavens ! what dreadful thing hath happened ? What malignant star hath struck with death one of the best and noblest hearts that ever beat ? Oh, where is the soul that but now shone in thy face ? Wretch that I am, shall I never behold it more ? Art thou fled, for ever fled, sweet guardian of my honour, my love, and peace ? But what will betide them now when every tongue will be busy with my fame ? Whither shall I turn for help, reduced to such sad extremities as I now am ? "

And while abandoned to her woe, the hapless girl thus poured her lamentations to the night, she never ceased her endeavours to restore the object of them by every means in her power, rubbing his heart and temples, joining his hands and lips to her own, and trying to breathe her soul into his. Finding that he yet gave no signs of life, she sweetly folded him in her arms and bathed his inanimate features with her tears. Ippolito's soul, just on the point of taking wing, seemed to welcome so much bliss ; and suddenly recovering his suspended powers, he heard the sweet words she uttered, and found himself alive in her arms. It was then he felt himself amply repaid for all the trials he had undergone, the sweetness and ecstasy of the reward far surpassing all he had been able to conceive, in breathing his vows thus closely into her ear. The moment before, she was about to transfix her breast with her lover's sword in a paroxysm of despair ; the next she found herself pressed to his breathing bosom, receiving, as it were, the gift of two lives restored to her at once.

For some time they both remained doubtful whether to believe that all was real, and gazed upon each other as if in a dream, until the fresh spirit of their joy being somewhat abated, they sat down by each other, side by side, with that serene and ineffable pleasure which the imagined certainty of their bliss inspired. But it was destined, alas ! to be of short duration ; a voice was heard calling upon the name of Gangenova, gradually approaching nearer and nearer, so that they were compelled to part almost without bidding each other adieu. The poor girl hastened, trembling, by the same path that she had left the house : she fancied in the disorder of her spirits that she suddenly heard the terrific howlings of wild beasts, accompanied by the most dismal screams and cries ; and such was the impression they made upon her imagination, just after having taken leave of Ippolito, as to deprive her of the power of motion. It was long before she recovered even strength enough to regain her apartment, and with panting breast and dishevelled hair she threw herself upon the couch, still unable to banish the terrific ideas that haunted her imagination.

In the meanwhile, the sisters of Gangenova, being likewise freed from the superintendence of their mother, had been innocently enjoying themselves in their chamber, frequently calling the fair girl by her name to come and join in their diversion. Paying little heed to her silence, they continued for some time to amuse themselves with their games, until one of them, by way of adding a little novelty to the scene, crept forward in the dark intending to surprise her in her own room. Still receiving no reply, she ran for a light, and on returning found her sister stretched upon the bed, resembling rather a lifeless statue than a breathing human form. Calling her second sister in great alarm, they made eager inquiries into the cause of her agitation, feeling assured that something extraordinary must have happened.

The poor girl was equally unwilling and unable to reply, and her sisters, in some anxiety, despatched a messenger for their mother, who lost no time in returning to resume her maternal charge. With a little more authority, she insisted upon knowing the cause of her alarm, and upbraided her sisters severely for not keeping a more vigilant watch. Gangenova declared herself quite unable to account for the manner in which she had been affected, and the others professed equal ignorance as to the cause of her indisposition. In this dilemma her mother had recourse to the advice of the most expert physicians the city had to boast, which brought no alleviation, however, to her daughter's alarming symptoms, not one of them being able to discover that her illness was owing to some sudden surprise, while she, far more jealous of her fair fame than of her life, concealed from every one the real cause of her sufferings. Growing rapidly worse, she became extremely anxious to behold once more her beloved Ippolito, and recollecting the old nurse, she instantly sent for her, entreating that she would as soon as possible acquaint him with her situation, and find some means by which they might at least meet to take an eternal farewell.

Upon receiving these sad tidings, Ippolito grew deadly pale and trembled, though at the same moment he hastened to comply with her wishes. He assumed the dress of a poor traveller, with a false beard, so as to render it almost impossibie to recognise him, and set out to beg alms at several houses adjacent to that of his beloved. As he approached the latter, the lady of the mansion herself made her appearance, half wild and distracted at the situation of her loveliest daughter. Informed of the occasion of her grief, the wily pilgrim, availing himself of the circumstance, bade her not despair, as the power of the Lord was infinite and His goodness equal to His power. Moreover, with His aid, he had himself become skilled in all the virtues of almost all the plants under the sun, and had devoted his knowledge of herbs and juices to the relief of his unhappy fellow-creatures, besides possessing secrets adapted to every species of disease.

The poor credulous old lady raised her hands to heaven in gratitude upon hearing such consolatory words, vowed that he had been peculiarly sent by Providence, and insisted that he should be instantly introduced to her unhappy girl. The moment Ippolito beheld her, he perceived that the tidings he had received were indeed too true. So much was he shocked, that he could with difficulty support his character; more particularly when he saw, from the brightening features of his beloved, that she instantly recognised him. Taking, then, the hand of the suffering girl within his own, as if to feel how fast her life-blood ebbed, he begged her attendants to stand apart while he proceeded to try his secret prayers and charms in his own way. Ippolito was thus enabled to learn the real source of her illness from her own lips. Beholding him with a mixture of tenderness and pity that added momentary lustre to her dying charms, she attempted, in those low soft tones he so much loved, to infuse balm into his wounded spirit. Painfully sensible of the extent of his loss, Ippolito from very grief was unable to utter a word, much less to ask the needful questions of his beloved. Wildly pressing his hand, she besought him never to forget the tender love he had borne her, and which she had seldom been happy enough to tell him how warmly and deeply she returned.

"For joyful, oh! very joyful, my Ippolito," she continued, "would my departure have been to me before now, had not solicitude for your fate detained me. As it is, I die content, nay, grateful, for two unexpected benefits: the one to have seen you thus, to hear you, and feel your hand in mine; and the other, to know that I lived and that I died beloved by my most noble and faithful-hearted Ippolito!"

It was now that the latter attempted to console and encourage her, declaring it would be his only pride to fulfil her wishes in the minutest point; but here his voice failing him through his fast-coming tears and sobs, he laid his aching head down by the side of his beloved's, and there remaining for a short time as he breathed forth a soul-distracting adieu, he raised it again painfully, passed his hand over his eyes, and looking his last look, left the apartment.

He then joined her weeping mother, and so far from holding out any hope, he said that pity for the sad and dying state in which he had found the poor patient had drawn scalding tears from his eyes. And he had not long been gone before the gentle spirit of his love, as if unable to continue longer without him, prepared to take wing, and in a few hours actually fled, as if to prepare in some happier scene a mansion of rest for their divided loves. For the wretched Ippolito, though able to bear up long enough to behold her beloved relics consigned to earth, had no sooner witnessed all the virtues and charms he had so fondly esteemed and loved for ever entombed in the vault of the Salimbeni, than, just as the ceremony was about to close, he fell dead at the foot of her marble monument. So strange and sudden an event threw the surrounding company, by whom it was regarded as little less than a miracle, into the utmost surprise and confusion, all of them believing that Ippolito Saracini was then on his way to the shrine of San Jacomo of Galicia. His unhappy parents, hearing of this his untimely end, hastened to join their tears with those of the mother of the beauteous Gangenova, by whose side the faithful Ippolito was laid.

GIOVAN-FRANCESCO STRAPAROLA
16th Century

ANDRIGETTO THE IMPENITENT

IN Como, a little city of Lombardy not very far from Milan, there once dwelt a citizen of the name of Andrigetto da Sabbia, whose immense possessions, surpassing those of any other person, did not, however, prevent him from adding to them by every means in his power.

Being perfectly secure against the attacks of conscience in all his dealings, he was never known to suffer remorse for the most unjustifiable actions. He was in the habit of disposing of the produce of his large estates to the poorer citizens and peasantry, instead of selling it to merchants and others who could command ready money; not from any charitable motives, but in order to obtain possession of their little remaining property, still uniting field after field to the great possessions he had already acquired.

It happened that so great a scarcity began to prevail in the city and its vicinity, that many persons actually perished of want, while numbers had recourse to our old usurer for assistance, to whom, from the urgent pressure of circumstances, they were compelled to make over, in return for the necessaries of life, such interest as they might possess either in houses or lands. The concourse of people in his neighbourhood was so great as almost to resemble a jubilee or a public fair.

Now there was a certain notary, Tonisto Raspante by name, a most notorious and wily practitioner of his art, and more successful than any other of his brethren in emptying the pockets of the poor villagers. He had still, however, so much regard for an ancient law in Como relating to usurious contracts, which required the money lent to be counted in the presence of proper witnesses, as to refuse to draw up such instruments as Andrigetto often directed him to prepare, observing that they were altogether against the form of the statute, and he would not venture to risk the penalty. But such were the overbearing manners of the old miser, and so great was his authority in the city, that sometimes threatening him with ruin, and at other times bribing him to his purpose, he compelled the attorney to obey his commands.

The time for confessing himself being at hand, before presenting himself at the confessional, Andrigetto took care to send to the priest an excellent dinner, with as much of the finest cloth as would make a pair of hose for himself and his servant, announcing at the same time his intention to confess on the ensuing day, when he thought that he was sure of meeting with a favourable hearing.

The priest undertook with pleasure the task of absolving from his sins so eminent and rich a citizen, and received his penitent with the utmost cordiality. Andrigetto fell on his knees before his spiritual father, accusing himself with very little ceremony of various sins and errors, not forgetting his usurious and illegal contracts, all which he recounted in the most minute manner. The priest, who had sense enough to perceive the enormous nature of his offences, conceiving himself bound to make some representations on the subject, ventured certain gentle hints on the impropriety of their repetition, and in the meanwhile strongly recommending restitution to the injured parties.

Instead of taking this in good part, Andrigetto turned very sharply round upon his confessor, observing that he was at a loss to understand what he meant, and that he had better go, and return no more until he had learned how to confess persons in a more rational manner. The priest, owing his preferment in a great measure to Andrigetto, and fearful lest he might lose his favour altogether, began to retract as well as he could, gave him absolution, and then imposing as slight a penance as possible, received a florin for his reward, after which Andrigetto took his leave in very excellent spirits.

Not long after this interview, our old usurer, while rejoicing in this absolution from all his sins, fell ill of a mortal distemper, and the physicians shortly despaired of his life. His friends and relatives having gathered round his bed, took the liberty of suggesting that it was now time to think of a sincere confession, to receive his last spiritual consolation, and make a final arrangement of his affairs, like a good Catholic and a Christian.

But the old gentleman, who had hitherto devoted all his thoughts and exertions, both day and night, to the hoarding of his wealth, instead of being at all impressed by the awfulness of his situation, only replied with great levity to their arguments, still amusing himself with arranging the most trifling concerns, and evincing not the least uneasiness at his approaching end. After long entreaties and persuasions, he was at last prevailed upon to comply with their request, and agreed to summon to his assistance his old agent, Tonisto Raspante the notary, and Father Neofito, his confessor.

On the arrival of these personages, they addressed the patient with a cheerful countenance, telling him to keep up his spirits, for that with God's help he would soon be a sound man again. Andrigetto only replied that he feared he was too far gone for that, and that he had perhaps better lose no time in first settling his worldly affairs and then arranging his ghostly concerns with his confessor. But the good priest, exhorting and comforting him to the best of his ability, advised him first of all to place his sole trust in the Lord, humbly submitting himself to His will, as the safest means of obtaining a restoration to health. To this, however, Andrigetto replied only by ordering seven respectable men to be called in as witnesses of his last will and testament.

These persons having been successively presented to the patient, and taken their seats, he proceeded to inquire from his friend Tonisto the very lowest charge which he was in the habit of making for penning a will.

"According to the strict rules of the profession," replied Tonisto, "it is only a florin; but in general the amount is decided by the feelings of the testator."

"Well, well, then," cried the patient, "take two florins, and set down what I tell you."

The notary having invoked the divine name, drew out the preliminaries in the usual manner, bequeathing the body of the testator to the earth and his soul to the hands of God who gave it, with humble thanks for the many favours vouchsafed by Him to His unworthy creature.

This exordium being read to Andrigetto, he flew into a violent rage, and commanded the notary to write down nothing but his own words, which he dictated as follows:

"I, Andrigetto da Sabbia, being of sound mind, though infirm of body, do hereby declare this to be my last will and testament: I give and bequeath my soul into the hands of the great Satan, the prince of devils."

Hearing these words, the witnesses stood aghast; Raspante's quill started from the paper, and, in evident horror and perturbation, he stopped. Looking the testator very earnestly in the face, he interposed :

" Ah ! Messer Andrigetto, these are the words of a madman ! "

" How ! " exclaimed Andrigetto, in a violent passion, " what do you mean ? How dare you stop ? Write word for word as I direct you, and nothing more, or you shall never be paid for a will of mine : proceed, I tell you ! "

Struck with the greatest horror and surprise, his friends attempted to remonstrate with him, lamenting that he should make use of language so opposite to his usual good sense, language which only madmen or blasphemers could be capable of using on such a subject and in so awful a situation as his.

" Desist, then," they continued, " for Heaven's sake, and consult your honour and the safety of your poor soul. Think of the scandal such a proceeding would bring upon your family, if you, who were esteemed so prudent and so wise, were to make yourself an example of all that is perfidious, ungrateful, and impious towards Heaven."

But Andrigetto paid no further attention to their reproaches than by observing that his business was with his attorney, and that as he had not yet finished his will, they had better take care what they were about ; on which there was soon a respectful silence throughout the room. He then turned towards his attorney, requesting to know, in a voice of suppressed passion, whether he was prepared to go on, as he had already offered to pay double the usual charge for his labours. Apprehensive that Andrigetto might expire before he had made a disposition of his property, the notary promised to do as he was required, more especially when he heard the patient beginning to hiccup with the violence of his emotions ; so that he was compelled to make a solemn vow to fulfil his client's instructions.

" Item," continued Andrigetto, " I hereby bequeath the wretched soul of my wicked agent, Tonisto Raspante, to the great Satan, in order that it may keep company with mine when it leaves this world, as it shortly must."

" The Lord have mercy on me ! " cried the poor attorney, shocked at the deep solemnity with which these last words were uttered ; " the Lord have mercy on my soul ! " and the pen dropped from his hand. " Recall," he continued, " my honoured patron, recall those wicked words ; do anything but destroy my eternal interests, my last, my dearest hopes."

" Go on, you rogue ! " cried the testator, " and do not venture to interrupt me again ; do not tell me about your soul. You have your pay, and that is enough ; so proceed quickly as I shall direct you. I leave my said attorney's soul to the devil, for this reason, that if he had not consented to draw up so many false and usurious contracts, but had driven me from his presence as soon as I proposed them, I should not now find myself reduced to the sad extremity of leaving both our souls to the king of hell, owing entirely to his shameful cupidity and want of common honesty."

The attorney, though trembling at the name of the king of hell, yet fearful lest his patron might enter into further particulars far from creditable to him, wrote as he was commanded.

" Item," continued the patient, " I bequeath the soul of Father Neofito, my confessor, into the claws of Lucifer ; aye, to thirty thousand pair of devils."

" Stop, Messer Andrigetto, pray stop," cried the priest ; " and do not think of applying those dreadful words to me. You ought to put your trust in the Lord, in the Lord Jesus, whose mercies always abound, who came to save sinners, and is still inviting them, night and day, to repentance. He died for our sins, and for your sins, Messer Andrigetto ; you have only to beseech pardon, and all will yet be well. The road is still open to restitution ; hasten to make restitution then ; for the Lord does not wish the death of a sinner. You have great wealth ; remember the Church ; you will have masses said for your soul, and may yet sit in the seats of paradise."

" Oh, thou wicked and most wretched priest ! " retorted the patient, " by thy vile avarice and simony thou hast helped thine own soul, as well as mine, into the pit of perdition. And dost thou now think of advising me to repent ? Confusion on thy villainy ! Write, notary, that I bequeath his soul to the very centre of the place of torments ; for had it not been for his bold and shameless conduct in absolving me from my numerous and repeated offences, I should not now find myself in the strange predicament in which I am placed. What ! does the rogue think it would be now just to restore my evilgotten gains, and thus leave my poor family destitute ? No, no ; I am not quite such a fool as to do that ; so please to go on. Item, To my dear lady Felicia I leave my pretty farm, situated in the district of Comacchio, in order to supply herself with the elegancies of life, and occasionally treat her lovers as she has been hitherto in the habit of doing, thus preparing the way further to oblige me with her company in the other world, sharing with us the torments of eternity. The remainder of my property, as well personal as real, with all future interest and proceeds accruing thereon, I leave to my two legitimate and beloved sons, Commodo and Torquato, on condition that they give nothing for a single mass to be said for the soul of the deceased, but that they feast, swear, game, and fight, to the best of their ability, in order that they may the sooner waste their substance so wickedly acquired, until, driven to despair, they may as speedily as possible hang themselves. And this I declare to be my last will and testament. as witness all present, not forgetting my attorney."

Having signed this instrument and put his seal to it, Andrigetto turned away his face, and uttering a terrific howl, finally surrendered his impenitent soul to Pluto.

ORTENSIO LANDO
16TH CENTURY

THE ASTROLOGER AND THE ASS

THERE was once a gentleman of Verona, named Messer Ugo da Santa Sofia, who devoted himself with such assiduity to the study of the arts and sciences, and especially to the contemplation of the heavenly bodies, that he had become famous throughout the whole country.

Whether planets, or fixed or wandering stars, fiery comets, satellites, or lunar orbs, he boasted the most intimate acquaintance with all their motions, and foretold their revolutions in heaven without the risk which he incurred when he ventured to prophesy respecting those which should happen on earth. He foretold the death of King Robert and the succession of a female to the throne. The confines of Hungary, he predicted, were to extend even as far as Greece, and would afterwards reach the plain of Troy; and he smelt the approach of that horrid pestilence which committed such dreadful devastations in the memorable year 1348. But suffice it to observe that the accuracy of his predictions was such, that his reputation spread through Europe, and none of its Princes ever found themselves in difficulty without sending for Messer Ugo to enjoy the advantage of his sage admonitions. We must not be surprised, therefore, to hear that he became a little vain of these his unearthly powers, which, in his own opinion, were altogether infallible.

Now it so fell out that one day during harvest-time he went to his country-house, for he took great pleasure in seeing the corn threshed in the barn, when one of his neighbours, an ancient villager, very well off in the world, called upon him to communicate what he considered to be rather important information at that season of the year. Being somewhat lame in one of his legs, he was in the habit of riding a beautiful ass, from which he now alighted at the door of Messer Ugo.

" I have called upon you, as I was riding by, just to tell you, Messer Ugo, that I think it would be prudent in you to take care of your corn, which has been cut so long, during this threatening weather; for within an hour hence we shall have such a tremendous storm, that you will imagine the very heavens are about to tumble upon our heads."

Our philosopher, with great coolness, inquired how his neighbour alone came to be in possession of this secret, and after gazing round the horizon on all sides, unable to detect the least black spot, which frequently portends the distant storm, he turned a look of quiet contempt upon the good countryman, observing :

" The sky is quite clear, the sun mild, and not even a cloud upon the mountains, and yet you are bold enough to prognosticate a storm. Why, there is a soft south wind blowing, and the sun is in the right sign and the right degree ; nothing less than a miracle can make it rain. Nature herself could not make it rain now. With the help of Providence, to be sure, she might ; but, as she stands disposed at present, it is impossible we can have any rain."

He continued to debate the point with the countryman for a long while without making the least impression upon him ; the only answer he received was, that Messer Ugo would be much better employed in giving orders to have his grain quickly housed than in wasting arguments upon him, as the approaching tempest would not merely destroy the corn, but beat down trees, scatter herds and flocks, and shake the houses to their foundations.

Messer Ugo's choler now rose to such a height at the countryman's strange pertinacity, that he was much inclined to bestow upon him a box on the ear ; but instead of this, he so far controlled his indignation as first to consult his telescope and compasses, with which he once more examined the heavens more narrowly than before, yet still drawing the same conclusion, that rain for that day, at least, was quite out of the question, expecting as soon to see the mountains levelled with the plains or the rivers flowing over the hills.

Finding that he could be of no use, the villager at length took his leave, and he had scarcely dismounted at home before a dark speck became visible in the horizon, and swelling with the rising wind, in a short time obscured the face of the sun itself. Strong lightnings soon afterwards began to play towards the north, while the wind changing gradually into the east, floods of rain, resembling water-spouts rather than a common shower, emptied themselves into the bosom of the west, already torn by the rising conflict of the elements. As the torrents of rain increased, the reverberating thunders and the livid lights, instead of dying away, seemed to gather double strength in an almost unheard-of manner, such as we may suppose pealed over the heads of the fierce Titans when, rising in rash revolt, they experienced the indignation of their father Jove. Towers and steeples tottered to their base, the loftiest oaks lay prostrate, the river Adige rose and burst its old embankments, while the proudest palaces with their royal inmates trembled, as if anticipating the dissolution of the groaning fabric of the world.

But where was poor Messer Ugo with his famous astrological observations during this time, and where was all his unhoarded grain ? It was an equally severe blow upon his property and his pride ; he almost wished he had never become versed in a knowledge of the stars, since he found himself thus shamefully imposed upon by the weather. His fine corn was flying all abroad, a prey to the fierce elements, and he sorely repented him of having turned a deaf ear to his neighbour, whose precaution would have so well availed him. Away he flung his square and compasses, his astrolabe, and his whole apparatus, in the rage of the moment, while he watched the wild progress of the storm, every moment appearing an age until it should have so far subsided as to permit him to creep with safety to his honest neighbour, to entreat his pardon and to inquire by what art he had foretold this dreadful tempest in the midst of a perfect calm.

At length, with some difficulty, during a pause of the awful blast, he contrived to reach his door ; and after apologising to him in a meek and faltering tone, he besought him to explain in what way he could possibly have foreseen such a calamity.

" There is certainly," he continued, " some superior master in the same art as my own, whom you must have applied to on this occasion."

" That is very true, Messer Ugo," replied the villager ; " I have consulted him, and he is no other than the pretty animal upon which you saw me mounted. My own ass unfolded the secret to me, as he has done many others of the same nature before. He can tell fair weather too, as well as foul ; and I never in my life was in need of any other weather-glass : he takes a more exact survey of the heavens than the best glass or compass could possibly do. I always remark that when the weather is going to be extremely rough, he sets up his back, his hairs stand on end, and he hides his tail between his legs, shaking as if he were in an ague. But if we are merely going to have a moderate breeze, it is quite another thing, for then he only holds his tail between his legs for a few moments, lashing his sides ; and if no thunder and lightning follow, he will scarcely do so much. But when we are to be visited with such a fierce tempest as we have had to-day, then you should mind what he says ; he never in all his life gave me such an awful warning before. For he first directed all his ears and eyes as it were up into the sky ; he stopped and listened ; and then he leaped up, and beat the earth with his four feet as if all the horse-flies in the world had been devouring him.

" So I thought I would just step and tell you our opinion upon the subject, for my noble beast and I are always perfectly of one accord on this point. Nor should you, with all your vast stores of learning, Messer Ugo, be surprised at this ; for how is it that the cock informs us so exactly of the hour, as if he had got a little piece of watch-work in his head ? How is it in the least more strange than what we hear of the dolphins gambolling before the luckless vessels, with their curved backs upon the surface, warning the poor sailors of the tempest at hand ? Why should not my ass be supposed to know something likewise upon the subject ? "

Messer Ugo da Santa Sofia had not a word to utter in reply ; he had now fairly the worst of the argument, and at length candidly confessed his admiration of the superior tact and foresight of the ass, grieving, however, at the same time, that the long-eared steed of Carabotto (the name of the good villager) should be, after all, a greater astrologer than himself, who had actually grown grey in the service of the stars, the tides, and the causes of everything which happens here below. He entreated his good neighbour to keep the matter secret, at least for a while, lest his reputation should suffer in the opinion of the world.

The countryman very kindly promised that he would do so, but whether he really did or not is uncertain, as the affair quickly took wind, though most probably from some witnesses who must have been present at the controversy previous to the storm. Certain it is that the whole country was speedily in possession of the secret, and of much amusement in consequence, it being everywhere said that the ass of Carabotto had turned out at last a greater astrologer than the great Messer Ugo da Santa Sofia di Verona himself.

The saying became at length quite proverbial, and nothing was more common than to hear a man answer a very pertinacious enemy by observing : " Yes, I daresay you think you know more astrology than Carabotto's ass " ; which generally brought another reply much as follows : " Go, go ! for you know less than poor Messer Ugo da Santa Sofia himself."

When our unhappy astronomer learned that the matter was publicly divulged throughout all Lombardy, he went into such a violent fit of passion, that he actually seized and committed to the flames more than two thousand crowns' worth of astrological books and instruments ; quadrants, spheres, and nativities all fell a prey to the fiery element ; and he used even to walk with his eyes fixed upon the ground to avoid contemplating the heavens, which, after all his long labours, had so egregiously deceived him.

EVIL FOR EVIL

Ortensio Lando

RICCARDO CAPPONI, a noble Florentine, having devoted himself in early life to trade, in the course of time realised a very handsome property. When advanced in years, he took his son, Vincenti, into partnership, and not long after gave his whole business into his hands; and falling into a bad state of health, owing either to his great exertions or to his subsequent high living, he became unable to leave the house.

His son, Vincenti, who was of an extremely avaricious disposition, finding his father continued to linger much beyond the period his covetous and ungrateful heart would have assigned him, and unwilling longer to support him, took measures, under pretence of obtaining for him better medical advice than he could at home provide, to have him conveyed to the city hospital. Yet his affairs were then in a flourishing state, and everything he possessed he owed to his unhappy parent, whose age and infirmities, whose tears and entreaties, he alike disregarded. This unnatural son could not, however, contrive to conduct the matter so secretly as to elude the observation and the reproaches of all classes of people in the city. He at first tried to impose, both upon his friends and the public, by the false representations that he set on foot; but finding these could not avail him, he resolved, in order better to disarm the popular voice against him, to send his own children with little presents to their grandfather.

On one occasion he gave to his eldest boy, about six years of age, two fine cambric shirts, desiring him, early the next morning, to take them carefully to his poor grandfather in the hospital. The little boy, with an expression of great respect and tenderness in his countenance, promised that he would do so; and on his return the next day, his father, calling him into his presence, inquired whether he had delivered them safe into the hands of his grandfather.

"I only gave him one, father," replied the little boy.

"What!" exclaimed Vincenti with an angry voice; "did I not tell you both were for your grandfather?"

" Yes," returned the little fellow with a steady and undaunted look, " but I thought that I would keep one of them for you, father, against the time when I shall have to send you, I hope, to the hospital."

" How ! " exclaimed Vincenti, " would you ever have the cruelty to send me there, my boy ? "

" Why not ? " retorted the lad ; " let him that does evil expect evil in return. For you know, you made your own father go there, old and ailing as he is, and he never did you any harm in his life, and do you think I shall not send you when I am able ? Indeed, father, I am resolved that I will ; for, as I have said before, let him that does evil expect evil in return."

On hearing these words, Vincenti, giving signs of the utmost emotion, as if suddenly smitten by the hand of Heaven, sorely repented of the heinous offence against humanity and justice that he had committed. He hastened himself to the hospital ; he entreated his father's pardon on his knees, and had him conveyed instantly home, ever afterwards showing himself a gentle and obedient son, and frequently administering to his aged parent's wants with his own hands.

This incident gave rise through all Tuscany to the well-known proverb above mentioned, " Let him that does evil expect evil in return " ; and from Tuscany it passed into many other parts of Italy.

COUNT CARLO GOZZI
1722–1806

THE GRAPE STEALERS

AS more lucky adepts than any lady in the art of thieving, I shall proceed to give an account of three very accomplished geniuses in their way, namely, Carlo Foschino, Girolamo Petrani, and Menico Cedola, belonging to the city of ——. And perhaps, as the scene of action did not lie in a church, and the spoils were but of inconsiderable value, Heaven permitted the rogues to make their escape, otherwise they would have been placed in an awkward predicament, and might have found the grapes they plucked uncommonly sour, and such as would effectually have disgusted them with the fingering art in future.

It happened to be a year of great scarcity, and more especially in the province of O——, insomuch that the villagers died of hunger, while the grain and vines of every kind looked as if they had been ridden over by troops of horse, affording such a prospect as nearly drove the farmers and their landlords distracted. A fine time indeed for those who had nothing to do but eat the fruits of others! So that the owners were compelled to keep watch day and night, though the harvest was hardly worth the pains.

More for whim than want, Carlo Foschino agreed with his companions to make an attack on one of the vineyards, celebrated for the sweetness of its grapes, at Santo Martino di ——, which is situated at a short distance from the city, intending not only to eat as much as they liked, but to fill a good basket or two for future use. With this view each of them took his pannier under his arm, and sallying forth about midnight, they arrived at the land of promise, into which they cautiously entered. When once fairly in possession, they proceeded to clear the ground before them in great style, whispering one another at intervals.

"How good they are!"

"Yes, so sweet! what a flavour! quite exquisite! It is a real paradise for us hapless mortals"; and thus feasting and applauding, they did great execution, sweeping everything before them in order to get at fresh bunches, until they were fairly weary and in danger of suffocation.

Then, drawing their well-sharpened knives, they began afresh the work of destruction, filling their panniers with all the expedition in their power. They were proceeding merrily through a fine plantation, having finished the better half of their task, but could not avoid making a rustling noise with the branches and scattering a few leaves; and the night being so still that a nest of ants at work would have been heard, this was enough to rouse the jealousy of three armed myrmidons on watch, who, like men of war, were scouring those coasts, to give all freebooters a warm reception with their great rusty blunderbusses and enormous slugs, in any shape but round.

Hearing a noise of the crashing of branches, one of the watchmen discharged his piece in that direction, while a sudden rush was made, and a cry set up enough to shake the soul of a hero.

"Thieves! thieves! that way! leap the ditch! shoot, kill them! oh, that is good, by San Bellino!"

Yet Heaven willed that the shot should miss its aim; and the wily robbers, not forgetting their panniers, started off at the sounds of vengeance they heard, using their utmost efforts to escape along a narrow path. The night was dark, and they often stumbled over the stalks of the vine or of the Indian corn growing in the field, though without paying attention to the circumstance, the entangling and tearing and trampling of leaves giving them little chance of escape from their fierce pursuers, whose threatening cries sounded nearer and nearer, till they imagined they felt themselves run through the body.

In this extremity Petrani whispered in a soft voice as he continued running:

"My friends, let us throw our panniers away and have a chance for our lives!"

To this Cedola replied, hardly able to draw his breath.

"You say well; let them go."

"No, no," cried Foschino; "take heart, brothers, and leave the matter to me!"

So forthwith he began to bellow as loud as he could:

"Mercy upon me! that last shot has pierced me through; I am dying, though I did not feel it before; my blood is spouting out like new wine from the barrel!——Confirm what I say, you blockheads, and make your escape."

Then Cedola began to cry, " Mercy, mercy upon us ! try to get a little farther ; the wound is perhaps not mortal, and we will fetch you a surgeon."

" No," replied the wily Foschino, in a dying voice, the better to keep up the cheat, " it is all over with me. Those cruel rascals have murdered a poor Christian for eating a bunch of grapes ; yet, by the Holy Virgin, they will have to swing for it, that is some consolation ! "

And thus saying, they proceeded with flying colours, their panniers heaped up with grapes. For the stupid watchmen, imagining all they heard to be true, began to consider the matter and take more time.

" Do you hear what he says ? " cried one.

" That I do," cried the second.

" And you, do you hear ? " they added to the third, one of the oldest cut-throats in all Italy.

" Let them take it, by all the saints, it is very well ; they will obey the seventh commandment in future. I will go nearer, for I daresay they must have left loads of grapes behind them, the wretches ! " and they proceeded more cautiously in pursuit.

Foschino hearing footsteps stealing along, afraid of discovery, and at the same time of losing the grapes and receiving a good bastinado from the watchmen, resolved, as he felt himself quite wearied out, to go no further.

" Leave me here to die, dear friends. I am only grieved that there is no priest at hand to confess me, but Heaven's will be done ! Fly, save yourselves ! Remember me to my poor wife and children, and perform my last wish ! "

During this time the foolish watchmen were listening, as he continued to add, " Be witness that I leave my wife all I have, in trust for the benefit of our children after her, in equal portions ; be kind to her and to them, and assist them to bring my body away to-morrow, that I may receive Christian burial, and persuade my friends to offer up a few alms and masses for my poor soul. I feel that I am going now, and do you go too ! "

The rustics hearing these sad words, stopped, and now began to hold a colloquy upon this unlucky case ; while Cedola and Petrani set up the most horrid lamentations, wringing their hands and sobbing as if their hearts would break.

" Nay, do not give way to despair. A plague upon the watchmen ! they will hang for it ; and upon the grapes ! we may indeed call them sour. Well, we have the comfort to think that the watchmen will be hanged if you die; they were only to take us into custody, not to take our lives. There never was such a piece of barbarity, such a wilful murder, since the world began. See how he bleeds, poor fellow! he will not live long. Come, let them even kill us all, since they have killed our best friend, a gentleman who only joined us for a frolic. Let the wretches dip their hands in the blood of us all; but we are men of quality, and they shall smart for it."

Upon hearing these words and cries so boldly uttered, the guards concluded it to be a serious affair, and being really afraid that they had killed the gentleman, began to think of running in their turn. But when they next heard him say, in a feeble and lamentable voice, "*In manus tuas, Domine, commendo spiritum meum,*" they could no longer control their fright, but took to their heels, just as they heard the others utter, "He is dead, he is gone for ever; cold, cold, my friend!" and a fresh ululation was set up, which added wings to the flight of the men.

This done, they departed at their leisure, the dead man leading the way with the panniers. When the watch ventured to stop, one of them said, "Who shot him, think you? It was not I, I am sure."

"Nor I."

"Nor I."

"Well, but," said another, "you agreed that I should fire."

"True, but you should have shot over his head and not through his body."

"Well," replied the man, "I thought I did shoot high up into the air. I wonder how it could have killed him"; and thus, each speaking in his own defence, full of fear and trembling, they returned home, but were unable to sleep a wink that night; while the three knaves, having recovered from their terror, were enjoying themselves comfortably over their panniers of grapes.

In the morning the thieves gave an account of their adventure, which threw their auditors into such fits of laughter that some have not ceased even to this day. As for the poor rustics, although they never found the corpse, or had any charge brought against them, they yet continued uneasy and suspicious, having the fear of the gallows perpetually before their eyes, and not having courage to make any inquiries into the affair, lest they should betray themselves, and raise suspicions that they had been guilty of so wicked a homicide.

GIOVANNI BOTTARI
17TH CENTURY

THE MONK AND THE WOMAN

IN the time of St. Jerome, one of the most learned doctors of Holy Church, there dwelt in Maronia, a village not far from the city of Antioch, a poor man, who supported himself upon the produce of a little farm which he cultivated with his own hands. He had an only son, of the name of Malco, whom he supported, as well as his wife, in pretty easy circumstances; this child being the sole pledge of their affection, and, from his pleasing and excellent disposition, the delight of both his parents. Having attained to years of maturity, their favourite object was now to behold him married; and with this view his father one day thus affectionately addressed him:

" As you know, my dear son, that you have neither brother nor sister, and are now arrived at manhood, while your parents are fast verging to old age, it would much gratify us both could we see you united according to your wishes in wedlock. As the consolation of our declining years, we shall thus be delighted to witness your happiness, bringing up your children, the sweetest solace of this our mortal state, in the fear of the Lord; whereas, should you defer such an engagement to a later period, you will encounter infinitely more risks and trouble, as may be learned from numerous examples which it were needless to specify."

After listening attentively to the kind advice offered by his father, Malco, with the greatest respect and reverence, begged to decline his proposal, alleging as a reason that he wished to devote himself wholly to a religious life—a resolution which gave equal surprise and concern to both his parents. They therefore gently reproached him for indulging wishes that involved the failure of their name, dying without any legitimate successors, of whom all men are more or less desirous; and urged besides a variety of other reasons, which were applied with as little success. All they could gather from him was, that upon mature deliberation he had resolved to provide only for the good of his soul, to the exclusion of all earthly considerations. In spite of all their tears and entreaties they could obtain only the same answer, and their threats proved as unavailing as their prayers.

Both parties persisting in their respective resolutions, to their mutual annoyance, Malco, in order to avoid its perpetual recurrence, as well as to execute the object he had in view, resolved to abandon his native place, which he took an early opportunity of doing. But not venturing to depart into the East from a dread of encountering the contending armies of the Romans and Persians, then engaged in cruel and sanguinary warfare, he took a secret route towards the desert of Calcis, and, after a few days of patient toil, he found himself amidst its vast solitude, relieved only by a solitary monastery which he discovered in the distance, where, the holy brotherhood receiving him on his arrival, he resolved to submit himself to their most rigid rules and discipline.

Joyfully assuming the monk's habit, he soon began to set an example to the whole fraternity, by the severity of his mortifications, his continual fasts and watches, which had shortly the effect of consuming all the vigour and freshness of his youth, along with his natural appetites, which he completely subdued by confining himself to the very scanty fare earned by his own hands.

Having continued this mode of life for some years, he accidentally heard of his father's decease, and feeling for the situation of his widowed mother, as well as being desirous of securing his little heritage, which he wished to convert into money as alms for the poorer brethren and other charitable purposes, he shortly came to the resolution of returning home. Going accordingly to the abbot, he entreated his permission to depart, at the same time bidding him a holy farewell. The good father, grown grey in experience and wisdom, was sore displeased to hear of his poor monk's intention, and pronounced it to be nothing better than a temptation of the devil, presented in this specious shape of charity the more surely to beguile his soul ; affirming that his only chance was to resist the ancient adversary in the outset, in default of which so many wise and holy men, even the fathers themselves, had oftentimes been deceived ; and that the more pious and excellent the object he had in view appeared to be, the more wily and diabolical was the plan laid for his spiritual destruction. This the holy father laboured to make manifest by many notable instances and examples ; but all in vain to deter the good monk, who was obstinately bent upon returning home.

For, though the eloquence of his superior appeared like the inspiration of the Holy Spirit, it had not the effect of shaking his resolution a jot, not even when his kind benefactor had recourse to prayers and entreaties, and charged him with the greatest ingratitude in thus turning his back upon the monastery and the poor brethren, who had so hospitably received and sheltered him. He would, moreover, bring into peril both soul and body, and provoke his eternal perdition, by wilfully traversing a country lying between Baria and Edessa, beset with heathen robbers and spoilers, who delighted to shed the blood of the innocent worshippers of the true faith.

"Besides," added the good father, appealing to the highest authority, "no man putting his hand to the plough, and looking back, is fit for the kingdom of heaven; and if he persist in this line of conduct, like the dog returning to his vomit, he will soon become the lost sheep of the fold, exposed to all the fury of ravenous wolves."

Malco, nevertheless, being by no means of a soft and yielding disposition, was neither to be persuaded nor terrified out of his purpose; and embracing the worthy abbot, who consigned him over to speedy destruction, he boldly set forth upon his route, heedless of the entreaties of the whole brotherhood. As a precaution against the Moors, he united himself to a body of travellers about to proceed in the same direction, who agreed to support and defend one another.

The caravan consisted of about sixty souls, men and women, of various ranks, and their courage was speedily put to the test; for they had hardly proceeded a day's journey, when they were suddenly assailed by a band of infidels, who sprang upon them in vast numbers from an ambush, crying, "Death, death to the unbelieving dogs!" at the same moment seizing their knives, and rapidly executing their threats. Great indeed was the outcry, the consternation, and confusion; some flying, some perishing, and some glad to be made prisoners.

Upon a division of booty after the tragedy, it happened that our friend Malco, along with a young woman, fell to the lot of one master, who, mounting his prisoners upon the same camel, took his way over a long and barren waste, beyond a vast river, during which they encountered infinite toil and trouble. And when they at length attained their destination, amidst some fertile solitudes in the heart of the desert, the poor monk was set to guard his heathen master's flocks, transformed into a shepherd boy; but possessing uninterrupted time and solitude, he soon became reconciled to his situation and quite contented, believing himself now better entitled to the character of a monk than he had ever before been; a monk, in the Greek tongue, signifying nothing more nor less than a recluse.

It thus became delightful to him to dwell upon the lives of the holy patriarchs, as described in the Old Testament, which it was his great ambition to emulate as nearly as possible, having merely dreamed or read of them in his convent, but never flattering himself that he should have the happiness so nearly to resemble them. Adding to this consideration the dangers through which he had passed, he had good reason to feel satisfied with his condition, and offer up thanks to Heaven for his preservation in hymns and psalms, which he could repeat extempore in great number.

Too happy had he been could he have continued in this tranquil state, had Fortune been so inclined ; but she was busily preparing new trials for him, while he imagined himself beyond the reach of her malice in the deep sequestered solitudes he so much enjoyed. For his master, becoming sensible of his faithful and assiduous services in the care and increase of his flocks, felt more kindly disposed towards him, and desirous of rewarding his poor slave in a manner which he thought at once agreeable and profitable. With this view, summoning his female slave into his presence, he addressed the pious Malco as follows :

" I am so well satisfied, Malco, with your conduct, that I am resolved to give you some signal proof of my favour, insomuch that if you had before a motive for promoting my interests, it will render you in future doubly assiduous. Behold, I am willing to give you this fair Christian here for your wedded wife ; you are fellow-prisoners, and I cannot do better than unite your fortunes in one, so that you may henceforward, though condemned to servitude, pass your days in peace and comfort in the joys of domestic life."

The poor monk was sadly grieved and disconcerted at this proposal, the worst in his opinion that he had to dread. He instantaneously declared his dislike to it, adding that he was prohibited by the rules of his order even from indulging such a wish ; and, besides, the lady in question had a husband most likely living, taken prisoner at the same time with themselves, though disposed of to a different master. Incensed at receiving the least opposition on the part of his slave, his master, giving way to an impulse of passion, suddenly drew his knife for the purpose of despatching Malco on the spot.

And this he would infallibly have done, had not his pious herdsman sought refuge behind the slighted lady, whom he was glad enough in this exigence to embrace ; and his dread was such that he became unable to utter a word, which his savage master luckily took for an acknowledgment of his error and an inclination to submit. Concluding such to be the case, he ordered both parties to be conducted home to Malco's hut, where they were safely secured for the night. In this great extremity the unfortunate monk stationed himself as far as possible from the hated object of his fears, considering her in the light of his spiritual adversary, whom he was to resist by every means in his power. He appeared to regard her with mingled scorn and detestation, which the fair Christian on her part returned; and, buried in their own thoughts, they sorrowfully contrasted their late freedom and happiness with their present miserable lot. Such, indeed, was its impression upon the spirits of the pious Malco, that added to his dread of being compelled sooner or later to violate his vows, he resolved to make an end of all his troubles at a single blow. With more of the hero than the Christian, he was already seen brandishing the fatal steel, and after muttering a few hasty prayers, he turned to his companion.

"Fear me not," he said, "unhappy woman; but fare you well. I am going to rid myself of this world, preferring to lose my life rather than to preserve it by entering into the marriage state."

Hearing his desperate intentions, and observing the deadly weapon glaring through the darkness that surrounded them, the kind lady seized the despairing man in her arms, and holding him as straitly as she could, she at the same time conjured him to have mercy on his own soul, and then falling at his feet, she thus continued:

"Nay, slay not thyself, my good Malco; but take heed, lest, in attempting to save thy soul alive, thou dost not by those very means contrive to lose it. If it be only a wish to preserve thy long-treasured virtue that tempts thee to such despair, pray let thy mind be easy on that score; for, believe me, I will sooner consent to be cut into pieces than sin against that commandment of God which thou well wottest of, being determined to preserve my conjugal faith at all hazards. So listen to me, and be at peace; for I will teach thee how to arrange thy affairs as well as my own in such sort as to leave us both at liberty to pursue our respective inclinations without incurring the tremendous vengeance of our lord and master. Let us affect submission to his wishes, while we continue to live with the affection only of brother and sister for each other, and in this way our misfortunes ought to render us dear to one another."

Such a proposal Malco received with gratitude, and they contrived to deport themselves so tenderly and affectionately one towards the other as completely to impose upon their master, who, pleased with this proof of their submission, every day granted more and more liberty to their actions. Some years elapsed in this manner without either of them having occasion to accuse the other of a wish to infringe upon the original conditions, their master indulging only a little surprise at not being sooner presented with a young progeny of slaves. But the pious brother, as well as his sister in captivity, becoming weary of the privations they endured, one day as our hero was standing in a desponding attitude alone in the desert, leaning upon his crook and gazing wistfully upon the sky (and little else, indeed, there was to be seen), he began to ponder seriously upon his past life. Surrounded by his flock, he dwelt upon his present lot as contrasted with the pleasant life he had before led with those holy monks by whom he had been so kindly educated and cherished. The figure of his venerable abbot appeared in all the odour of sanctity before him, and there were moments when his charitable acts and converse came fresh over his memory, seeming to say that he had wilfully forfeited the salvation which he would have secured to him, besides plunging his saintly director in holy grief for his premature departure.

While revolving these bitter thoughts, he chanced to cast his eyes on an anthill, where he observed thousands of little busy citizens labouring up and down the hill with all their might. Sometimes they marched in rank and file, as if conducting some important operations; some were pioneers, while others were employed in bearing provisions needful to the pigmy citadel. Another party was seen erecting earthen batteries against the wintry winds and floods, a second was busily biting off the heads of grains and seeds in order to prevent vegetation; and a third was seen, like pall-bearers, with the dead bodies of their brethren upon their shoulders, without in the least incommoding the proceedings of the others. More extraordinary still, such as were observed to be overburthened received immediate succour from a company in reserve, who speedily gave their shoulders to the task. And as the whole process appeared to be conducted according to certain rules and method, those that entered were seen as if inquiring the business of such as were going out, for the purpose of ascertaining their respective duties.

Poor Malco's thoughts began to dwell upon the delights of freedom and industry, as he contemplated the sight before him; slavery appeared to him in all its naked deformity, and he sighed once more for the arduous duties of a monastic life, of which he fancied he beheld so laudable an example in the busy scene before him. Upon returning to his rustic abode, he proceeded to address his female companion as follows, who expressed no little surprise at the sudden change which had taken place in his sentiments :

" I will tell you of what I have been thinking, and I hope it will meet with your approbation : I have an earnest desire to obtain my freedom."

" So have I," returned his companion ; " I am heartily weary of the severe and solitary life we lead here, and I am very much concerned to see your affliction. For this reason I would prevail upon you to seize the first occasion that offers of attempting our escape, as I will gladly run all risks in accompanying you."

This was mutually agreed upon by both parties, who had now only to study the best means of achieving so desirable an object. And it was not long before Malco, turning to the lady, said, " Are you still in the same way of thinking, and do you feel courage enough to avail yourself of such an opportunity as we were lately speaking of, should it speedily offer ? "

" Yes, indeed I do," was her reply.

" That is quite essential," continued Malco, " for if you indulge the least fear, it will necessarily involve us in greater troubles than ever. So listen while I explain all the particulars of the plan I have adopted " ; and this he proceeded to do, after which he lost no time in making all the preparations he considered necessary.

In the first place, he slaughtered two of the largest goats he could find in his master's flock, whose skins he converted into leather bottles, cooking the flesh so as best to preserve it for provisions upon their route. All being in readiness, they took a favourable opportunity towards nightfall of leaving their master, following the course of the adjacent river for about ten miles, over a toilsome and dangerous way. There Malco inflated his leather bottles, and boldly placing himself upon one of them, he let himself float in the direction of the current, inviting his companion to follow his example, which, with the utmost intrepidity, she did.

In this manner were they borne a long way down the river, until they found an opportunity of landing upon the opposite side, and flattered themselves that they should thus succeed in avoiding pursuit, as their master would be unable to track them beyond the banks of the river. Although they had the misfortune to lose the chief part of their stores during their passage, they pursued their way, allowing scarcely any time for refreshment or for rest, and dreading to look either behind or before them, lest they should behold the relentless features of their incensed master, or of robbers still more ferocious. The next day the heat of the sun was so excessive as to compel them to proceed for the most part by night, when they were infested with a variety of noxious insects, birds, snakes, and animals.

On the third day of their weary pilgrimage, while journeying between hope and despair, and at times stealing anxious looks around them, they heard footsteps hastily approaching, which from their direction they judged to be in pursuit. The form of their master seeming to rise before them, added wings to their flight; and such was the terror he inspired, that, losing all their presence of mind, they no longer knew the path they took, but eagerly looked out on all sides for some place of refuge. At the moment they found their pursuers fast gaining upon them, they perceived an immense cave not far from them, on the right hand, into which they rushed with the boldness of despair. But before they had entered very far, a fresh cause of alarm arose, even greater than the former: they discovered it to be in possession of poisonous reptiles and savage beasts, whose growlings were heard resounding in the distance. For such wild and deeply concealed caverns are eagerly resorted to during the hot and fiery season by the most ferocious animals, on account of their comparative coolness.

Affrighted at the appalling noises around them, the fugitives, venturing to advance no farther, hid themselves in a little recess on one side of the passage, and sunk almost lifeless upon the ground. In the meanwhile, their master and his attendant, for indeed it was no other, had approached the entrance of the cave, tracking the footsteps of their victims through the sand. Dismounting from their camels, the master ordered his servant to enter with his drawn sword, while he stood with a large knife at the mouth of the cavern, prepared to give them no agreeable reception. Now it so happened that the attendant, advancing in the obscurity of the place, passed by the recess where Malco and his companion lay. Impelled forward by the threats of his master, he began in his turn to call out with a loud voice, in order to affright the fugitives from their hiding-place, and penetrated into the more remote parts of the cavern, exclaiming:

"Vile wretches and slaves as you are, do you hear your master's voice ? Come forth, I say, and receive the just chastisement of your crimes ! come out, and see what sort of a reception he will give you."

He had hardly pronounced these words, that made the vaults of the cave echo back the sound, when, approaching the lair of a fierce and terrific lioness, she suddenly sprang upon the wretched slave, and, fastening upon his throat, bore him, howling, into the remotest recesses of that dismal place. His master, after awaiting his return, or the appearance of the fugitives, during a long period in vain, began to fear that his faithful slave had been overpowered by the other two, and, without reflecting longer upon the matter, he rushed forward, brandishing his huge knife, and shouting out his name, into the cave. At the same time he used the most opprobrious epithets towards his fugitive slaves, who lay trembling with dread upon the ground ; but he had not proceeded far beyond their hiding-place, when the same ferocious lioness that had just despatched his servant stood before his path. Before he could move a single step, he felt her talons at his throat, and in the next instant lay a corpse at her feet. The furious animal, supposing her retreat had been discovered, then rushed out of the cavern, bearing her cubs in her teeth, and, without returning to feast upon the dead bodies of the master and his slave, sought out for herself another lair.

During the whole time that this fearful tragedy was transacting, Malco and his companion had remained still as death, witnessing, at the same time, every circumstance as it occurred, while their hearts beat fearfully at the tremendous threats of the master and his servant as they were seen brandishing their weapons, and at the sudden and dreadful appearance and the howlings of the lioness, which made their very hair to stand on end.

Often was the wretched woman on the point of giving utterance to her fears, had not Malco restrained her ; and when they believed the danger to be passed, they were scarcely less affected than before, and offered up thanks to Heaven for their deliverance, which they continued until the evening, not venturing sooner out of their hiding-place. They then mounted the camels of the deceased, which they found supplied with provisions and wine, and recovering their spirits sufficiently to continue their journey, arrived amidst hymns of praise and gratitude about nightfall at the outposts of the Roman army.

An account of their long sufferings and adventures being conveyed to the tribune, he gave them a gracious hearing, and allowed them an escort as far as Mesopotamia, where they were recommended to the charge of the proconsul Labino. There, hearing of the decease of his worthy benefactor the abbot, Malco continued his journey into Maronia, along with the companion who had shared so many troubles with him, devoting himself wherever he came to the service of Heaven and the Church, and preserving his virtue free from the contamination of worldly vanities.

MICHELE COLOMBO
18TH CENTURY

FRIAR TIMOTHY AND THE WOODMAN

IN one of the districts of Montferrat dwelt a poor labourer, whose name was Gilbert. For the support of himself and family he cultivated a small enclosure, and whatever time he could snatch from the labours of his little farm he employed in gathering faggots from a wood which was at no great distance. These he brought home on the back of an ass, of which he was become the master, and afterwards, as opportunity served, conveyed them to the market of the next town, where, with the money they produced, he purchased such articles as were most wanted by his family. Gilbert was a simple fellow, and so credulous that you might have made him believe almost any absurdity.

It happened one day that, wishing to penetrate into the interior of the wood, he left his ass tied to a tree at the outskirts. Soon afterwards there passed that way two minor brethren of Saint Francis; Father Antony of Como, and Father Timothy of Casal Maggiore. Of missal or of breviary Father Timothy took little heed; he was one of those who, not yet on familiar terms with his alphabet, had attached himself to that holy order with no other aim than that of being useful in its most ordinary concerns. In company with Father Antony he rambled over the circumjacent districts, begging, for Christian charity's sake, contributions of bread, wine, fruit, and whatever else could be obtained for the maintenance and solace of the poor brotherhood.

Yet was there not one among them of quicker and acuter invention than he; a brain more fantastical it is impossible to imagine; and his most whimsical tricks were accomplished with such pleasantry and good humour, that he was the admiration of his associates.

Now these two friars having had a tedious tramp through roads somewhat muddy, and bending their course homewards with their bags well filled, were so fatigued that it was with great difficulty they could set one foot before the other; yet had they a good distance to travel ere they could reach their monastery. Accordingly, Father Timothy, observing that the ass was there unguarded, and considering it to be unreasonable that an animal made to carry burthens should stand there fresh and idle, while they, tired and breathless, bore on their shoulders no trifling weight, made up his mind without hesitation. Turning round to his companion, he asked with a smile :

" Brother Antony, what would you give if you could have this ass to carry our bags ? "

" Verily," answered the other, " so nearly am I exhausted, that just now it would suit me well."

" And do not you see," rejoined Timothy, " that it is Providence that has guided us to this beast ? Let us not reject the boon that is thus opportunely thrown in our way."

With these words, approaching the animal, he threw his wallet on its back, and invited his companion to do the same ; then loosing the halter from the ass's head, he fitted it upon his own, and proceeded to fasten himself to the tree, exactly in the position in which they had found the animal.

Next, turning to Father Antony, " Go," said he, " my good brother ; lead this beast back with thee to the convent, and there tell our brethren that I, suddenly attacked by fever, have found refuge in the house of a benevolent peasant, who, for the more expeditious conveyance of our collection of bread to the convent, has charitably lent thee this ass, which we may return to him next week, when, in quest of provisions, or for any other purpose, we may be coming this way. As for me, say that, please God, I hope to be with them in the course of to-morrow."

Hearing a proposal so extraordinary, Antony doubted if he were awake, and, used as he was to the whimsicalities of Timothy, yet this freak appeared to him so extravagant that he began to suspect his poor brother was really crazed, and fixing his eyes upon him with a stupid stare, stood motionless and mute.

" Away ! " cried Timothy, half angry ; " lose no time ; a moment's delay may defeat our purpose ; leave me to take care of myself, and this halter may chance not to gall my neck so grievously as you perhaps suspect. Have I not, Antony, shown you more than one sample of what I can accomplish ? Confide implicitly in me ; do what I desire, or you will repent it ; begone ! "

This he spoke in a tone so decisive and imperative, that Antony submitted, and replied, " Since so you command, so I will do ; look you to the consequences " ; and forthwith, driving the loaded beast before him, he punctually obeyed the directions his comrade had given.

The holy brotherhood, when they heard of the accident which had befallen Father Timothy, concluded that, since Providence orders all for the best, they must seek consolation for their brother's mischance in a pious reliance upon the Divine mercy, and in the meantime be thankful that Timothy's good host should have been disposed to despatch to them with so much provident expedition their supply of bread.

Gilbert, having at length gathered and bundled together his faggots, hastened from the wood to place them on the back of his ass; and seeing who it was that stood in the animal's place, exclaimed, " Lord, have mercy on us!" then crossed himself with trembling astonishment, and fearing that this was nothing less than a malicious trick played him by the devil, was about to run away. Recollecting, however, that the Evil One would be little inclined to assume the figure of a holy Franciscan, he somewhat checked his terror, but without any diminution of his stupor and amazement.

When Timothy observed his surprise and confusion, he could with difficulty refrain from laughing; but yet recollecting himself and composing his countenance, he thus addressed him:

" Thou art amazed, my friend, and truly not without reason, at that which thou heholdest; but what then will be thy astonishment when thou shalt learn the remainder of my story? Approach without dread; for thyself have no apprehension; but admire, in my case, the powerful hand and mysterious judgments of Heaven! It was thy belief that thou hadst an ass in thy stable, whilst, under the figure of that animal, thou wert harbouring there an unfortunate Franciscan, no other than myself!"

" Can you be serious, good father?" said Gilbert, interrupting him.

" Did I not tell thee," quickly rejoined the friar, " that this thy astonishment would be redoubled by my narration? Free me, I pray thee, from this disgraceful halter, the only vestige now left of my ignominy. Think not, oh, my son!" (continued Timothy when the rope was removed from his neck), " think not that, however sanctified be the life which a mortal leads here below, he therefore becomes sinless! So frail is humanity, so many the occasions of offence, and so strong and frequent the temptations that assail us, that it is a hard thing for a man to escape; he may resolve to fly from the world and to hide himself from its allurements, yet he carries still about him his carnal appetites, those treacherous enemies of his peace. What wonder, then, if occasionally he should yield to seduction, although dwelling in the sacred asylum of piety? Even I, I myself, had the ill fortune to fall, and my sins were of that nature and degree, that it pleased the Divine justice, by way of punishment, to transform me into a vile beast of burden, in order that in its shape I might undergo the penance I too well had merited. In this most wretched condition, so severe, as well thou knowest, have been the sufferings I have endured, that it has pleased God at length, in His compassion, to raise me from my degradation, and to restore me to the dignity of the human form."

Gilbert, who gave entire faith to the friar's story, recollecting all that he had made the poor ass endure, was filled with sorrowful contrition, and throwing himself upon his knees before the friar, cried in a supplicating tone:

"And can you, my good father, ever forgive me the blows, innumerable as they have been, which you have had from my hands, and the curses, moreover, which you have so often heard from my lips? Atrocious indeed do they now appear to me, since great is my veneration for your holy order, and for your pious founder, St. Francis!"

"Let not these recollections afflict thee," said Timothy, affectionately raising him from the ground; "for heaping as thou didst thy blows upon my back and sides, thou gavest to my flesh that salutary castigation which it was Heaven's will it should sustain; rebellious as it had too often proved, it was but right that it should suffer the punishment needful to bring it back into the path of duty. Nay, I will tell thee, that in this instance thou hast rendered me no inconsiderable service; for the more frequent and heavy were the blows of thy cudgel, the more speedily was by that means my sum of penance accomplished and the period of my deliverance accelerated. Far, therefore, from owing thee any grudge on that score, I ought to thank thee for it; and I give thee my word, that when once reseated in my cell, as I propose shortly to be, I will be mindful of thee, and put up for thy benefit prayers so fervent, that although just now thou appearest to suffer by the loss of thine ass, thou shalt, in ample recompense, receive manifold blessings poured down upon thy family, and upon the joyful harvest of thy fields. Take, then, my worthy friend, with a grateful heart, thy wood upon thy shoulder; go, and may peace attend thee!"

"But will not you, my good father," replied Gilbert, "abide with us this night? You shall want no accommodation which our cottage can afford; the hour, you see, is waxing late, and should rather suggest to you the thought of seeking for yourself a lodging than of adventuring on the high-road."

" Son, thou hast said well," answered the friar ; " but what must be my confusion on revisiting the spot where I have dwelt in such disgrace ! However, since to endure the survey of the scene of my humiliation may count for a becoming act of resignation, I submit, and with God's permission will follow wherever thou shalt direct."

So saying, they proceeded to the house, and when arrived there, Father Timothy pretended to be on terms of intimacy with all the family. He began to talk with great familiarity, first with one, then with another, as if they had been old acquaintances ; and when at this they one and all began to express surprise, he, in a joking way, said he wondered at their estrangement towards one who had for a long period been their guest. Gilbert, too, assured them that such was literally the fact ; and after keeping them awhile in suspense, informed them who this fellow of a friar was, and under what shape he had lived with them so long.

An aged man, Gilbert's father, a young woman, his wife, and two lads, his sons, whose age did not exceed twelve or fourteen, composed this simple group. Open-mouthed, half breathless, and with eyes fixed in motionless attention, each of them listened to Gilbert's story ; in their countenances you might have read a mixture of surprise, devotion, and gladness, not without marks of regret and compassion caused by a recollection of the long labours that the poor ass had sustained, the scanty nourishment of bad straw, worse hay, or vile garden weeds which at any time had reached his manger, and the many bastinadoes or goads with which every one of them had often galled or bruised him. In pity for his sufferings past, they strove with each other who should now caress him most, and show him the fondest regards. Two pullets, all that remained in the coop, were forthwith put to death, and by their help, together with whatever else the cottage could muster or the neighbourhood contribute, a repast was prepared ; to which a bottle of excellent wine, long hoarded by Gilbert, but which this evening it was his pleasure to uncork in honour of his guest, gave a relish.

Now, while the dishes and the cups went round, Father Timothy, naturally sociable and gay, indulged his mirthful vein to a degree that delighted them all, displaying from time to time some of his most original drolleries ; not forgetting, however, occasionally to recall his laughing circle to a more serious mood by introducing, in the midst of his facetious stories, some moral or religious precept, that he might appear to them as devout as they found him jovial and entertaining. Yet he could not so far command himself as not to awaken in the mind of Gilbert some little suspicion ; and this was principally occasioned by the notice which the friar took of Gilbert's wife, Dame Cicely, who was comely and well favoured for her station, and whom he eyed with glances that seemed to betoken how gladly he would, if he could, be on terms of greater intimacy with her.

She, on her part, with that veneration for the good brethren of the Church which belongs to her sex, and attracted, moreover, by his pleasant manners and conversation, could hardly look upon him with indifference. Of this the watchful husband was more than once aware ; and when at last he could no longer contain himself, thus addressed the friar :

" My good father, one may easily see how necessary to you is the mortification of the flesh ; even after the little indulgence that you have given to it this evening, it displays symptoms of rebellion and threatens you with a relapse into sin. If so recent an escape from your past sufferings prove thus unavailing to defend you from assaults of this nature, grieved am I to tell you that great is your danger of again assuming (aye, and very shortly too) an asinine form ; let me therefore advise you to return betimes to-morrow morning to your convent ; there stay, and bastinado your carcase without ceasing, unless you prefer that a service so necessary should be performed for you by others."

It is wonderful to observe how, at times, a man's passions have the power of quickening his understanding. Gilbert, who, in all his life before had never uttered a sentence which was above the common style of a labouring peasant, now that his slumbering intelligence was roused by the stimulating impulse of anxious jealousy, became all at once a fluent and able speaker. In consequence of an address so cogent and unexpected, the friar was aware that it became him to be upon his guard, and, by words and actions well considered and adapted, to steer clear of a flagellation of the flesh, which during the remainder of the evening he was careful to do.

Next morning, after a hasty breakfast, Timothy returned to his convent, and told the father guardian that it was for the benefit of the monastery that it had pleased Heaven to visit him with fever ; for that the good peasant, prompted by devotion towards the venerable St. Francis, had presented to the convent that useful animal which he had lent the preceding day to Friar Antony, intelligence which at first greatly rejoiced the worthy guardian ; but he subsequently reflecting that it might appear to the world inconsistent with the mendicant life of the brotherhood and with the strictness of their rules to maintain an ass, as if it were from indolence or self-indulgence ; that hence might ensue some diminution in the charity of the faithful and some abatement of fervent and zealous regard towards his order, prudently determined that it would be best to sell the ass, without the aid of which the brethren had hitherto gone on very well, and he therefore sent it forthwith, by a trusty person, to a neighbouring fair.

There, as chance would have it, that very day was Gilbert, who, as soon as he descried the ass, knew him from the circumstance of his having one of his ears cropped ; and going up to him, he placed his mouth close to the animal's ear in the action of talking to him, and whispered very softly :

" Lack-a-day, my good father ! the rebellious flesh, then, has played thee another trick ! Did I not forewarn thee that this would happen ? "

The ass, feeling a breathing and tickling in his ear, shook his head, as if not assenting.

" Deny it not," resumed Gilbert , " I know thee well ; thou art the self-same."

Again the ass shook his head.

" Nay, deny it not ; lie not ! " rejoined the worthy Gilbert, somewhat raising his voice ; " lie not, for that is a great sin ; thee it is : yes, in spite of thyself, it is thee ! "

The bystanders seeing a man thus holding a conversation with an ass, believed him crazy, and, gathering round him, began to put questions, some about one thing, some about another, and Gilbert advanced the strangest and most unaccountable facts, always maintaining that this was not an ass, however it might bear that resemblance, but in truth a poor miserable Franciscan, who, for his carnal frailties, was now unfortunately a second time transmuted into this form ; and he then told from the beginning all the story of the incontinent friar metamorphosed into a beast of burthen. The bursts of laughter which attended this narrative it is needless to describe.

Poor Gilbert was all that day the butt of the fair ; and as the owl draws after her a flight of birds, which flutter around her with various screams and chatterings, so was Gilbert, whichever way he turned, pressed upon by the surrounding crowd, who, with loud jeers and scoffs, made him their laughing-stock. At last some one among them recommended to him again to buy this unlucky animal, to feed him with the best hay he could procure, and by all kinds of good treatment to make him amends for what he had in times past caused him to suffer. This advice pleased Gilbert, who purchased the ass, and led him home. How was Dame Cicely astonished, how also the old father and the two youngsters, to see their well-known ass again!

Such was the welcome they gave him, such the attentions they paid him, that never was ass in the world so fed or so caressed. Plump beyond the costume of asses became his flesh; smooth and shining like velvet his skin; but the perverse animal soon grew vicious and prone to bad habits; already he began to give no little trouble, not to the old man, the wife, and the boys only, but even to Gilbert himself. With savage bites and rude kicks he assailed his generous benefactors, and brayed so loudly and so continually night and day that he became a very serious nuisance to the neighbourhood. He more than once broke the halter by which he was tied to the manger in order to satisfy his unruly appetite. How sadly scandalised all the family were at these brutal practices of Friar Timothy it is easy to imagine. Blamable as might seem to them all his former pranks, and unbecoming, as they doubtless were, in that probationary state to which he was condemned, they were peccadilloes compared with his last offence.

Gilbert, finding that day by day he became more intractable, concluded that, persevering as he did in a life thus vicious and depraved, he was condemned never more to fraternise with his Franciscan brethren. He began to suspect, too, that he himself might be in some measure to blame for what had happened.

"Asinine flesh and monkish flesh," said he to himself, "must not be too indulgently treated."

Gilbert saw the necessity there was for returning in good earnest to that system of flagellation which had on a former occasion produced so beneficial an effect. With this view he again had recourse to the cudgel and to hard labour; but whether it was that the unlucky ass had by a course of gentle treatment become of a constitution too delicate, or whether Gilbert, with an over-ardent zeal, carried his regimen of severity beyond the due limits, certain it is that the afflicted beast, unable to endure a discipline so rigid, soon died, and these good people had to deplore the eternal loss of the soul of Father Timothy, who, in spite of his having undergone two purgatories in an ass's shape, still died impenitent through the execrable vice of gluttony, from which may the Divine grace preserve all good Christians, not excepting the poor brethren of St. Francis!

ENRICO CASTELNUOVO
1839–

IT SNOWS

THE thermometer marks barely one degree above freezing, the sky is covered with ominous white clouds, the air is harsh and piercing; what can induce Signor Odoardo, at nine o'clock on such a morning, to stand in his study window? It is true that Signor Odoardo is a vigorous man, in the prime of life, but it is never wise to tempt Providence by needlessly risking one's health. But stay—I begin to think that I have found a clue to his conduct. Opposite Signor Odoardo's window is the window of the Signora Evelina, and Signora Evelina has the same tastes as Signor Odoardo. She too is taking the air, leaning against the window-sill in her dressing-gown, her fair curls falling upon her forehead and tossed back every now and then by a pretty movement of her head. The street is so narrow that it is easy to talk across from one side to the other, but in such weather as this the only two windows that stand open are those of Signora Evelina and Signor Odoardo.

There is no denying the fact: Signora Evelina, who within the last few weeks has taken up her abode across the way, is a very fascinating little widow. Her hair is of spun gold, her skin of milk and roses, her little turned-up nose, though assuredly not Grecian, is much more attractive than if it were; she has the most dazzling teeth in the most kissable mouth; her eyes are transparent as a cloudless sky, and—well, she knows how to use them. Nor is this the sum total of her charms: look at the soft, graceful curves of her agile, well-proportioned figure; look at her little hands and feet! After all, one can hardly wonder that Signor Odoardo runs the risk of catching his death of cold, instead of closing the window and warming himself at the stove which roars so cheerfully within. It is rather at Signora Evelina that I wonder; for, though Signor Odoardo is not an ill-looking man, he is close upon forty, while she is but twenty-four. So young, and already a widow—poor Signora Evelina! It is true that she has great strength of character; but six months have elapsed since her husband's death, and she is resigned to it already, though the deceased left her barely enough to keep body and soul together. Happily Signora Evelina is not encumbered with a family; she is alone and independent, and with those eyes, that hair, that little upturned nose, she ought to have no difficulty in finding a second husband. In fact, there is no harm in admitting that Signora Evelina has contemplated the possibility of a second marriage, and that if the would-be bridegroom is not in his first youth—why, she is prepared to make the best of it. In this connection it is perhaps not uninstructive to note that Signor Odoardo is in comfortable circumstances, and is himself a widower. What a coincidence!

Well, then, why don't they marry—that being the customary *dénouement* in such cases?

Why don't they marry? Well—Signor Odoardo is still undecided. If there had been any hope of a love-affair I fear that his indecision would have vanished long ago. *Errare humanum est.* But Signora Evelina is a woman of serious views; she is in search of a husband, not of a flirtation. Signora Evelina is a person of great determination; she knows how to turn other people's heads without letting her own be moved a jot. Signora Evelina is deep; deep enough, surely, to gain her point. If Signor Odoardo flutters about her much longer he will singe his wings; things cannot go on in this way. Signor Odoardo's visits are too frequent; and now, in addition, there are the conversations from the window. It is time for a decisive step to be taken, and Signor Odoardo is afraid that he may find himself taking the step before he is prepared to; this very day, perhaps, when he goes to call on the widow.

The door of Signor Odoardo's study is directly opposite the window in which he is standing, and the opening of this door is therefore made known to him by a violent draught.

As he turns a sweet voice says:

"Good-bye, papa dear; I'm going to school."

"Good-bye, Doretta," he answers, stooping to kiss a pretty little maid of eight or nine; and at the same instant Signora Evelina calls out from over the way:

"Good-morning, Doretta!"

Doretta, who had made a little grimace on discovering her papa in conversation with his pretty neighbour, makes another as she hears herself greeted, and mutters reluctantly, "Good-morning."

Then, with her little basket on her arm, she turns slowly away to join the maid-servant who is waiting for her in the hall.

" I am *so* fond of that child," sighs Signora Evelina, with the sweetest inflexion in her voice, " but she doesn't like me at all ! "

" What an absurd idea ! . . . Doretta is a very self-willed child."

Thus Signor Odoardo ; but in his heart of hearts he too is convinced that his little daughter has no fondness for Signora Evelina.

Meanwhile, the cold is growing more intense, and every now and then a flake of snow spins around upon the wind. Short of wishing to be frozen stiff, there is nothing for it but to shut the window.

" It snows," says Signora Evelina, glancing upward.

" Oh, it was sure to come."

" Well—I must go and look after my household. *Au revoir*—shall I see you later ? "

" I hope to have the pleasure—"

" *Au revoir*, then."

Signora Evelina closes the window, nods and smiles once more through the pane, and disappears.

Signor Odoardo turns back to his study, and perceiving how cold it has grown, throws some wood on the fire, and, kneeling before the door of the stove, tries to blow the embers into a blaze. The flames leap up with a merry noise, sending bright flashes along the walls of the room.

Outside, the flakes continue to descend at intervals. Perhaps, after all, it is not going to be a snowstorm.

Signor Odoardo paces up and down the room, with bent head and hands thrust in his pockets. He is disturbed, profoundly disturbed. He feels that he has reached a crisis in his life ; that in a few days, perhaps in a few hours, his future will be decided. Is he seriously in love with Signora Evelina ? How long has he known her ? Will she be sweet and good like *the other* ? Will she know how to be a mother to Doretta ?

There is a sound of steps in the hall ; Signor Odoardo pauses in the middle of the room. The door reopens, and Doretta rushes up to her father, her cheeks flushed, her hood falling over her forehead, her warm coat buttoned up to her chin, her hands thrust into her muff.

" It is snowing and the teacher has sent us home."

She tosses off her hood and coat and goes up to the stove.

" There is a good fire, but the room is cold," she exclaims.

As a matter of fact, the window having stood open for half an hour, the thermometer indicates but fifty degrees.

" Papa," Doretta goes on, " I want to stay with you all day long to-day."

" And suppose your poor daddy has affairs of his own to attend to ? "

" No, no, you must give them up for to-day."

And Doretta, without waiting for an answer, runs to fetch her books, her doll, and her work. The books are spread out on the desk, the doll is comfortably seated on the sofa, and the work is laid out upon a low stool.

" Ah," she cries, with an air of importance, " what a mercy that there is no school to-day ! I shall have time to go over my lesson. Oh, look how it snows ! "

It snows indeed. First a white powder, fine but thick, and whirled in circles by the wind, beats with a dry metallic sound against the window-panes ; then the wind drops, and the flakes, growing larger, descend silently, monotonously, incessantly. The snow covers the streets like a downy carpet, spreads itself like a sheet over the roofs, fills up the cracks in the walls, heaps itself upon the window-sills, envelops the iron window-bars, and hangs in festoons from the gutters and eaves.

Out of doors it must be as cold as ever, but the room is growing rapidly warmer, and Doretta, climbing on a chair, has the satisfaction of announcing that the mercury has risen eleven degrees.

" Yes, dear," her father replies, " and the clock is striking eleven too. Run and tell them to get breakfast ready."

Doretta runs off obediently, but reappears in a moment.

" Daddy, daddy, what do you suppose has happened ? The dining-room stove won't draw, and the room is all full of smoke ! "

" Then let us breakfast here, child."

This excellent suggestion is joy to the soul of Doretta, who hastens to carry the news to the kitchen, and then, in a series of journeys back and forth from the dining-room to the study, transports with her own hands the knives, forks, plates, tablecloth, and napkins, and, with the man-servant's aid, lays them out upon one of her papa's tables. How merry she is ! How completely the cloud has vanished that darkened her brow a few hours earlier ! And how well she acquits herself of her household duties !

Signor Odoardo, watching her with a sense of satisfaction, cannot resist exclaiming : " Bravo, Doretta ! "

Doretta is undeniably the very image of her mother. She too was just such an excellent housekeeper, a model of order, of neatness, of propriety. And she was pretty, like Doretta, even though she did not possess the fair hair and captivating eyes of Signor Evelina.

The man-servant who brings in the breakfast is accompanied by a newcomer, the cat Melanio, who is always present at Doretta's meals. The cat Melanio is old; he has known Doretta ever since she was born, and he honours her with his protection. Every morning he mews at her door, as though to inquire if she has slept well; every evening he keeps her company until it is time for her to go to bed. Whenever she goes out he speeds her with a gentle purr; whenever he hears her come in he hurries to meet her and rubs himself against her legs. In the morning, and at the midday meal, when she takes it at home, he sits beside her chair and silently waits for the scraps from her plate. The cat Melanio, however, is not in the habit of visiting Signor Odoardo's study, and shows a certain surprise at finding himself there. Signor Odoardo, for his part, receives his new guest with some diffidence; but Doretta, intervening in Melanio's favour, undertakes to answer for his good conduct.

It is long since Doretta has eaten with so much appetite. When she has finished her breakfast, she clears the table as deftly and promptly as she had laid it, and in a few moments Signor Odoardo's study has resumed its wonted appearance. Only the cat Melanio remains, comfortably established by the stove, on the understanding that he is to be left there as long as he is not troublesome.

The continual coming and going has made the room grow colder. The mercury has dropped perceptibly, and Doretta, to make it rise again, empties nearly the whole wood-basket into the stove.

How it snows, how it snows! No longer in detached flakes, but as though an openwork white cloth were continuously unrolled before one's eyes. Signor Odoardo begins to think that it will be impossible for him to call on Signora Evelina. True, it is only a step, but he would sink into the snow up to his knees. After all, it is only twelve o'clock. It may stop snowing later.

Doretta is struck by a luminous thought:

"What if I were to answer grandmamma's letter?"

In another moment Doretta is seated at her father's desk, in his arm-chair, two cushions raising her to the requisite height, her legs dangling into space, the pen suspended in her hand, and her eyes fixed upon a sheet of ruled paper, containing thus far but two words: *Dear Grandmamma.*

Signor Odoardo, leaning against the stove, watches his daughter with a smile.

It appears that at last Doretta has discovered a way of beginning her letter, for she replunges the pen into the inkstand, lowers her hand to the sheet of paper, wrinkles her forehead and sticks out her tongue.

After several minutes of assiduous toil she raises her head and asks: " What shall I say to grandmamma about her invitation to go and spend a few weeks with her ? "

" Tell her that you can't go now, but that she may expect you in the spring."

" With you, papa ? "

" With me, yes," Signor Odoardo answers mechanically.

Yet if, in the meantime, he engages himself to Signora Evelina, this visit to his mother-in-law will become rather an awkward business.

" There—I've finished ! " Doretta cries with an air of triumph.

But the cry is succeeded by another, half of anguish, half of rage.

" What's the matter now ? "

" A blot ! "

" Let me see ? . . . You little goose, what *have* you done ? . . . You've ruined the letter now ! "

Doretta, having endeavoured to remove the ink-spot by licking it, has torn the paper.

" Oh dear, I shall have to copy it out now," she says in a mortified tone.

" You can copy it this evening. Bring it here, and let me look at it. . . . Not bad,—not bad at all. A few letters to be added, and a few to be taken out ; but, on the whole, for a chit of your size, it's fairly creditable. Good girl ! "

Doretta rests upon her laurels, playing with her doll Nini. She dresses Nini in her best gown, and takes her to call on the cat, Melanio.

The cat, Melanio, who is dozing with half-open eyes, is somewhat bored by these attentions. Raising himself on his four paws, he arches his flexible body, and then rolls himself up into a ball, turning his back upon his visitor.

" Dear me, Melanio is not very polite to-day," says Doretta, escorting the doll back to the sofa. " But you mustn't be offended ; he's very seldom impolite. I think it must be the weather ; doesn't the weather make you sleepy too, Nini ? . . . Come, let's take a nap ; go by-bye, baby, go by-bye."

Nini sleeps. Her head rests upon a cushion, her little rag and horse-hair body is wrapped in a woollen coverlet, her lids are closed; for Nini raises or lowers her lids according to the position of her body.

Signor Odoardo looks at the clock and then glances out of the window. It is two o'clock and the snow is still falling.

Doretta is struck by another idea.

"Daddy, see if I know my La Fontaine fable: *Le corbeau et le renard.*"

"Very well, let's hear it," Signor Odoardo assents, taking the open book from the little girl's hands.

Doretta begins:

> "*Maître corbeau, sur un arbre perché,*
> *Tenait en son bec un fromage;*
> *Maître . . . maître . . . maître . . .*"

"Go on."

"*Maître . . .*"

"*Maître renard.*"

"Oh, yes, now I remember:

> "*Maître renard, par l'odeur alléché,*
> *Lui tint à peu près ce langage:*
> *Hè! bonjour . . .*"

At this point Doretta, seeing that her father is not listening to her, breaks off her recitation. Signor Odoardo has, in fact, closed the book upon his forefinger, and is looking elsewhere.

"Well, Doretta," he absently inquires, "why don't you go on?"

"I'm not going to say any more of it," she answers sullenly.

"Why, you cross-patch! What's the matter?"

The little girl, who had been seated on a low stool, has risen to her feet and now sees why her papa has not been attending to her. The snow is falling less thickly, and the fair head of Signora Evelina has appeared behind the window-panes over the way.

Brave little woman! She has actually opened the window, and is clearing the snow off the sill with a fire-shovel. Her eyes meet Signor Odoardo's; she smiles and shakes her head, as though to say: What hateful weather!

He would be an ill-mannered boor who should not feel impelled to say a word to the dauntless Signora Evelina. Signor Odoardo, who is not an ill-mannered boor, yields to the temptation of opening the window for a moment.

" Bravo, Signora Evelina ! I see you are not afraid of the snow."

" Oh, Signor Odoardo, what fiendish weather ! . . . But, if I am not mistaken, that is Doretta with you. . . . How do you do, Doretta ?"

" Doretta, come here and say how do you do to the lady."

" No, no—let her be, let her be ! Children catch cold so easily—you had better shut the window. I suppose there is no hope of seeing you to-day ? "

" Look at the condition of the streets ! "

" Oh, you men . . . you men ! . . . *The stronger sex* . . . but no matter. *Au revoir !* "

" *Au revoir.*"

The two windows are closed simultaneously, but this time Signora Evelina does not disappear. She is sitting there, close to the window, and it snows so lightly now that her wonderful profile is outlined as clearly as possible against the pane. Good heavens, how beautiful she is !

Signor Odoardo walks up and down the room, in the worst of humours. He feels that it is wrong not to go and see the fascinating widow, and that to go and see her would be still more wrong. The cloud has settled again upon Doretta's forehead, the same cloud that darkened it in the morning.

Not a word is said of La Fontaine's fable. Instead, Signor Odoardo grumbles irritably :

" This blessed room is as cold as ever."

" Why shouldn't it be," Doretta retorts with a touch of asperity, " when you open the window every few minutes ? "

" Oho," Signor Odoardo says to himself, " it is time to have this matter out."

And, going up to Doretta, he takes her by the hand, leads her to the sofa, and lifts her on his knee.

" Now, then, Doretta, why is it that you are so disagreeable to Signora Evelina ? "

The little girl, not knowing what to answer, grows red and embarrassed.

" What has Signora Evelina done to you ? " her father continues.

" She hasn't done anything to me."

" And yet you don't like her."

Profound silence.

" And *she* likes you so much ! "

"I don't care if she does!"

"You naughty child! . . . And what if, one of these days, you had to live with Signora Evelina?"

"I won't live with her—I won't live with her!" the child bursts out.

"Now you are talking foolishly," Signor Odoardo admonishes her in a severe tone, setting her down from his knee.

She bursts into passionate weeping.

"Come, Doretta, come. . . . Is this the way you keep your daddy company? . . . Enough of this, Doretta."

But, say what he pleases, Doretta must have her cry. Her brown eyes are swimming in tears, her little breast heaves, her voice is broken by sobs.

"What ridiculous whims!" Signor Odoardo exclaims, throwing his head back against the sofa cushions.

Signor Odoardo is unjust, and, what is worse, he does not believe what he is saying. He knows that this is no whim of Doretta's. He knows it better than the child herself, who would probably find it difficult to explain what she is undergoing. It is at once the presentiment of a new danger and the renewal of a bygone sorrow. Doretta was barely six years old when her mother died, and yet her remembrance is indelibly impressed upon the child's mind. And now it seems as though her mother were dying again.

"When you have finished crying, Doretta, you may come here," Signor Odoardo says.

Doretta, crouching in a corner of the room, cries less vehemently, but has not yet finished crying. Just like the weather outside,—it snows less heavily, but it still snows.

Signor Odoardo covers his eyes with his hand.

How many thoughts are thronging through his head, now many affections are contending in his heart! If he could but banish the vision of Signora Evelina—but he tries in vain. He is haunted by those blue eyes, by that persuasive smile, that graceful and harmonious presence. He has but to say the word, and he knows that she will be his, to brighten his solitary home, and fill it with life and love. Her presence would take ten years from his age, he would feel as he did when he was betrothed for the first time. And yet—no; it would not be quite like the first time.

He is not the same man that he was then, and she, *the other*, ah, how different *she* was from the Signora Evelina ! How modest and shy she was ! How girlishly reserved, even in the expression of her love ! How beautiful were her sudden blushes, how sweet the droop of her long, shyly-lowered lashes ! He had known her first in the intimacy of her own home, simple, shy, a good daughter and a good sister, as she was destined to be a good wife and mother. For a while he had loved her in silence, and she had returned his love. One day, walking beside her in the garden, he had seized her hand with sudden impetuosity, and raising it to his lips, had said, " I care for you so much ! " and she, pale and trembling, had run to her mother's arms, crying out, " Oh, how happy I am ! "

Ah, those dear days—those dear days ! He was a poet then ; with the accent of sincerest passion he whispered in his love's ear :

"I love thee more than all the world beside,
My only faith and hope thou art,
My God, my country, and my bride—
Sole love of this unchanging heart !"

Very bad poetry, but deliciously thrilling to his young betrothed. Oh, the dear, dear days ! Oh, the long hours that pass like a flash in delightful talk, the secrets that the soul first reveals to itself in revealing them to the beloved, the caresses longed for and yet half feared, the lovers' quarrels, the tears that are kissed away, the shynesses, the simplicity, the abandonment of a pure and passionate love—who may hope to know you twice in a lifetime ?

No, Signora Evelina can never restore what he had lost to Signor Odoardo. No, this self-possessed widow, who, after six months of mourning, has already started on the hunt for a second husband, cannot inspire him with the faith that he felt in *the other.* Ah, first-loved women, why is it that you must die ? For the dead give no kisses, no caresses, and the living long to be caressed and kissed.

Who talks of kisses ? Here is one that has alit, all soft and warm, on Signor Odoardo's lips, rousing him with a start.—Ah ! . . . Is it you, Doretta ?—It is Doretta, who says nothing, but who is longing to make it up with her daddy. She lays her cheek against his, he presses her little head close, lest she should escape from him. He too is silent —what can he say to her ?

It is growing dark, and the eyes of the cat Melanio begin to glitter in the corner by the stove. The man-servant knocks and asks if he is to bring the lamp.

" Make up the fire first," Signor Odoardo says.

The wood crackles and snaps, and sends up showers of sparks; then it bursts into flame, blazing away with a regular, monotonous sound, like the breath of a sleeping giant. In the dusk the firelight flashes upon the walls, brings out the pattern of the wall-paper, and travels far enough to illuminate a corner of the desk. The shadows lengthen and then shorten again, thicken and then shrink; everything in the room seems to be continually changing its size and shape. Signor Odoardo, giving free rein to his thoughts, evokes the vision of his married life, sees the baby's cradle, recalls her first cries and smiles, feels again his dying wife's last kiss, and hears the last word upon her lips,—*Doretta*. No, no, it is impossible that he should ever do anything to make his Doretta unhappy! And yet he is not sure of resisting Signora Evelina's wiles; he is almost afraid that, when he sees his enchantress on the morrow, all his strong resolves may take flight. There is but one way out of it.

" Doretta," says Signor Odoardo.

" Father?"

" Are you going to copy out your letter to your grandmamma this evening?"

" Yes, father."

" Wouldn't you rather go and see your grandmamma yourself?"

" With whom?" the child falters anxiously, her little heart beating a frantic tattoo as she awaits his answer.

" With me, Doretta."

" With *you*, daddy?" she exclaims, hardly daring to believe her ears.

" Yes, with me; with your daddy."

" Oh, daddy, *daddy*!" she cries, her little arms about his neck, her kisses covering his face. " Oh, daddy, my own dear daddy! When shall we start?"

" To-morrow morning, if you're not afraid of the snow."

" Why not now? Why not at once?"

" Gently—gently. Good Lord, doesn't the child want her dinner first?"

And Signor Odoardo, gently detaching himself from his daughter's embrace, rises and rings for the lamp. Then, instinctively, he glances once more towards the window. In the opposite house all is dark, and Signora Evelina's profile is no longer outlined against the pane. The weather is still threatening, and now and then a snowflake falls. The servant closes the shutters and draws the curtains, so that no profane gaze may penetrate into the domestic sanctuary.

" We had better dine in here," Signor Odoardo says. " The dining-room must be as cold as Greenland."

Doretta, meanwhile, is convulsing the kitchen with the noisy announcement of the impending journey. At first she is thought to be joking, but when she establishes the fact that she is speaking seriously, it is respectfully pointed out to her that the master of the house must be crazy. To start on a journey in the depth of winter, and in such weather! If at least they were to wait for a fine day!

But what does Doretta care for the comments of the kitchen? She is beside herself with joy. She sings, she dances about the room, and breaks off every moment or two to give her father a kiss. Then she pours out the fulness of her emotion upon the cat Melanio and the doll Nini, promising the latter to bring her back a new frock from Milan.

At dinner she eats little and talks incessantly of the journey, asking again and again what time it is, and at what time they are to start.

" Are you afraid of missing the train?" Signor Odoardo asks with a smile.

And yet, though he dissembles his impatience, it is as great as hers. He longs to go away, far away. Perhaps he may not return until spring. He orders his luggage packed for an absence of two months.

Doretta goes to bed early, but all night long she tosses about under the bed-clothes, waking her nurse twenty times to ask: " Is it time to get up?"

Signor Odoardo, too, is awake when the man-servant comes to call him the next morning at six o'clock.

" What sort of a day is it?"

" Very bad, sir—just such another as yesterday. In fact, if I might make the suggestion, sir, if it's not necessary for you to start to-day——"

" It is, Angelo. Absolutely necessary."

At the station there are only a few sleepy, depressed-looking travellers wrapped in furs. They are all grumbling about the weather, about the cold, about the earliness of the hour, and declaring that nothing but the most urgent business would have got them out of bed at that time of day. There is but one person in the station who is all liveliness and smiles—Doretta.

The first-class compartment in which Signor Odoardo and his daughter find themselves is bitterly cold, in spite of foot-warmers, but Doretta finds the temperature delicious, and, if she dared, would open the windows for the pleasure of looking out.

" Are you happy, Doretta ? "

" Oh, *so* happy ! "

Ten years earlier, on a pleasanter day, but also in winter, Signor Odoardo had started on his wedding-journey. Opposite him had sat a young girl, who looked as much like Doretta as a woman can look like a child ; a pretty, sedate young girl, oh, so sweetly, tenderly in love with Signor Odoardo. And as the train started he had asked her the same question :

" Are you happy, Maria ? "

And she had answered :

" Oh, *so* happy ! " just like Doretta.

The train races and flies. Farewell, farewell for ever, Signora Evelina.

And did Signora Evelina die of despair ?

Oh, no ; Signora Evelina has a perfect disposition and a delightful home. The perfect disposition enables her not to take things too seriously, the delightful home affords her a thousand distractions. Its windows do not all look towards Signor Odoardo's residence. One of them, for example, commands a little garden belonging to a worthy bachelor who smokes his pipe there on pleasant days. Signora Evelina finds the worthy bachelor to her taste, and the worthy bachelor, who is an average-adjuster by profession, admires Signora Evelina's eyes, and considers her handsomely and solidly enough put together to rank A No. 1 on Lloyd's registers.

The result is that the bachelor now and then looks up at the window, and the Signora Evelina now and then looks down at the garden. The weather not being propitious to out-of-door conversation, Signora Evelina at length invites her neighbour to come and pay her a visit. Her neighbour hesitates and she renews the invitation. How can one resist such a charming woman ? And what does one visit signify ? Nothing at all. The excellent average-adjuster has every reason to be pleased with his reception, the more so as Signora Evelina actually gives him leave to bring his pipe the next time he comes. She adores the smell of a pipe. Signora Evelina is an ideal woman, just the wife for a business man who had not positively made up his mind to remain single. And as to that, muses the average-adjuster, have I ever positively made up my mind to remain single, and if I have, who is to prevent my changing it ?

And so it comes to pass that when, after an absence of three months, Signor Odoardo returns home with Doretta, he receives notice of the approaching marriage of Signora Evelina Chiocci, widow Ramboldi, with Signor Archimede Fagiuolo.

" Fagiuolo ! " shouts Doretta, " *Fagiuolo !* " [1]

The name seems to excite her unbounded hilarity ; but I am under the impression that the real cause of her merriment is not so much Signora Evelina's husband as Signora Evelina's marriage.

[1] *Fagiuolo :* a simpleton.

THE LOST LETTER

ENRICO CASTELNUOVO

PROFESSOR ATTILIO CERNIERI, distinguished Egyptologist, Senator of the Kingdom, commander of numerous orders, active member of the Lincei, Corresponding Fellow of an infinite number of Italian and foreign societies and academies, was having his servant, Pomponio, open two cases of books arrived the evening before from Padua.

The books were the residue of a library that he had gathered at Padua when, twenty years before, he had filled the chair of neo-Latin in that university. Afterward he had travelled much for scientific purposes, had been called successively to the institute of higher learning in Florence, to the University of Naples, and finally the Ministry had solicited his presence in Rome, at the Sapienza, creating a chair especially for him, and offering him high emoluments.

For some time, during the Professor's peregrinations, the library, packed up and left with a colleague, had remained undisturbed at Padua. Then Cernieri had sent for a part of it when he was in Florence; another part later on when in Naples. Now having to come to Rome, with the intention of fixing there his permanent residence, he had determined to send for the two last cases.

To be sure, these books were not absolutely necessary to a man who, besides having recently refurnished his own library, had at his disposition the public and private libraries of the capital.

We live in a century in which everything proceeds by steam, even science. What is true to-day can readily be false to-morrow; and a volume runs the risk of being useless over night.

But in spite of its ten years of life, the monograph in which our hero had demonstrated, with ponderous arguments, that a group of roots hitherto believed to be of Celtic origin must be relegated to the Finnish Family, had not grown old. The book, small in weight but heavy in thought, had been translated into all the languages of Europe, and the genial information had placed our professor " at the top of the scientific pyramid," to quote the words of an enthusiastic disciple, by the side of the principal living philologist, the famous Lowenstein of the University of Upsala. But whether because the top of a pyramid is an uncomfortable place for two or not, Cernieri and Lowenstein had at first offered the interesting spectacle of two contestants who are vigorously striving to throw one another off, until, finally convinced of the uselessness of their struggles, they had changed rivalry into friendship.

The two learned men were, of course, two strugglers in the scientific arena, but instead of struggling with each other they struggled with the world at large. If by chance any mortal could be found rash enough to raise his crest and dare to endeavour to seat himself, too, on the top of the famous pyramid; had it been possible to penetrate the depths of the minds of the two "chers confrères," as they styled themselves in correspondence, it would probably have been discovered that each placed a very moderate estimate upon the virtues of the other. Lowenstein had very little faith in the Finnish roots; and Cernieri believed still less in the revolution brought about by Lowenstein in the study of the Hindu-Persian.

But let us leave Lowenstein in peace in distant Norway and turn our attention entirely to our illustrious compatriot. And to begin with, upon the afternoon in which Pomponio is opening the cases of books, the Professor was but forty, though looking much older.

He was slightly stoop-shouldered and his ample forehead was seamed with premature wrinkles; his near-sighted eyes were hidden behind glasses, and were generally half-closed, like those of a sleepy pussy-cat. His hair was thin and gray, his beard straggling, ill-cared for, and nearly white. When he was young, Cernieri used to shave; but after it had happened several times that he in his absent-mindedness had shaved but half his face, and in that unusual condition had entered his classes, he had thought best to leave well enough alone. For the rest, the abstraction of professors is proverbial, and need not be dwelt on here, though upon one occasion he had lost his train by persisting in looking through the whole station at Bologna for a package he had in his hand.

Absent-minded people are generally very good-natured, but our professor was an exception to the rule. Ordinarily his lips were visited but by the scientific smile, made up of the superiority and commiseration with which a learned man hears of the absurdities committed by a brother colleague or the world at large. In society, upon the rare occasions he forced himself to enter it, he preferred standing aside, avoiding women with horror, for he had not the faintest idea what to say to them, and the dear creatures themselves were equally at a loss what to say to him, though five or six years ago, owing to the scarcity of husbands in this vale of tears, more than one mother had cast her eyes over him as a convenient parti for one of her daughters.

So at one time the Countess Pastori had been brave enough to invite him to dinner, hoping to make him marry her second daughter, who had bad teeth and weak eyes, and had not found any one who would have her. The young girl, properly coached, had received the professor with marked deference, had prepared with her own hand an exquisite peach marmalade, and had even gone to the length of evincing interest in Finnish roots. Cernieri, however, did not take the bait; but, at once on guard, shortened his visit, and was careful never to set foot inside the doors of the Pastori mansion until the little Countess was betrothed to an importer of salt fish, who joined the cultivation of salmon with veneration for the titled nobility.

So warned by experience, he became gruffer than before, and more than ever inaccessible to any ideas of gallantry.

Every man has in the book of his life a secret page that a woman has made joyous or gloomy; as far as Professor Cernieri was concerned, this page had remained a blank. At least so his friends said; so would he have answered himself had he been asked, and he would have spoken in good faith. Absorbed as he was in research, he forgot things near at hand. Oh, why must he be made to remember the distant past?

. . . .

"Mercy on us!" exclaimed Pomponio, who had begun to take the books out of the box. "Mercy on us, what a dust!" Then added: "Really it would be much better if you would let me take them all downstairs, and dust them there."

But the Professor vigorously opposed the proposition. He wished it all to take place in his study, under his own eyes. He wanted, after they were dusted, himself to put the books in a case ready for their reception. And Pomponio, resigned to the inevitable, continued taking them out, dusting them as best he could, and handing them to his master, who, having glanced at the titles, put them in place.

The air was surcharged with dust, which covered the furniture, penetrated the pores, making both master and servant cough and sneeze constantly. "There is a spider's web on this," said Pomponio as he lifted a large folio. It proved to be an antique atlas of the world, printed at Gotha by Justus Perthès; and it so happened that while the man was dusting it a little square envelope, yellowed with age, dropped from its leaves and fell upon the floor.

"Gracious, what is that?" said Pomponio. "It looks like a letter." And putting down the atlas, he stooped to pick it up.

But the Professor had anticipated him, and, half-dazed, was turning the letter round and round. Without doubt it *was* a letter, and one of his own at that, still sealed, the stamp uncancelled, addressed in his own writing; the heavy, weighty writing of a man born to be a cavaliere of many orders; a fellow of many societies. It was a too distinct hand, giving assurance that the letter would reach its destination if it had been posted!

"Alla gentile Signorina Maria Lisa Altavilla, Firenze, Via dei Servi, No. 25—1 Floor."

That name appearing so unexpectedly under his eyes carried Professor Cernieri back twenty years, forcing from the mists of oblivion a slender, graceful girl, whose lovely countenance was crowned with an expression of rare sweetness. For her alone had his heart ever quickened. For her sake alone had he once for one day, for an hour, thought seriously of taking a wife. And then?—

Pomponio, who was consumed with curiosity, had noiselessly approached the professor and murmured: "But how in the world did it get hidden in that book?"

Cernieri turned bruskly—"What business have you here? Leave the room."

"Shall I not go on?"

"No, not now. Go away."

"Has anything happened?"

"Nothing. If I need you, I will ring."

Pomponio reluctantly retired. He would have given anything to know what sort of a letter that was which had so disturbed his employer.

When he was gone, the Professor sat down in his great armchair, and, with trembling fingers, broke the seal that Maria Lisa Altavilla had never been allowed to do. And this was what he had written in Padua, October 15, 1875:

"Cara Signorina—I have just received the sad announcement, and hasten to assure you of my sincere sympathy in your great grief. Last July, when I had the honour in Venice of being often with your father and yourself, I was a witness of your solicitude for that precious, highly esteemed soul.

"Do you remember (I can never forget it) that morning's trip to the sea? We had first visited San Lazzaro, where he had been good enough to listen with interest to my explanation in regard to the mummy preserved in the Museum of the Mechitaristi Fathers; then having crossed to Sant' Elizabeth on the Lido, we repaired to the baths lately established there. Your father, feeling rather tired, remained in the hotel with a friend while we went to walk on the beach.

"The day was deliciously balmy, the sun's rays tempered behind little clouds, so that you closed your red silk umbrella. The wavelets lapped the shore softly at our feet where our footprints marked the sand. You confided to me that for several years your father's health seemed to grow worse; how the various doctors, who had been called in, had suggested this remedy and that without being at all able to arrest the course of the disease, which was overwhelming you with terror. You told me of the tender affection that led him to hide his suffering from you; he who had never before concealed anything. Growing more confidential, you told me of your happy home life, of the full accord of your mutual thoughts and feelings, of your deep love each for the other, cemented by sorrow; for, from a large family, there now remained but you two in the world. Then, overcome by emotion, you ceased speaking, your eyes full of tears.

"What words struggled for utterance on my part! I cannot express all that was in my heart. I am naturally timid, and I will acknowledge a great horror of anything that will distract me from my studies or interfere with my habits; but I feel sure I made you understand, Signorina, how deeply I sympathised with you. I know I told you I was at your service whenever you might choose to call upon me. 'Thanks,' you murmured gently while your hand trembled in mine. Then you insisted upon going back to your father.

"We spoke no word as we went, but it seemed to me that our souls understood one another. In a day or two you had quitted Venice without my having the opportunity of seeing you again alone.

"Now, Signorina, the greatest of sorrows has come to you. Now is the time for you to test the true value of your friends.

"I would wish to come myself to Florence, but I am forced to leave in a few hours for London, in order to be present at the Congress of Orientalists, which opens there on the 19th inst.

"From England I may possibly start on a long journey out of Europe. My movements will depend upon you; one word from you will take me back to Italy. In any event, I shall be in London all October, and I beg you will let me have a line from you, Poste Restante. Think that I, too, and for a much longer period than you, have been alone in the world. Believe me always, yours sincerely,

"ATTILIO CERNIERI."

Twice the Professor read the four pages through, forcing himself to recall the day, the hour, the place in which he had written it; seeking to explain to himself how he could have forgotten to post it, as well as that the absolute silence of Maria Lisa Altavilla had not aroused some suspicion in his mind; why he had never written again to make sure. And this is what he remembered.

The mortuary notice had arrived one morning as he was in the midst of packing, and his thoughts had turned persistently to the young girl he had known three months before in Venice, and who had shown such perfect confidence in him. All day he had debated within himself whether he should merely send her his condolences or if he ought to say something more in regard to the sentiments with which she had inspired him, in which perhaps she shared. She was not an ordinary girl, this Maria Lisa. She seemed created to be the companion of a scholar.

Had she not been her father's secretary and could she not be his? To learn two or three languages so that she might help him; to take notes for him; to keep his work in order; to correct printer's proofs, and when he was leaving for a congress or scientific mission, to pack his trunks and accompany him to the station; perhaps sometimes go along to look after the nuisance of tickets, to treat with hotel proprietors, cabmen, et cetera. Viewed in this light, matrimony did not seem such a terrible abyss, but a tranquil port, in which to take shelter from storms. And that evening, at the same time with other letters, he had written that one to Maria Lisa; had written with an expansion and an abandon that had filled him with wonder; even now he was amazed, as he felt once again the unaccustomed sweetness of the thing.

Once again he was in his little room in his apartment at Padua; on the table an oil lamp was burning; spread out before him lay the atlas of Menke at the page that told of "Egyptus ante Cambysii tempus." He had been consulting it before answering his friend Morrison of the University of Edinburgh, who was insisting that they should together visit the ruins of Thebes in Upper Egypt, and he leaving his decision until after the Congress had, on the chance of the journey, corrected and amplified the itinerary to take in Ithaca, Apollonapolis, Syene, and then Cernieri remembered his landlady had knocked at his door to tell him the carriage was there and that she had already put his luggage, his plaid, and his umbrella in. He had shut the atlas and put it back upon the shelf hurriedly, hurriedly he had pushed the letters already stamped into his pocket ; hurriedly had rushed down and thrown himself into the cab.

By what strange fate had one of the letters been shut in the atlas ? By what carelessness, in putting the rest in the mail-box, had he not noticed that one was missing, the most important of all, was an enigma the learned professor was unable to solve. He was ready to swear that never for an instant had the thought occurred to him that he had not posted the letter ; indeed, he remembered, how for a number of days he was dumbfounded at his own rashness.

Why had he not considered the matter more fully ? Why, with one of those words which cannot be taken back, had he run the risk of sacrificing that greatest of blessings—independence ? Why had he played all his future on one card ? He was a man of honour ; had he received a favourable reply from Maria Lisa, nothing would have induced him to draw back. If she said no, then he had invited a needless repulse.

Dio buono, what madness had taken possession of him ? It was more than likely that a girl, who was not beautiful and hadn't a penny of dot, would remain single for two or three years at least and then he could have sought opportunities of seeing her and knowing her better, and of weighing the pros and cons.

So during the first week in London, while the temptation was increasing for the journey to the Orient with Morrison and a young " docente " from Heidelberg, who had offered himself as a companion, he was upset and nervous, and trembled at every distribution of letters, not knowing what he wished or feared. Then as time passed and he read his two theses, and became absorbed in the work of the Congress and drawn within the circle of illustrious scholars, who were greeting him as a new luminary in the world of science, the image of the poor absent orphan faded gradually away and a secret hope sprang up in his heart that he had regained his liberty through the continued silence of Maria Lisa without the humiliation of a refusal.

He could always remember he had done his duty; it was not his fault if his offer had not been accepted.

So one day, early in November, he could exclaim with Julius Caesar:

"Alea jacta est."

A rapid flight through Europe brought him with his companions to Brindisi, whence they embarked for Alexandria. Two years were passed in Upper Egypt and Abyssinia in the study of hieroglyphics and ruins, and in sending learned treatises to the principal European Reviews. Magazines, journals, letters from men of science, elections to academies poured in from Italy, from France, from Germany; some silly letters even came from his landlady in Padua. From Florence, from Maria Lisa Altavilla, not a word. Then when he got home, he almost forgot all about her. Only two years had passed, but they were worth a century to him, and preceding events assumed to his eyes a vague, nebulous distance. So when he had heard that three months before Maria Lisa had married a "Pretore residente" in an out-of-the-way corner of Sicily, he had not troubled himself more than he could help about it. He had to choose from the various offers of the Ministry, he had to write an article for the *Edinburgh Review* on Assyrian Antiquties; finally, he had to finish a weighty thesis on those Finnish and Celtic roots, for whose sake he had resolved to devote himself entirely to philology at the expense of everything else.

Maria Lisa was so small in comparison, and matrimony might have been such a nuisance. Only some time afterward, as he was on the point of accepting a Chair in Florence, he was assailed with scruples.

Suppose through the changing of her husband's jurisdiction the lady were now in Tuscany? How ought he to act? To seem indifferent and pretend not to recognise her, or to reproach her with the rudeness with which she had treated him?

Alas! the professor was soon relieved of all doubts.

La Maria Lisa Altavilla? the daughter of the Chevalier Altavilla? Who had married the pretore Carlucci? Poor thing! she had died in Sicily of malarial fever before she had been married more than ten months.

Dead! Attilio Cernieri felt penetrated through with pity and regret. Dead, so young; she, who might have been his wife! Then he would now be alone with his life all wrecked about him! Ah! it was indeed a thousand times better that Maria Lisa had not answered him! Better not to have gotten into habits that would now have to be broken! Better not to have grown accustomed to having a woman by his side. Those who know declare it is difficult to do without them then.

In a word, Cernieri had not been slow to comfort himself. And then, too, Time had fulfilled her part, spreading a thick veil over the fleeting episode; covering even the name of Maria Lisa with oblivion.

Now the old letter found within the pages of the ancient atlas had brought it all back. Before the middle-aged man, grown old in study, hardened with egotism, rose an enchanting picture of youth, clothed in shining colours, full of intangible sweetness. Pressing the poor, little yellow sheet between his hands, he beheld once more Maria Lisa's sweet face. As she sadly gazed at him she seemed to say: "Why in my hour of need did you not send me a word of sympathy? Chance acquaintances pitied my grief; thou, who hadst let me believe didst love me, alone remained mute and insensible. I called upon thee too. Ah! wretched indeed is she who trusts in a man!"

Cernieri seemed to hear Maria Lisa's voice pronounce the words.

And she had died without hearing his vindication, without knowing the truth. It is indeed "Sorrow's crown of sorrow," to be faded with the irrevocable, to be tormented with wrongs that cannot be repaired, with misunderstandings that cannot be removed.

But the letter, which the grave professor continued to hold unfolded before him, told, not only that Maria Lisa was dead, believing him worse than he deserved, but also that in his life there had been a moment of poetry, of abandon, and of love, and that that moment had remained barren. Never again could life bring him such another. Never again would his heart quicken for a woman's sake. Never again could flow from his pen words which might seem to us cold and conventional, but to him seemed burning with ardour and love. And he asked himself: "Suppose the letter had gone, had arrived at its destination and Maria Lisa had answered: 'I understand what thou wishest; I consent. I love thee and am willing to be thine. Come.'"

Then certainly, he would not have undertaken his great journey to Egypt and Assyria. Would not have deciphered hieroglyphics or interpreted the language of the ruins. Perhaps, though, he would have had sons of his own. Perhaps domestic cares might have retarded his fame, his activity might have been clogged and honours and decorations might not have fallen so abundantly upon his head. He might not even have made his luminous discovery about the Finnish roots. Perchance another would now occupy his enviable position on the very top of the scientific pyramid by the side of Lowenstein of the University of Upsala. If all that might have happened, a man like Professor Attilio Cernieri ought to rejoice that it had not. And still—and still! —A persistent, hungry doubt would not allow him to quiet his soul with this philosophic consolation. Would it not have been better to have sacrificed a little glory to have had a little love?

The Professor Attilio Cernieri lacked courage to tear or destroy the letter. He placed it in his desk, recalled Pomponio, and desired him to resume his interrupted labour.

But that evening in his study, the temptation to again behold those words of twenty years ago overcame him anew. And afterward there did not pass a day in which he did not take the poor little worn sheet from its envelope and read it over and over.

Then he would look at the envelope, at the stamp, upon which the Post had impressed no mark, and murmur once more:

"If the letter had only gone!"

THE THEOREM OF PYTHAGORAS

ENRICO CASTELNUOVO

"THE forty-seventh proposition!" said Professor Roveni, in a tone of mild sarcasm, as he unfolded a paper which I had extracted, very gingerly, from an urn standing on his desk. Then he showed it to the Government Inspector who stood beside him, and whispered something into his ear. Finally, he handed me the document, so that I might read the question with my own eyes.

"Go up to the blackboard," added the Professor, rubbing his hands.

The candidate who had preceded me in the arduous trial, and had got out of it as best he could, had left the school-room on tip-toe, and, in opening the door, let in a long streak of sunshine, which flickered on wall and floor, and in which I had the satisfaction of seeing my shadow. The door closed again, and the room was once more plunged into twilight. It was a stifling day in August, and the great sun-blinds of blue canvas were a feeble defence against the glass, so that the Venetian shutters had been closed as well. The little light which remained was concentrated on the master's desk and the blackboard, and was, at any rate, sufficient to illuminate my defeat.

"Go to the blackboard and draw the figure," repeated Professor Roveni, perceiving my hesitation.

Tracing the figure was the only thing I knew how to do; so I took a piece of chalk and conscientiously went to work. I was in no hurry; the more time I took up in this graphic part, the less remained for oral explanation.

But the Professor was not the man to lend himself to my innocent artifice.

"Make haste," he said. "You are not going to draw one of Raphael's Madonnas."

I had to come to an end.

"Put the letters now. Quick!—you are not giving specimens of handwriting. Why did you erase that G?"

"Because it is too much like the C I have made already. I was going to put an H instead of it."

" What a subtle idea ! " observed Roveni, with his usual irony. " Have you finished ? "

" Yes, sir," said I ; adding under my breath, " More's the pity ! "

" Come,—why are you standing there moonstruck ? Enunciate the theorem ! "

Then began my sorrows. The terms of the question had escaped my memory.

" In a triangle . . . " I stammered.

" Go on."

I took courage and said all I knew.

" In a triangle . . . the square of the hypothenuse is equal to the squares of the other two sides."

" In any triangle ? "

" No, no ! " suggested a compassionate soul behind me.

" No, sir ! " said I.

" Explain yourself. In what sort of a triangle ? "

" A right-angled triangle," whispered the prompting voice.

" A right-angled triangle," I repeated, like a parrot.

" Silence there, behind ! " shouted the Professor ; and then continued, turning to me, " Then, according to you, the big square is equal to each of the smaller ones ? "

Good gracious ! the thing was absurd. But I had a happy inspiration.

" No, sir, to both of them added together."

" To the sum then,—say to the sum. And you should say *equivalent*, not equal. Now demonstrate."

I was in a cold perspiration—icy cold—despite the tropical temperature. I looked stupidly at the right-angled triangle, the square of the hypothenuse, and its two subsidiary squares ; I passed the chalk from one hand to the other and back again, and said nothing, for the very good reason that I had nothing to say.

No one prompted me any more. It was so still you might have heard a pin drop. The Professor fixed his grey eyes on me, bright with a malignant joy ; the Government Inspector was making notes on a piece of paper. Suddenly the latter respectable personage cleared his throat, and Professor Roveni said in his most insinuating manner, " Well ? "

I did not reply.

Instead of at once sending me about my business, the Professor wished to imitate the cat which plays with the mouse before tearing it to pieces.

" How ? " he added. " Perhaps you are seeking a new solution. I do not say that such may not be found, but we shall be quite satisfied with one of the old ones. Go on. Have you forgotten that you ought to produce the two sides, DE, MF, till they meet ? Produce them—go on ! "

I obeyed mechanically. The figure seemed to attain a gigantic size, and weighed on my chest like a block of stone.

" Put a letter at the point where they meet—an N. So. And now ? "

I remained silent.

" Don't you think it necessary to draw a line down from N through A to the base of the square, BHIC ? "

I thought nothing of the kind ; however, I obeyed.

" Now you will have to produce the two sides, BH and IC."

Ouf ! I could endure no more.

" Now," the Professor went on, " a child of two could do the demonstration. Have you nothing to observe with reference to the two triangles, BAC and NAE ? "

As silence only prolonged my torture, I replied laconically, " Nothing."

" In other words, you know nothing at all ? "

" I think you ought to have seen that some time ago," I replied, with a calm worthy of Socrates.

" Very good, very good ! Is that the tone you take ? And don't you even know that the theorem of Pythagoras is also called the Asses' Bridge, because it is just the asses who cannot get past it ? You can go. I hope you understand that you have not passed in this examination. That will teach you to read *Don Quixote* and draw cats during my lessons ! "

The Government Inspector took a pinch of snuff ; I laid down the chalk and the duster, and walked majestically out of the hall, amid the stifled laughter of my school-fellows.

Three or four comrades who had already passed through the ordeal with no very brilliant result were waiting for me outside.

" Ploughed, then ? "

" Ploughed ! " I replied, throwing myself into an attitude of heroic defiance ; adding presently, " I always said that mathematics were only made for dunces."

"Of course!" exclaimed one of my rivals.

"What question did you have?" asked another.

"The forty-seventh proposition. What can it matter to me whether the square of the hypothenuse is or is not equal to the sum of the squares of the two sides?"

"Of course it can't matter to you—nor to me—nor to any one in the world," chimed in a third with all the petulant ignorance of fourteen. "If it is equal, why do they want to have it repeated so often? and if it is not, why do they bother us with it?"

"Believe me, you fellows," said I, resuming the discussion with the air of a person of long experience, "you may be quite certain of it, the whole system of instruction is wrong; and as long as the Germans are in the country, it will be so!"

So, being fully persuaded that our failure was a protest against the Austrian dominion, and a proof of vivid and original genius, we went home, where, for my part, I confess I found that the first enthusiasm soon evaporated.

My ignominious failure in this examination had a great influence on my future. Since it was absolutely impossible for me to understand mathematics, it was decided that very day that I was to leave school, especially as the family finances made it necessary for me to begin earning something as soon as might be.

It was the most sensible resolution that could have been come to, and I had no right to oppose it; yet, I confess, I was deeply saddened by it. My aversion to mathematics did not extend to other branches of learning, in which I had made quite a respectable show; and besides, I loved the school. I loved those sacred cloisters which we boys filled with life and noise,—I loved the benches carved with our names,—even the blackboard which had been the witness of my irreparable defeat.

I blamed Pythagoras' theorem for it all. With some other question—who knows?—I might just have scraped through, by the skin of my teeth, as I had done in past years. But, as Fate would have it, it was just that one!

I dreamt about it all night. I saw it before me—the fatal square with its triangle atop, and the two smaller squares, one sloping to the right, and the other to the left, and a tangle of lines, and a great confusion of letters; and heard beating through my head like the strokes of a hammer—BAC = NAF; RNAB = DEAB.

It was some time before I was free from that nightmare and could forget Pythagoras and his three squares. In the long run, however, Time, who with his sponge wipes out so many things from the book of memory, had nearly effaced this, when, a few weeks ago, the ill-omened figure appeared to me in one of my son's exercise-books.

"Has this curse been transmitted to my descendants?" I exclaimed. "Poor boy! What if the theorem of Pythagoras should be as fatal to him as it has been to me?"

I thought I would question him about it on his return from school.

"So," I began gravely, "you have already reached the forty-seventh proposition of Euclid in your geometry?"

"Yes, father," he replied simply.

"A difficult theorem," I added, shaking my head.

"Do you think so?" he asked with a smile.

"Oh! you want to boast and make me think you find it easy?"

"But I do find it easy."

"I should like to see you try it"—the words slipped out almost involuntarily. "It's no use—I can't bear vanity and boasting."

"At once," replied the dauntless youth. And action succeeded words. He took a piece of paper and a pencil, and quickly traced the cabalistic figure.

"As for demonstrations," he began, "there are plenty to choose from. Is it all the same to you which I take?"

"Yes," I replied mechanically. In fact it *had* to be all the same to me. If there had been a hundred demonstrations I should not have known one from the other.

"Then we'll take the most usual one," my mathematician went on; and proceeded to produce the lines which Professor Roveni, of respected memory, had made me produce twenty-seven years before, and, with the accents of the sincerest conviction, prepared to prove to me that the triangle BAC was equal to the triangle NAF, and so on.

"And now," said my son, when he had finished, "we can, if you wish, arrive at the same conclusion in another way."

"For pity's sake!" I exclaimed in terror, "since we have reached the journey's end, let us rest."

"But I am not tired."

Not even tired! Was the boy an embryo Newton? And yet people talk about the principle of heredity!

"I suppose you are at the top of your class in mathematics," I said, not untouched by a certain reverential awe.

" No, no," he replied. " There are two better than I. Besides, you know very well that everybody—except downright asses—understands the forty-seventh proposition."

" *Except downright asses!*" After twenty-seven years I heard, from the lips of my own son, almost the very identical words which Professor Roveni had used on the memorable day of the examination. And this time they were heightened by the savage irony of the added " *You know very well!*"

I wished to save appearances, and added in haste—

" Of course I know that. I was only in fun. I hope you would not be such a fool as to be proud of a small thing like that."

Meanwhile, however, my Newton had repented of his too sweeping assertion.

" After all," he went on, with some embarrassment, " there are some who never attend to their lesson, and then . . . even if they are not asses. . . ."

It seemed to me that he was offering me a loophole of escape, and with a sudden impulse of candour—

" That must be the way of it," I said. " I suppose I never paid attention."

" How! You? " exclaimed my boy, reddening to the roots of his hair. Yet . . . I would bet something that, at the bottom of his heart, he was longing to laugh.

I put my hand over his mouth.

" Hush," I said; " we will not pursue our inquiries into detail."

Well, the Theorem of Pythagoras has, as you see, cost me a new and very serious humiliation. In spite of this, I no longer keep up the old grudge. There will never be any confidence between us, but I consider it as a family friend whom we must not treat with rudeness, though he may not be personally congenial to ourselves.

LUIGI CAPUANA
1839–

THE RIVAL EARTHQUAKES

THERE was a long-standing rivalry—and one that was not professional alone—between the telegraph clerks of Pietranera and Golastretta. It is said to have begun at the Technical College, when the former carried off a silver medal hotly contested by the other ; but this is not quite certain.

What is certain is that Pippo Corradi could not undertake the smallest thing but Nino d'Arco immediately proceeded to do likewise. Thus when the former took a fancy to become an amateur conjurer, Nino at once went in search of the necessary apparatus for amusing his friends with the miracles of white magic. He was not a success ; he raised many a laugh by his want of skill ; but this did not prevent him from throwing away more money still on boxes with false bottoms, pistols to shoot playing cards instead of balls, wonderful balls which multiply and grow larger in your hands, and the like. Cost what it might, he was determined to astonish his Golastretta friends, who extolled in his presence the portents they had seen accomplished at Pietranera by Corradi, and derided him by way of contrast.

Then when Pippo Corradi, who was of a strange fickleness in his tastes, gave up white magic in order to devote himself to music, and the study of the clarionet in particular, Nino d'Arco suddenly laid aside the magic toys, which had already wearied him not a little, took music lessons from the parish organist, bought a brand new ebony clarionet, and rode over on a donkey to call on Corradi, under the pretext of consulting him on his choice, but with the sole intention of humiliating him. It was the only time he ever succeeded. He found him blowing into the mouthpiece of a boxwood instrument, which he had bought second-hand for a few francs from an old clarionet player in the town band. Nino swelled visibly with satisfaction at seeing the admiration and envy in his rival's eyes when he opened the leather case and showed him the polished keys of white metal, shining even more than the freshly varnished wood.

Nino put the instrument together delicately, and set it to his mouth, thinking to astonish Pippo with a scale in semitones, but he unluckily broke down in the middle. Then was Corradi able to take his revenge; and not content with having played scales in all tones, major, minor, diatonic, and chromatic, suddenly, without warning Nino, who kept staring at his fingers manœuvring over the holes and keys, he dashed point-blank into his *pièce de résistance, La Donna è Mobile,* tootling away quite divinely, till checked by the imperative need of taking breath. His eyes were nearly starting out of his head; his face was purple—but that was nothing! He chuckled inwardly at Nino's crestfallen look; and the latter, taking his instrument to pieces, put it back in the case, thus declaring himself vanquished.

Nino, returning to Golastretta, vented his vexation on his ass, because she would not go at a trot—just as though it had been she who taught Corradi to play *La Donna è Mobile.* So true it is that passion renders man unjust! He rushed at once to his master to learn *La Donna è Mobile* for himself, so as to be able, in a short time, to play it before his hated rival. The latter, however, had another great advantage, besides that of being able to murder *Rigoletto*; he was the local post-master. In this point it was useless trying to rival him, however much Nino might dream of a spacious office, like that at Pietranera, where Corradi, between the sale of one stamp and the next, between registering a letter, and administering a reprimand to the postman, could divert himself by blowing into his clarionet to his heart's content! Whereas he, Nino, was forced to escape from the house if he wished to practise and remain at peace with his family! Corradi, in his post-office, disturbed no one.

Nino did not know what a torment for the neighbourhood that clarionet was, shrilling from morning to night, with Corradi's usual obstinacy in anything he undertook. The shopkeeper opposite, poor wretch, swore all day long worse than a Turk, and did not know whether he was standing on his head or his feet every time that Pippo began to repeat the *Donna è Mobile*—that is to say, swore seven or eight times in the day. He made mistakes in his weights, he counted his change wrong;—though it is only fair to say that these errors were oftener in his own favour than in that of his customers. And if by any chance he saw Corradi at the window, he raised his hands towards him with a supplicating gesture, pretending to be jocular.

"You want to make me die of a fit! Good Lord!"

Of all this Nino d'Arco was quite ignorant when he started for

Pietranera a month later, to surprise Corradi with *Mira Norma*, which he had learnt, in addition to the air which first roused his emulation. He found Pippo adding up his monthly accounts, and not disposed to talk about music or anything else. The fact was that the shopkeeper opposite had indeed fallen down dead in a fit at the third or fourth rendering of *La Donna è Mobile*, as he had said, just as though he had had a presentiment of what was to happen. The occurrence had such an effect on Pippo that he felt as if he had killed the man, and could not bear to touch the clarionet again. He would not even mention the subject. Nino bit his lips and returned home, without having so much as opened his clarionet case. Once more it was the ass who paid the penalty. He had to relieve his feelings on some one or something.

If there were any need of an instance to prove that emulation is the most powerful agent in the development of the human faculties, this one would suffice. Seeing that Corradi had renounced the clarionet and all its delights, Nino no longer felt the slightest inclination to go on wasting his breath on his instrument, though it were of ebony, with keys of white metal. As a faithful historian, I ought to add that for one moment he was tempted by the idea of trying to attain to the glory of causing some one's death by a fit; but whether the Golastretta people had harder tympanums than those of Pietranera, or whether he himself was not possessed of the necessary strength and perseverance, certain it is that no human victim fell to Nino d'Arco's clarionet. And the fact of having no death on his conscience made him feel degraded in his own eyes for some time.

These had been the preludes to deeper and more difficult contests with his old schoolfellow.

Golastretta was situated between the central office of the province and the rival station of Pietranera; and thus it was Nino's duty to signal to his hated colleague the mean time by which he was to regulate his clock—a supremacy which Corradi could never take from him. But this was a joy of short duration.

Having very little to do, he was wont, after he had finished reading the *Gazette* or the last paper-covered novel, to snatch forty winks at his ease in the office. One morning, when he least expected it, the machine began clicking, and would not stop. It was his dear friend at Pietranera who kept sending despatches on despatches, and would not let him drop off comfortably.

By listening attentively, he soon made out what was the matter. The village of Pietranera had begun, on the previous evening, to dance like a man bitten by the tarantula, set in motion by earthquake-shocks repeated from hour to hour. The Syndic was telegraphing to the Vice-Prefect, the Prefect, the Meteorological Office of the province, in the name of the terrified population. And Corradi, too, was telegraphing on his own account, signalling the shocks as fast as they occurred, and indicating their length, or the nature of the movement—in order to gain credit with his superiors, said Nino d'Arco, vexed that Golastretta should not have its half-dozen earthquakes as well.

How cruelly partial was Nature! Scarcely twenty kilometres away she was rendering Corradi an immense service with eight, ten, twenty shocks—between day and night—within the week; and for him not even the smallest vestige of any shock whatever. He could get no peace, and kept his ear to the instrument.

One day, behold! there passed the announcement of a scientific commission on its way to Pietranera in order to study these persistent seismic phenomena. A few days later he became aware of the transit of another despatch appointing the Pietranera telegraph-agent director of the Meteorologico-Seismic station, which the commission had thought it advisable to establish at that place. In a month from that time the speedy arrival of a large number of scientific instruments was wired down from headquarters.

Nino d'Arco could stand it no longer; nothing would serve but he must go and see with his own eyes what under the canopy that Meteorologico-Seismic Observatory could be which would not let him live in peace.

He could not recover from the astonishment into which he was thrown by the sight of all these machines already set up in position, whose strange names Pippo Corradi reeled off with the greatest ease, as he explained the working of each. Rain-gauge, wind-gauge, barometers, maximum and minimum thermometers, hygrometers, and besides that a tromometer, and all sorts of devilries for marking the very slightest shocks of earthquake, indicating their nature, and recording the very hour at which they occurred, by means of stop-watches. . . . Nino was very far from understanding it all, but made believe to do so; and, at last, he remained quite a time gazing through a magnifying-glass at the pendulum constructed to register the movements of the earthquake by marking them with a sharp point on a sheet of smoked glass placed beneath it. . . . The pendulum was at that moment moving, sometimes from right to left, sometimes backwards and forwards, but with so imperceptible a movement that it could not be discerned by the naked eye. . . . Suddenly—*drin! drin!*—there is a ringing of bells, the pendulum quivers. . . .

"A shock!" And Pippo, triumphant, rushes to the telegraph instrument to announce it.

"I did not feel anything!" said Nino d'Arco, white with terror.

And he hastened to go. But he was simply knocked to pieces by all those machines and the satisfied air of his colleague. The latter already signed himself "Director of the Meteorologico-Seismic Observatory at Pietranera," and seemed a great personage—reflected Nino—even to him, who knew very well who he was, a telegraph clerk just like himself!

All along the homeward road, when he had finished settling accounts with the ass, he ruminated over the hundreds of francs which all that apparatus must have cost. . . . The seismographic pendulum, however, was only worth eighteen. . . . He would like to have at least a pendulum. . . . What would he do with it when he had it? No one could tell; least of all himself. But the pendulum kept vibrating in his brain all the week, backwards and forwards, right and left, scratching the smoked glass at every stroke. Nino seemed to himself to be always standing behind the magnifying-glass, as he had done at Pietranera. It was a diabolical persecution!

He had to humble himself before his detested colleague, in order to get information, explanations and instruments; but after all, in the end, the pendulum was there in its place, near the office window. It had cost him nearly half his month's salary. But what of that? Now, he too could telegraph the most beautiful earthquakes, on occasion.

But just look at the perversity of things! That infamous pendulum—as if on purpose to spite him—remained perfectly motionless, even if one looked at it through the magnifying-glass. Nino, who passed whole days ruining his eyes with that glass, anxious to observe the first trace of movement, so as to signal it, and thus begin his competition with the Pietranera observatory, ground his teeth with rage. Especially on the days when his fortunate rival seemed to be mocking him with the ticking of the messages which announced to the Provincial Office some little shock recorded by the instruments at Pietranera. For an earthquake—a real earthquake—Nino would have given, who can tell what? perhaps his very soul. In the meantime he dreamt of earthquakes, often awaking terrified in the night, uncertain whether it were a dream, or the shock had really taken place; but the pendulum remained stern and immovable. It was enough to drive the veriest saint desperate. Ah! Was that the game? Did the earthquakes obstinately refuse to manifest themselves? Well, he would invent them. After all, who could contradict him? And so that unlucky parish, which had been for centuries quietly anchored to the rocky mountain-side, began to perform in its turn—in the Reports of the Meteorological Office at Rome—an intricate dance of shocks, slight shocks, and approaches to shocks; there was no means of keeping it still any longer. And as Nino could not forego the glory of showing his friends the sheet where his name appeared in print beside those of several famous men of science, the report spread through the country that the mountain was moving, imperceptibly, and threatened to come down in a landslip.

"Is it really true?" the most timid came to ask.

"True, indeed!" replied Nino solemnly, and pointed to the pendulum; but he would allow no one to examine it at close quarters.

Just as though it had been done on purpose, the Pietranera observatory no longer signalled any disturbances since Golastretta had begun to amuse itself by frequent vibrations; and Pippo Corradi, suspecting the trick of his colleague, was gnawing his own heart out over all the false indications which were quietly being foisted in among the genuine ones of the official report, and making a mock of Science.

He, for his own part, did his work seriously and scrupulously, even leaving his dinner when the hour for observation came; and his reports might be called models of scientific accuracy. Ought he to denounce his colleague? to unmask him? He could not make up his mind. The latter, as bold as brass, went on making his village quake and tremble, as though it were nothing at all.

This time the proverb that "lies have short legs" did not hold good; for the lies in question reached Tacchini at Rome, and Father Denza at Moncalieri. Perhaps, even, they confused the calculations of those unfortunate scientists, who were very far from suspecting, in the remotest degree, the wickedness of Nino.

But one day, all of a sudden, the Golastretta pendulum awoke from its torpor, and began to move behind the magnifying-glass, although to the naked eye its motion was scarcely perceptible.

Nino gave a howl of joy. " At last ! at last ! "

To the first person who happened to come into the office he said, with a majestic sweep of the arm, " Look here ! "

" What does it mean ? "

" We shall have a big earthquake ! " and he rubbed his hands.

" Mercy ! "

The man, who had felt his head turning round with the continued agitation of the pendulum, and was struck with consternation to find that it could scarcely be perceived without the magnifier, rushed at once to spread the terrible news in streets, shops, and cafés. In an hour the telegraph office was invaded—besieged. Everybody wished to see with his or her own eyes, so as to be certain, and then take a resolution. And the people who had seen frightened the others with their accounts, exaggerating matters, giving explanations more terrifying than those they had received and half understood, and so increasing the panic, which now began to seize on the most sceptical spirits. An extraordinary success for Nino d'Arco ! He seemed to see before him the image of his colleague, jaundiced with envy, and again rubbed his hands with delight. Outside, the street was full of people discussing the affair with comments. Women were crying, boys shouting, " Is it still moving ? " " Worse than before." " Oh ! blessed Madonna ! " The parish priest hastened to the spot, frightened as badly as the rest by the news which had been carried to him by the sacristan ; and scarcely had he looked through the glass than he sprang from his chair as if he had felt the ground rocking under his feet.

" It is the judgment of God, gentlemen ! On account of our sins, gentlemen ! "

Then the people began to get away as fast as they could.

There was a banging of shutters, a hurried closing of doors, a rushing about, a shouting of each other's names. " Is it still moving ? " " Worse than ever ! " So that at last Nino d'Arco himself no longer felt easy. And from time to time he turned back to look once more at the pendulum, which continued to vibrate. It was the first time that Nino found himself indeed, as it were, face to face with a distinct indication of earthquake, after the hundred or so of shocks, of all sorts, strengths, and sizes, which he had invented and caused to be published in the Report at Rome. And now it was not exactly an amusing thing —that dumb menace, to which his ignorance gave a false significance. Pendulum of the devil ! Would it never be still ? A beautiful invention of science, calculated to kill a peaceful citizen with anticipatory fear! Who ever heard of the earth being shaken without people becoming aware of it?

It seemed to him that the vibrations increased from hour to hour, and that the danger of a general fall of buildings became more imminent every minute. He was alone in the office,—there was not a soul to be seen in the street,—every one had left the village, to seek safety in the open plain. And his duty, as telegraph operator, forbade him to move!

Towards evening he closed the office, and went out into the plain himself. The people were standing about in groups, telling their beads and chanting litanies. When they saw him they were near falling upon him, as the cause of the mischief. Was it not he who had turned the whole village upside down, with that accursed pendulum of his? The whole scene had a depressing effect on him, however much he might try to keep up his courage, and convince his fellow-townsmen of the great benefits of his warning, which might, for all they knew, have been the saving of many lives.

But at noon on the following day nothing had yet happened.

Every quarter of an hour some one of the bravest came in from the country to the telegraph office, to find out how things were going. The pendulum still vibrated—but there were no news of the predicted earthquake.

The evening came. Not the ghost of an earthquake! A few here and there began to turn the thing into ridicule. The syndic—who had a head on his shoulders—had sent a boy to the Pietranera. When the boy returned with Pippo Corradi's answer, "It's all nonsense—make your minds easy!" there was an explosion of "Oh!—oh!—oh!" and those who had been most frightened, and felt that they had been made fools of, began to yell, "Imbecile! Blockhead! Idiot!"

They rushed in a tumultuous noisy crowd to the telegraph office; and had they not met with the lieutenant of the Carbineers, who had hastened up on receipt of a cipher telegram from the chief constable, who knows how the matter might have ended for Nino d'Arco?

"What on earth have you been doing?" said the lieutenant. "You have been disturbing the public peace."

Nino was petrified for a moment; then, seeking to excuse himself by proof positive, pointed to the pendulum.

"Well?" said the lieutenant.

"Look—it moves!"

" You must be seeing double. There is nothing moving here."

" Do look carefully."

" Allow me. . . . Nothing moving ! "

In fact, the pendulum had stopped. Nino would not believe his own eyes.

" I confiscate it, for the present ! " cried the lieutenant.

And, raising the glass of the case, he took out the tube in which the pendulum was fixed.

" When one is as ignorant as you, sir, ..." Every one present applauded vigorously. " And I shall report the matter to head-quarters."

To Nino it mattered nothing that the crowd should applaud and hiss, or that the lieutenant of the Carbineers should report him at head-quarters. He was thinking only of Pippo Corradi, and how he would laugh behind his back when he heard it ; and the tears stood in his eyes.

And, as though all this had not been enough, behold, on the following day, the following message clicked along the wires from Corradi :

" To-day, 2 P.M., upward shock of first degree lasting three seconds ; followed, after interval of seven seconds, by undulatory shock, south-north, also first degree, lasting five seconds. No damage."

" Infamous fate ! " stammered Nino d'Arco. And he shut off the current, to escape from the clicks which seemed to deride him.

QUACQUARÀ

LUIGI CAPUANA

POOR Don Mario! No sooner was he seen coming round the corner with his rusty, narrow-brimmed, stove-pipe hat, nearly a foot high, and his overcoat with long tails fluttering in the wind, than every one—first the boys, then the men, the loafers on Piazza Buglio, and even the gentlemen at the Casino—began to salute him, on every side, with the cry of the quail, " *Quacquarà! Quacquarà!*" just because they knew that it enraged him.

He stopped and stood at bay, staring round, brandishing his great cudgel, and shaking his head threateningly. Then he would take two or three steps forward, looking fixedly at them, in order to discover one or other of the impudent wretches who so far forgot the respect due to him, the son and grandson of lawyers—to him who stood a hundred times higher than all those gentlemen of the Casino. . . . But in vain! On the right hand and the left, before and behind, rose the shouts and whistles, " *Quacquarà! Quacquarà!*"

" Don't excite yourself! Let them shout!"

" If I do not kill some one, they will never be quiet!"

" Do you want to go to the convict prison for nothing?"

" I will send them there!"

He became red as a turkey-cock, raving and gesticulating and foaming at the mouth.

" They would be quiet enough, if you did not get angry."

" They are cowards! Why don't they come out like men, and say it to my face?"

"*Quacquarà!*——"

" Ah! would you hit a child?" This time, if they had not stopped him, he would have broken the head of the barber's boy, who had boldly approached him near enough to utter the objectionable cry under his very nose. There was trouble enough before Don Mario would let himself be dragged away into the chemist's shop, which was filled with a laughing crowd. Vito, the chemist's young man, came forward, very seriously, and said to him:

"What does it matter if they *do* say *Quacquarà* to you? You don't happen to be a quail, do you?"

Don Mario turned furious eyes on him.

"Well; it's not as if they called you a thief!"

"I am a gentleman, and the son of a gentleman."

"Well? What does *Quacquarà* mean? Nothing at all. *Quacquarà* let it be!"

The chemist and the others present were writhing in convulsions of suppressed laughter at the serious countenance of Vito, who, under the pretext of lecturing Don Mario for his folly, kept on repeating the quail's cry to his very face, without his perceiving that it was done on purpose.

"Now I," said he, "if a man were to cry *Quacquarà* after me, I would give him a halfpenny every time. *Quacquarà! Quacquarà!* Shout yourselves hoarse, if you like!"

"And, meanwhile, you scoundrel, you're repeating it to my face," yelled Don Mario, as he raised his cudgel, perceiving at last that he had been made a fool of. At this point the chemist, who was terrified for the safety of his plate-glass windows, thought it time to interfere; and, taking his arm, drew him out of the shop, condoling with his grievances, and soothing his ruffled feelings as well as he could.

"Come out this way; no one will see you."

"Am I to hide myself? To please those louts? I am a gentleman, and the son of a gentleman!"

True—very true! The Majori had always been respectable people, son succeeding father in the notary's office from generation to generation, up to the year 1819; in which year there issued forth from the infernal regions that judgment of Heaven called the Code Napoléon, specially created for the despair of the notary Majori, Don Mario's father, who never could understand it, and was forced to retire from his profession.

"What? No more Latin formulas? . . . And documents to be headed 'In the King's Name'! But what has His Majesty the King to do with private contracts?"

And he relieved his conscience by having no more to do with the whole business. And so the ink had dried up in the great brass inkstand in his office, and the quill pens were all worn out; and the quiet in the house contrasted strangely with the bustle there had been formerly, when every one came to consult him, for he was honesty in person, and never set down on the papers a single word more or less than the interested parties wished. And thus Don Mario, who had hitherto acted as clerk in his father's office, and knew by heart all the Latin formulas, without understanding a syllable thereof, found his occupation gone. So did his brother Don Ignazio, who was not much more capable than himself; and after the old notary had died of a broken heart, on account of that unholy Code which had no Latin formulas, and insisted on having documents headed *In the King's Name*, the two brothers eked out a sordid livelihood on the little they inherited from him. But they were proud in their honourable poverty, and rigidly faithful to the past, even in their dress, continuing for a time to wear their old clothes, carefully brushed and mended, regardless of the fact that they were out of fashion and excited ridicule.

Don Ignazio, however, could not stand it long. When his beaver hat seemed to him quite useless, and his overcoat too threadbare, he bought a second-hand hat for a few pence from Don Saverio, the old clothes dealer, and a coat which had also been worn already, but presented a better appearance than his old one. Don Mario, on the other hand, stood firm, and went about in his rusty tall hat and long coat of half a century ago, shabby and darned, but without a spot. He was not going to derogate from his past—he, the son and grandson of notaries.

Then came hard times,—bad harvests,—the epidemic of 1837,—the cholera,—the revolution of '48;—and the two brothers passed disagreeable days and still more unpleasant nights, racking their brains for the means of procuring a glass of wine for the morrow, or a little oil for the salad or the soup.

"To-morrow I will go to So-and-so," Don Mario would say. "Meanwhile we must sweep out the house."

They did everything themselves; and while Don Ignazio cut up an onion to put into the evening's salad, Don Mario, in his father's indoor coat, all faded and mended, began carefully to sweep the rooms like a housemaid. He dusted the rickety tables and the old ragged, leather-covered arm-chairs; and then, having gathered up all the dirt into a basket, he would cautiously open the door, to make sure there was no one within sight, and, late at night, carried it out and deposited it behind the wall of a ruined house which had become the dust-bin of the neighbourhood.

And on the way he would pick up stones, cabbage-stumps, bits of orange or pumpkin-peel, so as to clean up the street also, seeing that no one troubled about it, every one being too much occupied with his or her own business to pay any attention to cleanliness. Cleanliness was his fixed idea—indoors and out. It often happened that Don Ignazio, finding that he was late in coming home, was forced to go out and call him in to supper.

" You are not the public scavenger, are you ? "

" Cleanliness is a commandment of the Lord ! " Don Mario would reply.

And, having washed his hands, he sat down to the meagre supper of onion salad and bread as if it had been the daintiest of dishes.

" This is Donna Rosa's oil ; and do you know there is no more left ?" said Don Ignazio one evening between two mouthfuls.

" To-morrow I will go to the Cavaliere ! "

" But his father was a peasant farmer ! "

" His grandfather was a day labourer ! "

" And now he is made of money ! "

" His grandfather became the Prince's agent—and made his fortune."

" Let us go to bed ; the light is going out."

They had to economise even their candles. But afterwards, in the dark, the interrupted conversation was continued—not very consecutively—from one bed to another.

" Have you seen the band in their new uniforms ? "

" Yes. . . . Farmer Cola has got in a hundred bushels of grain this year."

" Who knows if it is true ? Much good may it do him ! "

" To-morrow I will go to the Cavaliere for some oil. . . ."

" The wine is all gone, too."

" I will go for the wine as well. . . . *Ave Maria !* "

" *Pater Noster !* " And so they went to sleep.

In the morning, after carefully brushing his shabby and much mended coat and his rusty hat, Don Mario dressed hastily and began his day by going to mass at San Francesco. . . . This ceremony over, he proceeded on his errand, hugging the oil-flask tightly under his coat.

He presented himself with humble and ceremonious courtesy.

" Is the Cavaliere at home ? "

" No, but his lady is."

" Announce me to the lady."

Now all the domestics in the place knew perfectly well the meaning of a visit from Don Mario, and at most houses they would leave him to wait in the anteroom, or say to him without more ado:

" Give me the bottle, Don Mario."

It often happened that while they were filling it for him he could not control himself at the sight of the disorder in the room where they left him. He would mount a chair in order to remove, with the end of his stick, the cobwebs clustering on the ceiling; and if he found a broom within reach of his hand—what was to be done? he could not resist!—he began to sweep the floor, to dust the pictures, or to pick up the scraps of paper or stuff scattered about.

" What are you doing, Don Mario?"

" The Lord has commanded us to be clean. . . . Thank the lady for me!"

Donna Rosa, who was amused with him and his ways, always had him shown up to the drawing-room, and asked him to sit down.

" How are you, dear Don Mario?"

" Well, thank God. And how is your Excellency?"

" As well as most old women, dear Don Mario!"

" None are old but those that die. Your Excellency is so charitable that you ought to be spared for a hundred years to come."

Donna Rosa kept up the conversation as though she had no idea of the real object of this visit; and Don Mario, still hugging his bottle, awaited the favourable moment for presenting his request without appearing troublesome. From time to time, after wriggling on his chair, as if in pain, for a few minutes, he would rise, and with " Excuse me, my lady!" wipe the dust from a table, or stoop to pick up a flake of wool, or bit of thread from the floor, and throw it out of the window, —as though the sight of these things actually made him feel ill.

" Oh! never mind, Don Mario!"

" The Lord has commanded us to be clean. . . . I had come . . ."

" How does your brother like his new employment?" Donna Rosa interrupted him, one day.

" Very much indeed."

" You ought to try and get appointed inspector of weights yourself. There is one wanted at the Archi mill."

" But the addition, madam! the addition! Ignazio knows how to do it!"

He turned up his eyes, with a sigh—as if this arithmetical process were a most complicated calculation.

" Poor Ignazio ! " he went on. " He comes back from the mill so tired ! Just imagine, madam—four miles uphill, on foot ! . . . I had come for this. . . ."

And he produced the flask.

" With pleasure ! " Who was there that could say " No " to Don Mario ?

But when that unfortunate addition was mentioned, not even the gift of a bottle of wine could restore him to good humour. He had tried so many times to do an addition sum. The tens were the difficulty.

" Nine and one are ten. . . . Very good ! . . . But . . . put down nought and carry one. . . . Why carry one if there are ten ? "

He had found it utterly impossible to understand this. And yet he was no fool. You should have heard him read, quite correctly, all those old legal documents, with their strange Latin abbreviations, which the modern notaries and advocates could not succeed in deciphering. It is true that he recited them parrot-fashion, without understanding them ; but all the same he could earn half a franc at a time when required for this service ; and this meant two *litres* of wine and half a *kilo* of lamb—quite a festive meal, although, nowadays, with Don Ignazio's position, the two brothers were not quite so badly off as before.

They would even have been happy if it had not been for the irritating behaviour of the street boys. One day matters reached a crisis. Don Mario, administering a cuff to an ill-conditioned fellow who assaulted him with the cry of *Quacquarà*, received the same back with interest, and got his coat torn into the bargain. The magistrate, before whom the case was brought, kept the vagabond under arrest for a couple of hours, and got up a subscription at the Casino, to present Don Mario with a new coat and hat. But the latter would never consent to be measured for it, and when the coat—cut out by guess-work—was sent him, together with the most spick and span of hats, he thanked the donors politely, and sent the whole back.

" You have been a fool ! " said his brother, who, on his return from the mill that evening, found him intent on repairing his ancient garment. " You can't go out again in that."

" I shall stay at home," replied Don Mario loftily.

And he was no longer seen about the town.

He passed his days sitting on the front doorstep, talking to the neighbours, or wandering through the many empty rooms of the dilapidated house. No repairs had been undertaken for years past; the shutters were loose on their hinges. Two floors had given way, and had to be passed by means of planks, laid like bridges from one room to another; and the tiles were off the roof in many places, so that some of the upper rooms were flooded when it rained.

" Sell half the house," said one of the neighbours; " it is much too large for you two alone! "

But that evening, discussing the matter at supper, Don Mario and Don Ignazio found themselves greatly embarrassed.

" Sell! Easily said. . . . But what? The room that had been their father's office? "

" Oh! " exclaimed Don Mario indignantly.

It is true that the big volumes, bound in dark leather, were no longer in the shelves all round the walls. The government had taken possession of them, as though they had been its property, and not that of the notaries, who had drawn up all those documents. But what matter? The shelves, moth-eaten and rickety, reduced to receptacles for dishes, frying-pans, and utensils of all sorts, remained, to their eyes, living witnesses, as it were, to past glories. The two brothers looked at one another.

" Was it possible? . . . Well. . . . What *should* they sell? Their grandmother's room? "

A mysterious chamber, which had been kept locked for seventy years, and of which now even the key was lost. Their grandfather's wife—a saint on earth—had died there, and the widower had ordered it to be shut up, in sign of perpetual mourning. Every night the mice kept up a terrible racket there. But what matter? A master notary—one of the Majori—had willed that no one should open it and no one had done so. Were *they* to profane it? They were both agreed . . . it was impossible!

" What then? The portrait-room? "

There were arranged on its walls half-a-dozen canvases, blackened with years and smoke, on which you could make out—here, the severe profile of Don Gasparo Majori, 1592; there, the grey eyes, white moustache, and pointed beard of Don Carlo, 1690; beside it, the wig and round shaven face of Don Paolo, 1687; and farther on, the lean and narrow head of Don Antonio, 1805, framed in an enormous collar, with white neckcloth, and showy waistcoat with watch-chain and seals dangling from its pockets. Don Mario knew by heart the life, death, and miracles of each one, and so did Don Ignazio.

Could they turn them out of their own house? No; it was impossible. Better let the whole fall into ruins.

They went to bed and put out the light.

" Well, it will last our time. We are old, Mario ! "

" You are two years older than I ! "

" . . . To-morrow, Notary Patrizio is coming to get an old deed read out to him."

" So we shall be able to buy half a *kilo* of meat."

" Saverio the butcher cheats in his weights. I shall keep my eyes open."

" I have lent the rolling-pin to Comare Nina."

" I will get the wine from Scatá. . . . Vittoria wine this time. . . . *Pater Noster !* "

" *Ave Maria !* "

So they went to sleep.

They were growing old. Ignazio was right.

Don Mario sometimes wondered which of the two would die first, and the thought left him sad and depressed.

" I am the younger. . . . But, after me, the house will go to distant relatives, . . . they will divide it up and sell it. . . . But, after all, what does it matter to us? We shall both be gone then. . . . We are the real Majori ; when we are dead, the world is dead ! "

Yet he went on sweeping out the tumble-down old house with the same tenderness and care as ever, removing the cobwebs from the walls, and dusting the moth-eaten and ragged remnants of furniture ; driving a nail into the back of a chair or the leg of a table ; pasting a sheet of oiled paper in the place of a missing window-pane, and carrying out the dust and rubbish as usual, late at night.

Moreover, since he now frequently went to sleep in the daytime—with the loneliness, and having nothing to do—he sometimes passed the night out of doors, sweeping the whole length and breadth of the street, and pleased to hear the wonder of the neighbourhood next morning, and have people say to him:

" The angel passed by last night. Is it so, Don Mario? "

He would smile, without replying. He was now quite resigned to his voluntary imprisonment, as he could no longer wear his old coat and hat, which were still there, quite spotless and free from dust, though perfectly useless.

One day, however, Don Mario lost all his peace of mind.

Standing at a window in the portrait-room, he had been looking along the street at Reina's house, with its fantastically-sculptured gateway and the twisted stone monsters.

" A fine palace—quite a royal one," said Don Mario, who had never seen anything richer or more beautiful in his life.

" Yet, how was it the proprietor had never noticed those tufts of pellitory growing between the carvings over the arch of the great gateway, quite spoiling the building ? It was a sin and a shame ! "

Scarcely had Don Ignazio come home from the mill that evening, tired and out of breath, when his brother said to him:

" Look here ; you ought to go to Signor Reina. He is letting nasty weeds grow between the carvings of the gateway, under the middle balcony. It quite worries one to see them."

" Well ? "

" You ought to tell him of it—at least when you meet him again."

" I will tell him."

Don Ignazio, quite worn out with his long walk, had other matters to think of ; he wanted to have his supper and go to bed.

But from that day he too got no peace. Every evening, when he came home, Don Mario never failed to ask him, even before he had laid aside his stick : " Have you spoken to Reina ? "

" No."

" Go and tell him at once. It is a pity ; those weeds are spoiling the building."

They were quite an eyesore to him ; he could not make out how Reina could put up with such a sacrilege. And several times a day he would go to the attic window, mounting a pair of steps at the risk of his neck, in order to look out. Those weeds were always there ! They grew from day to day ; they made great bushes that waved in the wind. If they had been fungous growths in the interior of his own system, he could not have suffered more from them.

" Have you told Reina about them ? "

" Yes."

" What did he say ? "

" He swore at me."

That night Don Mario never closed his eyes. As soon as he found that his brother was snoring, then he lit the lamp, dressed himself, took the steps on his shoulder, which they nearly dislocated, and made his way to Reina's house, keeping in the shadow of the wall, and avoiding the moonlight, as if he had been a burglar.

As indeed the gendarmes thought him when they came upon him, perched on the top of the gateway, pulling away for dear life at the parasitic herbs, in spite of the proprietor, who did not care whether they grew there or not.

"What are you doing up there?"

"I am pulling out these weeds."

"Come down."

"Let me finish."

"Come down, I tell you!"

At this unceremonious summons poor Don Mario had to descend, leaving several bushes of pellitory to spoil the beautiful building unchecked. . . .

They were nearly taking him off to the police station! . . . And all for a good action! He died within three months, with the nightmare of those weeds weighing on his heart. . . . Poor old Don Mario!

GIOVANNI VERGA
1840–

CAVALLERIA RUSTICANA

AFTER Turridu Macca, Mistress Nunzia's son, came home from soldiering, he used to strut every Sunday, peacock-like, in the public square, wearing his rifleman's uniform, and his red cap that looked just like that of the fortune-teller waiting for custom behind the stand with the cage of canaries. The girls all rivalled each other in making eyes at him as they went their way to mass, with their noses down in the folds of their shawls ; and the young lads buzzed about him like so many flies. Besides, he had brought back a pipe with the King on horseback on the bowl, as natural as life ; and he struck his matches on the back of his trousers, raising up one leg as if he were going to give a kick.

But for all that, Master Angelo's daughter Lola had not once shown herself, either at mass or on her balcony, since her betrothal to a man from Licodia, who was a carter by trade, and had four Sortino mules in his stable. No sooner had Turridu heard the news than, holy great devil ! but he wanted to rip him inside out, that was what he wanted to do to him, that fellow from Licodia. However, he did nothing to him at all, but contented himself with going and singing every scornful song he knew beneath the fair one's window.

" Has Mistress Nunzio's Turridu nothing at all to do," the neighbours asked, " but pass his nights in singing, like a lonely sparrow ? "

At last he came face to face with Lola, on her way back from praying to Our Lady of Peril ; and at sight of him she turned neither white nor red, as though he were no concern of hers.

" It is a blessing to have sight of you ! " said he.

" Oh, friend Turridu, I was told that you came back around the first of the month."

" And I too was told many other things besides ! " he answered. " So it is true that you are going to marry Alfio the carter ? "

" If such is the will of God ! " answered Lola,, drawing together beneath her chin the two corners of her kerchief.

" You do the will of God by taking or leaving as it pays you best !

And it was the will of God that I should come home from so far away to hear such fine news, Mistress Lola!"

The poor fellow still tried to make a show of indifference, but his voice had grown husky; and he walked on ahead of the girl with a swagger that kept the tassel of his cap dancing back and forth upon his shoulders. It really hurt the girl to see him with such a long face, but she had not the heart to deceive him with fair words.

"Listen, friend Turridu," she said at length, "you must let me go on to join the other girls. What would folks be saying if we were seen together?"

"That is true," replied Turridu; "now that you are to marry Alfio, who has four mules in his stable, if won't do to set people talking. My mother, on the other hand, poor woman, had to sell our one bay mule and that little bit of vineyard down yonder on the highroad during the time that I was soldiering. The time is gone when the Lady Bertha span; and you no longer give a thought to the time when we used to talk together from window to courtyard, and when you gave me this handkerchief just before I went away, into which God knows how many tears I wept at going so far that the very name of our land seemed forgotten. But now good-bye, Mistress Lola, let us square accounts and put an end to our friendship."

Mistress Lola and the carter were married; and on the following Sunday she showed herself on her balcony, with her hands spread out upon her waist, to show off the big rings of gold that her husband had given her.

Turridu kept passing and repassing through the narrow little street, with his pipe in his mouth and his hands in his pockets, pretending indifference and ogling the girls; but inwardly he was eating his heart out to think that Lola's husband had all that gold, and that she pretended not even to notice him as he passed by.

"I'd like to take her from under his very eyes, the dirty dog!" he muttered.

Across from Alfio's house lived Master Cola, the vine-grower, who was rich as a porker, so they said, and had an unmarried daughter. Turridu said so much, and did so much, that Master Cola took him into his employ; then he began to haunt the house and make pretty speeches to the girl.

"Why don't you go and say all these fine things to Mistress Lola?" Santa answered him.

"Mistress Lola is a big lady! Mistress Lola is wife of one of the crowned heads now!"

"I suppose I am not good enough for the crowned heads."

"You are worth a hundred such as Lola; and I know one fellow who would never so much as look at Mistress Lola or her patron saint when you are around. For she isn't fit to carry your shoes for you, indeed she isn't!"

"When the fox found that he couldn't reach the grapes—"

"He said, 'how lovely you are, you sweet little grape!'"

"Oh! come, hands off, friend Turridu."

"Are you afraid I am going to eat you?"

"No, I am not afraid of you nor of him you serve."

"Ah! your mother was from Licodia, we all know that. Your blood boils quickly! Oh! I could eat you up with my eyes!"

"Then eat me up with your eyes, and leave no crumbs; but meanwhile pick up that bundle of twigs for me."

"For your sake I would pick up the whole house, that I would!"

To hide her blushes, she threw at him the fagot she happened to have in her hands, but for a wonder missed him.

"Cut it short! Talking doesn't bind fagots."

"If I was rich, I should be looking for a wife just like you, Santa!"

"I shall not marry a crowned head, as Mistress Lola did; but I shall have my dower, as well as she, when the Lord sends me the right man."

"We know that you are rich, yes, we know that!"

"If you know so much, then stop talking, for my father will soon be here, and I don't care to have him catch me in the courtyard."

The father began to make a wry face, but the girl pretended not to notice, for the tassel of the rifleman's hat had set her heart-strings quivering and was for ever dancing before her eyes. After the father had put Turridu out of the door, the daughter opened her window to him, and would stand chatting with him all the evening, until the whole neighbourhood could talk of nothing else.

"I am crazy about you," Turridu would say; "I am losing my sleep and my appetite."

"I don't believe it!"

"I wish I was the son of Victor Emanuel, so that I could marry you!"

"I don't believe it!"

" By our Lady, I could eat you up, like a piece of cake ! "

" I don't believe it ! "

" On my honour ! "

" Oh, mother mine ! "

Lola, listening night after night, hidden behind a pot of sweet basil, turning first pale and then red, one day called down to Turridu : " How is it, friend Turridu, that old friends no longer greet each other ? "

" Alas ! " sighed Turridu, " blessed is he who may greet you ! "

" If you care to give me greeting, you know where my home is," answered Lola.

Turridu came back to greet her so often that Santa took notice of it, and closed her window in his face. The neighbours pointed him out with a smile or a nod of the head when he passed by in his rifleman's uniform. Lola's husband was away, making a circuit of the village fairs with his mules.

" On Sunday I mean to go to confession, for last night I dreamt of black grapes," said Lola.

" Wait a while ! wait a while ! " begged Turridu.

" No, now that Easter is so near, my husband would want to know why I have not been to confession."

" Aha ! " murmured Master Cola's Santa, waiting for her turn on her knees before the confessional where Lola was washing herself clean of her sins. " On my soul, it is not to Rome I would send you to do penance ! "

Friend Alfio came home with his mules and a pretty penny of profit, and brought his wife a present of a fine new dress for the holidays.

" You do well to bring her presents," his neighbour Santa said to him, " for while you are away your wife has been trimming up the honour of your house ! "

Master Alfio was one of those carters who wear the cap well down over one ear, and to hear his wife talked of in this fashion made him change colour as though he had been stabbed. " Holy big devil ! " he exclaimed, " if you have not seen aright, I won't leave you eyes to weep with, you and your whole family ! "

" I have forgotten how to weep ! " answered Santa ; " I did not weep even when I saw with these very eyes Mistress Nunzia's son, Turridu, go in at night to your wife's house."

" Then it is well," replied Alfio ; " many thanks to you."

Now that the husband was home again, Turridu no longer wasted his days in the little street, but drowned his sorrow at the tavern with his friends ; and on Easter eve they had on the table a big dish of sausage. When Master Alfio came in, just from the way he fastened his eyes upon him, Turridu understood what business he had come on, and laid his fork down upon his plate.

" How can I serve you, friend Alfio ? " he asked.

" Nothing important ; friend Turridu, it is some time since I have seen you, and I wanted to talk with you of the matter that you know about."

Turridu had at once offered him a glass, but Alfio put it aside with his hand. Then Turridu arose and said to him : " Here I am, friend Alfio."

The carter threw an arm around his neck.

" If you will come to-morrow morning down among the prickly pears of Canziria, we can talk of this affair, friend Turridu."

" Wait for me on the highroad at sunrise, and we will go together."

With these words they exchanged the kiss of challenge. Turridu seized the carter's ear between his teeth, and thus solemnly bound himself not to fail him.

The friends had all silently withdrawn from the dish of sausage, and accompanied Turridu all the way to his home. Mistress Nunzia, poor woman, was accustomed to wait for him late every night.

" Mother," said Turridu, " do you remember when I went away to be a soldier, and you thought that I was never coming back ! Give me a kiss, such as you gave me then, for to-morrow I am going on a long journey ! "

Before daybreak he took his clasp-knife, which he had hidden under the straw at the time he went away as a conscript, and started with it for the prickly pears of Canziria.

" Holy Mother, where are you going in such a rage ? " sobbed Lola in terror as her husband started to leave the house.

" I am not going far," answered Alfio, " but it will be far better for you if I never come back."

Lola, in her night-gown, prayed at the foot of her bed, and pressed to her lips the rosary which Fra Bernadino had brought her from the Holy Land, and recited all the Ave Marias that there were beads for.

" Friend Alfio," began Turridu after he had walked quite a bit of the way beside his companion, who remained silent, with his cap drawn over his eyes, " as true as God Himself, I know that I am in the wrong, and I ought to let you kill me. But before I came here, I saw my old mother, who rose early to see me start, on the pretext that she had to tend the chickens; but her heart must have told her the truth. And as true as God Himself, I am going to kill you like a dog, sooner than have the poor old woman weeping for me."

"So much the better," replied Master Alfio, stripping off his jacket, "strike your hardest, and so will I."

They were both worthy foes. Turridu received the first thrust, and was quick enough to catch it on his arm. When he paid it back, he gave good measure, and aimed for the groin.

"Ah, friend Turridu, you have really made up your mind to kill me?"

"Yes, I told you so; ever since I saw my old mother going out to feed the chickens, her face floats all the time before my eyes."

"Then open your eyes wide," Alfio called to him, "for I am going to square accounts with you."

And as he stood on guard, crouching ever, so as to hold his left hand upon his wound which was aching, and with his elbow almost touching the ground, he suddenly caught up a handful of dust and threw it into his opponent's eyes.

"Oh!" howled Turridu, "I am done for!"

He sought to save himself by making desperate leaps backward; but Alfio overtook him with another blow in the stomach and a third in the throat.

"And the third is for the honour of my house, that you made free with. Now, perhaps, your mother will forget to feed her chickens."

Turridu stumbled about for a moment, here and there among the prickly pears, and then fell like a log. The blood gurgled in a crimson foam out of his throat, and he had no chance even to gasp out, "Oh, mother mine!"

THE SHE-WOLF

GIOVANNI VERGA

SHE was tall and lean ; her breast alone revealed the firmness and vigour of the brunette type ; and yet she was no longer a young woman. She was pallid, as though she always had the burden of malaria upon her ; and in the midst of that pallor two such great eyes and lips so fresh and ruddy that they seemed to devour you alive.

In the village they called her the She-Wolf, because she was never satiated—never with anything. The women all made the sign of the cross when they saw her pass by, with the skulking, prowling tread of a starving wolf ; for she made clean pickings of their sons and husbands with those rosy lips of hers, drawing them on behind her skirts merely with one glance of those eyes like the devil's own, even though they had been standing before the altar of St. Agrippina herself. Fortunately the She-Wolf never went herself to church, neither on Easter nor on Christmas, neither to hear mass nor to confess herself. Father Angiolino, of the Church of St. Mary of Jesus, a true servant of God, had lost his soul for her sake.

Maricchia—poor little thing !—a good and honest lass, wept in secret, because she was the daughter of the She-Wolf, and no one would take her to wife, even if she had had her share of fine things in a chest and her bit of good land in the sunshine, like every other lass in the village.

Once on a time the She-Wolf fell in love with a handsome lad who had just come home from soldiering and was mowing the hay beside her in the fields of the notary ; fell in love in the full sense of the term —love that sets the flesh on fire beneath a fustian jacket and makes you feel, when glances meet, a thirst like that which comes to you during the hot hours of June in the middle of an open pasture. But the lad continued tranquilly to mow, with his nose close down to his task, and would say to her :

" What is the matter with you, Mistress Pina ? "

In the silence of those vast fields, broken only by the whirring flight of the grasshoppers, when the sun beat down upon them like lead, the She-Wolf kept on steadily binding bundle after bundle, sheaf after sheaf, never wearying, never for a moment straightening up to relieve her back, never pausing to moisten her lips, but keeping ever close upon the heels of Nanni, who mowed and mowed, and time and again would ask her :

" What is it that you want, Mistress Pina ? "

One evening she told him what, while the men were dozing on the threshing floor, weary from a long day's labour, and the dogs were howling in the blackness of the vast open country. " It is you that I want ! You who are splendid as the sun and as tempting as honey ! It is you I want ! "

" And I, on the contrary, want your daughter ; the heifer, not the cow," retorted Nanni, with a laugh.

The She-Wolf left him like a hunted thing, with her hands in her hair, tearing at her temples without speaking a word, and roamed away to be seen no more at the threshing floor. But in October she saw Nanni again, because he was working alongside of her home, and the creaking of the oil press kept her awake all the night.

" Take the bag of olives," she said to her daughter, " and come with me."

Nanni was sending the olives by the shovelful into the machine and crying " Go along ! " to the mule, to keep it from stopping.

" Do you still want my daughter Maricchia ? " Mistress Pina demanded.

" What have you to give to your daughter Maricchia ? " retorted Nanni.

" She has what her father left her, and besides that I will give her the house. It is enough for me if you leave me a corner in the kitchen and a little straw to sleep on."

" In that case we can talk of it at Christmas," said Nanni.

He was all greasy and foul with oil and with the olives that had begun to ferment, and Maricchia did not want him at any price. But her mother dragged her by the hair before the hearthstone and told her, between clenched teeth :

" If you don't take him, I will kill you ! "

The She-Wolf was really ill, and people began to say that when the devil grows old he turns hermit. She no longer went prowling hither and thither; she no longer lurked in her doorway, staring out with her devil-haunted eyes. Her son-in-law, whenever he felt those eyes of hers fixed upon him, would try to laugh and would pull out his little scapular of the Madonna, to cross himself with it. Maricchia now stayed at home to nurse her babies, and her mother went forth into the fields to work beside the men, precisely like a man, weeding, spading, driving the cattle, pruning the vines, indifferent to the east winds of winter or the sirocco of August, the days when the mules droop their heads limply and the men sleep open-mouthed on the north side of the wall.

'Twixt nones and vespers, in the gloaming,
No honest woman goes a-roaming,

and Mistress Pina was the solitary living soul to be seen wandering across the country along the heated stones of the narrow lanes or through the parched stubble of the immense fields that melted away in a shimmering haze, far, far away toward nebulous Etna, where the sky sank to sleep on the horizon.

"Wake up!" the She-Wolf commanded Nanni, who was sleeping in the ditch beside the dust-laden hedge, with his head between his arms. "Wake up, for I have brought you a wine that will slake your thirst."

Nanni stared up with misty eyes, halfway between sleeping and waking; then finding her before him, erect and pallid, with swelling breast and eyes black like coals, he stretched out his arms uncertainly toward her. Then:

"No, no!

'Twixt nones and vespers, in the gloaming,
No honest woman goes a-roaming,"

sobbed Nanni, hiding his face against the dried grass of the ditch, as deep as he could, with his nails in his hair. "Take yourself off, take yourself off! Never come here again to the threshing floor!"

She took herself off, indeed, the She-Wolf, twisting up her superb tresses and looking down fixedly at her footsteps in the parched stubble, with her eyes black like coals.

But to the threshing floor she came back, time and time again, and Nanni ceased to tell her nay; and when she was late in coming between nones and vespers, in the hour of gloaming, he would go and wait for her, at the top of the little lane, white and deserted, with the sweat upon his brow—and afterward he would bury his hands in his hair, and repeat to her over and over:

" Take yourself off, take yourself off! Never come back again to the threshing floor! "

Maricchia was weeping night and day, but whenever she saw her mother coming back from the fields, always pallid and mute, she would insolently face her down, with eyes scorching with tears and jealousy, a veritable she-wolf's whelp herself.

" You vile beast! " she would say. " You vile beast of a mother! "

" Hold your tongue! "

" You thief! Oh, you thief! "

" Hold your tongue! "

" I'll bring the police; yes, I will! "

" Bring them then! "

And she really did go and bring them, with her children in her arms, fearless and dry-eyed, like a madwoman, because now, at last, she too loved this husband whom they had given her by force, all foul and greasy with the olives that had been put to ferment.

They summoned Nanni to the police-court and threatened him with the galleys and the scaffold. Nanni broke down and sobbed and tore out the hair of his head. He denied nothing, he attempted no sort of excuse.

" It is the temptation," he kept saying, " the temptation of hell itself! "

He cast himself at the feet of the official, begging to be sent to the galleys.

" Out of charity, Signor Officer, take me away from the hell I live in! Tell them to kill me or lock me up in prison; but don't let me see her again—never, never again! "

" No! " was the She-Wolf's decision, when the official argued with her. " I reserved a corner of the kitchen to sleep in, when I gave her my house as a dower. The house is mine. I won't get out of it! "

Not long after Nanni was kicked in the chest by a mule, and was like to die; but the parish priest refused to bring him the sacrament unless the She-Wolf left the house. The She-Wolf did leave the house, so that her son-in-law could prepare to make an end, even he, in good Christian fashion. He made confession and received communion with such signs of repentance and contrition that all the neighbours and curious idlers began to weep around the bed of the dying man. And better would it have been for him to die at that time, before the devil returned to tempt him and take possession of him, body and soul, when he was well again.

" Leave me in peace ! " he kept saying to the She-Wolf. " Out of charity, leave me in peace ! I have looked death straight in the eyes ! And there is poor Maricchia, half mad with despair. And now the whole land knows about it. The less I see of you, the better it is for you and for me."

And it would have been well for him to tear out his eyes, so as not to see those of the She-Wolf ; for whenever her eyes looked into his they destroyed him, body and soul. He no longer knew what to do next, to free himself from the spell she cast. He paid mass after mass for the souls in purgatory, and went to seek aid from the parish priest and from the police. At Easter he went to confession and publicly did penance on the holy paving stones in front of the church. And then, when the She-Wolf returned to tempt him,

" Listen ! " he said to her. " Never come again to the threshing floor, because if you come again to seek me, as truly as there is a God I will kill you like a beast ! "

" Kill me like a beast," replied the She-Wolf, " for all I care. But without you I do not care to live."

And when he saw her coming, from far off, across the budding green of new-sown fields, he paused from pruning the vines and went to take down his scythe from where it hung upon the elm. The She-Wolf saw him come to meet her, pallid and staring-eyed, with his scythe that gleamed in the sun ; yet she never shrank back a single step nor lowered her glance, but came steadily toward him, her hands full of great bunches of red poppies, her black eyes devouring him alive.

" May your soul go straight to hell ! " said Nanni brokenly.

THE WAR OF THE SAINTS

Giovanni Verga

ALL of a sudden, while Saint Rocco was quietly proceeding on his way, under his baldachin, with a number of wax candles lit all round him, and the band, and the procession, and the crowd of devout people—there came a general helter-skelter, tumult, and confusion worse confounded. There were priests running away, with the skirts of their cassocks flying wildly, drummers and fifers upset on their faces, women screaming, blood flowing in streams, and cudgels playing even under the very nose of the blessed Saint Rocco. The Praetor, the Syndic, the Carbineers all hastened to the spot ;—the broken bones were carried off to the hospital,—a few of the more riotous members of the community were marched off to pass the night in prison,—the saint returned to his church at a run rather than a processional step,—and the festival ended like the comedies of Pulcinella.

And all this through the spite of the people in the parish of Saint Pasquale. That year the pious souls of Saint Rocco had been spending the very eyes out of their heads in order to do things in grand style ;—they had sent for the band from town,—they had let off more than two thousand squibs,—and they had now got a new banner, all embroidered with gold, which, it was said, weighed over a quintal, and tossed up and down in the midst of the crowd, like a wave crested with golden foam. Which thing, by sheer contrivance of the Evil One, was a thorn in the sides of the followers of Saint Pasquale,—so that one of the latter at last lost patience, and began, pale as death, to yell at the top of his voice, " *Viva San Pasquale !* " Then it was that the cudgels began to fly.

Because, after all, to go and cry " *Viva San Pasquale* " in the very face of Saint Rocco, is really a good, sound, indisputable provocation ; —it is just like going and spitting in a man's house, or amusing yourself by pinching the girl who is walking arm-in-arm with him. In such a case there is no longer any sense of right and wrong,—and that slight amount of respect which people still have for the other saints—who, after all, are all related to each other—is trampled under foot. If it happens in church, seats are flung into the air,—if during a procession, there are showers of torch-stumps like swarms of bats, and at table the dishes fly.

"*Santo diavolone!*" cried Compare Nino, panting, heated, and dishevelled. "I'd like to know who has the face to cry *Viva San Pasquale* again!"

"I!" yelled Turi the tanner, who looked forward to being his brother-in-law, quite beside himself with rage, and nearly blinded by a chance blow received in the *mêlée.* "*Viva San Pasquale* till death!"

"For the love of Heaven! for the love of Heaven!" shrieked his sister Saridda, throwing herself between her brother and her betrothed. All three had been going for a walk in all love and good fellowship up to that moment.

Compare Nino, the expectant bridegroom, kept crying in derision, "Long live my boots—*viva San Stivale!*"

"Take that!" howled Turi, foaming at the mouth, his eyes swollen and his face like a tomato. "Take that for Saint Rocco, you and your boots! There!"

In this way they exchanged blows which would have felled an ox, till their friends succeeded in separating them by dint of cuffs and kicks. Saridda, who by this time had grown excited on her own account, now cried *Viva San Pasquale,* and was very nearly coming to blows with her lover, as if they had already been husband and wife.

At such times parents quarrel most desperately with their sons and daughters, and wives separate from their husbands, if by misfortune a woman of the parish of Saint Pasquale has married a man from Saint Rocco.

"I won't hear another word about that man!" cried Saridda, standing with her hands on her hips, to the neighbours, when they asked her how it happened that the marriage had not come off. "I won't have him, if they give him to me dressed in gold and silver from head to foot! Do you hear?"

"Saridda may stay where she is till she turns mouldy, for all I care!" said Compare Nino, in his turn, as he was getting the blood washed from his face at the public-house. "A parcel of beggars and cowards, over in the tanner's quarter! I must have been drunk when it came into my head to look for a sweetheart over there!"

"Since it is this way," had been the Syndic's conclusion, "and they can't carry a saint out into the square without sticks and fighting, so that it's perfectly beastly,—I will have no more festivals, nor processions, nor services; and if they bring out so much as one single candle—what you may call a candle—I'll have them every one in gaol."

In time, the matter became important; for the bishop of the diocese had granted to the priests of Saint Pasquale the privilege of wearing copes. The parishioners of Saint Rocco, whose priests had no copes, had even gone to Rome to raise an outcry at the foot of the Holy Father, carrying with them documents on stamped paper, and everything else; but all had been in vain, for their adversaries of the lower town—who, as every one remembered, had once been without shoes to their feet—had now grown as rich as Jews, through this new industry of tanning. And, in this world, one knows that justice is bought and sold like the soul of Judas.

At Saint Pasquale they were awaiting Monsignor's delegate, who was a person of importance, and had silver buckles on his shoes weighing half a pound apiece—and a fine sight they were to see—and he was coming to bring the copes to the canons. And for this reason, they, in their turn, had now sent for the band, and they were going to meet Monsignor's delegate three miles outside the town; and it was said that in the evening there were to be fireworks in the square, with *Viva San Pasquale* over and over again, in letters as big as those on a shop-front.

The inhabitants of the upper town were therefore in a great ferment; and some, more excited than others, were trimming certain staves of pear and cherry wood, as big as clothes-props, and muttering—

"If there is to be music, we shall want to beat time!"

The Bishop's delegate ran a great risk of coming out of his triumphal entry with broken bones. But the reverend gentleman was cunning enough to leave the band waiting for him outside the town, while he, taking a short cut, quietly walked to the parish priest's house, whither he summoned the principal men of the two parties.

When these gentlemen found themselves face to face—after all this time that the feud had lasted—each man began to look into the whites of his neighbour's eyes, as if he could scarcely keep his nails out of them; and it required all the authority of his Reverence—who had put on his new cloth soutane for the occasion—to get the ices and the other refreshments served without accidents.

"That's right!" said the Syndic approvingly, with his nose in his glass. " When you want me for the cause of peace, you'll always find me on the spot."

The delegate, in fact, said that he had come for the sake of conciliation, with the olive-branch in his mouth, like Noah's dove, and made his exhortation, distributing smiles and hand-clasps all round, and saying, " Gentlemen, will you do me the favour of coming into the sacristy to take a cup of chocolate on the day of the festival ? "

" Do leave the festival alone ! " said the Vice-Prætor ; " if not, more mischief will come of it."

" Mischief will come of it if this tyranny is to be allowed—if a man is not to be free to amuse himself as he likes, and pay for it with his own money ! " exclaimed Bruno, the carter.

" I wash my hands of the matter. The orders of the Government are explicit. If you celebrate the festival I shall send for the Carbineers. I am for order."

" I will answer for order ! " said the Syndic, tapping the ground for emphasis with his umbrella, and looking slowly around.

" Bravo ! as if we did not know that it is your brother-in-law Bruno who blows the bellows for you in the Town Council ! " retorted the Vice-Prætor.

" And you have joined the opposition party only on account of that bye-law about the washing, which you can't get over ! "

" Gentlemen ! gentlemen ! " entreated the delegate. " We shall do nothing if we go on in this way."

" We'll have a revolution, that we will ! " shouted Bruno, gesticulating with his hands in the air.

Fortunately the parish priest had quietly put away the cups and glasses, and the sacristan had rushed off at the top of his speed to dismiss the band, who, having heard of the delegate's arrival, were already hastening up to welcome him, blowing their cornets and clarionets.

" In this way we shall do nothing at all ! " muttered the delegate, worried to death by the thought that the harvest was already ripe for cutting in his own village, while he was wasting his time here talking to Compare Bruno and the Vice-Prætor, who were ready to tear one another's souls out. " What is this story about the prohibition of the washing ? "

" The usual interference. Nowadays one can't hang a handkerchief out of the window to dry without getting fined for it. The Vice-Prætor's wife—feeling safe because her husband was in a position of trust, for till now people always had some little regard for the authorities—used to hang out the whole week's washing—it was not much to boast of—on the terrace. . . . But now, under the new law, that's a mortal sin ; and now even the dogs and fowls are prohibited, and the pigs—saving your presence—that used to do the scavenging in the streets ; and now the first rain that comes it will be Heaven's mercy if we don't all get smothered in the filth. The real truth is that Bruno, the assessor, has a grudge against the Vice-Prætor, on account of a certain decision he has given against him."

The delegate, in order to conciliate the local mind, used to sit boxed up in his confessional, like an owl in its nest, from morning till evening, and all the women were eager to be shriven by the Bishop's representative, who had powers of plenary absolution for all sorts of sins, just as though he had been Monsignor in person.

" Your Reverence," said Saridda, with her nose at the grating, " Compare Nino makes me commit sin every Sunday in church."

" In what way, my daughter ? "

" He was to have married me, before there was all this talk in the place ; but now that the marriage is broken off, he goes and stands near the high altar, and stares at me, and laughs with his friends, all the time holy mass is going on."

And when his Reverence tried to touch Nino's heart, the countryman replied—

" No, it is she who turns her back on me whenever she sees me—just as if I were a beggar ! "

He, on the other hand, if Gnà Saridda passed across the square on Sundays, gave himself airs as if he had been the brigadier, or some other great personage, and did not even seem to see her. Saridda was exceedingly busy preparing little coloured paper-lanterns, and put them out in a row on the window-sill, in his very face, under the pretext of hanging them out to dry. Once they found themselves together in church, at a christening, and took no notice of each other, just as though they had never met before ; nay, Saridda even went so far as to flirt with the godfather.

" A poor sort of a godfather ! " sneered Nino. " Why the child's a girl ! And when a girl is born, even the beams of the roof break down !"

Saridda turned away, and pretended to be talking to the baby's mother.

" What's bad does not always come to do harm. Sometimes, when you think you've lost a treasure, you ought to thank God and Saint Pasquale; for you can never say you know a person till you have eaten seven measures of salt."

"After all, one must take troubles as they come, and the worst possible way is to worry one's self about things which are not worth the trouble. When one Pope's dead they make another."

"It's fore-ordained what sort of natures children are to be born with, and it's just like that with marriages. It's far better to marry a man who really cares for you and has no other ends to serve, even though he has no money or fields, or mules or anything. . . ."

On the square the drum was beating to give notice of the festival.

"The Syndic says we shall have the festival," was the murmur that went through the crowd.

"I'll go to law till doomsday, if it should leave me as poor as holy Job, with nothing left but my shirt; but that five francs' fine I will not pay! not if I had to leave directions about it in my will!"

"Confound it all!" exclaimed Nino. "What sort of a festival are they going to have, if we are all to die of hunger this year?"

Since March not a drop of rain had fallen, and the yellow corn, which crackled like tinder, was "dying of thirst." Bruno, the carter, however, said that when Saint Pasquale was carried out in procession it would rain for certain. But what did he care about rain? or all the tanners of his neighbourhood either? In fact they carried Saint Pasquale in procession to east and to west, and set him upon a hill to bless the country on a stifling May day, when the sky was covered with clouds,—one of those days when the farmers are ready to tear their hair before the burnt-up fields, and the ears of corn droop as if they were dying.

"A curse on Saint Pasquale!" cried Nino, spitting in the air, and rushing about among his crops like a madman. "You have ruined me, Saint Pasquale; you've left me nothing but the reaping-hook to cut my throat with!"

The upper town was a desolate place enough. It was one of those long years when the hunger begins in June, and the women stand at their doors with their hair hanging about their shoulders—doing nothing—staring with fixed eyes. Gnà Saridda, hearing that Compare Nino's mule was to be sold in the public square, to pay the rent of his farm, felt her anger melt away in an instant, and sent her brother Turi in hot haste, with the few *soldi* they had put aside, to help him.

Nino was in one corner of the square, with his eyes averted and his hands in his pockets, while they were selling his mule, with all its ornaments and the new headstall.

"I don't want anything," he replied sullenly. "My arms are still left me, please God. A fine saint that Saint Pasquale of yours, eh?"

Turi turned his back on him, to avoid unpleasantness, and went on his way. But the truth is that people's minds were thoroughly exasperated, now that they had carried Saint Pasquale in procession to east and west, with no more result than that. The worst of it was that many from the parish of Saint Rocco had been induced to walk with the procession too, thrashing themselves like asses, and with crowns of thorns on their heads, for the sake of their crops. Now they relieved their feelings in exceedingly bad language; and the Bishop's delegate was obliged to leave the town, as he entered it, on foot, and without the band.

The Vice-Prætor, by way of retaliation on his opponent, telegraphed that people's minds were excited, and the public peace compromised; so that one fine day a report went through the town that the soldiers had arrived, and every one could go and see them.

"They have come on account of the cholera," others said, however. "Down in the city, they say, the people are dying like flies."

The chemist put up the chain of his shop door, and the doctor left the place as speedily as possible, to escape being knocked on the head.

"It will not come to anything," said the few who had remained in the place, having been unable to fly into the country like the rest. "The blessed Saint Rocco will watch over his own town."

Even the lower town folks had begun to go barefoot to Saint Rocco's church. But not long after that, deaths began to come thick and fast. They said of one man that he was a glutton, and died of eating too many prickly pears, and of another, that he had come in from the country after nightfall. But, in short, there was the cholera, there was no disguising it,—in spite of the soldiers, and in the very teeth of Saint Rocco,—notwithstanding the fact that an old woman in the odour of sanctity had dreamed that the saint himself had said to her: "Have no fear of the cholera, for I am looking after that. I am not like that useless old ass of a Saint Pasquale."

Nino and Turi had not met since the mule was sold; but scarcely had the former heard that the brother and sister were both ill, than he hastened to their house, and found Saridda, black in the face, and her features all distorted, in a corner of the room. Her brother, who was with her, was recovering, but could not tell what to do for her, and was nearly beside himself with despair.

" Ah ! thief of a Saint Rocco," groaned Nino. " I never expected this. Gnà Saridda, don't you know me any more ? Nino, your old friend Nino."

Saridda looked at him with eyes so sunken that one had to hold a lantern to her face before one could see them, and Nino felt his own running over.

" Ah ! Saint Rocco," said he, " this is a worse trick than the one Saint Pasquale played me ! "

However, Saridda in time got better, and as she was standing at the door, with her head tied up in a handkerchief, and her face yellow as new wax, she said to Nino : " Saint Rocco has worked a miracle for me, and you ought to come too, and carry a candle at his festival."

Nino's heart was too full to speak, and he nodded assent. But before the festival came round, he too was taken with the pestilence, and lay at the point of death. Saridda tore her face with her nails, and said that she wanted to die with him, and she would cut off her hair and have it buried with him, and no one should ever look her in the face again as long as she lived.

" No, no," replied Nino, his face all drawn with agony. " Your hair will grow again, but it will be I that will never see you again, for I shall be dead."

" A fine miracle that Saint Rocco has worked for you ! " said Turi, by way of comforting him.

Both of them slowly recovered ; and when they sat sunning themselves, with their backs to the wall and very long faces, kept throwing Saint Rocco and Saint Pasquale in each other's teeth.

One day Bruno, the carter, coming back from the country after the cholera was over, passed by them, and said :

" We're going to have a grand festival to thank Saint Pasquale for having saved us from the cholera. We shall have no more demagogues and no more opposition, now that the Vice-Prætor is dead. He has left the quarrel behind him in his will."

" All very well ; a festival for the dead ! " sneered Nino.

" Perhaps it was Saint Rocco that kept you alive ? "

" There !—do have done with it ! " cried Saridda. " If you don't, we shall need another cholera to make peace between you ! "

ANTONIO FOGAZZARO
1842–1911

THE SILVER CRUCIFIX

"YOUR coffee, milady," said the maid.

The Countess did not reply. But although the curtains were closed, her handsome young face could be dimly discerned on the white pillow. The maid, standing tray in hand at the foot of the bed, repeated more loudly:

"Your coffee, milady."

The Countess sat up, while she yawned, with eyes still unopened, "Let in some light."

Her maid went to the window without putting down the tray, and, in turning the handle of the shutters, managed to knock over the empty cup on its saucer.

"Keep quiet!" whispered the mistress in a tone of irritation. "What is the matter with you this morning? Don't you see you are waking the baby?"

And as a matter of fact the infant was now awake and crying in its crib. The lady turned toward the child's bed, and peremptorily called out "Hush!"

This silenced her offspring at once, excepting for a few faint moans.

"Now, then, I will have my coffee," commanded the Countess. "Have you seen your master yet? Why, you are trembling all over! What is the matter with you?"

What, indeed, ailed the girl? Cup, saucer, sugar-bowl, and coffee-pot were rattling on the tray. "What is it?" repeated the Countess.

If the maid's face showed signs of alarm, no less was the mistress disturbed by doubts and fears.

"Nothing," replied the servant, still trembling.

The Countess hereupon seized her by the arm, shook it roughly, and exclaimed:

"Tell me!"

Meanwhile the pretty little head of a child of four was peering over the edge of the crib.

"It's a case," said the maid, half in tears, "it's a case of cholera."

Pale as death, the lady started up, and instinctively looked at her listening son. She jumped out of bed; by a single gesture she imposed silence on the girl, while motioning her to go into the next room. Then she darted to her child's crib.

The little fellow had begun to cry again, but his mother kissed and petted him, played and laughed with him until he forgot his woes, and stopped weeping. She pulled on her dressing-gown in great haste, and joined the servant, shutting the door behind her.

"Oh, my God, my God!" lamented the girl between her sobs, while the other woman too began to shed tears.

"Hush, for Heaven's sake! On no account must baby be frightened! What about this case—where is it?"

"Here, milady! Rosa, the steward's wife. She was taken ill at midnight."

"Heavens! And now—?"

"She is dead. She died half an hour ago."

The baby was shrilly clamouring for his mother.

"Go," said the Countess; "go in and play with him. Keep him happy; do anything you like. Be quiet, darling!" she exclaimed. "I shall be back in a moment." Upon which she rushed to the Count's room.

The lady was blindly, insanely afraid of the cholera; nothing but her passion for her child could have been more intense than this feeling. At the first rumours of the epidemic she and her husband had fled the city, escaping to their splendid country seat—her marriage portion—in the hope that the disease would not spread thither. The place had been spared in 1836, and had even remained untouched in 1886. And now there it was, in the farmyard attached to the villa.

Dishevelled and untidy, she flew into her husband's room. Before speaking she gave two violent tugs at the bell-rope.

"Have you heard?" she said, with flaming eyes.

The Count, who was phlegmatically shaving his beard, turned round, inquiring, with the soapy brush in his hand: "What?"

"Don't you know about Rosa?"

"Oh, yes, I know," was his calm response.

If, in the first place, the Count had cherished some vague illusion that his wife was ignorant of Rosa's death, it now also seemed proper to reassure her by his cool demeanour. Instead, however, her ladyship's eyes shot fire, and her features were savage with anger.

"What!" she shouted, "you know, and you can think of nothing better to do than shave? What sort of man are you—what sort of father—what sort of husband?"

"Good Lord!" cried the Count, throwing up his arms.

But before the poor man, soaped up to the eyes, and wrapped round with a towel, could add another word, in came the valet. Her ladyship commanded that not a peasant from the farmyard should be admitted to the house, and that no one should go thence to the farmyard. After this she gave orders for the coachman to be ready within an hour; he must harness to the landau the horses which his lordship would select.

"What are you going to do?" asked the latter, who had recovered himself meanwhile. "Nothing rash, I must insist."

"*Rash*—how dare you say that? I am willing to be obedient to you in everything, but when it comes to a question of life and death—my son's life, you understand—then I will listen to no parley from any one. I wish to leave here at once. Order the horses, please."

The Count grew annoyed. How could matters have come to such a pass as this? Was there any propriety in running away after such a fashion? And then, what about business affairs? In two days, or one day, or maybe in twelve hours, he would be ready to start. But not before—no. His wife, however, interrupted him violently: "Propriety, indeed, and business! For shame!"

"And clothes?" objected the husband. "We must certainly take some with us. You see, we shall really need more time."

The Countess made some contemptuous answer. She would see to it, she assured him, that the trunks were packed in an hour.

"But where do you expect to go?" persisted the Count.

"To the railway station, first of all, and then wherever you like. Now order the horses."

"I have had enough of this!" cried the other. "I'll give such orders as I choose! I'll let the business affairs go, and everything else! Your clothes, too! The sorrels," he added, enraged, to the domestic who was standing by impassively.

The Countess dressed and did her hair with the utmost speed, at moments clasping her hands in silent prayer, distributing commands, summoning servants from various parts of the house by frantic pulls at the bell. There was running up and down stairs, banging of doors, shouting, laughing, calling out of names, suppressed swearing. All the windows facing the fatal farmyard were immediately closed. Thus the cries of the unfortunate children who had lost their mother were shut out; besides a disagreeable odour of chlorin had penetrated into the villa, and even into the Countess's room, smothering the delicate Viennese perfume she habitually used.

"Heavens!" she exclaimed angrily, "now they are doing their best to ruin everything! Pack up quickly, and get those trunks locked! This frightful smell is enough to kill one! Don't they know that chlorin has no effect? They ought to burn the things. The steward will be dismissed if any thieving goes on."

"Some things are being burnt already, milady," observed one of the maids. "The doctor is having sheets, coverlid, and mattress burnt."

"That's not enough!" snapped the Countess.

Here the Count, shaved and dressed, entered his wife's apartment. He began talking to her aside.

"What shall we do with these servants? We can't take all of them with us."

"Anything you please. Send them away. Nothing will be safe in the house if they remain. I don't want them to get the cholera, and then fumigate the rooms with that vile chlorin, and perhaps burn up some of my best gowns. They have no respect whatever for their master's property, and—"

Furious at having yielded, the Count now broke in with:

"A pretty state of things! A shame, I tell you, a scandal, to sneak off like this!"

"That's it!" retorted the woman. "That's just how you men always are! To appear strong and courageous is more important to you than the life and safety of your family. You are afraid of becoming unpopular. Well, if you want to keep up your reputation, why don't you send for the mayor, and present him with a hundred lire for the cholera patients of the place?"

He thereupon suggested that he would stay at the villa alone, and that she should go with the child. Only he had not enough stability to carry out his own idea.

During this conversation the trunks were being filled. The little boy's playthings, his most expensive apparel, prayer-books, bathing-suits, jewellery, crested notepaper, furs, underlinen, many superfluous and few necessary articles were thrown in helter-skelter, and the lids closed down by sheer force. Then the Countess, followed by her spouse—who made a great show of activity, but really accomplished nothing—hurried through the whole house, opening drawers and cupboards, taking a last look into them, and locking them up with their own hands. The Count stated his opinion that it might be advisable to partake of some refreshment before commencing the journey.

" Yes, yes ! " ironically said his consort, " we'll take some refreshment ! I'll show you what to take ! "

And she drew up her husband and all the servants, including those who were going home for a holiday, and dosed each one with ten drops of laudanum. Her son she regaled with some chocolates.

At last the landau stood before the door. Prior to actually departing, her ladyship, who was extremely pious, withdrew to the seclusion of her bedchamber for a final prayer. Kneeling at a chair, in her tight-fitting costume of white flannel, her black, eight-button gloves reaching to the elbows, and her gold and platinum bracelets, she raised her eyes devoutly to heaven—under the overshadowing plume of her black velvet hat—and murmured a feverish supplication. Not a word did she say to God about the poor wretches who had lost their mother ; nor did she ask that the cholera might spare the humble workers chained to the rich soil which had given her this house, her jewels, clothes, Viennese perfume, her education, her dignity, her husband and child, her accommodating God. Neither did she ask anything for her own person. She, who already saw herself and her family smitten down with the dread disease on the journey, offered up no prayers excepting for her son. In fact, her lips simply muttered Paters and Aves and Glorias, while her mind was altogether with the child, thinking of the fearful fate which might befall him, of the danger to his health in this precipitate journey, of his possible loss of appetite, sleep, spirits, or colour. Oh, if he could but be kept unconscious of any peril or pain assailing others !

Rapidly she crossed herself, donned a long, grey cloak, and shut a window that had remained open. Before the strong morning breeze clouds were chasing across the sky, the grass was bending on the lawn, and the tall poplars were swaying in the avenue leading to the villa. But the Countess, though brought up on family traditions, had no thought for reminiscences of her youth belonging to this country estate. She merely closed the window and went downstairs.

The mayor was conversing with his lordship by the carriage door.

" Have you just come from there ? " she asked the official, and, being informed that he had come from his home, she upbraided him for not having kept off the epidemic. He excused himself with polite smiles, to which the lady confusedly replied: "Never mind, then; never mind," as she hastened her child into the vehicle.

"Did you give him the money?" she whispered to her husband as soon as she was seated beside him. He made a sign in the affirmative.

"I should like to thank her ladyship, too," began the obsequious mayor, "for the generosity with which——"

"Oh, it was nothing—nothing!" interrupted the Count, scarcely knowing what he said.

Established in the carriage, the Countess made a rapid survey of bags and boxes, coats and shawls, umbrellas and parasols. Her husband in the meantime turned round to see if all the luggage was in its place in the barouche, which had been fastened on behind to the landau. "But," he suddenly remarked, "what is the matter with that little boy?"

"Yes, who is that crying?" excitedly called out the Countess, leaning far out of the carriage.

"All ready!" exclaimed the peasant who had been assisting the servants with the luggage, and to whose side clung a small, ragged urchin. "Stop, can't you?" his father bade him, sharply, then repeating the words, "All ready!"

The Count, with his eye on the boy, plunged into one of his pockets. "Don't give way, my boy; you shall have a soldo all to yourself."

"Mother is ill," whined the lad sorrowfully; "mother has the cholera."

Up jumped the Countess. Her face livid and contorted, she brought down her folded sunshade across the coachman's back:

"Drive on!" she shrieked; "drive on—quick!"

The menial whipped up the horses. They began to prance, and then went off at a gallop. The mayor barely had time to leap out of the way, and his lordship to fling out a handful of coppers, which scattered on the ground at the peasant's feet. He stood motionless—while the boy continued weeping—and stared after the flashing wheels of the carriage that rolled swiftly away, whirling up the dust.

"Damn those rich pigs!" he said.

Pretending not to hear, the mayor discreetly departed.

The peasant, a man of middle age and stature, pale, meagre, evil-looking, and as rugged as his offspring, made the youngster pick up the coins. Then they went home together.

They inhabited, in the yard belonging to one of the Countess's farmhouses, a tumble-down, unplastered brick hovel, situated between a dunghill and a pigsty. Before the door gaped a dark ditch, from which issued an indescribable stench, and which was bridged by a single rough plank. Upon entering, one found oneself in a dingy, unpaved sort of cavern. There was no flooring, either wood or stone, but there was an irregular brick fireplace, and in front of it the ground had been depressed by poor wretches kneeling to cook their mess of cornmeal. A wooden stair—three steps missing—conducted to the room, foul with dirt and rubbish, where father, mother, and son were wont to pass the night in a single bed. Standing by this article of furniture, one might look down into the kitchen below through the broken boards. The bed occupied the only spot not soaked by the rain that dripped from the roof.

Crouching on the floor, her head leaning against the edge of the bed, sat the peasant's cholera-stricken wife. Although but thirty, she looked old; at twenty she had been a blooming girl, and even now preserved remnants of mild beauty. At the first glance her husband understood; he swallowed an imprecation. The child, frightened by his mother's discoloured face, kept in the doorway.

"For Christ's sake, send him away," she moaned feebly. "I have the cholera; send him away. Go to your aunt's, dear. Take him away, and send me the priest."

"I'll go," said the man to her; and to the boy, motioning toward the farmyard gate, "You go to your aunt's."

From the porch of the yard he fetched an armful of straw, carried it into the kitchen, and went upstairs to his wife, who by exerting all her strength had contrived to get on the bed.

"Listen," said the man, in accents of unusual tenderness; "I am sorry, but if you die in the bed it will have to be burnt. You understand, don't you? I have brought some straw into the kitchen—a nice lot."

Too weak to answer, she made a mute signal of assent, and then a faint effort to rise from her couch. But the man took her up in his arms. By a gesture she begged him to reach first for a small silver crucifix hanging on the wall; she pressed it fervidly to her lips while her husband carried her down to the kitchen. Here he made her as comfortable as he could on the straw, before going for the priest.

And now she, too, this poor creature lying alone like a beast in a cage on the already infected straw—she, too, before departing to an unknown world, began to pray. She prayed for the salvation of her soul, convinced that she was guilty of many sins, and tormented by her inability to remember them.

When the timid doctor, sent by the mayor, arrived, he asked in great fright whether there was any rum or marsala in the house. There was neither; so he recommended hot bricks for her stomach, put up a notice of quarantine, and left her. The priest, who knew no fear, carelessly reeled off what he termed " the usual things," obscuring the divine message with words of his own. Nevertheless, though benighted and ignorant, the dying woman derived comfort and serenity therefrom.

His task done, the priest went. Meanwhile the husband had put a few more handfuls of straw under her back, and lit the fire to heat the bricks. His wife went on praying—less for her child than for the man whom she had pardoned so often, and who was embarked on the road to perdition. Finally, kissing the cross, her mind turned to its giver. She had received it sixteen years back, at her confirmation, from the Countess, the mistress of the splendid manor where it was a joy to live and of the wretched hovel where it was a joy to die. At that time the Countess was a young girl, and had presented the silver crucifix to the labourer's daughter at the suggestion of her mother, then mistress of the estate, a kind, gentle lady, long dead, but unforgotten by her humble tenants.

The dying woman acknowledged having thought ill of the new mistress, of having complained sometimes, so that *her* husband had cursed because, despite repeated petition, neither roof, nor flooring, nor staircase had ever been repaired, and because the window frames had not been filled with linen panes. Feeling truly penitent, in her heart she implored forgiveness of his lordship and her ladyship; and she besought the Holy Virgin to bless them both.

At the moment when her husband placed the scorching bricks on her stomach, a spasm ran through her body, and she gave up the ghost. The man flung some straw over her blackening face, wrenched the little cross out of her hand, stuffed it into his pocket with a scowl at its small value, mumbling some customary pious sentiment the while.

But he did not say, for he did not know, and we do not know, how much good this poor woman's crucifix had done, invoked and kissed by her on so many occasions. Still less can we tell how much benefit may yet spring from that charitable thought of an old lady, descending to an innocent child, and afterward reascending as a prayer from a pure heart to the Throne of Infinite Mercy.

The same evening the servants at the villa, who had been given leave of absence during the journey of the Count and Countess, got drunk in the drawing-room on rum and marsala.

MARIO PRATESI
1842–

DOCTOR PHŒBUS

MANY years ago a company, with capital to back it, took a lease of the manganese mines in the province of Valle Amena. Perhaps the " Pleasant Valley " may at one time have deserved its name ; but nowadays there is nothing pleasant about the monotonous barren hills, of no use to any one but the goats, and the distant woods, too scanty to lend any tint of green to the dry and desert landscape. The company's employés were scarcely to be blamed for not liking the place ; everything was scarce, even pretty faces—at least such as had had the benefit of soap and water. But the pay was good, and more than one among them had hopes of becoming a shareholder, or at least cashier ; and so things went on somehow or other. Two hundred navvies pushed the work rapidly forward, and enormous trucks full of the grey metal blocked the postal road day and night.

But all that glitters is not gold ; and one day the report spread that the flourishing company had failed, as though prosperity had undermined its foundations like stagnant water. It made a great talk in the neighbourhood, and every one concluded his or her comments by long exclamations of astonishment.

" *Mah !* " ejaculated the old, dried-up chaplain of the Charity Society, with his hands in the pockets of the threadbare shooting-coat which he always wore except when he put on his surplice to go and fetch the dead. " In my opinion it was just like when a set of people leave the gaming-table, where low cards have been dealt ; but they do not all leave with the same advantages."

" There is no getting at the exact truth," remarked the landlord of the village inn, who did not repent nearly so much of his sins as he did of having given credit ; " but in this business I too believe that the rogues have done the honest men who trust their neighbours, and never suspect any cheating."

" What nonsense ! " exclaimed Signor Vincenzino ; and perhaps he would have said more, only that, being syndic, and very rich, he thought it possible he might be risking the chance of a decoration. He rose from his seat in the Caffé del Giappone. " In any case," he continued, keeping his back turned to the host, " there is the law."

" I'd like to see it ! " replied mine host. " But it's very seldom that rogues who have grown rich do not find some one to help them, in one way or another, in keeping what they have stolen."

" Precisely ! " retorted the chaplain, holding up his finger like Dante under the Uffizi. " There are certain experts and certain lawyers who show a most extraordinary ability in this respect, and acquire enormous credit, so that sometimes the Government is even forced to raise them to the rank of *Commendatore*. You alone, poor Phœbus . . ."

And so on, and so on. . . . It would be tedious to repeat all the conversation that took place at the Caffé del Giappone. As to Phœbus, however, I should not be altogether disposed to agree with the chaplain. If Phœbus found no one to make the best of the arguments on his side when—having been blinded by the effects of an explosion at the works —he asked for a miserable little pension, which the Company refused, saying that his misfortune was due to his own carelessness, and not to the necessities of his work,—if, I say, he had no one to plead his cause, this must be regarded merely as an accident, which happened to him, as it may happen to hundreds of others in a like condition. Then came the crash ; and if a company were going to give every man what he wants, what motive could it have for declaring itself insolvent ? In this case, to recommend the fulfilment of any humane duties is like running after a mist-wreath, or asking a routed army, in full retreat, to think of the dead and wounded they are leaving behind.

I do not deny that the consequences were certainly unpleasant for Phœbus, who had now eaten nothing for three days, and sat in the chimney-corner, yawning and stretching his arms to such an amazing extent, first in one direction, and then in another, that he looked like the castle of St. Angelo when the fireworks are being let off on Easter Day. A miserable hen, which sat motionless, not daring to attract attention to itself, and a cat which seemed to have nothing more to wish for in this life, having now reached the very utmost degree of leanness, and lay curled up, with half-closed eyes, on the dead ashes of the hearth, were the only creatures not audibly complaining in the melancholy darkness of the hut, which covered so much misery. It seemed as though they were meditating on the infinite vanity of things. But not so Phœbus's wife, nor Vittorino, his little son ; for the one, by continual whimpering, and the other with her reproaches, added notes of sickening despair to the symphony of those sonorous, expansive, and well-nourished yawns of the blind man. Yet the wife had not the slightest reason for envying the cat; she was dry and thin as though she had nothing left for hunger and grief to gnaw at;—she was near her confinement, poor soul, and, with her face the colour of sodden dead leaves, and her black eyes, greedy, feverishly bright, and sunken in their sockets, she was a very different person from the comely young Rosalinda whom Phœbus had married when he returned from serving in the *Bersaglieri*. That was six months before the accident at the quarries; and now she was more like one of the thirsty, dropsical wretches in Dante's "Malebolge."

"Go to Sor Vincenzino," said Phœbus.

His wife did not reply.

"Go to the doctor."

"Don't you know that a hundred poor sinners might die before either of *them* would stir a finger? Don't you know that the doctor keeps on asking me for a franc for that tooth he pulled out last year?"

Phœbus moved his jaws for a little while, like an animal chewing the cud; then he gave seven or eight more yawns, and rubbed his hands as if he had just concluded a good stroke of business.

"Go to Nannone—go to the chaplain, to the archdeacon, to Lisetta—only go to some one!"

"I went to Nannone this morning—he was not at home. I went to the chaplain yesterday, and he gave me that bread. I went to Lisetta the day before yesterday, and she gave me that *polenta*. And who's going to the archdeacon's, with that vixen of a Modesta there? Not I!"

"Then, you ugly slug, you cannot be hungry, and must just eat your own talk!"

The wife rose, sobbing and muttering curses, and went out, dragging the water-jar with her as usual, as an excuse for knocking at people's doors. When they opened, however, it was something more than permission to draw water at the well that she wanted—her errand was more serious than that.

To-day she did not find them disposed to listen to tales of misery, for it was the last day of the carnival, and the weather was bright and clear. A cold wind kept the sky cloudless, and the sun, going down in the west, seemed to embrace the whole sky and earth with its rays, and smiled among the shadows and on the peaks of the snowy Apennines, which gradually faded away into the distance on the last clear rim of the horizon. But the village, all but the great ruined tower on the little piazza, the upper part of which was still in light, began to grow dark; and it was already dusk in the ancient, narrow streets, black as if after a conflagration, filled with crowds of country folk, among which the red shawls of the jolly peasant women made bright points here and there, and noisy with cymbals and other instruments, laughter, and shouting.

This, then, was not a propitious moment. In fact, Rosalinda was not long in returning, with her pitcher and her hands both empty. The people, nearly all poor, were tired of her continual requests, and by this time the pitcher trick was becoming stale.

"Eh!" said her husband, rubbing his hands as usual. "I suppose they would not open their doors to you, because it is winter, and they are afraid of the cold coming in?"

"Be quiet!" screamed Rosalinda to the child. "Be quiet, or I'll make an end of you!"

"Be quiet, Vittorino," repeated Phœbus. "This evening we shall have twenty loaves and some roast meat! Wife! you be quiet too, and give me those things that ought to be in the box!"

The things were a heap of rags, on the top of which lay a worn-out tall hat, very old, but seeming still to remember its former owner; for to those who had never seen him in any other hat for years and years it was impossible not to be instantly reminded of that wrinkled, benevolent, patient face, whose serious sadness was rather added to than diminished by the somewhat long chin and Dantesque nose. The other things—a waistcoat, knee-breeches, and a very long black overcoat—had very evidently belonged to an extremely poor and unfortunate priest.

But Vittorino began to laugh and dance when he saw his father put on not only this Court suit, as it seemed to him, which his wife handed him, grumbling and crying at the same time, but a pair of huge horse-hair whiskers and an enormous paper collar, the points of which reached nearly to the tip of his nose.

Not only this, but a wave of merriment ran through the whole village, like the ripple which a puff of wind makes in the surface of the lagoon, when Phœbus issued from his door thus dressed, with a huge book containing the whole series of ancient medical prescriptions under his arm. Some people insisted on recognising in his icy smile, in those remedies so learnedly prescribed in his slow, pompous manner, in that awkward, straddling walk, Doctor Ambrogio, the village physician for forty years, who was also surgeon, veterinary surgeon, and dentist. As dentist his renown had attracted people from the remotest villages; and for the expense and trouble he had undergone to acquire it he expected compensation even from the poor, though in justice it must be said (and this shows Doctor Ambrogio's fair-mindedness), much less than from the rich.

Other masks made a cheerful variation in the crowd—*stenterelli*, with painted faces and pigtails curled up like a point of interrogation, harlequins, Turks, madmen, wizards, and big, bearded creatures got up as nurses, and carrying turkeys swathed up in baby-clothes; which birds, pushing their red-wattled heads out from among the bandages, never imagined—though they seemed astonished and confused enough already—the slaughter which was to befall them later on. The women, with bright eyes and laughing lips, hung over each other's shoulders, in the windows and on the balconies, to get a sight of Phœbus. Only when he began to give utterance to certain jokes at which no girl—and not even a married woman—can very well laugh in public, then they knitted their brows, while the men, looking at them, laughed fit to kill themselves. Then his popularity grew; then it seemed as though Plenty thought fit to empty her cornucopia over Phœbus; then the public liberality knew no limits, and down were showered steaks, and bread, and sausages, and dumplings, and pine-kernel buns, and boiled chestnuts, and pears and apples, and flat cakes, and rosemary cake, and millet puddings—all poured on the devoted head of Phœbus, who, without putting the smallest morsel into his mouth, stuffed the whole into the front of his waistcoat, into his hat, and into all the pockets of his overcoat and trousers.

Yet none the less did he continue to look like Famine, or Lent personified, come to play the fool in the midst of all that courteous and kindly merriment. The clumsy black spectacles—with the glasses broken and mended with black sealing-wax—with which he covered the horrible sight presented by his burnt eyes, seemed of themselves to darken him, and take away every touch of life and mobility from his worn face, white as old wax, which might have been taken for that of an old man or one far gone in consumption, if it had not been for the intensely black hair, and the figure, which, though below the middle height, was broad in the chest, and all muscles and sinews. If his hair had been white he would not have moved people's compassion so much as he did when they saw him still fresh and robust ; for thus his lot appeared peculiarly unjust and cruel, paralysing his strong arms, and robbing him of so many years of ease gained by hard labour, and reducing him instead to the necessity of asking alms, which were so limited, and not always kindly given. Nevertheless, on account of that habit he had of smiling and rubbing his hands when speaking, many people thought him a merry and light-hearted man who was fond of his joke.

The shouting crowd hustled him out on the little square, where rises the gloomy tower—at that moment lit up by the last rays of the sun, with the hawks wheeling, in the blue sky, round the top.

Doctor Ambrogio, standing at the door of the chemist's shop, looked like Æsculapius himself, with his ruddy, well-nourished face, full of severe learning, and his long white beard, under which appeared, wound several times round his neck, a heavy scarlet woollen scarf. If this physician, who was great at blood-letting and cupping, had remained a little behind the times, the chemist had by no means done so ; and in this instance the old and the new generation joined hands. For the chemist, emulous of his city colleagues, had sold to a Florentine dealer in antiquities the phials and vases of glazed terra-cotta and the dried Nile crocodile, which, hanging with widely-opened jaws from the middle of the ceiling, had formerly given an uncanny idea of medical science and the apothecary's art, as though they had been devouring monsters. Moreover, he had decorated his shop with all the latest improvements—gilt boxes and ornamental stoppers, chalybeate water, and purgative syrups enclosed in cut-glass bottles ; and he never sold an ounce of cream of tartar or bitter salts without doing it up in a little bag of glazed paper. All this elegance certainly raised the price of his commodities ; but only consider how much it added to the efficiency of the drugs !

Here, right in front of this luxurious establishment, Phœbus stood still, in the midst of the crowd, opened his book, turned over the pages, and after discoursing for some time, concluded by prescribing Dr. Ambrogio, who was still standing in the doorway, and who suffered from sciatica, *a decoction of asinine cucumber*.

Dr. Ambrogio turned his back, closed the glass door, and said to Sor Vincenzino, who was seated on the sofa reading the paper : " This blind man is a public nuisance, and I cannot think why you don't get him out of the way. If I were syndic . . ."

" If you were syndic you would know what red-tape and difficulties and formalities are! Last year I tried to send him to the hospital for the blind at . . . , and they sent him back because he was not a native of the place."

" Yes, I remember. I gave him as full a certificate as I could to get him away from here. Good heavens! If this town is not a nest of wretchedness, I don't know what is."

The chaplain, who was also in the shop waiting for the chemist, seemed touched to the quick, and said—

" It is the fault of the rich. If the rich were to think more about giving work——"

But the doctor interrupted him.

" Here we are with the rich again! Can't you understand, sir, that the rich have too many taxes?" The syndic nodded approvingly. " It's the Government that's in fault," said the doctor. " Here's the dilemma, and there's no getting out of it:—Either they ought to take off the income-tax, or they, and not we, should see to the feeding of these starving wretches."

" Very true! Just the thing I have so often thought," answered the syndic. " Because if they were to take off the income-tax, that sum would remain in the treasury; but it cannot remain there, because the funds have to be turned to account; and for doing this labour is needed, and labour being needed it has to be paid for, and being paid for, why, there you are. Then people have something to eat! Why, that's quite clear, gentlemen! No difficulty in understanding that!"

" There was no need for your explanation," returned the chaplain, shrugging his shoulders with a slightly vexed look as he rose from the sofa, stretching out his legs, which appeared, long and thin as those of a blackbird, under the skirts of his wretched coat. " Even the poor Countess paid income-tax; yet at the end of the year she had spent a pretty large sum in good works. But her heirs have inherited her money and not her merciful heart."

" That is just the sort of speech you might be expected to make, belonging as you do to the Charity Society," said the doctor, with a quietly contemptuous smile.

" And a ruined man into the bargain!" whispered Sor Vincenzino into the doctor's ear. " Later on, some time, I'll tell you a little story about his niece."

" Throwing away one's own money in that fashion," the doctor went on, with a solemn air of wisdom, " is not charity; it is merely carrying out the whims of hysteria; and the Countess was hysterical from the tip of her great toe to the ends of her hair. It's a question of organisation. You're far behind the times, chaplain!"

"You had better take care. I may be in advance of you!"

"Everything *may* be; but that there ought to be methods and limits even in charity, for otherwise even great fortunes would fall into ruin, this indisputable and precious axiom of economic science, I am afraid—excuse me—you are not acquainted with. And with interest, you know, there is no joking."

Sor Vincenzino concluded his approving nods by one of final and comprehensive assent; and wishing to convey clearly to the chaplain that, in short, he thought nothing of him, he turned his back on him, and set himself, with a diplomatic countenance, to meditate over his newspaper. The chaplain understood that, and with his simple face full of grave sadness, and his white hair curling over his temples, remained standing, waiting patiently for the medicine for his poor, pretty niece, who was ill. The doctor kept looking out of the window, and saying to himself, "I should like to know what has become of the police! They ought to make an example and dismiss them both! If I saw one of them I'd tell him to make that rascal hold his tongue!"

"To-day I cure every one for nothing!" Doctor Phœbus was shouting in the midst of the crowd. "To-morrow it will be too late! Yes, it will be too late, unhappy people! If you have not enough to live upon—if you do not pay me a proper fee for every visit—if you don't want to pay a high price for medicines, and buy them here of my good friend the chemist, who is the only man who sells good ones—why then, unhappy wretches, you can be no patients of mine! Then you will have to go to the hospital—our hospital!—where he who goes in never comes out any more! What with fasting, and poultices, and gruel without salt, mallow-water and cuppings, in a week you will either be cured or gone where you want no more curing."

At this point the last glimmer of the fiery sunset, the sound of the great church bell, and the rattle of a drum which was going round announcing the "Last Wonderful Comedy of the Burattini," distracted the audience. A man slipped out of the Caffé del Giappone, in the dusk, with baking-pan full of pastry, just out of the oven, and hastened to carry it to the Casino for the evening's festivity. It was duly evident from all the going and coming that there were great things in the air.

Not only at the Casino, but there was to be dancing at Sora Carmelinda's and at Sor Gregorio's; there was to be dancing at the taverns, in the space between the wine-casks, and in the hay-lofts at the farms; for all which occasions there had been secretly stored up in every house masks and half-masks and *papier-mâché* noses, in which one could be perfectly certain of not being recognised. Time was pressing; the drum had ceased to beat and the bell to ring, and instead one could hear stray barrel-organs, to whose sound little companies of peasants came trooping in along the dark lanes; and here and there, scattered through the streets of the merry little town, the shouting and laughter which had previously been all concentrated in the square. Then Phœbus found that he had been left alone, in a deeper darkness than before. He stretched out his numbed hands in order to give them a joyful rub; but the long tight overcoat, now stuffed out with the bounty showered on him, got in his way; he tried to stoop and to raise his arms, but this too was a failure. He was impatient to get home quickly, and instead of being able to do so he was forced to grope his way slowly along those noisy streets, where he could scarcely find room to set his stick down.

"Wife! Vittorino! help! I can get no farther! Wife! Come and help me unload the casks full of presents my patients have given me!" he began to shout when he was a few paces from the house.

His wife and Vittorino hurried to meet him, and relieved him of his load in a twinkling; and having entered the house, all three ate like wolves, finding, moreover, here and there among the spoils, a piece of cod's head or a rotten apple, flung for a joke, which were thankfully received by the cat and the hen, now awakened; so provident is Nature.

Then, unluckily, Phœbus said to his wife, "This evening, at least, dear, you are not going to complain!" Alas! it was like putting the match to the powder-magazine. She had been quiet; but the words seemed to set her going afresh, and she began again—shrieks, tears, and lamentations; how much reason she had for complaining, and how much for thinking of the next day, and how much better it would have been if she had always remained single.

Then Phœbus began, in good earnest, to blaspheme like a heretic, in the brutal Tuscan way. Yet, being quick-witted and kind-hearted beyond the average, he understood that such a burst of temper, after all anxiety had been removed by so abundant a supper, could only have been caused by the state of her health ; and he resisted the temptation of bringing her to her senses by a good beating. Instead of that, he shuddered, pitied her, and sat down comfortably in the chimney-corner without saying another word.

But poor little Vittorino, cheered by the unaccustomed supper, began to sing and jump about in that gloomy den, just like a bird which has seen the sun rise. Only the poor woman felt as if her nerves were being torn to pieces by the noise ; and she thought the child, young as he was, ought to have understood that there was cause rather for crying than laughing. Then he began to cry ; but that, also, would not do ; he was to be quiet and not let himself be heard in any way. The child obeyed with a sigh, and the mother then took him in her arms, soothing, petting, and kissing him. But these caresses of his mother's who was sobbing after having beaten him (the blind man was singing to himself the whole time), could not draw a smile from him ; tired out and very serious, he fell asleep in her arms, and she laid him down on the ghastly mattress and stretched herself beside him. And after that there was nothing more to be seen or heard in the room. . . .

They were all asleep, even Phœbus, who loved sleep because it gave him back his liberty. By day, when he was awake, there was always a cloud surrounding him, and he fancied that he had to bore his way through it, as a mole bores through the ground, to find the sun he had lost. But that dark path went on and on, and never came to an end ; it was only in the darkness of night that he could even see the sun again, when he slept and dreamed that he was no longer blind, but could move about freely as before, with his eyes open and seeing. Then he saw them all again—not his little Vittorino, for the child had been born since his misfortune, and the father had never looked on his bright eyes and pretty features ; but his wife, and his parents, and his mates, and sometimes lovely distant landscapes that he had never seen before. . . . He had never had such beautiful dreams before he became blind. . . .

But that night he did not sleep sound, for a hand shook him roughly as he sat in the dark corner of the hearth, and recalled him to the reality of things—namely, to the belfry tower to ring the bells, according to orders received from the archdeacon, from eleven o'clock to midnight, in order to announce the beginning of Lent, and warn people against breaking in on the fast and vigil.

At the command, then, of Phœbus, still masquerading as the doctor, two beggars, acting as his subordinates, who had already entered the tower and seized the bell-ropes, began bending their backs and rising again to the swing of the bells—a " double " so loud and eloquent in the gloomy silence as to reach even the most distant cabins, where some ancient oaks marked the boundary of the parish. But for a great many the bells tolled in vain. Nay, some masks even went and stood under the archdeacon's windows, making unseemly noises, howling and whistling with the intention of annoying him. And in some hay-lofts the young men, laughing at the remonstrances of the old and the continued tolling of the bells, kept up the dancing till daybreak, amid the smoke of the pipes and the sawing of the violins. The girls, it is true, were somewhat recalcitrant ; but with a few scruples of conscience and a little remorse, they let themselves be whirled away, after a while, willingly enough.

After ringing for an hour, Phœbus, hearing the archdeacon's maid-servant call him from a window, entered, with his companion, the corridor of that dignitary's house, and having cautiously knocked at a door, was told to come in. They entered a large room lit by an old-fashioned brass lamp. Facing the door, at a little round table, smoking and sipping punch, after having finished their game at chess, sat the good archdeacon, a jolly man of portly presence, verging upon seventy ; Cavalier Vincenzino, the syndic, with bye-laws and civic enactments clearly written on the folds of his brow and the curves of his mouth ; and the preaching friar, an elderly and hypocritical Franciscan, with red hair and a round face, who had arrived that very day to preach the Lenten sermons. When Phœbus and his companions entered, the friar hid his modest little pipe in his wide sleeve, and produced instead a snuff-box, from which he immediately offered a pinch to the syndic and the archdeacon, who readily accepted. The archdeacon, seeing Phœbus appear before him in that burlesque costume, and with that crushed and battered chimney-pot hat, threw back the tassel of his black skull-cap, which was dangling close to his left ear, and nearly choked himself with laughter. Modesta, the maid, who made a glorious entry, carrying a large dish of steaming meat-dumplings, hastened to set them down on the other table, which was ready laid in the middle of the room, so that she might scratch her head and laugh, like her master—or even louder and longer. This pleased neither the preaching friar nor the syndic, and they whispered together, looking deeply scandalised.

"*Persicomele!*" exclaimed the archdeacon, "are you going about masked after the stroke of twelve? And what sort of a costume might this be?"

"It is the costume of a doctor of medicine!"

"Dear archdeacon, my dear sir!" said the Franciscan, pointing at Phœbus, "this suit of clothes has belonged to a priest; do you not see the black stockings, the knee-breeches, the waistcoat? Archdeacon, it is not the proper thing to let the clothes of the clergy be seen in a masquerade."

"*Persicomele!*" exclaimed the archdeacon, looking more closely, as he passed his hand over his knees, as if dusting his breeches. "Who gave you these clothes?"

"The chaplain!"

"Good! very good!" exclaimed the syndic, chuckling with delight, but he immediately resumed the calm, severe, and munificent aspect of the person who has to sign municipal edicts.

"It seems impossible that, at the present day, certain priests should have so little respect for their cloth!" said the Franciscan indignantly. "Fatal effects, my dear sir! . . ." And he took an enormous pinch of snuff, with both hands.

"You must not believe, reverend father," replied the syndic, with some heat, "that the chaplain gives the law to our commune; he is a——"

"Sir!" exclaimed the archdeacon.

"But you don't know——"

"I don't want to know. The chaplain is a priest, and that's enough! Find me another who for 260 francs will take the services of the Charity Society the whole year round, who will go ten or twelve miles on foot, in the depth of winter, or in the dog-days, to attend a funeral, and that with seventy years on his back! And then he has all his brother's family to keep—seven persons! But you were only joking, Cavalier!—so never mind, let it pass. . . . And as for you, you blind rascal, I must speak to you again about this. You had no business to go masquerading in these clothes, which were given you in charity. To-morrow, I shall tell the chaplain to take them away from you again!"

"What a pity!" thought Doctor Phœbus to himself; "I was going to make the overcoat into a nice jacket to wear only on feast-days!"

" But, to make a short story of it," resumed the archdeacon after some moments of anxious silence, " what did you come here for—eh ? "

" We came to see whether it is time for the meat dumplings."

" The dumplings are on the table ; sit down, therefore, and eat."

" Fair and softly," exclaimed one of the guests a little later, giving Phœbus a tremendous nudge with his elbow.

" Blind man, you're going too fast ! " cried the archdeacon, looking at him.

" May I lose my sight if I have eaten more than two ! "

" Two !—you've eaten a dozen ! "

" The blind man has a good appetite ! Well, there's no harm—his teeth will stand it ! " said Modesta, who was seated close by, counting the mouthfuls.

" Well then, Modesta, my dear," said Phœbus, " when his reverence says, ' Modesta, give the blind man a piece of bread and some meat, poor fellow ! ' why do you give me nothing but little dry crusts and cheese-parings ? Do you take me for a mouse, Modesta ? "

" Blind man, blind man, you are never satisfied ! "

" Bless your reverence ! " said Modesta, " it would take a great deal to satisfy him ! "

" Nay, 'twould take little enough. I would be quite content if I had the sight of my eyes again."

" Good luck to you ! " exclaimed the syndic at last, after having for some time looked on in admiring silence at the process of mastication and deglutition. " The like of us would be dead in three days if they ate in that fashion ! "

" Just try a little abstinence ! " said Doctor Phœbus. " Try living all the year round on wild herbs and roots boiled without salt, or roasted in the ashes. That's my prescription for you, sir ! "

" Well, well," said the syndic, " I would willingly exchange my life for yours. You have no expenses ; you pay no taxes—do you think that a small thing ? Now, I have to spend the very soul out of my body ; a little for the cat and a little for the dog, and what remains for me ? At the end of the year—so much received, so much spent, everything paid, and nothing over ! "

" I should just like to take you by the neck and hold you down to our life for a month or so, so that you could try it ! "

" Is that the way to speak to me ? " said the syndic, somewhat offended. " You ought to be more respectful."

" Oh! you must not think, my dear sir," said the archdeacon, " that the blind man is really wanting in respect towards the authorities. Not at all! He may be a little quick-tempered now and then, but when he recollects himself he is a perfect lamb! "

" A kind of lamb which——" began the Franciscan.

" What do you expect? " interrupted Phœbus. " I used to be as sweet as sugar; but now I am a little spoilt with doing nothing. Now that I have tried it I find, in truth, that the labour of a porter is better than the idleness of a gentleman. Just set me to work in your factory, sir; let me turn the wheel, and give me thirty centimes a day, and you'll see how the blind man works! "

" Oh! indeed; you and your blarney!" retorted the syndic. " Look here, I would willingly help you, but I cannot. I shall have to shut up the works soon, to turn off every one, even my cook. Are they making game of us with these taxes? I don't know how we can go on; I haven't ten shillings left in the world. It is not my place as syndic to say so, but the fault certainly lies with the Government. . . ."

" Heigho! " said the blind man, " we shall be disappointed indeed, if we are putting our trust in you, Mr. Government! "

" You should put your trust in Providence, young man," said the preaching friar, " and come and hear my sermons! "

" Indeed and he shall come to the sermons, and be hanged to him!" exclaimed the archdeacon. " I'll give him a couple of eggs for every sermon; at Easter, so many sermons and so many eggs. But if you miss one sermon, you blind rascal, you shall get nothing at all! "

" Put it in writing, sir! "

" Why, you blind scoundrel, are you afraid of my dying first? "

" You, sir?—why, you'll live to the age of Noah on the clerical soups that Modesta makes for you! No; it's I that may die before Easter, and I should like to bequeath that little legacy of eggs to my family! "

" Come, come, Modesta! never mind the blind man; it's time to clear the table. Don't sit there keeping the brazier warm."

" Goodness gracious! " exclaimed Modesta, looking into the dish; " there were sixty, and there are only eleven left! "

" I'm very sorry I didn't eat them too! " replied Phœbus, " but I'll come to breakfast after the sermon to-morrow and finish them! "

" Yes, come by all means; they'll just do for you! " said the archdeacon, giving a glance at the dish.

"Are they made of meat or potatoes?" asked the Franciscan, with another great pinch of snuff.

"Of meat, of meat," said Modesta testily.

"Yes, there's just enough meat to swear by!" said Phœbus.

"Even though there were but a piece the size of a pin's head," said the friar as he took another pinch, "that would be enough! To-morrow, you know, archdeacon, it's a black vigil."

"The friar is right! Do you want to go to hell for eating dumplings to-morrow! *Persicomele!* there'll be no more dumplings now till next year,—so good-bye, my fine fellow! Modesta, light the syndic to the door. Don't you see that he has put on his cloak, and wants to go? Good-night, sir!"

"Good-night, archdeacon!" said the syndic, and then turned to whisper in his ear, "By the bye, the chaplain always stands up for all bad characters . . . and his niece. . . ."

"Why, whatever has the chaplain done to you? Modesta, light these other people out!"

"Never mind me, I can see in the dark!" replied Phœbus, going towards the door. "Modestina, dear, don't you bother yourself with the light; you're using up too much oil; you should be saving with it, Modestina!"

"What are you thinking of, poor blind man?—such a trifle as that!" cried Modesta. "Good gracious! we're all of us baptized Christians, and a little light costs nothing."

The blind man, in going out, closed the door with such a tremendous bang that he put out Modesta's lamp; and returning to his disconsolate hut, wished two or three apoplexies to that meddling vagabond of a friar who had deprived him of those poor clothes and the remains of the supper, with which it was the archdeacon's annual custom to reward the four poor wretches for their labours in the belfry. Having reached his house, he told his wife the good tidings of the eggs at Easter, and fell asleep in the time it takes to tell it. But that night he saw in his dreams neither flowers, nor cities, nor seas bright in the sunshine. He dreamed instead that he was the stout director of the manganese mines, and that he was sitting in a nicely-warmed room at a well-spread table, and just tasting the full flavour of a fat roast fowl. He was just at work on one of the legs when his wife began to turn him over and call him to get up. He struggled with his hands, feeling the director of the mines gradually disappear, and a moment later he became aware that he was only blind Phœbus. Then he hit himself a great thump on the head, and started up because he heard the bells ringing for sermon. When he had got into church he sat down close to the sacristy door, so that the archdeacon might be sure to see him. The preacher seemed to be flinging squalls of rain and wind, and all the devils of hell down from the pulpit on all the crowded, uncovered heads. Phœbus paid no attention to him. When he came out, certain good-for-nothing youngsters, loafing outside, shouted after him:

"Phœbus! Phœbus! what has the preacher been saying?"

"I don't know!" he replied. "I was thinking of the eggs!"

"By Bacchus! the archdeacon is quite right in thinking him a little cracked! But I do believe that he would be a true believer if he saw the Divine Master's teachings practised a little better, and also a little to his advantage!"

This was what the chaplain said to himself as he came out from the service, with displeasure still written on his face, and also a certain timid disgust, whether provoked by living men or by the dead, whom he was constantly obliged to see, I do not know.

EDMONDO DE AMICIS
1846–1908

THE LITTLE SARDINIAN DRUMMER

ON the 24th of July 1848, the first day of the battle of Custoza, sixty soldiers belonging to one of our regiments of infantry, were ordered to garrison a lonely house on a height near by. But they were suddenly attacked by two companies of Austrians, who, assaulting them on several sides, scarcely gave them time to take refuge within the house and barricade the door, leaving their dead and wounded on the field.

The door being well secured, our soldiers hastened to the windows on the ground floor and upper floor, and opened a deadly fire on the besiegers, who replied vigorously as they slowly approached in the form of a semicircle.

The sixty Italian soldiers were commanded by two subaltern officers, and by a tall, silent, grim old captain, with white hair and whiskers.

With them was a little Sardinian drummer, a boy scarcely more than fourteen years old, but who did not look even twelve, with his dark, olive skin, and black, deep-set eyes with fire in them.

From a room on the upper storey the captain directed the defence, every order sounding like a pistol shot, his iron countenance showing not the slightest emotion.

The little drummer, pale, but with his feet firmly planted on the table, and holding fast to the walls, stretched out his head and neck to look from the window, and saw through the smoke the Austrians steadily advancing over the fields.

The house was near the top of a very steep hillside, so that only one small high window in the upper floor looked out over the crest. The Austrians did not threaten that side, nor was there anybody on the hill-top. The fire was directed against the front and the two sides.

The firing was infernal—a close, heavy hailstorm of balls rained upon the walls and through the broken roof, tearing out the ceiling, shattering the beams, doors, furniture, filling the air with fragments, plaster, and clouds of lime and dust, utensils and broken glass whizzing, clattering over their heads, rebounding from the walls with a terrifying noise and clash.

Now and then a soldier stationed at the windows fell inward, and was pushed to one side; others staggered from room to room, stanching their wounds with their hands. In the kitchen lay one soldier, pierced through the forehead. The enemy was closing in. At last the captain, until then impassive, began to show signs of uneasiness, and hurriedly left the room, followed by a sergeant. In a few moments the sergeant came rushing back, called the drummer, telling him to follow.

The boy raced up the stairs after him, and entered a dilapidated garret, in which he saw the captain with pencil and paper in hand, leaning on the window-sill, and lying on the ground at his feet was a rope belonging to the well.

The captain folded the paper, and, fixing on the boy those cold, grey eyes before which every soldier trembled, said abruptly:

" Drummer! "

The little drummer's hand went up to his cap.

The captain said:

" Thou art brave."

The boy's eyes flashed.

" Yes, captain," he answered.

" Look down yonder," said the captain, taking him to the window, " on the ground, near the house of Villafranca, where those bayonets glisten. There is our regiment, motionless. Take this paper, grasp this rope, let yourself down from the window, cross the hill like lightning, rush through the fields, reach our men, and give this paper to the first officer you see. Take off your belt and knapsack."

The drummer took off his belt and knapsack, and hid the paper in his breast pocket; the sergeant threw out the rope, holding fast one end; the captain helped the boy to jump through the window, his back toward the fields.

" Be careful," said he, " the salvation of this detachment depends on thy valour and thy legs."

" Trust me, captain," said the drummer, sliding down.

" Crouch low on dropping," again said the captain, taking hold of the rope, too.

" Have no fear."

" God speed thee! "

In a few moments the boy was on the ground, the sergeant drew up the rope, and disappeared, while the captain hastened to the little window, and saw the drummer racing down the hill. He now hoped he would escape unseen, but five or six little clouds of dust rising from the ground warned him that the boy had been discovered by the Austrians, who were firing down from the top of the hill. Those little clouds were the earth torn up by the balls. But the drummer continued running at full speed. After a while the captain exclaimed in consternation : " Dead ! " but scarcely was the word out of his mouth when he saw the little drummer rise.

" Ah, it was but a fall ! " said he, and breathed again.

The drummer again ran on, but he limped.

" He has sprained his foot," said the captain.

A little cloud of dust rose here and there around the boy, but always farther from him.

He was beyond their reach. The captain uttered a cry of triumph ; but his eyes followed him, tremblingly, for it was a question of minutes. If he did not soon reach the regiment with the note, asking for immediate succour, all his soldiers would be killed, or he would be obliged to surrender, and become a prisoner of war with them.

The boy ran for a while rapidly, then he stopped to limp ; again he ran on, but every few minutes he stopped to limp.

" Perhaps a ball has bruised his foot," thought the captain, and he tremblingly noted all his movements, and in his excitement he talked to the drummer as if he could hear him. Every moment his eyes measured the distance between the boy and the bayonets that glistened below on the plain, in the midst of the golden wheat-fields.

Meantime he heard the whistling and the crash of the balls in the rooms below, the voice of command, the shouts of rage of the officers and sergeants ; the sharp cries of the wounded, and the noise of broken furniture and crumbling plaster.

" Courage ! Valour ! " he cried, his eyes following the drummer in the distance. " Forward ! Run ! Malediction ! He stops ! Ah, he is up again, forward ! "

An officer out of breath comes to tell him that the enemy, without ceasing the fire, wave a white handkerchief, demanding their surrender.

" Let no one answer ! " shouts the captain, without taking his eyes from the boy, who was now in the valley, but who no longer ran, and who seemed hopeless of reaching the regiment.

" Forward ! Run ! " cried the captain with teeth and fists clenched.

" Bleed to death, die, unfortunate boy, but reach your destination ! " Then he uttered a horrible oath. " Ah, the cursed idler has sat down ! "

In fact, up to that moment the boy's head, that could be seen above the wheat, now disappeared as if he had fallen. After a moment his head was again seen, then he was lost behind the wheat-field, and the captain saw him no more.

Then he hurried downstairs. The balls rained, the rooms were full of wounded, some of whom rolled over like drunken men, catching at the furniture ; the walls and floors were covered with blood. Dead bodies lay across the threshold ; the lieutenant's arm was broken by a ball. Smoke and powder filled the rooms.

" Courage ! " shouted the captain. " Stand to your post ! Succour is coming ! Courage a little longer ! "

The Austrians had approached closer. Their disfigured faces could be seen through the smoke. Through the crash of balls could be heard the savage cries insulting them, demanding their surrender, and threatening to cut their throats. A soldier, terrified, withdrew from the window, and the sergeants again pushed him forward.

The fire of the besieged slackened. Discouragement showed on every face ; resistance was no longer possible. The moment came when the Austrians redoubled their efforts, and a voice thundered, at first in German, then in Italian :

" Surrender ! "

" No ! " shouted the captain from a window. The fire became more deadly, more furious on both sides. Other soldiers fell. There was more than one window without defenders. The fatal moment was imminent. The captain's voice died away in his throat as he exclaimed :

" They do not come ! They do not come ! "

And he ran furiously from side to side, brandishing his sabre convulsively, ready to die. Then a sergeant, rushing down from the garret, shouted with stentorian voice :

" They come ! "

" Ah, they come ! " joyfully shouted the captain.

On hearing that cry all—the well, the wounded, sergeants and officers—crowded to the windows and again the fierceness of the defence was redoubled. Soon there was noticed among the enemy a kind of vacillation and a beginning of disorder. Suddenly the captain gathered a few soldiers together on the lower floor to resist with fixed bayonets the impetuous attack on the outside. Then he went upstairs. Scarcely had he mounted when he heard the sound of hurried footsteps, accompanied by a formidable " Hurrah ! " and the pointed hats of the Italian carbineers appeared through the smoke, a squadron at double-quick, a brilliant flash of swords whirled through the air above their heads, their shoulders, their backs ; then out charged the little detachment, with fixed bayonets, led by the captain. The enemy wavered, rallied, and at last began to retreat. The field was evacuated, the house was saved, and shortly after two battalions of Italian infantry and two cannon occupied the height.

The captain and the surviving soldiers were incorporated with their regiment, fought again, and the captain was slightly wounded in the hand by a spent ball during the last bayonet charge. The victory on that day was won by the Italians.

But the following day the battle continued. The Italians were conquered, in spite of their heroic resistance, by superior numbers, and on the morning of the 26th they were in full retreat toward the Mincio.

The captain, though wounded, marched at the head of his company, weary and silent, arriving at sunset at Goito on the Mincio. He immediately sought his lieutenant, who, with his arm broken, had been picked up by the ambulance, and who must have arrived before he did. They pointed out to him a church in which the field hospital had been installed. He went there, the church was filled with the wounded lying in two rows of cots, and mattresses laid on the floor. Two physicians and several practitioners were busily coming and going, and nothing was heard but groans and stifled cries.

Scarcely had the captain entered when he stopped and glanced around in search of his subordinate.

At that moment he heard, near by, his name called faintly :

" Captain ! "

He turned. It was the little drummer. He was stretched upon a wooden cot, covered up to the neck with a coarse old red and white check window curtain, his arms lying outside, pale and thin, but with his eyes burning like two coals of fire.

" What ! is it thou ? " asked the captain in a surprised, abrupt manner. " Bravo, thou hast fulfilled thy duty."

" I did all that was possible," replied the drummer.

" Art thou wounded ? " asked the captain, glancing around at the beds, in search of his lieutenant.

"What could you expect?" replied the boy, who was eager to speak of the honour of being wounded for the first time, otherwise he would not have dared to open his lips before his captain.

"I ran as long as I could with my head down, but, though I crouched, the Austrians saw me immediately. I would have arrived twenty minutes earlier had they not wounded me. Fortunately I met a captain of the general's staff, to whom I gave the note. But it was with great effort I got along after that. I was dying with thirst. I was afraid I could not arrive in time. I cried with rage, thinking that every minute's delay sent one of ours to the other world. But I did all I could. I am content. But look, captain, and excuse me, you are bleeding!"

In fact, from the palm of the badly bandaged hand the blood was flowing.

"Do you wish me to tighten the bandage, captain? Let me have it for a moment."

The captain gave him his left hand, and stretched out his right hand to help tie the knot; but scarcely had the little fellow risen from the pillow when he turned pale, and had to lie back again.

"Enough! enough!" said the captain, looking at him, and withdrawing his bandaged hand, which the drummer wished to retain. "Take care of yourself instead of thinking of others, for slight wounds, if neglected, may have grave consequences."

The little drummer shook his head.

"But thou," said the captain, looking attentively at him, "thou must have lost much blood to be so weak."

"Lost much blood?" repeated the boy, smiling. "Something more than blood. Look!" and he threw down the coverlet. The captain drew back in horror.

The boy had but one leg; the left leg had been amputated above the knee. The stump was wrapped in bloody cloths.

Just then a small, fat army physician in shirt-sleeves passed.

"Ah, captain," said he rapidly, pointing out the little drummer; "there is an unfortunate case. That leg could have been easily saved had he not forced it so much, caused inflammation; it was necessary to amputate it. But he is brave, I assure you. He did not shed a tear or utter a cry. I was proud, while operating, to think he was an Italian boy, my word of honour! Faith, he comes of good stock!"

And he went on his way.

The captain wrinkled his bushy white eyebrows, and looked fixedly at the little drummer while covering him up with the coverlet. Then, slowly, almost unconsciously, yet still looking at him, his hand went to his képi, which he took off.

" Captain ! " exclaimed the astonished boy. " What, captain, for me ? "

The rough old soldier, who had never spoken a gentle word to an inferior, replied in a soft and exceedingly affectionate voice :

" I am but a captain, thou art a hero ! "

Then he threw his arms about the little drummer and kissed him with all his heart.

A GREAT DAY

Edmondo de Amicis

THE G——s were living in the country, near Florence, when the Italian army began preparations to advance upon Rome. In the family the enterprise was regarded with disapproval. The father, the mother, and the two grown daughters, all ardent Catholics and temperate patriots, talked of *moral measures*.

"We don't profess to understand anything about politics," Signora G—— would say to her friends; "I am especially ignorant; in fact, I am afraid I should find it rather difficult to explain *why* I think as I do. But I can't help it; I have a presentiment. There is something inside me that keeps saying: 'This is not the right way for them to go to Rome; they ought not to go, they must not go!' I remember how things were in forty-eight, and in fifty-nine and sixty; well, in those days I never was frightened, I never had the feeling of anxiety that I have now; I always thought that things would come right in the end. But now, you may say what you please, I see nothing but darkness ahead. You may laugh as much as you like . . . pray heaven we don't have to cry one of these days! I don't believe that day is so far off."

The only one of the household who thought differently was the son, a lad of twenty, just rereading his Roman history, and boiling over with excitement. To mention Rome before him was to declare battle, and in one of these conflicts feeling had run so high that it had been unanimously decided not to touch upon the subject in future.

One evening, early in September, one of the official newspapers announced that the Italian troops had actually entered the Papal States. The son was bursting with joy. The father read the article, sat thinking awhile, and then, shaking his head, muttered: "No!" and again: "No!" and a third time: "No!"

"But I beg your pardon, father!" shouted the boy, all aflame.

"Don't let us begin again," the mother gently interposed; and that evening nothing more was said. But the next night something serious happened. The lad, just before going to bed, announced, without preamble, as though he were saying the most natural thing in the world, that he meant to go to Rome with the army.

There was a general outcry of surprise and indignation, followed by a storm of reproaches and threats. No decent person would willingly be present at such scenes as were about to be enacted; it was enough that, as Italians, they were all in a measure to blame for what had happened, without deliberately assuming the shame of being an eye-witness; there was nothing one could not forgive in a lad of good family, except (it was his mother who spoke) this craze to go and see *a poor old man bombarded.* A fine war! A glorious triumph, indeed!

When they had ended the lad set his teeth, tore in bits the paper clutched between his fingers, and, lighting a candle, flung out of the room, stamping his feet like an Italian actor representing an angry king.

Half an hour later he stole gently back to the dining-room. His father and mother sat there alone, sad and silent. He asked pardon of his father, who grumblingly shook hands; then he returned to his room, followed by his mother.

"Then we shall hear no more of these ideas?" she tenderly suggested, laying her hands on his shoulders.

He answered her with a kiss.

The next day he crossed the borders of the Papal States.

The discovery of his flight was received with tears, rage, and invectives. They would never consent to see him again; if he came back, they would not even rise from their seats to welcome him; they would not speak to him for a month; they would cut off his allowance; they had a hundred other plans for his discomfiture. With the mother it was only talk; but the father meant what he said. He was a good but hard man, averse to compromises, and violent in his anger; his son knew it and feared him. It was incomprehensible that the lad should have ventured upon such a step.

The news of the 20th of September only increased the resentment of his parents.

"He will see," they muttered. "Only let him try to come back!"

Their words, their gestures, the manner in which they were to receive him, were all thought out and agreed upon: he was to receive a memorable lesson.

On the morning of the 22nd they were all seated in the dining-room, reading, when there was a great knock at the door, and the boy, flushed, panting, sunburnt, stood erect and motionless on the threshold.

No one moved.

" What ! " cried the boy, extending his arms in amazement, " you haven't heard the news ? "

No one answered.

" Hasn't any one told you ? Has no one been out from Florence ? Are you all in the dark still ? "

No one breathed.

" We have heard," one of the girls at length faltered, after exchanging glances with her father, " that Rome was taken——"

" What ! Is *that* all ? "

" That is all."

" But what a victory ! What a victory ! " cried the son, with a shout that set them trembling. " So I am the one to tell you of it ! "

They sprang up and surrounded him.

" But how is it possible ? " he went on, with excited gestures—" how is it possible that you haven't heard anything ? Have there been no rumours about the neighbourhood ? Haven't the peasants held a meeting ? What is the municipality about ? Why, it's inconceivable ! Just listen—here, come close to me, so—I'll tell you the whole story ; my heart's going at such a rate that I can hardly speak . . ."

" But what has happened ? "

" Wait ! You sha'n't know yet. You must hear the whole story first, from beginning to end. I want to tell you the thing bit by bit, just as I saw it."

" But *what* is it ?—the Roman festival ? "

" The *plébiscite* ? "

" The King's arrival ? "

" No, no, no ! Something much more tremendous ! "

" But tell us, tell us ! "

" Sit down, lad ! "

" But how is it that we haven't heard anything about it ? "

" How can I tell ? All I know is that bringing you the first news of it is the most glorious thing that's ever happened to me. I reached Florence this morning—they knew all about it there, so I rushed straight out here. I fancied that perhaps you mightn't have heard yet—I . . . I'm all out of breath. . . ."

" But tell us, tell us quickly ! " the mother and daughters cried, drawing their chairs around him. The father remained at a distance.

" You shall hear, mother—*such* things ! " the boy began. " Here, come closer to me. Well, you know what happened on the morning of the twenty-first ? The rest of the regiments entered ; there were the same crowds, the same shouting and music as on the day before. But suddenly, about midday, the noise stopped as if by common consent, first in the Corso, then in the other principal streets, and so, little by little, all over the city. The troops of people began to break up into groups, talking to each other in low voices ; then they scattered in all directions, taking leave of each other in a way that made one think they meant to meet again. It seemed as though the signal had been given to prepare for something tremendous. Men said a hasty word to each other in passing and then hurried on, each going his own way. The whole Corso was in movement ; people were rushing in and out of the houses, calling out from the street and being answered from the windows ; soldiers dashed about as though in answer to a summons ; cavalry officers trotted by ; men and boys passed with bundles of flags on their shoulders and in their arms, all breathless and hurried, as if the devil were after them. Not knowing a soul, and having no way of finding out what it all meant, I tried to guess what was up from the expression of their faces. They all looked cheerful enough, but not as frantically glad as they had been ; there was a shade of doubt, of anxiety. One could see they were planning something. From the Corso I wandered on through some of the narrower streets, stopping now and then to watch one of the groups. Everywhere I saw the same thing—crowds of people, all in a hurry, all coming and going, with the same air that I had already noticed in the Corso, of concealing from somebody what they were doing, although it was all being done in the open. Knots, bands, hundreds of men and women passed me in silence ; they were all going in the same direction, as though to some appointed meeting-place."

" Where were they going ? " the father and mother interrupted.

" Wait a minute. I went back to the Corso. As I approached it I heard a deep, continuous murmur of voices, growing louder and louder, like the noise of a great crowd. The Corso was full of people, all standing still and facing toward the Capitol, as though they expected something to come from that direction. From the Piazza del Popolo to the Piazza di Venezia they were jammed so tight that nobody could budge. I heard whispers flying about: 'Now they're coming!'—'They're coming from over there!'—'Who's coming?'—'The main column—here's the main column!'—'Here it is!'—'No, it isn't!' 'Yes, it is!' All at once there was a stir in the crowd, and a big shout, 'Here they are!' and down the middle of the street a wide passage-way seemed to open of itself, as though to make room for a procession. Every head was uncovered. I fought my way through from the outer edge of the crowd, to get a look at what was coming. I can feel the shiver down my back now! First, a lot of generals in full uniform, and gentlemen in civilian's dress, with the tricoloured scarf; in the midst of them, girls, women, and ragged, tattered men; workmen, peasants, women with babies, soldiers of all arms; smartly-dressed ladies, students, whole families clutching hold of each other's hands, for fear of getting lost in the crowd; all jammed together, trampled upon, so that they could barely move; and with it all not a sound but a buzzing, monotonous murmur; silence on both sides of the street; silence in the windows. It was awfully solemn; half strange and half fearful. I felt as if I were in a trance."

"But where were they going to?" his parents and sisters interposed with growing impatience.

"Wait a bit!" he returned. "I fought my way into the thick of it, with the crowds on both sides of the street piling in on top of me. Lord, what a crush! They spread out like a torrent, pouring into every cranny, sweeping people on ahead of them, into shop-doors, into the courtyards of houses, wherever there was a yard of vacant space. As we went on, other streams of people kept surging into the Corso from all the side streets, which were just as closely packed; on we swept from the Capitol; and they said that there were thousands more in the Forum. Hordes kept pouring in from the Piazza di Spagna, from the Via del Babbuino, from the Piazza del Popolo. Every one had something in his hand: a wreath of flowers, a branch of olive or laurel, a banner, a rag tied to a stick. Some carried holy images uplifted above their heads; inscriptions, emblems, pictures of the Pope, of the King, of the Princes, of Garibaldi; never under the sun was there such a medley and confusion of people and things! And all the while only that low murmur, and the great multitude moving on with a calmness, a dignity that seemed miraculous. I felt as though I were dreaming!"

They gathered close round him without a word.

"Suddenly I noticed that the crowd had turned to the left. Round we all went; very slowly, with the greatest difficulty, shoved, trampled on, knocked about; with our arms pinned to our sides, and hardly able to breathe, we fought our way, street by street, to the little square by the bridge of St. Angelo. The bridge itself was crammed with people; beyond it there were more crowds, which seemed to stretch all the way to St. Peter's. The right bank of the Tiber swarmed like an ant-hill. Crossing the bridge was a hard job; it took us over a quarter of an hour. The poor devils on each side, in their fear of being pushed over the edge, clutched the parapet madly, and shouted with terror; I believe there were several accidents.

"Well, at last we got across. All the streets leading to the Piazza of St. Peter were choked with human beings. When we reached the foot of one of the two streets that run straight to St. Peter's we heard a great roar, like the noise of the sea in a gale; it seemed to come to us in gusts, now near by, now a long way off. It was the noise of the crowd in the square before St. Peter's. We rushed ahead more madly than ever; climbing over each other, carried along, pushed, swept, and dragged, till at last we reached the square. God, if you could have seen it!—What a spectacle!—The whole huge square was jammed, black, swarming; no longer a square, but an ocean. All around the outer edge, between the four lines of columns, on the steps of the church, in the portico, on the great terraced roof, in the outer galleries of the dome, on the capitals of the columns, on the very pilasters; in the windows of the houses to the right of the square, on the balconies, on the leads, above, below, to the right and to the left, wherever a human being could find foothold, wherever there was some projection to cling to or to dangle from, everywhere there were heads, arms, legs, banners, shouts, gesticulations. The whole of Rome was there."

"Heavens! . . . And the Vatican?" the women cried, in a tremble.

"All shut up. You know that a wing of the Vatican overlooks the square, and that the Pope's apartments are in that wing. Every window was closed; it looked like an abandoned palace; like a cold, rigid, impassive face, staring straight ahead with wide-open motionless eyes. The crowd looked up at it with a murmur.

"Over by the church steps I noticed a lot of officers and gentlemen moving about and giving orders, which seemed to be handed on through the crowd. The excitement was increasing. Every head in the square was uncovered; white heads of old men, brown heads of soldiers, fair heads of little children. The sun blazed down on it all. Thousands of shapes, colours, sounds, seemed to undulate and blend; banners, green boughs, fluttering rags, were tossed back and forth as though upon a dancing sea. The crowd seethed and quivered as if the ground underfoot were on fire.

"Suddenly there was a shout that swept over the whole square: 'The boys! The children! Let's have the children!'

"Then, as if every one were following some concerted plan of action, all the children in the square were lifted up above the crowd, and the men and women who carried them fought a way through to the front of the Vatican. The bigger boys made their own way. Bands of ten and twenty of them, holding each other by the hand, wriggled between people's legs; hundreds of children, some on their own feet, some carried, some pushed, a whole world of little folk, hidden till then in the crowd, suddenly swarmed in one corner of the square; and how the women screamed! 'Take care!—Make room!—Look out for my child!'

"Presently there was another shout: 'The women now! The women!' and another shuffling up and settling down of the crowd. Then a third shout, louder than any of the others: 'The army! The troops!' this time. Then came the most indescribable agitation, but underneath it all a sense of order and rapidity; none of the ordinary confusion and delay; every one helped, made way, co-operated; the whole immense multitude seemed to be under orders. Gradually the disturbance ceased, the noise diminished, the gesticulation subsided; and looking about one saw that all the soldiers, women, and children in the crowd had disappeared as if by magic.

"There they all stood, on the right side of the square, divided into three great battalions that extended from the door of St. Peter's to the centre of the colonnade, all facing the Vatican, packed together and motionless. The crowd burst into frantic applause."

"But the Vatican?" the whole family cried out for the third time.

"Shut up and silent as a convent; but wait. Suddenly the applause ceased, and every head turned backward, whispering: 'Silence!' The whisper travelled across the square and down the length of the two streets leading to it; gradually the sound died out, and the crowd became absolutely, incredibly silent: it was supernatural. All at once, in the midst of this silence, we heard a faint mysterious chirping ; a vague, diffused sound of voices, that seemed to come from overhead. Gradually it grew louder, and there was an uncertain gathering of shrill, discordant tones, now close by, now far off, but growing steadier and more harmonious, until at length it was blent in a single tremendous silvery chant that soared above us like the singing of a choir of angels. Thousands of children were singing the hymn to Pius IX.—the hymn of forty-seven."

"Oh, God—oh, God!" cried the mother and daughters, with clasped hands.

"That song re-echoed in every heart ; it touched something deep down and tender in every one of us. A thrill ran through the crowd ; there was a wild waving of arms and hands, as though to take the place of speech ; but the only sound was a confused murmur.

"'Holy Father,' that murmur seemed to say, 'look at them, listen to them ! They are our children, they are your little ones, who are looking for you, who are praying to you, who implore your blessing. Yield to their entreaty ; give them your blessing ; grant that our religion and our country may dwell together as one faith in our hearts. One word from you, Holy Father, one sign from you, one glance even, promising pardon and peace, and every man of us shall be with you and for you, now and for ever ! Look—these our children and your little ones !"

"Thousands of banners fluttered in the air, the song ceased, and a deep silence followed."

"Well ?" they cried breathlessly.

"Still shut up," the lad answered. "Then the women began to sing. There was a deep thrill in the immense voice that rose ; a something that throbs only in the breast of mothers ; it seemed a cry rather than a hymn ; it was sweet and solemn.

"At first the crowd was motionless ; then a wave of excitement passed over it, and the hymn was drowned in a great clamour : 'These are our mothers, these are our wives and sisters ; Holy Father, listen to them. They have never known hatred or anger ; they have always loved and hoped ; all they ask is that you should give them leave to couple your name with that of Italy on their children's lips. Holy Father, one word from you will spare them many cruel doubts and many bitter tears. Give them your blessing, Holy Father !'"

The boy's listeners questioned him with look and gesture.

"Still closed," he answered ; "still closed. But then a tremendous chant burst out, followed by a wild surging of the crowd : the soldiers were singing.—' These are our soldiers,' the people cried ; ' they shall be yours, Holy Father. They come from the fields and the workshops ; they will keep watch at your door, Holy Father, they will attend upon your steps. They were born under your rule, as children they heard your glorious cry for liberty, they fought the stranger in your name and in that of their King ; in the hour of danger, you will find them close about your throne, ready to die for you. One word, Holy Father, and these swords, these breasts, this flesh and blood are yours ! They ask your blessing on their country, Holy Father, they ask you to repeat your own glorious words ! ' . . .

" A window in the Vatican opened. The song ceased, the shouts died out—silence. There was not a soul in the window. For a few seconds the immense multitude seemed to stop breathing. It seemed as though something moved behind the window—as though at the back of the room a shadow appeared and then vanished. Then we fancied that we caught a glimpse of people moving to and fro, and heard a vague sound. Every face was turned towards the window, every eye was fixed upon it. Suddenly, as if by inspiration, every arm in the multitude was stretched out towards the palace ; mothers lifted their children above their heads, soldiers swung their caps on the points of their bayonets, every banner was shaken out, and a hundred thousand voices burst into one tremendous shout, ' *Viva ! Viva ! Viva !* ' At the window of the Vatican something light-coloured appeared, wavered, fluttered in the air. God in heaven ! " cried the boy, with his arms about his mother's neck, " it was the flag of Italy ! "

The delight, the joy, the enthusiasm which greeted his words are indescribable. The lad had spoken with so much warmth, had been so carried away by his imagination, that he had not perceived that, gradually, as the story proceeded, he had passed from fact to fiction ; and his eyes were wet, his voice shook, with the spell of his hallucination. His words carried conviction, and not a doubt clouded the happiness of his listeners. They laughed and cried and kissed each other, feeling themselves suddenly released from all their doubts and scruples, from all the miserable conflicts of conscience that had tortured them as Italians and as Catholics ! The reconciliation between Church and State ! The dream of so many years ! What peace it promised, what a future of love and harmony ! What a sense of freedom and security !

" Thank God, thank God ! " the mother cried, sinking into a chair.

worn out by her emotions. And then, in a moment or two, they were all at the lad again, clamouring for fresh details.

" Is it really true ? "

" Haven't you dreamed it ? "

" Go on, tell us everything. Tell us about the Pope, about the crowd, about what happened next . . ."

" What happened next ? " the boy began again, in a tired voice. " I hardly know. There was such an uproar, such confusion, such an outburst of frenzy, that the mere recollection of it makes my brain reel. All I saw was a vortex of arms and flags, and the breath was almost knocked out of me by a thundering blow on the chest. After a while, I got out of the thick of it, and plunged into one of the streets leading to the bridge of St. Angelo. People were still pouring into the piazza from Borgo Pio with frantic shouts. I heard afterwards that the crowd tried to break into the Vatican ; the soldiers had to keep them back, first breast to breast, then with blows, and then with their bayonets. They say that some people were suffocated in the press. No one knows yet what happened inside the Vatican ; there was a rumour that the Pope had given his blessing from the window—but I didn't see him. I was almost dead when I got to the bridge. The news of what had taken place had already spread over the whole city, and from every direction crowds were still pouring towards the Vatican. Detachments of cavalry went by me at a trot ; orderlies and *aides-de-camp* carrying orders dashed along the streets. Hearing their shouts, the people in the windows shouted back at them. Decrepit old men, sick people, women with babies in their arms, swarmed on the terraces, poured out of the houses, questioning, wondering, embracing one another. . . . At last I got to the Corso. At that minute there was a tremendous report from the direction of the Pincio, another from Porta Pia, a third from San Pancrazio : all the batteries of the Italian army were saluting the Pope. Soon afterwards the bells of the Capitol began to ring ; then, one after another, a hundred churches chimed in. The crowds of Borgo Pio surged frantically back towards the left bank of the Tiber, invading the streets, the squares, the houses, stripping the coverings from the papal escutcheons, carrying in triumph busts of Pius IX., portraits and banners. Thousands assembled with frantic cheers before the palaces of the Roman nobles who are known for their devotion to the Holy See. In answer to the cheers, the owners of the houses appeared on their balconies and unfurled the Italian flag.

" Wait a minute, I'm out of breath . . ."

As soon as he had recovered his breath he was assailed with fresh questions.

" Well, and what then ? And the Vatican—? The Pope—? "

" I don't know.—But Rome that night . . . how can I ever tell you how beautiful, how great, how marvellous it was ! The night was perfectly clear, and I don't believe such an illumination was ever seen since the world began. The Corso was on fire ; the churches were jammed with people, and there was preaching in every one of them. The streets were full of music, dancing, and singing ; people harangued the crowds in the *cafés* and the theatres.

" I wanted to see St. Peter's again. There had been a rumour that His Holiness needed rest, and Borgo Pio was as still as it is on the stillest night. The piazza was full of moonlight. A silent throng was gathered about the two fountains and on the steps of the church. Many were sitting down, many stretched at full length on the ground ; the greater number had fallen asleep, worn out by the fatigue and excitement of the day ; women, soldiers, children, lay huddled together in a confused heap. Hundreds of others were on their knees, and sentinels of all the different corps moved about here and there, with little flags and crosses fastened to the barrels of their guns. The ground was strewn with flags, foliage, flowers, and hats lost in the crush ; the windows of the Vatican were lit up ; there was not a sound to be heard, the crowd seemed to be holding its breath.

" I turned away, beside myself with the thought of all that I had seen, of the effect that it would produce in Italy, and all over the world ; of what you would all say to it, and you most of all, father ! I found myself at the station without knowing how I had got there. It was full of noise and confusion. I jumped on to the train, we started, and here I am. The news reached Florence last night ; they say the excitement was indescribable ; the King has left for Rome ; the news is all over the world by this time ! "

He sank into a chair and sat silent, as though his breath had failed him. Then he sprang up and rushed out to intercept the papers, which usually reached the villa at eleven o'clock in the morning.

In this way he succeeded in maintaining the blissful delusion until evening. The dinner was full of gaiety, the lad continued to pour out detail after detail, and his listeners to heap benediction upon benediction.

Suddenly a hurried step was heard on the stairs, and the bell rang violently. The door opened, and a tall, pale priest, with a drawn mouth, appeared on the threshold. He was a recent acquaintance of the family, who felt no great sympathy for him, but who received him courteously more out of respect for his cloth than out of regard for his merits.

As he entered, all but the son sprang up and surrounded him with excited exclamations.

" Well, have you heard the news ? Thank God, it's all ended ! The hand of God is in it ! What do you think of it all ? Tell us, let us hear your opinion ! "

" But what news ? " asked the priest, looking from one to the other with astonished eyes.

In wild haste, and all speaking at once, they poured out the story of the festival, the forgiveness, the reconciliation.

The priest stared at them, with the look of a man who finds himself unexpectedly surrounded by lunatics ; then, with a withering glance at the boy, and a smile of malignant triumph—

" Fortunately," he said, " there is not a word of truth in it ! "

" Not a word of truth in it ? " they clamoured, turning upon their informant.

The boy, unmoved by their agitation, returned the priest's look half-scornfully, half-sadly.

" Your reverence, don't say fortunately. Since you are an Italian, rather say, ' Alas, that it is not so ! ' "

For a moment the others stood aghast ; then, angered, as people will be, rather against those who undeceive them than against those who delude them, they turned towards the priest, involuntarily echoing the boy's words : " He's right, your reverence ! Say rather, 'Alas, that it is not so ! ' "

The priest pointed to his own breast with a long knotty finger.

" I ? " he exclaimed bitterly, " never ! "

At these words, the boy's father, rudely roused from his mood of tender exaltation, and bursting, after his wont, into sudden fury, stretched his arm towards the priest, with a cry that rang through the room like a pistol-shot : " Out of my house this instant ! "

The priest stalked out, slamming the door. The lad's arms were about his father's neck ; and the old man, laying his hands on his son's head, said gently : " I forgive you."

GABRIELE D'ANNUNZIO
1863

SAN PANTALEONE

I

THE great sandy piazza glittered as if strewn with powdered pumice. Its whitewashed houses held a strange metallic glow, like the walls of an immense furnace cooling off. The glare of the clouds, reflected from the stone pillars of the church at its far end, gave them the appearance of red granite. The church windows blazed as with inward fire. The sacred images had assumed life-like colours and attitudes, and the massive edifice seemed lifted now, in the splendour of the new celestial phenomenon, to a prouder domination than ever, above the houses of Radusa.

Groups of men and women, gesticulating and talking loudly, were pouring from the streets into the square. Superstitious terror grew in leaps and bounds from face to face. A thousand awful images of divine punishment rose out of their rude fancies ; and comments, eager disputes, plaintive appeals, wild stories, prayers, and cries were mingled in a deep uproar, as of a hurricane approaching. For some time past this bloody redness of the sky had lasted through the night, disturbing its tranquillity, illumining sullenly the sleeping fields, and making dogs howl.

"Giacobbe ! Giacobbe ! " shouted some, waving their arms, who till then had stood in a compact band around a pillar of the church portico, talking in low tones, "Giacobbe ! "

There came out through the main door, and drew near to those who called him, a long, emaciated man, apparently consumptive, whose head was bald at the top, but had a crown of long reddish hair about the temples and above the nape of the neck. His little sunken eyes, animated with the fire of a deep passion, were set close and had no particular colour. The absence of his two upper front teeth gave to his mouth when speaking, and to his sharp chin with its few scattered hairs, the strangeness of a senile faun. The rest of his body was a wretched structure of bones ill-concealed by his clothes. The skin on his hands, his wrists, the backs of his arms, and his breast was full of blue punctures made with a pin and india-ink, the souvenirs of sanctuaries visited, pardons obtained, and vows performed.

When the fanatic approached the group at the pillar, a swarm of questions arose from the anxious men. "Well, then? what did Don Cónsolo say? Will they send out only the silver arm? Would not the whole bust do better? When would Pallura come back with the candles? Was it one hundred pounds of wax? Only one hundred? And when would the bells begin to ring? Well, then? Well, then?"

The clamour increased around Giacobbe. Those on the outskirts of the crowd pushed towards the church. From all the streets people poured into the square till they filled it. And Giacobbe kept answering his questions, whispering, as if revealing dreadful secrets and bringing prophecies from far. He had seen aloft in the bloody sky a threatening hand, and then a black veil, and then a sword and a trumpet.

"Go ahead! Go ahead!" they urged him, looking in each other's faces, and seized with a strange desire to hear of marvels, while the wonder grew from mouth to mouth in the crowd.

II

The vast crimson zone rose slowly from the horizon to the zenith and bade fair to cover the whole vault of heaven. An undulating vapour of molten metal seemed pouring down on the roofs of the town; and in the descending crepuscule yellow and violet rays flashed through a trembling and iridescent glow. One long streak, brighter than the others, pointed towards a street which opened on the river-front, and at the end of this street the water flamed away between the tall slim poplar-trunks, and beyond the stream lay a strip of luxuriant country, from which the old Saracen towers stood out confusedly, like stone islets, in the dark. The air was full of the stifling emanations of mown hay, with now and then a whiff from putrefied silkworms in the bushes. Flights of swallows crossed this space with quick, scolding cries, trafficking between the river sands and the eaves.

An expectant silence had interrupted the murmur of the multitude. The name Pallura ran from lip to lip. Signs of angry impatience broke forth here and there. The waggon was not yet to be seen along the river-road; the candles had not come; Don Cónsolo therefore was delaying the exposition of the relics and the acts of exorcism; the danger still threatened. Panic fear invaded the hearts of all those people crowded together like a flock of sheep, and no longer venturing to raise their eyes to heaven. The women burst out sobbing, and at the sound of weeping every mind was oppressed and filled with consternation.

Then at last the bells began to ring. As they were hung low, their deep quivering strokes seemed to graze the heads of the people, and a sort of continuous wailing filled the intervals.

"San Pantaleone! San Pantaleone!"

It was an immense, unanimous cry of desperate men imploring aid. Kneeling, with blanched faces and outstretched hands, they supplicated.

"San Pantaleone!"

Then, at the church door, in the midst of the smoke of two censers, Don Cónsolo appeared, resplendent in a violet chasuble, with gold embroidery. He held aloft the sacred arm of silver, and conjured the air, shouting the Latin words:

"*Ut fidelibus tuis aeris serenitatem concedere digneris, Te rogamus, audi nos.*"

At sight of the relic the multitude went delirious with affectionate joy. Tears ran from all eyes, and through glistening tears these eyes beheld a miraculous gleam emanate from the three fingers held up as if in the act of benediction. The arm appeared larger now, in the enkindled air.

The dim light awoke strange scintillations in the precious stones. The balsamic odour of incense spread quickly to the nostrils of the devotees.

"*Te rogamus, audi nos!*"

But when the arm was carried back and the tolling stopped, in that moment of silence a tinkling of little bells was heard near at hand coming from the river-road. Then of a sudden the crowd rushed in that direction and many voices cried:

"It is Pallura with the candles! It is Pallura coming! Here's Pallura!"

The waggon came screeching over the gravel, drawn at a walk by a heavy grey mare, over whose shoulders hung a great shining brass horn, like a half-moon. When Giacobbe and the others made towards her, the pacific animal stopped and breathed hard. Giacobbe, who reached the waggon first, saw stretched out on its floor the bloody body of

Pallura, and screamed, waving his arms towards the crowd, " He is dead! He is dead! "

III

The sad news spread like lightning. People crowded around the waggon, and craned their necks to see, thinking no longer of the threats in the sky, because struck by the unexpected happening and filled with that natural ferocious curiosity which the sight of blood awakens.

" He is dead? What killed him? "

Pallura lay on his back upon the boards, with a broad wound in the middle of his forehead, with one ear torn, with gashes on his arms, his sides, and one thigh. A warm stream flowed down to his chin and neck, staining his shirt and forming dark, shining clots on his breast, his leathern belt, and even his breeches. Giacobbe hung over the body; all the rest waited around him; an auroral flush lighted up their perplexed faces; and at that moment of silence, from the river-bank arose the song of the frogs, and bats skimmed back and forth above the heads of the crowd.

Suddenly Giacobbe, straightening up, with one cheek bloody, cried:

" He is not dead. He still breathes."

A hollow murmur ran through the crowd, and the nearest strained forward to look. The anxiety of those at a distance commenced to break into clamour. Two women brought a jug of water, another some strips of linen. A youth held out a gourd full of wine.

The wounded man's face was washed; the flow of blood from his forehead was checked; his head was raised. Then voices inquired loudly the cause of this deed. The hundred pounds of wax were missing; only a few fragments of candles remained in the cracks of the waggon-bed.

In the commotion their minds grew more and more inflamed, exasperated, and contentious. And as an old hereditary hatred burned in them against the town of Mascálico, on the opposite bank of the river, Giacobbe said venomously, in a hoarse voice:

" What if the candles have been offered to San Gonselvo? "

It was like the first flash of a conflagration! The spirit of church-rivalry awoke all at once in these people brutalised by many years of blind, savage worship of their own one idol. The fanatic's words flew from mouth to mouth. And beneath the tragic dull-red sky, the raging multitude resembled a tribe of mutinous gypsies.

The name of the saint broke from all throats, like a war-cry. The most excited hurled curses towards the river, and waved their arms and shook their fists. Then all these faces blazing with anger, and reddened also by the unusual light,—all these faces, broad and massive, to which their gold ear-rings and thick overhanging hair gave a wild, barbaric character,—all these faces turned eagerly towards the man lying there, and grew soft with pity. Women, with pious care, tried to bring him back to life. Loving hands changed the cloths on his wounds, sprinkled water in his face, set the gourd of wine to his lips, made a sort of pillow under his head.

"Pallura, poor Pallura, won't you answer?"

He lay supine, his eyes closed, his mouth half open, with brown soft hair on his cheeks and chin, the gentle beauty of youth still showing in his features contracted with pain. From beneath the bandage on his forehead a mere thread of blood trickled down over his temples; at the corners of his mouth stood little beads of pale red foam, and from his throat issued a faint broken hiss, like the sound of a sick man gargling. About him attentions, questions, feverish glances multiplied. The mare from time to time shook her head and neighed in the direction of the houses. An atmosphere as of an impending hurricane hung over the whole town.

Then from the square rang out the screams of a woman, of a mother. They seemed all the louder for the sudden hushing of all other voices, and an enormous woman, suffocated in her fat, broke through the crowd and hurried to the waggon, crying aloud. Being heavy and unable to climb into it, she seized her son's feet, with sobbing words of love, with such sharp broken cries and such a terribly comic expression of grief, that all the bystanders shuddered and averted their faces.

"Zaccheo! Zaccheo! My heart, my joy!" screamed the widow unceasingly, kissing the feet of the wounded man and dragging him to her towards the ground.

The wounded man stirred, his mouth was contorted by a spasm, but although he opened his eyes and looked up, they were veiled with damp, so that he could not see. Big tears began to well forth at the corners of his eyelids and roll down over his cheeks and neck. His mouth was still awry. A vain effort to speak was betrayed by the hoarse whistling in his throat. And the crowd pressed closer, saying:

"Speak, Pallura! Who hurt you? Who hurt you? Speak! Speak!"

Beneath this question was a trembling rage, an intensifying fury, a deep tumult of reawakened feelings of vengeance; and the hereditary hatred boiled in every heart.

"Speak! Who hurt you? Tell us! Tell us!"

The dying man opened his eyes again; and as they were holding his hands tightly, perhaps this warm living contact gave him a momentary strength, for his gaze quickened and a vague stammering sound came to his lips. The words were not yet distinguishable. The panting breath of the multitude could be heard through the silence. Their eyes had an inward flame, because all expected one single word.

"Ma—Ma—Mascálico—"

"Mascálico! Mascálico!" shrieked Giacobbe, who was bending over him, with ear intent to snatch the weak syllables from his dying lips.

An immense roar greeted the cry. The multitude swayed at first as if tempest-swept. Then, when a voice, dominating the tumult, gave the order of attack, the mob broke up in haste. A single thought drove these men forward, a thought which seemed to have been stamped by lightning upon all minds at once: to arm themselves with some weapon. Towering above the consciousness of all arose a sort of bloody fatality, beneath the great tawny glare of the heavens, and in the electric odour emanating from the anxious fields.

IV

And the phalanx, armed with scythes, bill-hooks, axes, hoes, and guns, reunited in the square before the church. And all cried: "San Pantaleone!"

Don Cónsolo, terrified by the din, had taken refuge in a stall behind the altar. A handful of fanatics, led by Giacobbe, made their way into the principal chapel, forced the bronze grille, and went into the underground chamber where the bust of the saint was kept. Three lamps, fed with olive oil, burned softly in the damp air of the sacristy, where in a glass case the Christian idol glittered, with its white head surrounded by a broad gilt halo; and the walls were hidden under the wealth of native offerings.

When the idol, borne on the shoulders of four herculean men, appeared at last between the pillars and shone in the auroral light, a long gasp of passion ran through the waiting crowd, and a quiver of joy passed like a breath of wind over all their faces. And the column moved away, the enormous head of the saint oscillating above, with its empty eye-sockets turned to the front.

Now through the sky, in the deep, diffused glow, brighter meteors ploughed their furrows; groups of thin clouds broke away from the hem of the vapour zone and floated off, dissolving slowly. The whole town of Radusa stood out like a smouldering mountain of ashes. Behind and before, as far as eye could reach, the country lay in an indistinctly lucent mass. A great singing of frogs filled the sonorous solitude.

On the river-road Pallura's wagon blocked the way. It was empty, but still soiled, here and there, with blood. Angry curses broke suddenly from the mob. Giacobbe shouted:

"Let us put the saint in it!"

So the bust was placed in the wagon-bed and drawn by many arms into the ford. The battle-line thus crossed the frontier. Metallic gleams ran along the files. The parted water broke in luminous spray, and the current flamed away red between the poplars, in the distance, towards the quadrangular towers. Mascálico showed itself on a little hill, among olive trees, asleep. The dogs were barking here and there, with a persistent fury of reply. The column, issuing from the ford, left the public road and advanced rapidly straight across country. The silver bust was borne again on men's shoulders, and towered above their heads amid the tall, odorous grain, starred with bright fireflies.

Suddenly a shepherd in his straw hut, where he lay to guard the grain, seized with mad panic at sight of so many armed men, started to run up the hill, yelling, "Help! Help!" And his screams echoed in the olive grove.

Then it was that the Radusani charged. Among tree-trunks and dry reeds the silver saint tottered, ringing as he struck low branches, and glittering momentarily at every steep place in the path. Ten, twelve, twenty guns, in a vibrating flash, rattled their shot against the mass of houses. Crashes, then cries, were heard; then a great commotion. Doors were opened; others were slammed shut. Window-panes fell shattered. Vases fell from the church and broke on the street. In the track of the assailants a white smoke rose quietly up through the incandescent air. They all, blinded and in bestial rage, cried, "Kill! kill!"

A group of fanatics remained about San Pantaleone. Atrocious insults for San Gonselvo broke out amid waving scythes and brandished hooks:

"Thief! Thief! Beggar! The candles! The candles!"

Other bands took the houses by assault, breaking down the doors with hatchets. And as they fell, unhinged and shivered, San Pantaleone's followers leaped in, howling, to kill the defenders.

The women, half-naked, took refuge in corners, imploring pity. They warded off the blows, grasping the weapons and cutting their fingers. They rolled at full length on the floor, amid heaps of blankets and sheets.

Giacobbe, long, quick, red as a Turkish scimitar, led the persecution, stopping ever and anon to make sweeping imperious gestures over the heads of the others with a great scythe. Pallid, bare-headed, he held the van, in the name of San Pantaleone. More than thirty men followed him. They all had a dull, confused sense of walking through a conflagration, over quaking ground, and beneath a blazing vault ready to crumble.

But from all sides began to come the defenders, the Mascalicesi, strong and dark as mulattos, sanguinary foes, fighting with long spring-bladed knives, and aiming at the belly and the throat, with guttural cries at every blow.

The mêlée rolled away, step by step, towards the church. From the roofs of two or three houses flames were already bursting. A horde of women and children, wan-eyed and terror-stricken, were fleeing headlong among the olive trees. Then the hand-to-hand struggle between the males, unimpeded by tears and lamentations, became more concentrated and ferocious.

Under the rust-coloured sky, the ground was strewn with corpses. Broken imprecations were hissed through the teeth of the wounded; and steadily, through all the clamour, still came the cry of the Radusani:

"The candles! The candles!"

But the enormous church door of oak, studded with nails, remained barred. The Mascalicesi defended it against the pushing crowd and the axes. The white, impassive silver saint oscillated in the thick of the fight, still upheld on the shoulders of the four giants, who refused to fall, though bleeding from head to foot. It was the supreme desire of the assailants to place their idol on the enemy's altar.

Now while the Mascalicesi fought like lions, performing prodigies on the stone steps, Giacobbe suddenly disappeared around the corner of the building, seeking an undefended opening through which to enter the sacristy. And beholding a narrow window not far from the ground, he climbed up to it, wedged himself into its embrasure, doubled up his long body, and succeeded in crawling through. The cordial aroma of incense floated in the solitude of God's house. Feeling his way in the dark, guided by the roar of the fight outside, he crept towards the door, stumbling against chairs and bruising his face and hands.

The furious thunder of the Radusan axes was echoing from the tough oak, when he began to force the lock with an iron bar, panting, suffocated by a violent agonising palpitation which diminished his strength, blind, giddy, stiffened by the pain of his wounds, and dripping with tepid blood.

"San Pantaleone! San Pantaleone!" bellowed the hoarse voices of his comrades outside, redoubling their blows as they felt the door slowly yield. Through the wood came to his ears the heavy thump of falling bodies, the quick thud of knife-thrusts nailing some one through the back. And a grand sentiment, like the divine uplift of the soul of a hero saving his country, flamed up then in that bestial beggar's heart.

V

By a final effort the door was flung open. The Radusani rushed in, with an immense howl of victory, across the bodies of the dead, to carry the silver saint to the altar. A vivid quivering light was reflected suddenly into the obscure nave, making the golden candlesticks shine, and the organ-pipes above. And in that yellow glow, which now came from the burning houses and now disappeared again, a second battle was fought. Bodies grappled together and rolled over the brick floor, never to rise, but to bound hither and thither in the contortions of rage, to strike the benches, and die under them, or on the chapel steps, or against the taper-spikes about the confessionals. Under the peaceful vault of God's house the chilling sound of iron penetrating men's flesh or sliding along their bones, the single broken groan of men struck in a vital spot, the crushing of skulls, the roar of victims unwilling to die, the atrocious hilarity of those who had succeeded in killing an enemy,—all this re-echoed distinctly. And a sweet, faint odour of incense floated above the strife.

The silver idol had not, however, reached the altar in triumph, for a hostile circle stood between. Giacobbe fought with his scythe, and, though wounded in several places, did not yield a hand's breadth of the stair which he had been the first to gain. Only two men were left to hold up the saint, whose enormous white head heaved and reeled grotesquely like a drunken mask. The men of Mascálico were growing furious.

Then San Pantaleone fell on the pavement, with a sharp, vibrant ring. As Giacobbe dashed forward to pick him up, a big devil of a man dealt him a blow with a bill-hook, which stretched him out on his back. Twice he rose and twice was struck down again. Blood covered his face, his breast, his hands, yet he persisted in getting up. Enraged by this ferocious tenacity of life, three, four, five clumsy peasants together stabbed him furiously in the belly, and the fanatic fell over, with the back of his neck against the silver bust. He turned like a flash and put his face against the metal, with his arms outspread and his legs drawn up. And San Pantaleone was lost.

MASTRO PEPPE'S MAGIC

GABRIELE D'ANNUNZIO

MASTRO PEPPE LA BRAVETTA was a stout, stupid, good-natured man. He lived in Pescara, sold pots and pans, and was terribly in awe of his wife, the severe and miserly Donna Pelagia, who ruled him with a rod of iron. Besides the income derived from his business, he possessed a piece of land on the other side of the river which produced enough to keep a pig. To this property the couple were wont to repair every January, to preside over the killing and salting of the pig which had been fattening through the year.

Now one year it so happened that Pelagia was not very well, and La Bravetta was to attend the execution alone. And to him, in the course of the afternoon, came two of his friends, graceless vagabonds, Matteo Puriello, nick-named Ciávola, who was a poacher, and Biagio Quaglia, better known as Il Ristabilito, whose most serious occupation was that of playing the guitar at weddings and on other festive occasions.

When he saw these two approaching he welcomed them enthusiastically, and then, leading them into the building where the wonderful pig was laid out on the table, asked—

"What do you say to this, now? Isn't he a beauty? What do you think of him?"

The two friends contemplated the pig in silent wonder, and Ristabilito clicked his tongue appreciatively against his palate. Ciávola asked, "What are you going to do with it?"

"Salt it down," replied La Bravetta, in a voice which trembled with greedy delight of future banquets.

"Going to salt it?" cried Ristabilito suddenly. "Going to salt it? But, Ciá, did you ever see any man so stupid as this fellow? To let such a chance slip!"

La Bravetta, quite dumbfounded, stared first at one and then at the other with his calf-like eyes.

"Donna Pelagia has always kept you under her thumb," continued Ristabilito. "This time she can't see you; why shouldn't you sell the pig, and then we'll feast on the money."

" But Pelagia ? " stammered La Bravetta, who was filled with an immense consternation by the image of his wrathful wife presented to his mind's eye.

" Tell her that the pig was stolen," said Ciávola, with a gesture of impatience.

La Bravetta shuddered.

" How am I to go home and tell her that ? Pelagia won't believe me—she'll drive me—she'll . . . You don't know what Pelagia is ! "

" Uh ! Pelagia ! uh ! uh ! Donna Pelagia ! " jeered the two arch-plotters in chorus. And then Ristabilito, imitating Peppe's whining voice, and his wife's sharp and strident one, acted a comic scene in which Peppe was utterly routed, scolded, and finally cuffed like a naughty boy.

Ciávola walked round the pig, scarcely able to move for laughing. The unfortunate butt, seized with a violent fit of sneezing, waved his arms helplessly, trying to interrupt the dramatic representation. All the window-panes trembled with the noise. The flaming sunset streamed in on three very different human faces.

When Ristabilito stopped, Ciávola said:

" Well, let's go away ! "

" If you'll stay to have supper——" began Mastro Peppe, somewhat constrainedly.

" No, no, my dear boy," interrupted Ciávola, as he turned towards the door, " you do as Pelagia tells you, and salt the pig."

As the two friends walked along the road Ristabilito said to Ciávola:

" *Compare*, shall we steal that pig to-night ? "

" How ? " said Ciávola.

" I know how, if they leave it where it was when we saw it."

" Well, let's do it. But, then ? " said Ciávola.

The other's whole face lit up, and fairly vibrated with a grin of delight.

" Never mind—*I* know," was all he said.

They saw Don Bergamino Camplone coming along in the moonlight—a black figure between the rows of leafless poplars with their silvery trunks. They immediately quickened their pace to meet him ; and the jolly priest, seeing their festive looks, asked with a smile:

" What's up now ? "

The friends briefly communicated their project to Don Bergamino, who assented with much cheerfulness. And Ristabilito added, in a low voice:

" Here we shall have to manage things cunningly. You know that Peppe, ever since he took up with that ugly old hag of a Donna Pelagia, has been getting very stingy, and at the same time he's very fond of wine. Now we must go and fetch him and take him to Assaù's tavern. You, Don Bergamino, must treat us all round. Peppe will drink as much as ever he can, seeing it costs him nothing, and will get as drunk as a pig ; and then——"

The others agreed, and they went to Peppe's house, which was about two rifle-shots distant. When they were near enough Ciávola lifted up his voice :

" Ohé ! La Bravetta-a-a ! Are you coming to Assaù's ? The priest is here, and he's going to pay for a bottle of wine for us. Ohé-é-é ! "

La Bravetta was not long in descending, and all four set off in a row, joking and laughing in the moonlight. In the stillness the caterwauling of a distant cat was heard at intervals, and Ristabilito remarked :

" Oh ! Pé ! don't you hear Pelagia calling you to come back ? "

. . . .

They crossed the ferry, reached the tavern, and sat till late over Assaù's wine, which Mastro Peppe found so good that he was at last discovered to be incapable of walking home. They assisted him back to the house and left him to go upstairs alone, which he did with some difficulty, talking disconnectedly all the time about Lepruccio the butcher and the quantity of salt needed for the pig, and quite oblivious of the fact that he had left the door unfastened. They waited a while, and then, entering softly, found the pig on the table, and carried it off between them, shaking with suppressed laughter. It was very heavy, and they were quite out of breath when they reached the priest's house.

In the morning, Mastro Peppe having slept off his wine, awoke, and lay still a little while on his bed, stretching his limbs and listening to the bells as they rang for the Eve of St. Anthony. Even in the confusion of his first awakening he felt a contented sense of possession steal through his mind, and tasted by anticipation the delight of seeing Lepruccio cutting up and covering with salt the plump joints of pork.

Under the impulse of this idea, he rose, and hurried out, rubbing his eyes the while to get a better view. Nothing was to be seen on the table but a stain of blood, with the morning sun shining on it.

" The pig ! Where is the pig ? " cried the bereaved one hoarsely.

A furious excitement seized upon him. He rushed downstairs, saw the open door, struck his forehead with his fists, and burst into the open air yelling aloud—calling all his farm labourers round him, and asking them if they had seen the pig—if they had taken it. He multiplied his complaints, raising his voice more and more ; and at last the doleful sound, echoing along the river-bank, reached the ears of Ciávola and Il Ristabilito.

They therefore repaired to the spot at their ease, fully agreed to enjoy the sight and keep up the joke. When they came in sight, Mastro Peppe turned to them, all afflicted and in tears, and exclaimed, " Oh, poor me ! They have stolen the pig ! Oh ! poor me ! What shall I do ?—what shall I do ? "

Biagio Quaglia stood for a while, looking at this most unhappy man out of his half-shut eyes, with an expression midway between derision and admiration, and his head inclined to one shoulder, as if critically judging of some dramatic effort. Then he came closer and said :

" Ah ! yes, yes—one can't deny it. . . . You play your part well."

Peppe, not understanding, lifted his face all furrowed with the tracks of tears. . .

" To tell the truth, I never thought you would have been so cute," Ristabilito went on. " Well done ! Bravo ! I'm delighted ! "

" What's that you're saying ? " asked La Bravetta between his sobs. " What's that you're saying ? Oh ! poor me ! How can I ever go home again ? "

" Bravo ! bravo ! that's right ! " insisted Ristabilito. " Go on ! Yell harder !—cry !—tear your hair ! Make them hear ! That's it ! Make them believe it ! "

And Peppe, still weeping :

" But I say they have really and truly stolen it ! Oh, dear ! oh, dear ! "

" That's it ! Go on ! Don't stop ! Again ! "

Peppe, quite beside himself with exasperation and grief, redoubled his asseverations.

" I'm telling the truth ! May I die now, at once, if they haven't stolen that pig from me ! "

" Oh, poor innocent ! " jeered Ciávola. " Put your finger in your eye ! How can we believe you, when we saw the pig here yesterday evening ? Has St. Anthony given him wings to fly away with ? "

" Oh, blessed St. Anthony ! It is just as I say ! "

" It's not so ! "

" It is."

" No ! "

" Oh ! oh ! oh ! It is ! it is ! I'm a dead man ! I don't know how in the world I am to go home. Pelagia won't believe me, and if she does, I shall never hear the end of it. . . . Oh ! I'm dead ! . . ."

At last they pretended to be convinced, and proposed a remedy for the misfortune.

" Listen here," said Biagio Quaglia ; " it must have been one of the people hereabouts ; for it is certain that no one would have come from India to steal your pig, would they, Pé ? "

" Of course, of course," assented Peppe.

" Well then—attend to me now," continued Ristabilito, delighted at the devout attention accorded to his words ; " if no one came from India to rob you, it is certain that one of the people hereabouts must have been the thief ; don't you think so ? "

" Yes, yes."

" Well, what have we to do ? We must get all these labourers together, and try some charm to discover the thief. And if we find the thief, we've found the pig."

Mastro Peppe's eyes brightened with eagerness, and he came closer, for the hint at a charm had awakened all his innate superstition.

" Now, you know, there are three kinds of magic—the black, the red, and the white. And you know there are three women in the village skilled in the art : Rosa Schiavona, Rosaria Pajara, and Ciniscia. You have only to choose."

Peppe remained a moment in doubt. Then he decided for Rosaria Pajara, who enjoyed great fame as a sorceress, and had in past times performed several marvellous feats.

" Very well," concluded Ristabilito ; " there is no time to be lost. Now, just for your sake, and only to do you a pleasure, I am going to the town to get everything that will be wanted. I will talk to Rosaria, get her to give me everything, and come back before noon. Give me the money."

Peppe took three *carlini* from his waistcoat pocket, and held them out hesitatingly.

" Three *carlini ?* " shouted the other, putting back his hand, " *Three carlini !* She'll want ten at least ! "

On hearing this Pelagia's husband was almost struck dumb.

" What ? Ten *carlini* for a charm ? " he stammered, feeling with trembling fingers in his pocket. " Here are eight for you. I have no more."

" Well, well," said Quaglia drily ; " we'll see what we can do. Are you coming along, Ciá ? "

The two companions set off at a smart pace for Pescara, along the poplar-bordered path, in Indian file, Ciávola demonstrating his delight by mighty thumps on Ristabilito's back. When they reached the town, they entered the shop of a certain Don Daniele Pacentro, a chemist of their acquaintance. Here they purchased certain drugs and spices, and got him to make them up into little balls the size of walnuts, which were then well coated with sugar and baked. Biagio Quaglia (who had disappeared in the meantime) then returned with a paper full of dirt swept up in the road, of which he insisted on having two pills made, in appearance exactly similar to the others, but mixed with bitter aloes, and only very slightly coated with sugar. The chemist did as he was desired, putting a mark on the two bitter pills, at Ristabilito's suggestion.

The two jokers now returned to Peppe's farm, and reached it about noon. La Bravetta was awaiting them with great anxiety, and as soon as he saw them shouted, " Well ? "

" Everything is in order ! " replied Ristabilito triumphantly, showing the little box of magic confectionery. " Now, seeing to-day is the Eve of St. Anthony, and the peasants are taking a holiday, you must call them all together, out here in the open air, and give them a drink. You have some casks of Montepulciano ; you might as well have some of that out for once. And when they are all assembled it will be my business to do and say all that has to be said and done."

Two hours later, the afternoon being very warm, bright, and clear, and La Bravetta having spread the report, all the farmers of the neighbourhood and their labourers came in response to the invitation. A great flock of geese went waddling about among the heaps of straw in the yard ; the smell of the stable came in puffs on the air. They stood there, quietly laughing and joking with one another, as they waited for the wine,—these rustics, with their bow-legs, bent by heavy labour,—some of them with faces wrinkled and ruddy as old apples, and eyes that had been made gentle by long patience, or quick with years of cunning ; others young and limber, with beards just coming, and home care evidenced in their patched and mended clothes.

Ciávola and Ristabilito did not keep them waiting long. The latter, holding the box in his hand, directed them to make a circle round him, and then, standing in the middle, addressed them in a short oration, not without a certain gravity of voice and gesture.

"Neighbours," he began, "none of you, I am sure, knows the real reason why Mastro Peppe de' Sieri has summoned you here. . . ."

A movement of astonishment at this strange preamble passed round the circle, and the joy at the promised wine gave place to uneasy expectations of various kinds. The orator continued:

"But, as something disagreeable might happen, and you might afterwards complain of me, I will tell you what it is all about before we make the experiment."

The listeners looked into one another's eyes with a bewildered air, and then cast curious and uncertain glances at the little box which the orator held in his hand. One of them, as Ristabilito paused to consider the effect of his words, exclaimed impatiently:

"Well?"

"Presently, presently, neighbours. Last night there was stolen from Mastro Peppe a fine pig which was going to be salted down. No one knows who the thief is; but it is quite certain that he will be found among you, because no one would come from India to steal Mastro Peppe's pig."

Whether it was a happy effect of the strange argument from India, or the action of the mild winter sun, La Bravetta began to sneeze. The rustics took a step backward, the whole flock of geese scattered in terror, and seven consecutive sneezes resounded freely in the air, disturbing the rural stillness of the spot. The noise restored some cheerfulness to the minds of the assembly, who in a little while regained their composure, and Ristabilito continued as gravely as ever—

"To find out the thief Mastro Peppe intends to give you to eat of certain good *confetti*, and to drink of a certain old Montepulciano, which he has tapped to-day on purpose. But I must tell you one thing first. The thief, as soon as he puts the sweets into his mouth, will find them bitter—so bitter that he will be forced to spit them out. Now, are you willing to try? Or perhaps the thief, rather than be found out in this way, would like to go and confess himself to the priest? Answer, neighbours."

"We are willing to eat and drink," replied the assembly, almost with one voice. And a wave of suppressed emotion passed through all these guileless folk. Each one looked at his neighbour with a point of interrogation in his eyes ; and each one naturally tried to put a certain ostentatious spontaneity into his laughter.

Said Ciávola : " You must all stand in a row, so that no one can hide himself."

When they were all ready he took the bottle and glasses, preparing to pour out the wine. Ristabilito went to one end of the row, and began quietly to distribute the *confetti*, which crunched and disappeared in a moment under the splendid teeth of the rustics. When he reached Mastro Peppe he handed him one of the pills prepared with aloes, and passed on without giving any sign.

Mastro Peppe, who till then had been standing staring with his eyes wide open, intent on surprising the culprit, put the pill into his mouth almost with gluttonous eagerness and began to chew. Suddenly his cheeks rose with a sudden movement towards his eyes, the corners of his mouth and his temples were filled with wrinkles, the skin of his nose was drawn up into folds, his lower jaw was twisted awry ; all his features formed a pantomimic expression of horror, and a sort of visible shudder ran down the back of his neck and over his shoulders. Then, suddenly, since the tongue could not endure the bitterness of the aloes, and a lump rising in his throat made it simply impossible for him to swallow, the miserable man was forced to spit.

" Ohé, Mastro Pé, what are you doing ? " exclaimed the sharp, harsh voice of Tulespre dei Passeri, an old goatherd, greenish and shaggy as a swamp tortoise.

Hearing this, Ristabilito, who had not yet finished distributing the pills, turned suddenly round. Seeing that La Bravetta was contorting his features and limbs in agony, he said, with an air of the greatest benevolence—

" Well, perhaps that one was too much done ! Here is another ! swallow it, Peppe ! "

And with his finger and thumb he crammed the second aloe-pill into Peppe's mouth.

The poor man took it, and, feeling the goatherd's sharp, malignant eyes fixed on him, made a supreme effort to overcome his disgust ; he neither chewed nor swallowed the pill, but kept his tongue motionless against his teeth. But when the aloes began to dissolve, he could bear it no longer ; his lips began to writhe as before, his eyes filled with tears, which soon overflowed and ran down his cheeks. At last he had to spit the thing out.

" Ohé, Mastro Pé, and what are you doing *now* ? " cried the goatherd again, with a grin which showed his toothless, whitish gums. " Oh ! and indeed, now, what does this mean ? "

All the peasants broke from their ranks and surrounded La Bravetta, some with laughing derision, others with angry words. The sudden and brutal revulsions of pride to which the sense of honour of the rustic population is subject—the implacable rigidity of superstition—now suddenly exploded in a tempest of abuse.

" What did you make us come here for ? To try and lay the blame on us with a false charm ? To cheat us ? What for ? Thief ! liar ! son of a dog ! Would you cheat us ? You scoundrel, you thief, you ! We are going to break all your pots and dishes ! Thief ! son of a dog ! "

Having smashed the bottle and glasses, they went their ways, shouting back their concluding imprecations from among the poplars.

There remained on the threshing-floor Ciávola, Ristabilito, the geese, and La Bravetta. The latter, filled with shame, rage, and confusion, and with his mouth still sore from the bitterness of the aloes, could not utter a word. Ristabilito, with a refinement of cruelty, stood looking at him, shaking his head ironically, and tapping the ground with his foot. Ciávola crowed, with an indescribable mockery in his voice—

" Ah ! ah ! ah ! ah ! Bravo, La Bravetta ! Now do tell us—how much did you make by it ? Ten ducats ? "

THE END OF CANDIA

GABRIELE D'ANNUNZIO

I

THREE days after the Easter banquet, which was traditionally a great occasion in the Lamonica household, both in its lavishness and in the number of its guests, Donna Cristina Lamonica was counting the table linen and silver service, and replacing them one by one, methodically, in drawer and cupboard, in readiness for future banquets.

As usual, she had with her, to help in the task, the chambermaid, Maria Bisaccia, and the laundress, Candida Marcanda, familiarly known as Candia. The huge hampers, filled with fine linen, stood in a row upon the floor. The silver platters and other table service gleamed brightly from the sideboard—massive vessels, somewhat crudely wrought by rustic silversmiths, and of more or less liturgical design, like all the plate which rich provincial families hand down from generation to generation. A fresh fragrance of soapy water pervaded the room.

From the hampers Candia took tablecloths, napkins, and towels; she made the mistress take note that each piece was intact, and then passed them over to Maria, who laid them away in the drawers, while the mistress sprinkled lavender between them and entered the numbers in a book. Candia was a tall, lean, angular woman of fifty, with back somewhat bent from the habitual attitude of her calling, with arms of unusual length, and the head of a bird of prey mounted on a turtle's neck. Maria Bisaccia was a native of Ortona, a trifle stout, with a fresh complexion and the clearest of eyes; she had a soft fashion of speech, and the light, leisurely touch of one whose hands were almost always busy over cakes and syrups, pastry and preserves. Donna Cristina, also an Ortonese, and educated in a Benedictine convent, was of small stature, with a somewhat too generous expanse of bosom, a face overstrewn with freckles, a large, long nose, poor teeth, and handsome eyes cast downward in a way that made one think of a priest in woman's clothing.

The three women were performing their task with the utmost care, giving up to it the greater part of the afternoon. All at once, just as Candia was leaving with the empty baskets, Donna Cristina, in the course of counting the small silver, found that a spoon was missing.

"Maria! Maria!" she cried, in utter dismay, "count these! There's a spoon missing! Count them yourself!"

"But how could it be? That's impossible, Signora!" replied Maria, "let me have a look." And she in turn began to count the small pieces, telling off the numbers aloud, while Donna Cristina looked on, shaking her head. The silver gave forth a clear, ringing sound.

"Well, it's a fact!" Maria exclaimed at last, with a gesture of despair; "what's to be done about it!"

She herself was safe from all suspicion. For fifteen years she had given proofs of her fidelity and honesty in this very household. She had come from Ortona together with Donna Cristina at the time of the wedding, almost as though she were a part of the marriage settlement; and from the first she had acquired a certain authority in the house, through the indulgence of her mistress. She was full of religious superstitions, devoted to the saint and the belfry of her birthplace, and possessed of great shrewdness. She and her mistress had formed a sort of offensive alliance against Pescara and all pertaining to it, and more particularly against the saint of the Pescarese. She never missed a chance to talk of her native town, to vaunt its beauty and its riches, the splendour of its basilica, the treasures of San Tommaso, the magnificence of its religious ceremonies, as compared with the poverty of San Cetteo, that possessed only one single little silver cross.

Donna Cristina said:

"Take a good look in there."

Maria left the room to extend the search. She explored every nook and corner of the kitchen and the balcony; but in vain. She came back empty-handed.

"It isn't there! It isn't there!"

Then the two together tried to think, to make conjectures, to ransack their memories. They went out upon the balcony that communicated with the court, the balcony back of the laundry, to make one last research. As they talked together in loud tones, women's heads began to appear at the windows of the surrounding houses.

"What has happened, Donna Cristina? Tell us about it."

Donna Cristina and Maria related the occurrence with many words and many gestures.

"Lord, Lord! Then there have been thieves here?"

In a moment the report of the theft had spread through the neighbourhood, through all Pescara. Men and women fell to discussing, to imagining who could have been the thief. By the time the news had reached the most distant houses of Sant' Agostino it had gathered volume; it was no longer a question of a mere spoon, but of all the silver plate in the house of Lamonica.

Now, since the weather was fine and roses were beginning to bloom upon the balcony, and a pair of linnets were singing in their cage, the women lingered at their windows, for the pleasure of gossiping across the grateful warmth of the outdoor air. Female heads continued to appear from behind the pots of sweet basil, and a chatter arose that must have rejoiced the cats upon the house-tops.

Clasping her hands, Donna Cristina asked: "Who could it have been?"

Donna Isabella Sertale, nicknamed the Pole-cat, who had the lithe and stealthy movements of a beast of prey, asked in a strident voice: "Who did you have with you, Donna Cristina? It seems to me that I saw Candia on her way——"

"Aha!" exclaimed Donna Felicetta Margasanta, nicknamed the Magpie because of her continuous garrulity. "Aha!" repeated the other gossips.—"And you hadn't thought of it?"—"And you never noticed?"—"And you don't know about Candia?"—"We can tell you about Candia!"—"Indeed we can!"—"Oh yes, we can tell you about her!"

"She washes clothes well, there is no denying it. She is the best laundress in Pescara, there's no question about it. But the trouble with her is that she is too light-fingered—didn't you know that, my dear?"

"She got a couple of towels from me once."—"And a napkin from me."—"And a night-gown from me."—"And three pairs of stockings from me."—"And a new petticoat from me."—"And I never got them back again."—"Nor I."—"Nor I."

"But I didn't discharge her. Whom could I get? Silvestra?"

"Oh! oh!"

"Angelantonia? The African?"

"Each one worse than the other!"

" We must put up with it."

" But it's a spoon this time ! "

" That's a little too much ! "

" Don't you let it pass, Donna Cristina, don't you let it pass ! "

" Let it pass, or not let it pass ! " burst forth Maria Bisaccia, who, in spite of her placid and benign appearance, never let an opportunity pass for displaying her superiority over her fellow-servants. " That is for us to decide, Donna Isabella, that is for us to decide ! "

And the chatter continued to flow back and forth from windows to balcony. And the accusation spread from lip to lip throughout the whole countryside.

II

The following morning, Candia Marcanda already had her arms in a tubful of clothes, when the village constable, Biagio Pesce, nicknamed the Little Corporal, appeared at her door.

" His Honour, the mayor, wants you up at his office at once," he told the laundress.

" What's that ? " demanded Candia, wrinkling her brows into a frown, yet without interrupting the task before her.

" His Honour, the mayor, wants you up at his office, at once."

" Wants me ? What does he want me for ? " Candia demanded rather sharply, for she was at a loss to understand this unexpected summons, and it turned her as stubborn as a horse balking at a shadow.

" I can't tell you what for," replied the Little Corporal, " those were my orders."

" What were your orders ? " From an obstinacy that was natural to her, she would not cease from asking questions. She could not convince herself that it was a reality. " The mayor wants me ? What for ? What have I done, I should like to know ? I'm not going. I haven't done anything."

The Little Corporal, losing his temper, answered : " Oh, you won't go, won't you ? We'll see about that ! " and he went off, muttering, with his hand upon the hilt of the ancient sword he wore.

Meanwhile there were others along the narrow street who had overheard the conversation and came out upon their doorsteps, where they could watch Candia vigorously working her arms up and down in the tubful of clothes. And since they knew about the silver spoon, they laughed meaningly and interchanged ambiguous phrases, which Candia could not understand. But this laughter and these phrases awoke a vague foreboding in the woman's mind. And this foreboding gathered strength when the Little Corporal reappeared, accompanied by another officer.

"Come on!" said the Little Corporal peremptorily.

Candia wiped her arms, without replying, and went with them. In the public square, people stopped to look. One of her enemies, Rosa Panura, called out from the door of her shop, with a hateful laugh: "Drop your stolen bone!"

The laundress, dazed by this persecution for which she could find no reason, was at a loss for a reply.

Before the mayor's office a group of curious idlers had gathered to watch her as she went in. Candia, in an access of anger, mounted the steps in a rush and burst into the mayor's presence, breathlessly demanding: "Well, what is it you want of me?"

Don Silla, a man of peaceful proclivities, was for the moment perturbed by the laundress's strident tones, and cast a glance at the two faithful custodians of his official dignity. Then, taking a pinch of tobacco from his horn snuff-box, he said to her, "My daughter, be seated."

But Candia remained standing. Her beak-like nose was inflated with anger, and her wrinkled cheeks quivered curiously. "Tell me, Don Silla."

"You went yesterday to take back the wash to Donna Cristina Lamonica?"

"Well, and what of it? What of it? Was there anything missing? All of it counted, piece by piece—and not a thing missing. What's the matter with it now?"

"Wait a moment, my daughter! In the same room there was the table silver——"

Candia, comprehending, turned like an angry hawk, about to swoop upon its prey. Her thin lips twitched convulsively.

"The silver was in the room, and Donna Cristina found that a spoon was missing. Do you understand, my daughter? Could you have taken it—by mistake?"

Candia jumped like a grasshopper before the injustice of this accusation. As a matter of fact she had stolen nothing.

"Oh, it was I, was it? I? Who says so? Who saw me? I am

astonished at you, Don Silla! I am astonished at you! I, a thief? I? I?"

And there was no end to her indignation. She was all the more keenly stung by the unjust charge, because she knew herself to be capable of the action they attributed to her.

"Then it was you who took it?" interrupted Don Silla, prudently sinking back into the depths of his spacious judicial chair.

"I am astonished at you!" snarled the woman once more, waving her long arms around as though they had been two sticks.

"Very well, you may go. We will see about it."

Candia went out without a salutation, blindly bumping into the doorpost. She was beside herself. As she set foot in the street and saw the crowd which had gathered, she realized that already public opinion was against her; that no one was going to believe in her innocence. Nevertheless, she began to utter a vociferous denial. The crowd continued to laugh as it dispersed. Full of fury, she returned home, and hopelessly began to weep upon her doorstep.

Don Donato Brandimarte, who lived next door, said mockingly: "Cry louder, cry louder! There are people passing by!"

Since there were heaps of clothing still waiting for the suds, she finally calmed herself, bared her arms, and resumed her task. As she worked, she thought out her denials, elaborated a whole system of defence, sought out in her shrewd woman's brain an ingenious method of establishing her innocence; racking her brain for specious subtleties, she had recourse to every trick of rustic dialectic to construct a line of reasoning that would convince the most incredulous.

Then, when her day's work was ended, she went out, deciding to go first to see Donna Cristina.

Donna Cristina was not to be seen. It was Maria Bisaccia who listened to Candia's flood of words, shaking her head but answering nothing, and withdrawing in dignified silence.

Next, Candia made the circuit of all her clients. To each in turn she related the occurrence, to each she unfolded her defence, continually adding some new argument, amplifying her words, growing constantly more excited, more desperate, in the face of incredulity and distrust. And all in vain; she felt that from now on there was no further defence possible. A sort of blind hopelessness took possession of her—what more was there to do? What more was there to say?

III

Meanwhile Donna Cristina Lamonica gave orders to send for Cinigia, a woman of the people, who practised magic and empirical medicine with considerable success. Cinigia had several times before discovered stolen goods; and it was said that she was secretly in league with the thieves.

"Find that spoon for me," Donna Cristina told her, "and you shall have a big reward."

"Very well," Cinigia replied; "twenty-four hours are all I need."

And twenty-four hours later she brought back her answer; the spoon was to be found in a hole in the courtyard, near the well.

Donna Cristina and Maria descended to the courtyard, made search, and, to their great amazement, found the spoon.

Swiftly the news spread throughout Pescara.

Then triumphantly Candia Marcanda went the rounds of all the streets. She seemed to have grown taller; she held her head erect; she smiled, looking every one straight in the eye, as if to say, "I told you so! I told you so!"

The people in the shops, seeing her pass by, would murmur something and then break forth into a significantly sneering laugh. Filippo La Selvi, who sat drinking a glass of liqueur brandy in the Café d' Ange, called Candia in.

"Another glass for Candia, the same as mine!"

The woman, who was fond of strong spirits, pursed up her lips covetously.

"You certainly deserve it, there's no denying that!" added Filippo La Selvi.

An idle crowd had gathered in front of the café. They all had the spirit of mischief in their faces. While the woman drank, Filippo La Selvi turned and addressed his audience:

"She knew how to work it, didn't she? Isn't she a clever one?" and he slapped the laundress familiarly upon her bony shoulder.

The crowd laughed. A little dwarf, called Magnafave, or "Big Beans," weak-minded and stuttering, joined the forefinger of his right hand to that of his left, and striking a grotesque attitude and dwelling upon each syllable, said:

"Ca—ca—ca—Candia—Ci—ci—Cinigia!" and he continued to make gestures and to stammer forth vulgar witticisms, all implying that Candia and Cinigia were in league together. His spectators indulged in contortions of merriment.

For a moment Candia sat there bewildered, with the glass still in her hand. Then in a flash she understood—they did not believe in her innocence. They accused her of having brought back the silver spoon secretly, by agreement with the sorceress, to save herself further trouble.

An access of blind anger came upon her. Speechless with passion, she flung herself upon the weakest of them, upon the little hunchback, in a hurricane of blows and scratches. And the crowd, at the sight of this struggle, formed a circle and jeered at them in cruel glee, as at a fight between two animals, and egged on the two combatants with voice and gesture.

Big Beans, badly scared by her unexpected violence, tried to escape, hopping about like a little ape ; and held fast by the laundress's terrible arms, whirled round and round with increasing velocity, like a stone in a sling, until at last he fell violently upon his face.

Some of the men hastened to pick him up. Candia withdrew in the midst of hisses, shut herself within her house, and flung herself across her bed, sobbing and gnawing her fingers, in the keenness of her suffering. The new accusation cut her deeper than the first, and all the more that she knew herself capable of such a subterfuge. How was she to clear herself now ? How was she to establish the truth ? She grew hopeless as she realized that she could not allege in defence any material difficulties that might have interfered with carrying out the deception. Access to the courtyard was perfectly simple ; a door, that was never fastened, opened from the ground floor of the main stairway ; people came and went freely through that door, to remove the garbage, or for other causes. So it was impossible for her to close the lips of her accusers by saying, " How could I have got in ? " The means of successfully carrying out such a plan were many and easy.

Candia proceeded to conjure up new arguments to convince them ; she sharpened up her wits ; she invented three, four, five different cases to prove that the spoon never could have been found in that hole in the courtyard ; she split hairs with marvellous ingenuity. Next she took to making the rounds of the shops and the houses, seeking in every possible way to overcome the people's incredulity. They listened to her, greatly entertained by her captious reasoning ; and they would end by saying, " Oh, it's all right ! "

But there was a certain tone in their voice that left Candia annihilated. So, then, all her trouble was for nothing! No one would believe her! Yet with marvellous persistence she would return to the attack, spending whole nights in thinking out new arguments. And little by little, under this continued strain, her mind gave way; she could no longer follow any sustained thought but that of the silver spoon.

Neglecting her work, she had sunk to a state of actual want. When she went down to the river bank, under the iron bridge, where the other wash-women congregated, she would sometimes let slip from between her fingers garments that the current swept away for ever. And she would talk continually, unweariedly, of the one single subject. In order not to hear her, the young laundresses would begin to sing, and would mock her with the improvised rhymes of their songs. And she meanwhile would shout and gesticulate like a crazy woman.

No one could give her work any longer. Out of pity, some of her former employers would send her food. Little by little she fell into the habit of begging, and wandered through the streets, bowed over, unkempt, and all in rags. The street urchins would run behind her, shouting: "Tell us the story of the spoon, 'cause we never heard it, Auntie Candia!"

She would stop strangers sometimes as they passed by, to tell them the story and to argue out her defence. Young fellows would sometimes send for her, and pay her a copper to tell it all over, two, three, or four times; they would raise up difficulties against her arguments; they would hear her all the way through, and at last stab her with a final word. She would shake her head, and go on her way; she found companionship among other beggars and would reason with them endlessly, indefatigably, invincibly. Her chosen friend was a deaf woman, whose skin was a mass of angry blotches, and who limped on one leg.

In the winter of 1874 she was at last stricken with serious illness. The woman with the blotches cared for her. Donna Cristina Lamonica sent her a cordial and a scuttle of coals.

The sick woman, lying on her pallet, still raved of the silver spoon. She would raise herself on her elbow and struggle to wave her arm, to give emphasis to her fevered arguments.

And at last, when her staring eyes already seemed overspread with a veil of troubled waters that rose from within, Candia gasped forth:

"It wasn't I, madam—because you see—the spoon——!"

SALVATORE FARINA
1846–

SEPARATION

I

MY room in the Via Bagutta was really situated a little higher than was necessary. I said it to myself every day, for I had so often to climb the hundred and twelve stairs that separated me from the world below; but whenever I reached the top, and gazed through the window over the splendid panorama of roofs and chimneys, I so much enjoyed the view that I remained living there. I made the acquaintance of all my neighbours; and among a bachelor's neighbours there are sure to be some from whom it is better to keep aloof.

Thus I made the acquaintance of the most eccentric married couple that can be imagined. If I were to say that Signor Sulpicio and Signora Concetta were each the actual half corresponding to the other, the statement need hardly be metaphorically taken; for, in truth, both of them together owned only as much flesh and muscle as usually belong to one ordinary mortal. If their years were added together, their sum was considerably over that of a century and a half. And if I imagined to myself—a funny, but not improper notion—Signora Concetta standing on her husband's head, it seemed to me as if the worthy lady would just touch, or, perhaps, even project, a very little beyond the ceiling; and my room was only three and a half yards high.

After the establishment of these mathematical proportions, it will be easy for the reader to form a picture of this couple; and they will live in his memory as in mine, a pair of lank, haggard thin forms, grey-headed, their faces furrowed with wrinkles, and their eyes sunk and sparkling.

For fifty-five years they had shared bed and board and all the vicissitudes of life with one another; they had so grown into one another, and had so lived themselves one into another, even their faces, with the exception of their noses, had grown like one another, that they might easily have been taken for brother and sister. But those noses, those noses! They had obstinately retained their own original shape; and I must confess that never in my life did I see two more differently shaped noses. The man's was hooked—eagle-fashion—as though inquisitively to watch whatever entered the mouth; while the woman's was small and retreating, as though it stepped aside to leave the way to her mouth open for a good morsel. This simile was not made by me in the first instance, but had its origin with the couple.

It happened at dinner fifty-four years and eleven months ago, in an unfortunate moment of mutual anger about some sauce that tasted of smoke.

This was the first cloud that appeared on the fair sky of their conjugal happiness; but it was an ugly dark cloud, and it mounted from the sauce into their noses, from their noses into their heads, from their heads into their minds. At last they discovered that never on this earth had a married pair more unwillingly borne the burden of the conjugal yoke than they. Concetta spoke of returning to her relatives, and Sulpicio wished her to go at once; but considering that they were on their wedding journey, and that Concetta's relatives lived two hundred miles away from the scene of this first matrimonial quarrel, the execution of this plan was, for the time being, deferred.

But "Separation" was, and remained, the password between them. Next day it occurred to Sulpicio that his companion had been entrusted to him as a maiden treasure; he remembered a touching conversation which he had had with his father-in-law; he bethought him of his vow to make her happy; a whole host of good thoughts and wise resolves rose up in his soul, and at length brought him to the conviction that it was his place to persuade Concetta not to forsake the domestic hearth.

Concetta, too, on the whole a sensible woman, thought of her mother's advice; of the vow she had taken at the altar; of the envy of her friends who remained unmarried; of the secret joy and pretended pity of her youthful companions. Then she considered that Sulpicio was not really a bad man, and that it was only the unfortunate smoky sauce that was at fault in the whole matter.

When Sulpicio approached her with his pleasantest smile, Concetta also met him with her pleasantest manner; they pressed each other's hands, embraced warmly, and peace was concluded.

But in their hearts there remained the consciousness that they had made trial of one another. This trial was followed by others no less stormy; and lodgers on the fourth floor in the Via Bagutta, and sometimes the whole neighbourhood, were occasionally witnesses to sudden shrieking sounds.

"That is Concetta," the people would say. It was Concetta. After the unfortunate victim had vainly cast at her tyrant's head all the flattering terms she had collected during the last fifty-five years, without being able to trump his supply, she would finish by giving a terrible scream. At the end of such scenes old Sulpicio generally fled downstairs, so that Concetta sent her last abusive words after him from one of the steps.

Then the good neighbours came to her assistance. They let her talk till the attack of rage was over; then they joined in her lamentation, and pitied her, and declared her fate to be undeserved, and her husband a brute. Suddenly she seemed quieted, and then she contradicted every one most passionately, and defended her Sulpicio with incredible warmth, whom she alone could understand, whose heart only she could read, and who was really better than any one else.

When the attack was over, and the landing cleared again, the old woman crept quietly and secretly back into their apartment, and buried her trembling head in a large black-silk hood; thereupon she descended two flights of stairs, and knocked at the door of Madame Nina, who lived with a weak-headed uncle, a friend of Sulpicio's. Concetta knew that her husband thought very highly of the young woman; yet she was so far from being jealous of her, that she even made use of her assistance in re-establishing peace.

Almost at the same moment the husband returned secretly to the house, came panting up the stairs, and burst into my room. As he knew that Concetta cherished almost motherly feelings towards me, and that a word from me would go a long way with her, he did me the troublesome honour of entrusting me with the restoration of his domestic peace.

II

From me this office of peacemaker required no great sacrifice, nor from Nina either, I believe.

As soon as Concetta saw me, she met me cordially, seized my hand in both hers, and by mutely nodding her head and casting up her eyes, she declared to me all her sorrow for what had occurred, her intention of returning to her conjugal duties, and her gratitude for my successful efforts. It was evident that neither could Concetta live without her

Sulpicio, nor Sulpicio without his Concetta. They loved each other, as they had always loved each other ; and in spite of being ever ready to quarrel, they loved as much as any two people can love.

As I had expected, as soon as Sulpicio appeared at the door after his conversion, hiding his emotion from me by assumed indifference, Concetta would have given him any atonement in her power, and in her confusion she sought through all her pockets for her thimble and needle-case.

Meantime I occupied myself with the lock of the door, or looked out of the window, or examined some book or picture. Then the two came a little nearer to one another ; my backward glances revealed two trembling hands that pressed one another, two faces sparkling with glad smiles, and two tears rolling down along the furrows of the wrinkles. At last they fell into each other's arms. I then looked elsewhere, or I turned round as if accidentally and said that it was beautiful weather—unless it happened to be pouring with rain ; but I thought to myself that in those tears youth had come back to life, and that these smiles were well worthy the rosy cheeks and foreheads of spring.

But one day the storm raged so terribly that the diplomatic transactions lasted many hours, and had to be very skilfully managed before the two ships could be got to run into the calm matrimonial harbour. The word " Separation " was pronounced by both parties with the greatest decision, and neither would give way.

In order to avoid any diplomatic transactions, both parties had left the house and gone in opposite directions. The servant, a half-silly little thing, whom the two old people had turned up somewhere and taken in, knew nothing except that her master and mistress had gone out one after another. I seated myself by the grate, stirred the fire, and awaited the events that might come. It was a beautiful winter's day, the sun shone brightly and the fire crackled merrily on the hearth.

My thoughts too were cheerful. I tried to guess which of the two would be the first to return to the domestic hearth. Who ? Doubtless Concetta. Suddenly I heard a dress rustling ! I rose, turned round, and saw before me—Signora Nina, the young widow from the third floor.

The lady seemed surprised to find me. She was the more embarrassed as she had entered with her usual easy familiarity ; and to avoid the appearance of having committed an indiscretion, she acted as though she had not observed my presence, and thus made me understand that in so entering she had only made use of an old privilege. All the more I felt it to be my place to salute and address her ; but she anticipated me.

"Is Signora Concetta not at home ?" she asked.

"Neither she nor Signor Sulpicio. I am waiting for both."

"And I wanted to speak to one of them. I will come again."

The information that both husband and wife had left the house seemed to make her anxious ; still she remained.

"I really meant to wait, but I will come again."

"Thank you. Probably you come for——"

"For the same reason."

With these words I stepped a little aside, as though to invite her to remain. The next minute she was seated at my former place, near the fire, and I—did not go.

Signora Nina did not know me, but I knew her well. From my window, which was over hers, I had often examined the colour of her hair, and vainly hoped some time to be able to behold that of her eyes. Once I had sent her away by coughing ; since then I had never coughed at the window. Now those little white hands, that I had once seen playing the scales, were resting on the mantelpiece, and I might openly look into that face which had hitherto been to me a veiled picture.

Yes, Nina was beautiful, at least she seemed so to me.

As I was still standing before her, she invited me, by a polite movement of her hand, to seat myself. I did so. One moment of silent expectation followed. No one came.

The silence began to become uncomfortable. She broke it by speaking of Sulpicio. I spoke of Concetta.

When I told her of the office whose duties I had faithfully fulfilled ever since I had the good fortune to be the neighbour of this couple, she smiled. What a beautiful smile ! What splendid teeth !

"What a misfortune !" said she, after a short pause. "To live with one another fifty-five years without being able to understand each other !"

"An eternal fight and squabble ! I have been a witness to it. But in reality they are fond of one another."

The widow's face showed a curious smile, but she did not answer.

"Such contradictions are like contrary winds," continued I, "which stir up wave after wave, and toss them up to the sky ; then, when the storm is over, the sea becomes calm again, and once more shows the smooth surface of its clear waters. I scarcely think that two people could live with one another for any length of time without quarrelling."

Still the widow did not answer. She shook her head, and stirred impatiently among the ashes in the grate.

I was silent.

" What time is it ? " asked she, as though she thought her silence offended me.

" Four o'clock."

" It is late. I must go. I will come again."

" By the right time, it is still thirteen minutes to four."

Nina smiled, and—did not go.

I did not know why, but in my heart there was a sound as of joy-bells.

Suddenly we saw Sulpicio and Concetta coming along hand-in-hand.

" Is peace restored ? " both Nina and I inquired with our eyes.

" It is," answered husband and wife, in the same language.

" I had come to offer my congratulations on the peace," said the widow. " Now it is late, and I must go."

Concetta was in good spirits ; her wrinkles revealed a kindly smile, and her eyes sparkled.

" It was not a bad thing that Signor Carlo kept you company," said she to the young widow.

Nina blushed, and I felt my heart beat faster.

She went, and soon after I took my leave.

The whole day long I only thought of Signora Nina, and only dreamt of her all night. All next morning I stood at the window to see her. I was fortunate enough to be observed by her, and to be allowed to bow to her. For a whole month I stood regularly at the window at the same time, and rejoiced in the same good fortune ; now I smiled at her, now she at me. Seven months and eight days after I was permitted to press Signora Nina to my heart. She was no longer a widow.

III

We were happy. We inhabited a little house far removed from the noisy bustle of the town. Our windows did not open on to the dwellings of troublesome neighbours. We had the sun every day from morning to noon, and our new furniture shone in festive light.

She said her old uncle would on no consideration remain alone with his infirmities, and had gone to live with a sister in the town.

We were alone with our dreams, our plans, and thoughts; and that was sufficient for us. Any other society would only have been wearisome.

Our room was rose-coloured, like the happy spirits that presided over it. The future appeared to us as a beautiful dream. Nina was as graceful as she was dignified. She could smile so sweetly; her glance was as bright and as clear as the moon's beam; her voice was gentle and harmonious; and then she had such a bewitching way of approaching me, laying her hands on my shoulders, and, without one spoken word, saying to me, "I love you!" that I could have gazed on her for hours, and devoured her with my eyes.

She had only one fault: she could not go from one room into another without banging the door behind her. Often, when I was startled from my thoughts and dreams by the slamming of a door, I was on the point of giving expression to the unpleasant sensation; but then I saw her rosy face, and was silent. None the less did it constantly irritate me, and I tried in vain to endure it more calmly.

I must testify to myself that I was an almost perfect husband to Nina. I left her alone as seldom as possible, and then only for a short time. I never contradicted her. I tried to anticipate all her wishes, always spoke kindly to her, and committed a thousand little absurdities to keep her in good humour. But I, too, had one little fault: I was terribly absent. Sometimes, when I was absorbed in some stupid thought, I did not notice that she, herself smiling, demanded a smile from me; and then I would answer some joking fancy by a serious shake of my head.

Certainly Fate, when it mated together two such serious faults, could not have intended to produce an image of conjugal peace.

One day I was even more absent, and she slammed the doors even more violently than usual; a loud "O!" escaped from me. She had heard it and I repented it. In vain. Next time Nina did not disturb me in my contemplation; she walked softly on tiptoe, and when she closed the door, she did it with the greatest care, to avoid making the least sound.

The roar of Vulcan's smithy would not have made me spring up faster from my chair. I rushed towards her, embraced and kissed her, and we laughed together in the fulness of our hearts.

But the ice was broken ; a thought had come to open expression between us : we were not perfect. In spite of all her exertions, Nina did not succeed in curing herself of her fault ; only as soon as she had committed it she assumed a half-sorry, half-teazing manner, which made her seem even more beautiful.

As for me, as often as my thoughts carried me away, I continued to shake my head and open my eyes wide ; and so everything remained as before.

Our honeymoon lasted several months without the faintest shadow of a cloud resting on the brows of the lovers.

One day—it was one of those sultry July days on which the cruel hot sun mocks us—she swears to this day that she first said to me, " I should like to know in what you are always so deeply absorbed. I really should like to know ! " And would you believe it, honoured reader, I am said first to have offended her by a slight imprecation, which I did not notice myself until it was more than half out of my lips ? Yet, however that may be, one of us replied with a rude speech, the other with a somewhat ruder one, then now and then was added a touch of scorn and bitterness ; and at last Nina's eyes were as full of tears as my heart of wounded pride.

Another time, the same beginning, the same end ; and that was repeated again and again.

" This life is becoming unendurable," said she.

" So I think too," answered I.

" Indeed ! Do you think so too ? But I for my part am thoroughly tired of it. And we have borne these chains now for nearly a year ! "

" Ten months," I answered.

" To you it may seem ten years, to me it does not yet seem quite so long. But I suppose our happiness has already lasted too long ! O, how unhappy I am ! I can see it already ; you will come to hate me, if indeed you do not hate me already. But I, too, shall at last hate you."

I longed to take her in my arms, and to carry her with her wrath through all the rooms, until at last she should laughingly exclaim, " Now it is enough." Best of all, I should have liked to kneel before her, to confess my conjugal sins, and beg for absolution, or to fall upon her neck and kiss it until it was so red with my embraces that fright would have brought her back to her senses ; in short, all the good thoughts that can only occur to the best sort of husband rose up in me.

I give her a sidelong glance ; she sees my look, and shrugs her shoulders. I make a step towards her, she leaves the room, and I—do the same ; but in the opposite direction, down the stairs, deeply hurt, yet full of conscience-pricks before even I began to carry out my terrible plans of vengeance.

For a long time I continued walking round and round in a circle. I could not leave the spot, and involuntarily my looks always rested on the house in which dwelt my happiness.

Then all at once I remembered Concetta and Sulpicio, our good friends of former times ; and I thought that I had no one to undertake the office of peacemaker with Nina for me, and besides that I would never entrust such an office to any one, or ever permit it.

I said to myself, " It is the first time ; but who knows whether it is the last time ? You must return to her, shorten her punishment as much as posible ; you must speak kindly to her, and say that we will not quarrel any more. But what if she, instead of listening kindly to me, should prove refractory ? O, what nonsense ! She will certainly answer my first kind word with a hearty kiss. Then we shall no longer talk or complain, but only laugh together."

Two or three times these reflections had brought me as far as the threshold of my house, and just as often I had gone away again. At length I ventured to cross the Rubicon, ran quickly through the doorway, sprang up the stairs, three or four steps at a time, and a moment after I stood before her, who had already come weeping to meet me on the landing.

She covered her face with her hands, and did not speak a word. I put my arm round her and drew her into the room ; then I took her on my lap, gently forced her hands away from her eyes, laid my face next hers, and begged her forgiveness. But instead of forgiving me she broke out into fresh sobs, threw her arms round my neck, and laid her head on my shoulder. My heart was beating violently. Nina's behaviour seemed to me to tell of some misfortune. What could have happened during my absence ? New caresses in kiss and word. When at length I ventured to address her with an anxious inquiry, she burst out afresh into more violent sobs.

" She is dead ! "

" Who ? "

" Concetta, poor Concetta ! "

I was silent. To tell the truth, the matter did not affect me very deeply ; the worthy lady was a good deal past seventy, and her place in heaven had long been reserved for her. Still I felt it my duty to pay some regard to Nina's sincere distress. When she had finished crying she said, in a voice of deep emotion :

" Now they are separated ! "

" And who brought you the news ? "

" A friend who visited me. Poor Concetta died quite suddenly the day before yesterday."

" And Sulpicio ? "

" Is in despair. He does not speak a word, and seems quite stunned."

" I must go and see him."

" Yes, do, my friend ; go at once."

I went. When I arrived— Alas, the poor old heart had not been able to endure the grief of desolation ! In that same night, a few hours after they had carried out his life's companion, he lay down in his widowed bed in the certain conviction that he should not see the next morning.

The dead man's smiling face seemed to say to me, " Even death has not been able to separate us."

With my heart full of sadness, but of mild beneficent sadness, I returned home. We were alone. I said not a word to Nina. She fell sadly round my neck and pressed me to her heart.

" Carlo ! "

" Nina ! "

She cast up her eyes, as though she wished to read my thoughts in mine ; then she whispered :

" We too ! Is it not true ? "

MATILDE SERAO
1856–

AN INTERVENTION

I

GUIDO certainly looked perfectly happy ; indeed, any one would have thought that he had not a care in the world. He was on his way home from a political banquet, where he had been explaining in detail his programme to his electors. He had been complimented on all sides, and, added to this, the dinner itself had been excellent and the champagne all that could be desired. Guido felt quite easy in his own mind about the result of the election, and now this evening he was going to a ball, where he would enjoy a flirtation with the Baroness Stefania. He was just returning home now to have an hour's rest and a nap, like Napoleon on the eve of a battle. On entering the dining-room his faithful old servant, Giuseppe, followed him respectfully in, and stood for a minute evidently desiring to speak to his master.

" What is it, Giuseppe ? " asked Guido.

" If you will excuse me, sir, I wanted——"

" Be quick about it, my good fellow, for I have not much time."

" Do you not remember what day it is, sir ? "

" No—what do you mean ? "

" It is your birthday——"

" Ah ! so it is," said Guido, and his face clouded over.

" There always *used* to be flowers everywhere, sir——"

" There *used* to be—but that's over—there are none in these days," and Guido smiled bitterly.

" You'll please to excuse me, sir," said the old man, stepping forward and uncovering a huge bouquet on the table.

" Oh, Giuseppe—there's no need to apologise, my good fellow. Thank you very much ; this little surprise has given me great pleasure."

Guido could not help feeling melancholy all the same at the thought that on this day, when he was accustomed to being *fêted*, there was only his old servant now to remember it. It was only a passing regret, for

Guido was too much a man of the world not to be able to throw off all *appearance* of emotion.

" I am going to my room to get a little rest," he said to Giuseppe ; " you can wake me at eight."

" You'd better not, sir," said the servant, earnestly.

" And why not, pray ? "

" Because, sir, when Girolamo was here alone this morning a lady called, and when she found that you were out, she said : ' Tell your master, when he comes in, that I will call again at seven, and ask him to be sure and wait in for me, as I want to see him on particular business.' "

" And her name ? "

" She would not give it."

" H—m ! more and more mysterious ! Did Girolamo say what she was like ? "

" Yes, she was young, tall, dark, and very well dressed."

" Oh ! it's getting decidedly interesting and I feel curious. And you think, then, Giuseppe, for the sake of this unknown lady, I ought to forego my nap ? "

" Well, it is just seven o'clock, sir. If she is anything like punctual, you wouldn't have time to lie down before she is here."

" Oh, well. I will make the sacrifice. Get my newspaper, Giuseppe, and I'll read until she arrives. Dark !—the Baroness Stefania is fair—nothing like a change," murmured Guido to himself when the old man had gone out of the room.

It certainly sounds very much as though the young politician were a veritable Don Juan, but in reality it was nothing of the kind. Guido had had a great disappointment in his life. He had loved one woman passionately and devotedly—but his happiness had been suddenly snatched away from him, and the love still smouldered in his heart, half smothered and stifled as it had been. For the last two years Guido had been striving to forget—and he had thrown himself headlong into all the gaieties and diversions of society life.

" If you please, sir ! " exclaimed Giuseppe, re-entering the dining-room hastily.

" Has she arrived ? "

" She is in the drawing-room."

" Do you know her ? "

" No—no, sir," stammered the old servant.

Guido was soon in the drawing-room. He opened the door quietly and stood for a few seconds contemplating his visitor. She was standing near a table turning over the leaves of an album. Her back was turned towards the door, but Guido could see that she was tall and graceful. She wore a very handsome dark silk dress, and was decidedly elegant.

"Madam——," said Guido, advancing towards her.

She turned suddenly, and her host felt as though he had received an electric shock. He bowed, however, profoundly, in order to hide the surprise on his face. "I am not inconveniencing you by coming this evening?" she asked, after returning his bow, and then she sat down very deliberately.

"Certainly not, I am entirely at your service."

"If you say that merely out of politeness, so much the worse for you, as I should like to take it literally."

"Do so, by all means. I take upon myself all risk, and shall be glad to hear what you have to say," answered Guido, smiling.

The lady, whose name was Emma, stroked her muff, evidently hesitating as to how she was going to express what she had to say.

Guido was watching her—yes, she was just as beautiful as ever—just as fascinating as that first time he had seen her; it seemed to him even that her beauty was perhaps more complete, more wonderful than ever. The profile was more decided, she had a faint colour in her cheeks, and her eyes, which were always so intelligent, had now another expression in them, a more beautiful expression than ever. It was very evident that the woman before him had suffered—that she had had some great trouble.

"Have you ever taken part in a comedy?" she asked at length.

"Oh, yes! I am still acting in one that never comes to an end."

"My question was needless, I see. To-morrow, then, I want you to continue, that is all; but you will have an important *rôle* to take, and it will be difficult to succeed."

"All depends on the actors and the public."

"You will have me as a partner."

"I know what talent you have."

"For acting?"

"For declaiming. Is it a proverb we are to act?"

"Yes, but the moral of it is in the motive for which it is given—

not in the comedy itself. Tell me, do you still write regularly to my father ?"

"Yes ; but for the last three weeks he has not answered my letters."

"I received a letter from him yesterday, in which he tells me that he is very well, and that he will arrive to-morrow in Milan by the train at twenty past ten."

Guido could not conceal his surprise now.

"To-morrow ?"

"Yes."

"Your father—who never stirs from home !"

"He is on his way back to Naples after a journey that he was obliged to take, and is coming round this way to see——"

"His daughter," put in Guido.

"And his son, he says."

"So that——?"

"So that I think it is a very pleasant sort of position for us," said Emma, putting her small foot on a velvet stool by her chair.

"You think it pleasant ?"

"It is scarcely worth while discussing mere words ; it would be better to find a way out of the difficulty."

"I do not see any way out."

"And yet you are a politician and an intelligent man ! Of what use has it been, then, for you to learn the art of clever subterfuges, to undertake transactions of the most delicate nature, and to have accustomed yourself to using phrases which are no doubt both sincere and diplomatic ?"

"If you continue in that strain I shall have fewer and fewer ideas every minute."

"I have a plan."

"Yes, I knew you had."

"It is very evident that you are trying to be obliging."

"I wish you always thought so."

"Well, listen. I would not have my father, upon any account, know the truth."

"The wretched truth," interrupted Guido.

"It is no use putting adjectives in everywhere. My father would be nearly heartbroken if he knew, and I should feel such remorse. It seems to me that it is not right for the mistakes and faults of the children to be visited on the parents. Until now, as you have helped me in this, thanks to the distance and to his not knowing any one in Milan, he has been spared this grief. But now, to-morrow, all the pious lies and all our hypocrisy would be discovered, and Heaven knows what would be the result. It must be prevented, and I am counting on you to help me. He must see us together when he comes to-morrow, and we must not betray, either by word or look, the true situation. This is what we must do."

Emma had spoken earnestly and firmly, and Guido had listened attentively. He was silent for a moment when she stopped speaking, and she began again, impatiently:

"It is merely a comedy, as I told you at first. A play given for a charitable purpose. It ought not to cost you so much."

"Oh, I am quite ready and willing," said Guido; "but are you not afraid that something may go wrong and compromise everything?"

"In what way?"

"Well, there are the servants."

"Send your new valet out to-morrow for a day's holiday, and then I will speak to Giuseppe."

"Very well. But supposing some friend should happen to drop in?"

"You must tell Giuseppe you are not at home to any one."

"I suppose we should go to the station to meet your father. What will everyone say when they see us together?"

"They won't see us. We can go in a close carriage and drive fast."

"Your father will be here all day: no matter how unsuspicious he may be, don't you think the house looks very much like a bachelor's dwelling now?"

"Oh! that can soon be altered. My work-table and other little things, and then my music, can be brought here this evening. That will all be our *mise en scène*, you know."

"But——"

"Oh! you have perhaps had some alterations made in the other rooms?"

"No! nothing has been altered," said Guido, speaking very seriously; "everything is—as you left it."

"By way of sentiment?"

"It was out of respect."

" A thousand thanks. Have you any other objections ? "

" None whatever ; the great thing is now whether we shall succeed in deceiving M. Giorgianni."

" By acting a sentimental couple ? We must think of the past and try to remember all our nonsense during our honeymoon," said Emma sarcastically.

" Oh ! I had completely forgotten all that," replied her husband promptly. They both glanced at each other questioningly, as though measuring strength like two duellists.

" It is perhaps selfish of me to ask you to give up your day like this to-morrow. Have you no engagements ? "

" None ; and if I had I should break them."

" Thanks, again. But this evening you are free, at any rate ; I do not need any company."

" What do you mean ? "

" Well, I must stay and arrange the things, and send for my part of the stage scenery, so that it may look more as it used to. I do not want you, though, to feel you have to stay here and watch me—it would be too dull for you. Go out—anywhere—for until ten o'clock to-morrow you are quite free."

" I was going to a ball—but if you like I will stay in——"

" Why ? Oh no ! for we should have to keep up a conversation, and now that we have nothing more to say to each other——"

" Nothing—or else, perhaps—too much ! Well, then, if you will excuse me, I will go and dress."

Emma bowed, and Guido left the room, *looking* as though he had nothing in the world to trouble him. In reality, he felt by no means as calm as he appeared.

At the ball he was most absent-minded, and the Baroness Stefania did not know what to make of him. After two or three dances, he managed, during a quadrille, to slip away unobserved, and on returning home he found that a complete transformation scene had taken place. The large drawing-room, which had not been used for some time, was open, and candles were lighted everywhere. The wardrobes and cupboards, too, were all open, and there was a strong scent of violets. A copy of one of the newest songs was on the piano ; the furniture had been moved about to give a less stiff appearance ; flowers were in all the vases, and Emma herself in a pretty tea-gown was just standing on tip-toe to put a small statue upon a bracket.

Was it all a dream? Emma there! And these two long years of separation, had he forgotten them—and their terrible quarrel?

"Good-night!" said Guido, as he passed through the room.

"Good-night," she replied, without turning round.

II

And yet before their marriage they had been so foolishly in love with each other. Guido had followed Emma from Florence to Naples, and had passed whole nights under her window. Emma had written letters of eight pages to him every day, and had stayed out on her balcony till quite late in the evenings. The young couple had been blissfully happy and devotedly in love with each other for three years. They had had their little differences, for Emma had been greatly indulged by her father, and she was quick-tempered and very jealous. Guido, like all well-balanced temperaments, was very calm always, and his cool manner and ironical or contemptuous smile when she was fuming had frequently had the effect of fuel added to a fire. Sometimes they had offended each other seriously, but the making-up the quarrel afterwards had always been all the more tender. One day, however, it happened that Guido happened to meet a girl whom he had formerly very much admired, and with whom he had in the old days fancied himself deeply in love. Somehow or other, Emma had become aware of this, and reproached him with never having told her. Guido, angry at being dictated to, and also at his wife's want of confidence, put on a careless, indifferent manner.

All Emma's deep love for her husband seemed to change suddenly into cold contempt and scorn. She was very proud, and she had been deeply wounded at the thought of having a rival in her husband's affections, for with her quick imagination she had convinced herself that Guido still loved this other woman.

She sent for her husband, and very calmly, without her voice trembling in the least, she announced to him that she had decided it would be better for them to separate quietly, without any fuss or any scene.

Guido was stupefied; at first he protested, and then tried to take it all as a joke, and wanted to explain matters to her; but his wife answered so coldly and so proudly, that there was nothing left for him but to maintain a frigid silence. It seemed to him that it was beneath his dignity to plead his cause, and so he merely agreed to all her conditions and let her go, judging her to be both proud and heartless. Ever since then he had busied himself with politics, gone out a great deal into society, and putting on a careless, indifferent air, pretended to be sceptical, and quite happy in his second bachelorhood. When he was alone, however, and when he had the courage to face his own soul, he owned to himself that his whole life was ruined, and that he felt utterly desolate. He had happened to meet his wife since their separation several times. They had bowed to each other almost like strangers, and had passed on their respective ways.

Emma had withdrawn from society, so her husband was sure never to meet her at the balls and theatres, where he now spent the greater part of his spare time. They had, before separating, agreed on one point, and that was to continue writing to the old father as though nothing had happened.

Guido used to put in his letters : " Emma is well, but I suppose she has given you all the news about herself ; she sends her love," etc., and then Emma wrote in her letter : " Guido is very well, but very busy. He was not able to get off in order to stay with me at the sea."

And so M. Giorgianni's happiness had gone on hanging by this fragile silken thread. To meet and speak to each other thus, for the first time after that supremely cruel day of their separation, had been no easy matter for either of them.

Emma had had to put aside her pride before she could thus bring herself to enter her husband's house, ask him this favour, and put on that hypocritical mask of indifference and of sarcasm. " It is for my father's sake ! " she had kept repeating to herself in order to brace herself up to it.

Guido's cold politeness had given her strength. Their conversation had been, on the whole, courteous and satisfactory. There had been no allusion to past, present, or future, with the exception of just one or two stinging remarks ; but there had been no scene, no reproaches. They had both behaved like wise practical individuals. Yes, but what about the next day ? The next day would probably be the same ; a little courage, and very much hypocrisy, no blunders, and a whole series of white lies, as they brought the old man home from the station. Then afterwards, when it was all over, why, they would bow again most formally to each other, and would go on their way as though nothing had happened. Of any attempt at a reconciliation there was not the least idea. Guido would never make the first advance, and Emma would never forgive. Such were the thoughts of both husband and wife, and then they each concluded with the idea that, after all, they were quite satisfied and perfectly resigned to their present arrangement.

III

Dinner was just over, and Signor Giorgianni was smiling, for he felt so happy—he had had such a hearty reception, and everything seemed so very satisfactory.

The two actors managed to get up a smile also—but the fact was, all that had appeared so easy to them the night before had proved very difficult when it came to the point. For instance, when Emma's father had arrived, he had put his arms round both of them as he kissed his daughter. Then they had been obliged to call each other by their old familiar pet names, and to show those little attentions to each other which come quite naturally to a husband and wife who adore each other, as they were supposed to ; and all the time, a word or an intonation of the voice which recalled the past would make Guido turn pale with emotion and would bring the colour into Emma's cheeks, and make them both feel awkward for a moment. Prepared as they had been for the ordeal, and try as they did to forget themselves and their own personalities, the reality would keep coming to their minds, and they could not stifle entirely the old interest in each other. Added to all this was the fear lest some careless, thoughtless remark might escape them, and thus cancel all the efforts they had made ; and then more vague and undefined was an idea which was growing more and more persistent, that somehow, in some strange way, this comedy would lead to some unforeseen change, that henceforth a new era would begin for them.

Whilst M. Giorgianni was going upstairs in front of them, Emma glanced despairingly at her husband, and he knew she was thinking,

" How shall we go on with this comedy until the end of the day ? "

He replied by another glance which meant : " We must do our best, and have faith for the rest."

The worst was yet to come, for no sooner had M. Giorgianni taken an arm-chair comfortably in the drawing-room than he began asking all kinds of embarrassing questions, and making remarks which were not calculated to put the young husband and wife at their ease, considering the circumstances.

"Yes," he said, putting down his coffee-cup, "I am thoroughly enjoying this day with you, my children. You see, Emma, *mia*, letters are all very well in their way, but I prefer a visit, even though it be a short one. Do you know, my child, you look very well, and prettier than ever, I declare—isn't she, Guido?"

"Yes, that is what I am always telling her," replied the son-in-law, smiling.

"Yes; and what you tell me, too, in your letters. Yes, Emma, that is a fact; Guido writes of nothing else but his wife in his letters. It's my belief you have quite bewitched him. What a model husband!"

"Yes, indeed, he is," said Emma, quietly.

There was silence for a moment after this remark. Guido's head was bent, he appeared to be counting the flowers on the carpet.

"Your Aunt Elizabeth sends all kinds of messages to you both—and Rosalia, your cousin, too. Poor girl, she's had a lot of trouble!"

"Why, she married her Piero!" exclaimed Emma, a shade of sarcasm in her tone.

"Yes, yes, she married him, and they were very fond of each other. But, I don't know, they did not hit it off very well; there were scenes and tears, and Rosalia went back home."

"Oh, well, she did quite right."

"Quite wrong, you mean. A wife ought never to leave her husband. Well, it's all right now, thanks to my eloquence. I persuaded her to forgive all she had against her husband."

"You, papa?"

"Yes, and I glory in my intervention. It was your mother's creed, my child; she was so merciful and so tolerant—ah! she was a good woman! She always used to say: 'Those who love the most pardon the most.'"

Every one was silent again, and then M. Giorgianni suddenly said:

"Come, my children, I want to go all through the house and see everything. There seems to me to be plenty of silk and velvet everywhere, but I have only glanced round. I want to see everything now."

"Come along," said Guido; "we will begin with the large drawing-room."

"It's magnificent, this room," said M. Giorgianni, on entering. "Just the thing for a large reception. Do you have many parties?"

"Well, we used to give more than we do just now."

"Yes, yes, I understand; your business affairs and your political engagements must take up your time a great deal; but it's a lovely room. Ah! and this is the boudoir? Exquisite taste, to be sure. Did you choose the furniture, Emma?"

"No, it was Guido who chose it."

"Well, my compliments, then," said the father, turning to his son-in-law. "I suppose you are always to be found here, Emma? Are you not afraid of every one coming to make love to her, Guido?"

"I! I know my wife too well for that!"

"And you, Emma, are you ever jealous?"

"I know my husband too well, papa!"

Both these answers had been given so spontaneously that M. Giorgianni was quite satisfied.

"This bedroom is lovely, the colours harmonize so well." He turned round and looked about as though he missed something.

"Emma!" he said.

"Yes, papa, what is it?"

"Where is your mother's portrait—I do not see it anywhere?"

She did not know what to reply, and her husband interposed.

"We have been away from home, and we have not all our luggage here yet."

"That portrait, though, should not have been left behind. It's all the same, though: Emma would never forget her mother. Ah! Guido, *mia*, you ought to have known her. When she was dying she made me promise that I would sacrifice everything for our child's happiness, so you see she helped you in your marriage. When Emma came and said to me, 'Papa, I shall never be happy if I do not marry Guido'—well, I thought of my poor dead wife, and that decided me. It was as though you were intended for each other, and you had been in love then for about a year. Emma was getting pale and wretched looking, and as for you, Guido, you were like a madman. Ah! young lovers! how foolish they are. Do you remember that ball at the English Consul's, Emma, where we went with Guido?"

"Yes, I remember," said Emma, mechanically.

"When every one saw you that evening there was no need to tell the news, it was very evident that you were engaged, and every one began congratulating me. Oh! but you know you were really too much in love."

"Yes, too much!" assented Guido.

"Oh! I mean it, though. Well, well, let us hope it will always continue, eh! Emma?"

"Yes, let us hope so."

"What's this room? Why, it's locked!"

It was the room Guido now used, and which Emma had not entered. They had not counted on the old man wanting to see every room.

Emma came to the rescue, for it was Guido's turn not to know what to answer.

"It is the spare room, papa."

"Ah! the one you would have put me in if I could have stayed? Yes, I must go to-night; it's a pity!"

"Yes, indeed it is," said Guido.

"Well, never mind, I'll look at my room by way of consoling myself——"

"But, papa——" began Emma.

"I understand. It is not in order; oh! That does not matter, child—not at all."

Guido turned the key, and opened the door, courageously, for he saw there was nothing else to be done.

"Ah! A very nice room, and quite in order, my child. Ah! and there's your portrait. I'm sure it was Guido who put that there for me. Thank you, my dear fellow; it was very thoughtful, but I really cannot stay this time, although I should like to very much."

They went back into the drawing-room and sat down. Both husband and wife were very absent-minded, and certainly if Signor Giorgianni had been endowed with much perspicacity, he would have discovered that something was wrong. Fortunately, the excellent old man was not good at guessing enigmas.

"What a pity for you to leave such a beautiful house!"

"Why, papa?"

"Well, if Guido should be elected member, why, you will have to live in Rome six months of the year, and I suppose he won't leave you alone in Milan. You will have to have two houses—it will be a nuisance for you—but I shan't be sorry. If you come to Rome, I shall be able to see you at least once a month—from Naples to Rome, it is quite a short, easy journey; whilst from Naples to Milan—no, that is too far, too far! We shall be sure to see each other often then."

IV

When our two actors, after conducting Signor Giorgianni to the station, got into the carriage to drive home, they both involuntarily gave a sigh of relief.

The comedy was over, and they were going back again to their ordinary life. Emma looked out of the window at the rain, and Guido did not stir: they were strangers again to each other now. By accident Guido touched his wife's arm.

" I beg your pardon," he said.

" It is granted," she replied carelessly.

Strangers, indeed! And yet they were now both of them going over in their mind the events of the day, and recalling to themselves the sensations they had felt.

" Would you prefer driving straight to your house ? " asked Guido, just before they reached the place where their roads separated.

" No, I must go and help my maid to collect all the little things I put about in your rooms. I will go home as soon as we have finished."

" Very well."

When they arrived, Emma went straight upstairs and through the large drawing-room to her boudoir.

Guido threw himself on a divan in the drawing-room and pretended to be reading a newspaper. In reality, he was listening to her footsteps as she moved slowly about in the other room. He saw her pass the open door once or twice.

" Are you not tired ? " he called out at last. " Can I help you ? "

" No, thank you, I have almost finished."

Presently she came into the drawing-room and sat down, very wearily. The excitement of the day had completely exhausted her. She looked round the room as though she missed something.

" It's raining still, is it not ? " she asked Guido, for he had put his paper down.

" Yes, it's still going on."

" The carriage is not there yet ? "

" I really don't know, but I'll go and see."

" No, it does not matter ; it was to be round in ten minutes from now."

" Shall I see you home ? "

" No, it isn't worth while, thank you."

Did these ten minutes appear to them like a century or like an instant ? Perhaps in a way like both. When the footman announced that the carriage was at the door, Emma rose deliberately, and walking across to the large mirror, put on her hat. It took her some time to fasten it on with the pins, for her fingers were trembling slightly.

She then put her gloves on very slowly, and gave a few finishing touches to herself at the glass. When she was quite ready, she turned towards Guido to say good-bye.

He had risen from his seat and his face was deadly pale.

" Good-bye," said Emma.

Guido did not reply. She turned away and walked across the drawing-room proudly, without wavering an instant, her step firm, but she knew that her husband was following her.

When she reached the door she lifted her hand to raise the velvet curtain, but Guido was more prompt, and her hand touched his as he held the curtain down.

" You have forgotten to tell me that you have forgiven me, Emma ! " he said, very quietly, in a voice in which grief and passion were each struggling for the mastery.

She turned towards him abruptly and hid her face on his shoulder, for the old love had sprung up again between them with a stronger force than ever.

" You will never go away any more, darling, never ? "

" No, Guido, we will fetch my mother's picture back here."

GRAZIA DELEDDA
1872–

TWO MEN AND A WOMAN

AMONG the prisoners who arrived at the Penitentiary on the 23rd of March, as the setting sun was flooding with crimson its cold, grim walls, was a young man of distinguished appearance ; he was dressed in grey, and the folds of his large, soft grey hat, adorned with a knot of grey ribbon, quite hid his pale, thin face, with its aquiline nose and carefully-kept pointed beard. During the journey he had not spoken once, but sat with bent head and knitted brows, his eyes intently fastened upon his thin, nervous hands with their long, polished nails, enclosed in the shining bands of the steel handcuffs. On reaching the Penitentiary he had for an instant raised his head and fixed his shining, burning eyes upon the countenance of the Direttore, who on his side returned the gaze coldly and at length. By a queer coincidence, the prisoner and the Direttorre had the same name—Cassio Longino! And they both knew it ; and the prisoner, who in his distant country across the sea where " Cassio " means " a white petticoat," had often been the subject of many a caricature, experienced now a sort of bitter satisfaction, on seeing himself on that account sought by the cold, scornful glance of the Signore Direttore. With the first glance, the two men hated each other. The Direttore was approaching middle life, was small and stooped a little. His feet and hands were small, and the latter were always plunged in the pockets of his long, black overcoat. His clean-shaven face bore the marks of physical suffering, which was accentuated in deep lines about the pale, thin lips ; his eyes were small and green and full of an almost cruel indifference ; his hair was blond and short, and his ears large and prominent. For all these reasons, but chiefly because he was the commandant of the prison, he was exceedingly displeasing to No. 245 ; and No. 245 was displeasing to the commandant on account of his haughty manner, the fiery look with which he observed him, and especially on account of his vigorous, superb youth.

While the prisoners were being consigned to their quarters, the Direttore did not open his mouth, and for several days Cassio, shut up in a private cell, did not again see him. His cell faced the east, and through the tiny aperture pierced in the great stone rampart he could see the distant Apennines, still covered with snow, and the Tuscan landscape, over which the early spring was scattering a vivid green sward, and the pale, tender colouring of bursting twig and blossom. In the Penitentiary garden, which was cultivated by prisoners clad in white linen suits and red caps, Cassio, who by especial permission of the Government retained his gentleman's clothes, watched the peach trees burst into a glory of intensest pink, and the apple trees toss their delicate bloom in rich masses through the balmy fragrant air.

A prey to keen anguish and despair, he never wandered far from his cell. The long, silent evenings overwhelmed him with despair; often he did not sleep at night, but tossed feverishly upon his hard straw pallet. When, in the morning, the guard, a great, tall fellow, whose red head brushed against the ceiling of the cell, would come in to make up the bed, Cassio was always dressed and standing before his tiny, barred window.

Outside the swallows were wheeling and fluttering about, their wings and breasts flashing in the sunshine. The prisoner did not deign to speak a word to the guard, nor did he take the slightest notice of the continual complaints, whistles, or gestures of his neighbour on the right; but when the exercise hour arrived and he was allowed to walk in the courtyard, he paced in haughty indifference, without even a glance at his companions, up and down the sad, dew-covered pavement.

The rumour spread through the prison that he was a very rich lord from Sardinia, a relation of the Direttore, and since the Direttore was feared and hated (though none of the prisoners knew the reason of this hate and fear, for the poor man had never done them any evil, except with his look of icy indifference), No. 245, within a week after his arrival, was hated, and strange to say, was feared.

Having requested permission to write, on the first of April, he was sent for into the office; through the barred window there penetrated a ray of pale sunshine, in whose light danced the shadows of a distant tree-top. The Direttore, bent more than usual, was working at a grey table; he neither moved nor spoke for a long time, during which Cassio, standing upright and stiff, his eyes fixed on the branches trembling in the sunshine, grew hot with humiliation.

Ah! in the presence of the others, of that crowd of criminals, and the vile guards, he could at least give himself the satisfaction of taking refuge in a certain, scornful dignity; he was stronger than those who bound him, greater than those whom he would not even deign to call companions in misfortune, but in the presence of this little man, so ill and full of disdain, he must bow, must reply, must humiliate himself.

"You," said the Direttore brusquely, turning around, but not rising, "are condemned to three years of simple detention for forgery; and you may write only once a month."

His voice was rather weary, but the tone was pure Tuscan.

"I know it," replied Cassio, "but I have not asked to be allowed to write to my own home, but on my own account, in my own cell."

"It is not possible. Why do you not ask to be placed in the office of the clerks?"

"Is there chance of being allowed to do so?"

"Yes, there is every chance."

That very day Cassio proffered his request, and on the next was placed in the office, where a great quantity of work was badly executed by three other prisoners. The room, which was next to that of the Direttore, was even more desolate and gloomy, and the three clerks, the first, fat and bald, with small, bleared eyes; the second, fair, pale, and with a transparent look, and the third a tall muscular young man, with black curly hair, and the face of a Roman emperor, made a bad impression on the new arrival.

They appeared resigned to, and even contented with, their melancholy fate. Cassio, on the other hand, experienced a profound disgust, which was but accentuated by the stupid resignation of his companions in misfortune—a very anguish of impotent desperation, and regretted his request. Better to have remained alone in his cell, with his hands clasping the bars of the little window, and before him the distant Apennines, that brought to him memories of his own native mountains, resounding with the neighing of his black charger, dashing in pursuit of the straying sheep—alone with his sentence and his sorrow!

He of the curly head, bolder than the other two, who contented themselves with casting stealthy glances at him, sought promptly, though respectfully, to make his acquaintance. (They knew that he had the same name as the Direttore, and so it was told among the other prisoners.)

"Are you a Sardinian?"

"Yes," replied he coldly.

"Since Fate has sent you to this place, allow me——"

"A beautiful Fate!," interrupted Cassio bitterly, and cut off sharply the compliment the unfortunate man was about to present to the presumed great Sardinian signore. But he said nothing more himself, nor asked anything of the others.

Three days later, there arrived for him from Sardinia a letter bearing an air of indefinable elegance. The handwriting was large and firm, while a delicious, almost imperceptible fragrance escaped from the sheets.

The Direttore opened it, and read it with a certain hesitation and half feeling that he had been expecting it.

After all, he was a man who was still young; he had suffered much and loved much, and if his own sufferings had produced that profound indifference which passed for cruelty among the unhappiness it was his fate to control, there still remained in his heart something of sympathy and compassion. Had No. 245 been a poor devil, like almost all the other prisoners, instead of a most interesting personality, the Direttore, after the first day, would never have given him another thought. But this handsome young stranger, with his haughty, distinguished air, who had arrived surrounded by a romantic mystery, had attracted the attention of every one, as well as his own.

The queer stories current in the gloomy cells and dark corridors had also reached his ears.

The thought that there might be something of truth in them had even begun to pierce his customary indifference with a faint interest, which was augmented as he perused the letter.

Not that it contained anything of especial interest. It was written by a half-sister of Cassio.

An intense affection manifested itself through all the four sheets, a certain nameless sweetness, and exquisite suggestion of comfort and resignation.

"Have courage, Cassio, do not despair nor suffer too much; remember that we two are alone in the world, alone to love and believe in one another. The time will pass, and when God reunites us I will know how to recompense thee for the immense sacrifice thou hast made for me. Do not feel humiliated nor cast down; the good know that thy fault was an act of heroism——"

"Indeed," thought the Direttore, "prisoners are always innocent, generally are victims, but that they should be heroes!"

This letter, so different from the vulgar epistles that were accustomed to come to the Penitentiary, so good, delicate, and loving, gave him food for reflection.

A sort of morbid curiosity took possession of him, against which he struggled in vain, to find out, to know everything. So that in spite of himself, though not contrary to the regulations of the establishment, which he scrupulously observed, he sent for No. 245, and on his arrival he opened the conversation by explaining some difficult work to be done in the office, and then, fixing a look of close scrutiny upon him, said:

" Here is a letter for you."

Cassio proffered never a word, but raised his head, and his face turned red to the tips of his ears.

And for the second time a wonderful thing happened. The Direttore of the Penitentiary envied his prisoner. For to the prisoner in his profound wretchedness had come a voice of comfort and affection, illuminating his dark horizon with a glory that was mirrored on his countenance, and to him, free and powerful, alone and lost in the infinite sadness of deep suffering, there never came one word of tenderness, one ray of light.

In spite of his emotion, Cassio perceived something abnormal was passing in the mind of the Direttore, and, astute Sardinian that he was, he took advantage to ask eagerly if he might not have the letter at once and read it there in the office.

Better there, under the badly concealed indifference of the little green eyes, than in the repulsive surroundings of his workroom, subject to the vulgar curiosity of the three clerks.

From that day he became more sociable, more resigned, and the Signore Direttore showed him a certain deference which did not escape the eyes of the others, and but confirmed the report of an assumed relationship.

But still he did not receive permission to write until he had been there a month, though on the very day he was given two sheets. And his letter was not less affectionate than had been his sister's, though less sweet and delicate; in every line was displayed the agony of helplessness:

" I have been here but a month, though it seems thirty years. I am beginning to be more resigned. They have put me in the clerk's office, with three terrible strangers [this the Direttore erased], the work is hard, but it helps to pass the time. At first I could not accustom myself to it, now I am less desperate. The Signore Direttore is very kind to me. Yes, I know the time will pass somehow or other, but still I feel as if my sentence would be eternal; that the 987 days yet remaining are as boundless as the waves; but most of all do I suffer when I think of thee; and yet the thought brings me much comfort. Thou art so good. Please do not forget me and get married while I am away! But I am ashamed, my dear Paola, such a thing I well know is impossible. How could a good sister forget her unhappy brother? But all the same, when I am tossing sleeplessly on my narrow bed, the thought fills me with terror. Who could believe such a thing possible?

"Though I am now resigned to all, I did once believe in the justice of men. But what have they done to me? Write very soon and do not forget me. If that were to happen I would soon find a termination to my sufferings."

Not a word nor thought for any one else, only for her! The answer arrived by return mail, together with clothes, books, and money.

The Signore Direttore felt anew the strange fascination of envy and longing, as he read the delightful tender letter of Paola. She had not a word of reproach for the lack of confidence the unhappy man had shown in her, but said how grieved she was that he should be so sad, and assured him she would never marry until his return. She had, too, a good word for the Signore Direttore. "Love and respect him; he can do much for thee; can be like a father to thee" [" a brother, young lady," thought the Direttore]. "I pray for thee and for him."

"Thanks," he murmured rather bitterly.

In the third letter, Cassio having asked what she was doing and how she passed the days:

"The days pass sadly in thy absence. I look after my affairs as well as I can, and often go into the country with my foster-parents. Poor things, they are a great comfort to me! We go on horseback, and these trips are my only diversion. In the house nothing new has happened. I am embroidering the tapestry I began at school, when my dreams were so different from the present reality. I am working into it certain Sardinian embroideries ferreted out by the foster-mother.

"I never see any one, but am always thinking of thee and counting the days."

"Why in the world do not these people, who seem rich and cultivated, think of asking for a pardon?" the Direttore asked himself, and, rising, he went into the garden—where the Tuscan spring was rioting amid a very glory of roses, crimson, white, and yellow; while gleaming among the deep green of the shrubbery, like brilliant butterflies, moved about the little red caps of the prisoner gardeners—and fell into a strangely sweet strain of thought of which the tender strong sister of No. 245 was the subject. In fancy he saw her, tall and dark, like her brother, with the pallor and distinguished appearance so marked in the prisoner; or bending patiently over her embroidery; or else trotting on her little Sardinian horse, her eyes half closed as she faced the ardent beams of the midday sun. Then, lost in wonder, he took himself to task for such boyish romance, till he worked himself into quite a frenzy of anger at his foolishness, which left him exhausted and more indifferent even than was his wont.

And so the months rolled by, bringing three or four more letters from Paola. In the last she promised to send her picture, if Cassio was quite sure he would be allowed to receive it.

"It is allowed," wrote the Direttore at the bottom of the page before sending it to the prisoner.

For one, two, three weeks, in that great pile, under the overarching blue sky and ardent sunshine that turned it into a very furnace, two souls were awaiting with passionate eagerness, though under different aspects, that picture of a woman.

The waiting of Cassio was sweet and full of peace, amid the passive resignation that habit and hope had begun to plant in his heart. The pleasure of anticipation brought him almost a sentiment of happiness; he would rise up early in the morning with the thought that perhaps to-day he would receive it, and as he waited for the guard who came to conduct him to the office, he would turn to his little window and reach out his hands as if striving to gather in some of the freshness of the morning; and he was always thinking of the picture.

Outside the swallows were flitting and wheeling as they sang, their wings and tails gleaming in the sunshine; the yellow corn surrounded with its golden glory the shining green of the distant vineyards, while farther away the watching Apennines shone in the luminous morning air. The prisoner called to mind the crimson dawns of his native mountains, brilliant with flowering yellow broom, then his thoughts turned to the expected picture, till he felt a vague feeling that was almost happiness.

The Direttore quitted his bed with a face even paler than was its wont, and he, too, thought of the picture ; but his waiting was made up of a strange mingling of restlessness, bitterness, and anger against himself, because he could not overcome his foolish curiosity, his foolish sentimentalism, the foolish interest " these people " awakened in him.

He went into the garden, and then into his bureau, and did his duty, performing all his tiresome work, and with cold eyes, and hands in his pockets, inspected those men clad in their prison garb of shame, but all the time he was waiting for the picture. In the bottom of his heart, under his anger and cruel indifference, there glimmered a spark of joy, from which a tiny ray sprang into his eyes and stayed there. And this spark, this hidden ray of light, burst into brilliant flame on the arrival of the picture, so instinct with life and loveliness and charm. She was not in the least as his fancy had pictured her ; for hers was a blond and delicate loveliness. The beautiful dark eyes, and the delicately curved lips and dimpled chin were suffused with an infinite sweetness. It was the same ineffable sweetness as filled her letters, a fragrance exhaled from every word, and this mysterious and suggestive fascination it was which had conquered the soul of this silent man, who was thought cruel and was feared and hated only because he was a poor dreamer.

The letter accompanying the photograph was, as usual, full of sweetness and charm.

" I was thinking of thee and smiling when the picture was taken ; may it bring thee a little joy and comfort in hoping for better days. Read in my eyes all that I would fain say to thee."

Just here, the Direttore, too, looked into the eyes of the picture, then finished reading the letter, only to return to gaze on the picture, turning it so that the full light should fall upon it, until the face seemed to assume a sort of reality, the lovely eyes to shine, the lips to smile.

" Oh, Dio ! What a fool I am ! " said Signore Longino to himself ; but in his heart he was thinking : " How would this exquisite creature write to her lover, if she writes thus to her brother ! " And then he fell to thinking sadly, that he was small, ugly, almost old, hated and feared by all those unfortunates whom his cold eyes dominated.

Once more he read the letter and gazed at the glowing picture, and —and that day neither the one nor the other was given to the prisoner.

That night the Signore Direttore had a queer dream ; he thought a mutiny had broken out among the prisoners and they yelled and shook their chains and rushed upon him. He held Paola's picture in his hands and could neither move nor defend himself, for then the picture would fall to the ground and No. 245 would know that he had stolen it. But just as he was about to be killed by the prisoners, Cassio threw himself between, crying: "Leave him alone, for he is to marry my sister, and then he will become good because she is so good."

He waked up bathed in perspiration, and passed the rest of the night sleeplessly tossing about his bed.

Cassio, in the meanwhile, was waiting patiently, though, as the days passed, a vague anxiety disposed his new-found repose. A week went by and still no picture came, and he had waited so long! so long! What could be happening over yonder, beyond the sunlit sea among the purple solitudes of the fragrant thyme-scented mountains? Paola must be ill—or had she forgotten him? Cassio fell back into the agonised despair of his first days. He asked, but was refused, permission to telegraph. With difficulty he got permission to write two days sooner than his allotted month.

His letter was so sad and full of despair that the Direttore felt more than ever ashamed of his deed; for two weeks he had lived in torment, and while he seemed more cruel and hard than ever, his little green eyes fell sadly upon the prisoners, for at last he understood how, against his will, a man might be led into crime. As he read the sad letter of No. 245, he murmured again: "But why do not they ask for pardon?" And he became aware that with the new-found pity awakened for No. 245 mingled a certain egotism of hope, that then he could speak frankly to the prisoner—one no longer—and say: "Signore, I may be a fool, but all the same I have fallen desperately in love with your sister, whom I have never seen. Will you give her to me for my wife?"

Paola telegraphed at once that she had sent another photograph by registered mail. In the eagerness for the peace of her poor prisoner, she pretended she had not sent a picture, and had been unable to write on account of a lot of reasons, which she detailed at length, principally she had been unable to be photographed before.

"How good she is!" thought the Direttore in admiration, and he felt inclined to write and tell her everything.

But of course he did not do so. "She will think I am mad, and will fear for her brother."

And so the summer passed and autumn approached; prisoners came and went. In the office the three clerks were not only resigned, but even happy, but showed an ill-concealed dislike for the haughty Sardinian, who, to an extent, was himself resigned. Only amid the sweetness of the autumn, when the dawn flooded the pure sky with crimson and gold or the setting sun threw his red beams on the sad walls, he was tortured with longing for freedom and home ; and he fretted like a horse taken from his free pastures and shut up in confinement ; but he was learning to control these rebellions and to immerse himself to the lips in hope and dreams of the future, till the present seemed scarcely a reality. But when winter came and the Apennines were black with storm clouds, and the angry rain pelted incessantly the grim fortress, Cassio felt his nerves snap like cords stretched too far. During the day the three heads of the clerks, pinched with cold, the blear blue eyes, the transparent profile, the head like the Roman emperor, appeared to him as in some tortured vision, awakening within him a brutal desire to seize some object and crush them to pieces. This desire increased from day to day, and was at times so intense that Cassio experienced the strange sensation of having realised it. Once in his cell he would come to himself and understand that he hated the three unfortunate clerks because they represented during those terrible winter days all the human power that was torturing him, against which his inmost soul revolted. His nights were almost sleepless. Outside the wind was roaring with a suggestion of distant torrents. Amid the darkness and roar of elements Cassio lost all perception of time, and as he tossed on his narrow bed, blessed visions came at last to his storm-tossed heart. The sighing of the wind in his distant well-loved mountains ; the prints of the wild boar among the green ferns ; the noisy stream bounding from rock to rock ; the partridges flitting among the flowering oleanders ; the joyful neighing of his black horse, and, above all else, the smile of Paola.

But with the grey dawn the sweetness of dreams was turned into bitter reality, and no one knows what might have happened to the three clerks had he not been one day providently summoned to the Direttore's office.

The Signore Direttore deigned to ask a favour. He had been sent a little fragrant plant with a few slender, dry branches ; it had come from Sardinia, and he wanted to know if the prisoner could tell him anything about it.

Cassio took the slender branches in his long, delicate hands, and inhaled its fragrance with closed eyes. The perfume brought him a vision of the green mountains of Gennargentu. An intense homesickness thrilled him.

" It is the tirtillo."

" The tirtillo. I thought so. The precious secret of the Sardinian shepherds that gives its especial aroma to the Sardinian cheese."

Cassio bowed in assent.

" The famous tirtillo," continued the Direttore, " the new cure for epizootic."

" In Sardinia it has been used for centuries," replied Cassio humbly. " Many things that on the continent pass for discoveries are well known on the island."

The Direttore did not reply, but turned his back and resumed his writing, and apparently all was over, when, suddenly turning around, he addressed Cassio without looking at him.

" Has a pardon been asked for you ? "

" Yes ; after the sentence in the Court of Cassation I appealed in the Giudiziarie of Cagliari."

" To whom did you appeal ? "

" To the Ministry."

" That was unfortunate. The Ministry when appealed to never decides. Often the prisoner has finished his term before they arrive at any conclusion."

Cassio looked very grave.

" It would be better to send your request to the Queen ; it would sooner be obtained."

" Pardon me," returned Cassio, bowing his head, " but is there a chance that it would be obtained ? "

" If the request should be made by your sister, it would be granted," answered the other brusquely, and again he turned his back so that he should not see the prisoner's emotion, and the latter should not see the Direttore's confusion.

This time the conversation was really over, and Cassio was reconducted to his office. But he was really another man ; the presence of his three unhappy companions aroused his compassion, but no longer his hatred. Around his thin fingers still lingered the fragrance of the tirtillo, and, raising them to his mouth, he inhaled the fresh sweetness of his distant meadows.

And probably for the first time, the Direttore was sincerely loved by one of his prisoners.

Cassio wrote to Paola begging her to ask the Queen for a pardon.

" You can make the request for yourself, without having recourse to the formal process of the law. Explain things as they are. I hope, and bless him who has counselled it."

And so the winter passed. In the limpid dawn of a February day, Cassio was standing before his grated window ; his face was pale and bloodless, but his eyes were shining with hope. From the Apennines, which raised their lofty, white crests into the crystal azure of the sky, there came a delicious odour of snow ; long strips of vivid green were scattered over the valley, and already in the garden the apricot trees were displaying their rosy blossoms.

Cassio felt his blood dance through his veins with the mysterious expectation of coming happiness ; all the glories of the opening spring seemed reflected in his soul.

Another man, free, in his cold and melancholy rooms, felt the same tumultuous, though sweet sensation ; his green eyes reflected the tender splendour of the budding season, his heart enclosed a precious shrine.

There came a day when the inquiry of the Ministry into the conduct of the prisoner, Cassio Longino de Isidoro, reached him. The Direttore's reply was of the best. He did not know why No. 245 had been guilty of forgery, but he believed him to be an honest young man, of fine morals and excellent education. By the same mail he also sent to an intimate in the Bureau a letter that, coming from such a person as Signore Longino, could not fail of effect.

Whether it was instrumental in bringing about the result or not, the decree of pardon and order for freedom arrived very soon after—when Cassio had been there just a year.

Once more he was summoned to the Direttore's office. Outside, the air was balmy and fragrant, and the sky of deepest blue. Inside, the shadows of distant branches trembled in the sunshine that poured in through the barred window. The Direttore was seated at his table, but this time he rose as Cassio entered. The youth noticed it, but did not dare to give words to the wild hope that sprang up within him, but he felt his heart beat with a violence that well-nigh choked him.

" The decree has arrived," said the Direttore, and he was holding something in his hand.

" The decree ? "

" The decree of pardon."

" For whom ? " asked Cassio eagerly.

The Direttore began to lose patience.

" For whom but for you ? " And he rejoiced in the deep emotion shown by the young man. So much the better ; if the thing was so great as to seem impossible, so much the greater would be his gratitude. But then he thought sadly : Suppose his efforts should result in failure ! If in the excess of his gratitude Cassio should give him false hopes !

" For me ! for me ! " stammered the poor youth. " For me ! For how long ? "

" For all the rest of your sentence. You are free—that is, not at once, but after a few formalities, in a week at most."

Gradually Cassio pulled himself together. At first he had gazed at the Direttore without seeing him. Now he began to look at him. He observed his pale face was flushed, that the air of physical suffering had disappeared, that the small, green eyes were shining.

He, on the other hand, was trembling violently, his face was ashy, his hands cold, and a mist floated before his eyes.

" This man is fine, when he is rejoicing in the happiness of another. How I have misjudged him," he thought. Then he asked himself : " But why did he do it ? "

He was to know very soon.

The Direttore begged him to be seated ; he showed him the decree, and profited by the moment in which Cassio was looking at the King's signature to begin :

" Now, I have something else to tell you. Listen and do not judge hastily. I have long been awaiting this moment, and the thing seemed easy, but now I see I need great courage and you great indulgence if we are to understand each other."

He smiled sadly, and the old expression of suffering returned once more.

Cassio looked at him stupidly, still confused with the weight of his happiness, but beginning to gain his self-control. The other understood that his opportunity was slipping away and hastened to speak, though, in spite of every effort, his voice trembled.

" I scarcely know how to express myself so that you may understand everything ; but I have confidence in your intelligence. Listen. I have done everything in my power to obtain that piece of paper there " —and he pointed to the decree, and Cassio, following his gesture, sat gazing at the sheet—" and, above all, I did so because I felt you deserved it." (" Does he know my story ? " Cassio asked himself, feeling that his deserts in prison had been very few.) " I do not ask for gratitude, indeed I will be thankful if you will not allow that sentiment to influence you at all. I wish to speak to you as one gentleman to another." (" Heavens! does he think me a grand Signore and wish to ask me for money?" thought Cassio. "I am not ungrateful, but what *can* he want of me?") " Now you are free and are at liberty to act as seems good to you."

" Speak," returned the other, with a sad impatience, " whatever lies in my power——"

" I do not know if it lies in your power."

" Speak! Speak!"

" Listen, but do not ill-judge me, nor think me insane. While reading your sister's letters, I have learned to appreciate so good and noble a soul, and——" (" Oh, Dio mio! he has fallen in love with her!" cried Cassio to himself, and the world grew suddenly dark.) " I have learned to love her. Do not laugh at me. I am still young!"

But Cassio felt small inclination to laugh.

" Have you written to her?" he asked brusquely.

" No, certainly not. Pray do not be offended. I have not allowed myself so great a privilege. Only to you——"

" But it is impossible, not to be thought of—impossible!" interrupted Cassio, striking as he spoke the paper which was lying on his knees, till it rustled.

" It seems impossible, but it is true; and though it may be strange, it is not the first time it has happened. My demand is serious, Signore Longino. Can your sister accept it?"

" What demand?"

The other thought a moment. " This young man is labouring under too much excitement; I was wrong to speak to him so suddenly. He is not in a state to hear it."

" My proposal of marriage."

Cassio did not reply at once. By a terrible effort he controlled himself. When the mist cleared from his eyes he turned and looked at the Direttore, and beheld him as in the past, pale, suffering, and ugly, and into his terrible pain there fell one drop of comfort—she would not accept him, he felt sure.

" But," he asked, " have you reflected on what you are doing? Have you written to my country and obtained information? In such cases——"

"I have not written. What would be the good? I know your sister, that she is good and noble, I desire nothing more. I, too, am all alone."

"You are too good. I do not know how properly to express my gratitude. Do not fear you are not understood. I both understand and admire you. I feel myself greatly honoured by your offer, and if it remained with me—but let me assure you I will do all in my power. Do not despair."

He rose and rolled up the pardon, looking at it with ill-concealed bitterness as he towered over the small person of the Direttore, who approached with extended hand to express his thanks. He asked permission to return to his cell and unroll his bed. Everything was granted him. As he threw himself on his comfortless cot he groaned in agony. Paola was not his sister, but his fiancée. For her he had soiled his honour, compromised his future, and broken with his family. She alone remained to him. She had feigned to be his sister in order that she might write to him. And must he lose her now? That other possessed a splendid position, was good and noble. Had he a right to snatch such a brilliant future from Paola? He had sacrificed to her his honour and well-nigh two years of liberty, but she had not asked the sacrifice of him, and was it right that in exchange he should ask for her whole life? In any case she must decide for herself, and at the bottom of his heart he felt secure of her—but it made him wretched to think he had deceived and was still deceiving so noble and excellent a man.

"I will tell him everything, come what may," he decided after an hour of anxious thought, then uncertainty took possession of him once more. "No, I will say nothing. After all, he has no right to know, and I will write when I reach home. After all, he did it only because he wanted to on his own account. His cat-like eyes fill me with distrust; perhaps he would do me some harm."

Later he grew ashamed of his distrust, and cried out aloud in his lonely cell, "Am I indeed vile?"

Approaching the grating, he stood gazing at the white, diaphanous clouds piled up on the horizon; they had assumed the shape and colouring of an alabaster staircase whose luminous steps disappeared into the unscaled heights. Cassio, as he looked, was overwhelmed with an intense homesickness, and suddenly he felt good and pure, as if he had indeed mounted to the last step of those silver stairs and caught from that height a glimpse of his beloved native land. He murmured :

" Had it not been for him I should have languished here for yet a weary time. I might have died or committed some madness. I will tell everything, let the result be what it may."

He waited anxiously the hour when it would be possible for him to see the Direttore, then addressed him in clear tones :

" See, Signore Direttore, I have been thinking of what you were very good enough to tell me this morning."

" Very well," answered the other, though he feared for the result.

" Before entering upon the subject, please allow me to tell you in a few words of the strange circumstances of my condemnation, for," he added, smiling sadly, " I am bold enough to believe you do not think me guilty."

The other man said never a word.

" Listen. For ten years I have loved a maiden of my own country. She was rich, but an orphan living with her guardian. I was sent away to college and was absent many years. On my return I learned that the poor girl, although she had attained her majority, was kept in subjection and badly treated by her guardian, who had possessed himself of all her property. He gave her nothing, but kept her shut up and frightened with terrible threats. I succeeded in communicating with her, and, finding that she loved me, I vowed to free her and restore her property. ' Let us be married,' she said, ' and I will fly with you.' But as my intentions might involve me in many difficulties, I would not accept her offer. I assisted her to take refuge with friends, and when she was in safety I began my operations.

" And can you guess what I did ? I almost think so. I forged the name of her guardian, and since he was very rich and well known at home and abroad, and his credit was illimitable, I obtained a good deal of money. I placed all in the name of the young girl and waited. When the notes fell due, all became known. I had foolishly hoped I should be considered a hero. Instead I was seized, vilified, condemned. My little property was taken, my family disowned me. She, alone of all the world, remains to me, and she, Signore Direttore, is Paola."

The Signore Direttore remained absolutely silent. What, indeed, could he say ? He only felt that Cassio's story and his own seemed impossible, though he knew but too well it was but too true. Cassio understood him perfectly.

"It is strange, impossible, is it not? Had I been told it, I would not have believed it."

"Life is strange," said the other at last, and he clenched his hands till the nails penetrated the flesh. "The ways of destiny are indeed mysterious."

"He is resigned," thought Cassio, and he hazarded another remark.

"Life is often a terrible romance." But looking the Direttore in the face he saw an expression of such agony imprinted as caused him to retract his thought of a moment before.

"But see," he continued, "in spite of everything I will do all in my power to prove my gratitude."

"What do you mean?"

"Let me speak. It was my duty to let you know the exact truth, but you have been so good to me that I give you my word of honour, as a gentleman, that I will do everything——"

"What are you saying? What are you saying?" repeated the other in a strange tone, as if he were listening to distant voices, and not to Cassio's words.

"After all, Paola alone can decide. I will tell her everything, as if I were indeed her brother and nothing more."

"Oh, no! No! What are you saying?"

"Nay, if you will allow it I will write this very day, and we will await her reply. Perhaps when it comes I will not need to return to my own country."

"What are you saying?" repeated the Direttore; but now his voice had regained its strength, and, raising his eyes, he looked Cassio full in the face. "You must not write, but return at once to your home, where, I prophesy, every happiness awaits you. From the bottom of my heart I hope so. And yet, who would ever have imagined it! You are right. Life *is* a terrible romance."

"But," Cassio persisted, "let me write. I beg it of you as a personal favour. You will see the debt I owe you can never be cancelled, and duty should be stronger than love. Paola will be much more fortunate with the Direttore than with me, and above all things I desire her happiness and well-being."

The other listened patiently; once his eyes flashed with a vivid light, but he remained immovable.

"See," he concluded, after having expressed his appreciation of Cassio's generosity, "if your duty is to prove yourself grateful and generous toward the signorina, her duty is no less to make you happy and recompense you for all you have suffered."

" But——" interrupted Cassio.

" One moment—let me finish, please. If the signorina were to act otherwise, she would not be the noble, lofty being I have imagined her, and then my offer would no longer exist. Do you understand ? Am I not right ? "

But Cassio answered never a word, and the Direttore turned toward the window. And the soul of each was full to overflowing. Cassio thought but of his happiness, and the Direttore reminded himself with bitterness that in any case his dream was lost to him for ever.

ROBERTO BRACCO

FOR THE SAVING OF SOULS

SISTER FILOMENA, her lips close to the grating of the confessional, began humbly :

" Father, I am not sure that I have sinned. Sometimes my conscience tells me that I have and sometimes it tells me that I have not. And when it tells me that I have not, I suffer more than when it tells me that I have."

The father-confessor did not understand. " Speak more clearly, my daughter. And tell me everything. You are so young! At eighteen one's conscience cannot be trusted. Let me judge. The Lord will give me light. Speak."

" Listen, father ; this is the whole truth. Toward midnight on Monday, No. 7 in ward five, where I have been substituting for Sister Maria since I entered the hospital, received the consolations of religion. The physician on duty said there was no longer any hope. He told me that the suffering could not last long and that death would surely come before dawn.

" ' There will not be many paroxysms,' the doctor added, ' but if you think I am needed, call me without hesitation. The other patients need no attention. They will give no trouble either to you or to me,' and he went to get some sleep.

" I had nothing to do but to administer a teaspoonful of medicine every half-hour. I took my accustomed place beside the bed, and as I sat there, thinking, I began to pray for the soul that was passing."

" For whose soul ? "

" For the soul of the poor man who was suffering."

" It was a man, then ? "

" Did I not say so, father ? "

" You spoke of No. 7, if I am not mistaken, and No. 7, my daughter, has no sex. It does not matter ; go on."

" It was almost three o'clock, when in a weak voice—I could almost hear the death-rattle—he gasped :

" ' Sister Filomena, it has come.' Since midnight he had lain silent almost in a stupor.

" ' Courage, my brother,' I whispered in his ear ; ' courage.'

" Then slowly, slowly, forcing himself to utter every word clearly, he continued : ' I am ready. It is sad to die at twenty-five, but I am resigned. And perhaps it is better so. I was alone, I was poor. I thought I was a poet, and I was nothing. I thought I was loved, and no one loved me. If I did not have you beside me now, I should die as if abandoned in a desert.'

" He was silent, and I repeated : ' Courage, my brother, God is with you.'

" After a few moments I saw that his deep blue eyes were dim with tears.

" ' Will you grant me a favour, Sister Filomena ? ' he asked.

" ' Any that I can, my brother.'

" And he said : ' Do you wish me to die in peace ? Do you wish me to die blessing Him who made me ? '

" ' Every good Christian should die so,' I answered."

" You answered well, my daughter."

" The dying man said softly : ' Help me to do so.'

" ' How, my brother ? ' I asked.

" ' Help me to cross without bitterness the threshold of the life I am leaving. Let me carry with me into the next life the memory of a kindness. Sister Filomena, have pity on a dying man. Give me—a kiss.' "

" A kiss ! " the priest exclaimed.

" I repeated again, ' Courage, my brother ; prepare yourself for the kiss of God.' "

" Well said, my daughter."

" But with failing breath he begged : ' Grant me this favour. Do you not understand, Sister Filomena, that you will be my salvation ? Would you be for ever weighed down with remorse ? Would you have me lose my soul ? Would you be the cause of my damnation ? ' "

" And you, my daughter ? And you ? "

" Father, I was frightened by those words. I reflected that, dying in bitterness, he might run the risk of everlasting damnation, and I, too, if I should be the cause. I reflected that every minute that passed death took a step toward him, and that the end must come before dawn. In the quiet room, I could hear his laboured breathing. There were but few patients in the ward, and they were sleeping peacefully. The lights had been lowered. The white beds, in the dim light, looked like tombs. A great sadness came upon me. I stooped and kissed him. I barely caught the words, 'Thanks, thanks.' Then I began to pray again."

"And where did you kiss him?" The father-confessor by his quiet voice tried to conceal his anxiety, the perplexity that was troubling his judgment.

"Father, it was almost dark," Sister Filomena answered quietly, "but I think I kissed him on the mouth."

"An imprudence, an imprudence, to say the least! I understand that it was done with good intentions, my daughter. You were moved by a sentiment of Christian piety—sublime, if you will, but mistaken—I might almost say dangerous. On the brow instead of the mouth would have been better; and that would have been sufficient to save his soul. Still, you kissed a man who was almost dead."

"That is what I said, also."

"And now that he is duly dead and buried—*requiescat in pace*—we will think no more about him."

"But, father, it is not quite so. He is living."

"Living!"

"Yes. He was in a dying condition until dawn. With the first rays of the sun came relief. The doctor, on entering the ward, could not conceal his surprise from the sick man, on whose lips there was a slight smile. He made a careful examination, gave him a hypodermic injection, and said in a low tone: 'It is strange, strange. Perhaps we shall get the better of the disease.'"

"But that is a disaster!" exclaimed the father in dismay.

"Father, what are you saying!"

"This is a serious matter, my daughter. If you kissed a living man on the lips and he continues to live, I do not know what is to be done. With death at the door it was different. All would have adjusted itself in the sight of the Lord. But if he lives, the Divine Clemency may be seriously perplexed. Let as speak openly. We must save appearances."

After pondering a little, he questioned further. "Tell me, daughter, what sort of a man is this doctor?"

"Oh, a good man!"

"But his standing as a physician?"

" He is one of the best."

" And how is the sick man to-day ? "

" He is better."

" You are lost ! "

" Oh, my God ! "

" You still dare to utter his name ? "

" I am a wicked sinner, father ? "

" Unworthy to wear that habit ! " But as Sister Filomena burst into bitter sobbing, the priest spoke less cruelly. " I cannot yet see my way clear. You told me just now that when your conscience tells you you have not sinned, you suffer more than when it tells you the opposite. How is such a contradiction possible ? How am I to understand that ? "

" I do not know, father. I feel what I feel, and I am confessing it to you just as it is."

" And you repent, now, of what you have done ? "

" If it is a sin, I must repent."

" But do not think that I will give you absolution now. We will wait a few days. Who knows ? We will see what turn the illness of this young man takes, and act accordingly. Now go. I do not wish to hear more to-day. And when you approach the bed, blush ; you understand ? "

" I always blush, father."

" That is well."

A few days later Sister Filomena came again to her father-confessor.

" Well, how is No. 7 ? "

" I think he is much improved."

" And what do the doctors think ? "

" They say that he will recover."

" My child, there is no longer any hope for you ! "

" That is what I told him."

" What did you tell him ? "

" I told him that I was lost on account of him, and that if I had known that he would live I should not have kissed him."

" And what did this healthy poet answer ? "

" He answered that he did not desire my perdition, and that he, in his turn, would save my soul."

" He might have done that by dying ! "

" Yes, father ; and so he has sworn to me that on the day when they tell him he has fully recovered he will kill himself for me."

This was a new complication. The priest reflected for a few moments ; then with an air of resignation and resolve, he said :

" On the whole, it is better to give you absolution. If that sort of a man begins to die again, we shall have to begin once more at the very beginning."

GIULIO DE FRENZI

A SURVIVOR

MY dear Ugo—After three years of absolute silence, I suppose it will seem somewhat impertinent to say that this is an answer to the long letter in which, barely landed in New York, you narrated to me your impressions of the voyage, and your plans for a new and industrious life. Yet really this is no falsehood. This morning, while arranging some papers, I accidentally came across your good letter of April 19, 1900.

" Poor Ugo ! " I exclaimed, " he was so quick to send me news of himself, while I——" Then a lightning inspiration of rescue flashed to my mind, one of those great ideas which cause in even a mediocre man like me the proud feeling that he is the Napoleon or the Bismarck of his own life. " Suppose I write to Ugo ! " And instantly seizing upon this idea with an incredible fervour of hope, I asked myself what had led me to discover your letter, and with it the precious recollection of your friendship, just to-day ? I am sorry that I am an atheist, for I should like to thank some one, and do not know whom.

But I diverge. Still, old friend, it is all very well to be a sceptic, but a day like this does somewhat upset one's mind. Do you know why I was arranging my papers ? I intended to kill myself. I had made an appointment with the last friend, the only one who never betrays us. At eight o'clock in the evening, the dinner hour, I had ordered a dinner worthy of the tête-à-tête. Hardly should the champagne have slightly intoxicated me, when I would have sunk into the loving arms of the one who would never allow me to escape. Or if, as in your merry days in Rome, you still prefer gastronomy to gallantry, let me tell you that a good revolver was to have been my dessert. Instead, nothing of the kind has happened ; I dined alone, drank my modest chianti, and burned neither my brain nor anything else for a single reason ; this morning I found your letter !

I seem to see your handsome prosperous countenance assume an expression of justifiable amazement. " Have I then become a thaumaturgist ? What the devil could that letter of mine have contained to check a candidate for suicide on the verge of the abyss ? " and as dramatists would say, " And how can that egotist Piero Galleschi, who, when we were together from evening till morning, did nothing but flee draughts and violent emotions, ever contemplate, even for one moment, a proposition so notoriously contrary to the most elementary principles of hygiene ? "

Ah, I understand that I must tell you all. After three years of silence, this seems to you an unexpected and excessive change. Have patience, my poor Ugo, and listen ; that is to say, read.

You left me three years ago, fairly happy. Alone in the world, decorously ignorant, gifted with those small vices that lend charm to existence. Absolutely lacking passions good or evil, a moderate spender of my income, which I enjoyed to the last cent without ever spending a cent more. For my age, my position, and my character I had all the requisites for a man to have the right to call himself happy. Possibly, to escape the tedium of restaurants and extempore love affairs, I should have ended by marrying, had I met a woman who would not disturb the marvellous equilibrium of my life.

But this equilibrium was disturbed soon enough. Toward autumn of that same year 1900, I began no longer to feel well. A draught not avoided in time, an unusual occurrence, gave me a cough ; I suffered with fever and weakness, lost energy, and after a few months had grown thin. It was nothing. The doctors so agreed in reassuring me of this that finally I began to suspect that I was threatened with, at least from my point of view, premature death. This suspicion, together with all the symptoms of disease, aggravated by the various treatments, was not exactly calculated to enliven my days, still less my nights ; I lost patience for the first time in my life. It was the beginning of the transformation.

I therefore went to Trabalza to ask his illustrious and expensive opinion. I went to him—why should I deny it ?—somewhat anxious, and when, entering his luxurious consulting room, I felt his cruel glance, which in a moment had laid bare my soul, I was tempted to lie to him, or to ask of him the usual compassionate falsehood. But then, mechanically repeating, with the words already meditated, the story of my illness, almost without realising, I led us both to the opinion of the dreaded truth. He frowned in silence, then requested me to disrobe. I assure you, Ugo, I was unnerved, but to conceal my distress, I said tragically : " Listen, doctor. I do not wish to be deceived, whatever your opinion."

He made me recline on a couch that seemed a catafalque, then began pounding me and listening all over my body. Under those icy hands I shivered. He suspended his examination for a moment, and remained absorbed in thought, without even looking at me. I tried to read my fate in his wrinkled face. But almost immediately he ordered me to rise. Again, this time standing, I must submit to the torture. Sounding my thin chest, he tried to surprise the secret of my malady, while my anxiety became more unendurable. All cowardice vanished in my desire for the truth. I desperately implored him:

"Tell me, tell me! I am alone in the world, and death does not alarm me. I do not wish to be deceived like a child."

Trabalza took off his spectacles, polished them methodically and put them back on to his nose. I, nude before him, waiting, felt compassion for and ashamed of myself.

"Dress yourself!" he ordered, his voice so much softened that my heart swelled almost to tears. Why this softened voice? Because he would liberate me from terror or deprive me of all hope?

"Speak! speak! I wish to know. I must know!"

The good doctor, instead of answering, repeated some questions as to my age, the appearance of the first symptoms, the illnesses of which my parents died, etc. Then, with the air of one who hopes to be forgiven for bad news:

"I will obey your orders," he said, "although I am sincerely sorry. You have tuberculosis."

"A bad case?" I stammered stupidly.

Dr. Trabalza made a vague gesture. "You have no right to conceal anything from me," I burst out. "How long can I live?"

The doctor seemed absorbed for a few moments in deep meditation. He was calculating the residue of my life.

"Three years at the most," was his final judgment.

Three years, and then the forces of life would be exhausted! There would be the melancholy sunsets contemplated from a bed; clumsy indifferent nurses; two or three impatient envious cousins; the notary, perhaps, the priest certainly, summoned in the fatal terror of the nothingness beyond, and then, then, a gasp, a groan, one's eyes distended to receive the last ray of sunlight, rigid hands outstretched to clutch the fleeting life! Then I would be dressed in a frock-coat, like poor Peppino Canepa. A fine casket, lined with silk; a great funeral, with wreaths of flowers sent by the heirs and my friends of the restaurants;

ten lines of the usual death notice. My friends every now and then would tell of my pranks; but of my name, my person, my deeds—all would sink into oblivion, save those student escapades, which might for a time serve to enliven the company.

Thus coldly was my immediate future outlined before my anguished soul as I left Trabalza's house. When one is or believes himself healthy, he lives from one day to the next, forgetting, almost unconscious, of the inevitable end, as if his life were to go on indefinitely; passions, thoughts, plans, are with him based on an illusion of permanency and only the fatigue of old age gradually insinuates to his mind the feeling of decay. What matters it then? He has already accomplished his destiny. But for a condemned one who knows he is to die, and die young, the idea of totally disappearing from the world, of being absolutely and irrevocably separated from all that he loves, makes him suffer. The thought that soon no one will trouble more about him, neither pity nor curse him, that the children once caressed by him will grow up in ignorance of him, that he will be, in short, as though he had never lived!

Had I at least a son—some one in whom I might hope that my existence would be perpetuated! But would not he, too, have been a predestined victim of fate, a sickly being? Besides, why should I regret that an insignificant man, a solitary egotist, left no record of himself on earth?

I must die. Very well. I would die gaily, thoughtlessly; I would pass beyond without seeing the road, without realising that I was traversing it.

I possessed about 400,000 francs. I divided it into three annuities and prepared to spend it to do honour to what was to come.

With a splendid racing automobile I carried Henriette Sonillard, who was all the rage at the Olympia, off to Nice with me. Gay, cold, extravagant, this girl was exactly suited to my case. She introduced me to the *demi-monde* society of the Riviera, where she had many acquaintances.

Carnival arrived in a merry whirl of gaiety, and my automobile, covered with red roses, triumphed in the *course des fleurs*. Henriette scattered roses and twenty-franc pieces right and left. Thanks to her, I had secured just what I needed—never to be alone with my secret thought. And gradually this thought had retired to a corner of my mind, waiting——

Early in the spring I liquidated my relations honourably, with Henriette, to return to the capital, in pursuit of a Roman lady whom I had met six or seven times at Monte Carlo.

Months passed rapidly. When summer came, I followed Sisi to St. Moritz, then to Viareggio. Here I happened to run my auto over a good-for-nothing, who, having had his leg broken, found it convenient to sue me, which cost me ten thousand francs and many annoyances; but even this was useful in helping me not to think.

That winter was most brilliant. I did not miss a ball or reception. A year passed; another, in a perpetual whirl of artificial but intense enjoyment. I had two thoroughbreds for morning rides in the villa Borghese. I flirted with patrician beauties, was elected vice-president of the Lawn Tennis Club. All thought me a happy man.

I had consulted no other physicians, taken no temperatures, and abolished mirrors in my bathroom. While dressing I avoided looking at my form. I wished to forget, ignore. Sometimes, facing my secret thought suddenly, the idea of my impending death amazed me like the record of a tormenting nightmare which I had shaken off. But instantly I drove the thought back into shadows, that it might not dissipate the kindly stupor which helped me to run gently down the last slope. I turned my eyes away from the goal. From sports and orgies I demanded the heavy sleep that knows no dreams. And the third year: this year began like the others, but full of worse follies, more prodigal insanities.

One day, early in April, my administrator considered it his duty to warn me that there remained to me barely 38,000 francs of my capital.

Half an hour later I rang Dr. Trabalza's door-bell. Fortunately, I could see him at once.

The doctor gazed at me in his usual scrutinizing way, but did not seem to remember ever having seen me. Two years and five months had elapsed. I had to recall to his mind the consultation, the diagnosis, the verdict. He stroked his beard, silent and thoughtful. Then:

"Take off your clothes," said he, brusquely.

The examination was even longer and more minute than before. While the doctor was sounding my chest, and listening with his icy ear, his cold hands upon it, a diabolical suspicion suddenly came into my mind and caused a sudden outburst of rage. The doctor and I from time to time exchanged almost hostile glances. His questions and my answers were pronounced in tones of sarcastic impertinence.

" What treatments have you had during this time ? " he asked at a certain point.

" None of any kind," I said boldly and haughtily.

" I thought so ! " murmured he, as though under the weight of extreme and dreaded disillusion.

He began wandering uneasily about the room. But when he passed me I seized him inexorably by the coat sleeve——

" Well ? " I asked. I know not whether ironically or threateningly.

He decided to speak.

" I have something to tell you which will please you greatly——"

He smiled and spoke almost with set teeth. He hated me.

"——yes, greatly. If not my diagnosis, at least my prognosis was wrong. You are cured ! "

I grasped him by the shoulders, pushing him to and fro, nude as I was, in a momentary paroxysm of rage.

" Cured ! " I cried. " You are jesting ! It is not possible—it is not allowable ! This is a fraud ! I must not be cured ! "

The doctor believed me actually insane.

" No, no. I am not jesting. Calm yourself. I repeat, you are cured. And I am surprised that this news does not fill you with joy——"

" Of course ! and my money ? " I cried in his face, like a frantic creditor.

" Your money ? "

I had to tell him the wretched story. But as I told it, recalling the irreparable ridiculousness of the situation, I was so overcome by a sense of degradation that it served to calm me and restore my exact perception of the reality.

" You have learned, I fancy, not to trust too much to the verdicts of science," pronounced Dr. Trabalza, like a moralist, when I had finished. Then, possibly dissimulating a scruple under a slight smile: " How much have you spent for this instruction ? "

" About 400,000 francs," I groaned.

The doctor was thoughtful for a moment, as though hesitating to express the idea that passed through his mind. But finally he took courage and uttered it.

" You will see that, in time, the lesson is worth it."

I shook my head, incredulous.

He no longer hated me. He understood that the scattering of my

400,000 francs was a disaster at least equal to the failure of his scientific glory. Such was my opinion, and I went in haste to express it to a lawyer friend, to ask if he believed it possible to bring suit for damages against Dr. Trabalza. A new sentiment was born in me—a sentiment of sympathy, I might almost say, of fellow feeling for the poor scamp who, two years before, having been run over by my automobile, had caused me quarrels, expenses and annoyances of all sorts. Had I not been ruined by Dr. Trabalza? And had I not a right to an adequate indemnity? But the lawyer, although a friend, laughed in my face, and did not even condescend to accompany me to the door. This lack of regard was sufficient to prove to me that I was ruined indeed, and hopelessly so.

There were three courses open to me: work, suicide, or to continue by expedients and deceit the life I had led of late. This at first seemed to me of the three the most practical method. I knew so many others who lived thus like gentlemen, and who often, plucking their geese, could not have, like me, justified themselves by remembering that in their turn they had once been plucked.

But, Ugo, when one thinks the matter over carefully, the profession of elegant scoundrel is considered easy by those moralists who praise the virtue of human sweat only when this, so to speak, is shed upon the soil of the field, or the desk of an office. But rest assured that from my small observations, the man of the world, forced to live by expedients, earns his living by the sweat of his brow as much, if not more, than the farmer or clerk; and, believe me, even the gesture with which he signs a note is as sacred as that of one who sows grain. Oh, no one can ever say how hard some rascals work that they may live without working!

Now, since my earliest infancy I had been accustomed to actual idleness, the idleness ignorant of its true value, natural idleness. It is not so simple a matter as might at first sight appear, to liberate oneself in a day from all the precepts and moral prejudices with which tradition, education, religion, and various other venerable things have inoculated our blood. Lombroso and his disciples, whom may the god of lunatic asylums bless, have studied hereditary depravity. Why, so far, has it never occurred to any one that hereditary nobility was worthy of study? In short, I ended by discarding the idea of rascality. There remained for me, therefore, two courses: actual work or suicide.

Work; but how? For whom? And where? In the city over

which my automobile and mistresses had scattered the double perfume of *Cœur de Jeanette* and benzine, could I transform myself into a clerk, an insurance agent, a journalist ?

During my long hesitation the remnant of my patrimony was vanishing.

I saw that, all things considered, it suited me better to choose suicide. I had been accustomed to the thought of death for some time, and was convinced that Dr. Trabalza, in predicting my death within not more than three years, had proved himself a poor physician, but an excellent prophet. I forgot that the origin of a predicted fact is not seldom found in this same prophecy. But suicide seemed to me a much more dignified end to my life than the horrible suffering of a chronic malady. I should die when and as I pleased, since I had relative liberty as to the hour, the day, perhaps the month.

This morning, discovering that I had only nine thousand three hundred and twenty-five francs and a few sous, I saw that this liberty was becoming restricted. It was necessary to kill myself before suicide should become for me a vulgar or cowardly act.

And it was then, old fellow, that your saving letter came into my hands. If you do not wish to resign the office which you will presently occupy in regard to my destiny, listen with kind attention to the following proposition :

Can you take me as partner, as clerk, as porter in your transatlantic business ?

You were an idle, good-for-nothing, worse than I, when you left Naples ; you have made a fortune with Marsala ! Ungrateful one, how many times have I paid your bill at restaurants ?

Ugo, I await your yes, because it must be a yes—for two months, until the middle of September, at Frascati, where in the strictest economy I am preparing myself to become, within sixty days, a hard-working, self-made man.

Even as a porter, you know, I have the health—the health of—I cannot describe it. I embrace you.

PIERO.

LUCIANO ZÙCCOLI

THE MERRY COMPANY

GIGI CAVALIERI, better known as Pivione, came out of the Porta Romana and, disregarding the fact that his shoes lacked heels and that he had no umbrella, struck out towards the open country in the pouring rain. He heard his feet splash in the mud and felt the water dripping from the brim of his faded hat and falling upon his neck. His drenched coat gave off the odour of damp wool. His trousers were bespattered with mud.

But this man had no thought for the inconveniences which had often been the lot of his laborious existence. He advanced at a rapid pace and at the same time with great caution. At one moment he glanced backward and at the next he fixed his eyes on a row of poplar trees ahead, which were somewhat obscured by the rain and fog. At that hour, about three o'clock in the afternoon, and in such adverse weather, Gigi Cavalieri had the luck to meet nothing more than a wagon and a mendicant friar during his entire walk of ten kilometres.

Just as his legs were beginning to feel heavy, partly from fatigue and partly from the weight of the mud that clung to his shoes, Pivione stopped before a small hut and, casting a few hurried glances around, quickly took a key from his pocket, opened the door, entered and shut it after him. Once within he clambered up a ladder and reached a squalid little room.

Here there was a bed, and lying on it, fully dressed, a blond-haired girl. Her swollen lips and bloodshot eyes were evidence of a strong fever. At the sound of the creaking of the ladder she slowly turned her head towards the door, and at the sight of Gigi she opened her lips in a forced smile.

" How is she ? " he asked in an undertone of a lean old woman seated at the foot of the bed.

" How do you suppose she is ? Always the same ! " answered the old woman without moving.

Gigi made a gesture of displeasure and drew from his pocket a parcel carefully wrapped in waxed paper.

" I have brought the quinine," he said.

Wherever he stood he left footprints of mud and little pools of water. Taking off his hat and coat, he bent over the girl, who was doing her utmost to maintain a smile. The poor fellow looked at her for a long time. His pale face, bearing the marks of vice, sleeplessness, crime and fear, suddenly assumed an expression of kindly tenderness. He passed his hand through the beautiful blond hair of the sick girl and then placed his palm on her feverish forehead.

" How are you, Giulia ? " he asked very gently.

With an effort Giulia answered, " Better—I feel better."

Pivione continued looking at her in silence. At times it seemed as if his eyes were attempting to gaze into her soul. He did not alter his position until the old woman took him by the arm and handed him a glass of water. " Are you going to give her the medicine you have brought ? "

Gigi took a single powder from the package, poured its contents on a wafer, and then, gently raising the girl's head, administered the first dose of quinine.

" If she could undress and go to bed, she would feel much better," he said to the old lady.

" She is not strong enough and I cannot manage it," answered the woman. " Perhaps you could help me."

Gigi roughly intercepted the arm that she was already reaching toward the girl. " No," he said. " Listen to me." He threw a glance in the direction of the sick girl, who had already closed her eyes, and then descended the ladder followed by the old lady. " Listen ! " he repeated, when they were but a few paces from the door. " You must give Giulia one or two of those powders every two hours and by to-morrow evening the fever will have disappeared. But don't undress her ; cover her up well if she is cold, but remember, don't undress her."

Then, lowering his voice, he added : " It is necessary that both of you be prepared for flight."

The poor old woman wrung her hands in despair and opened wide her diminutive eyes.

" What on earth has happened now ? " she exclaimed.

Instinctively, Pivione looked about him ; then, in a low and rapid tone, speaking with clenched teeth, he added, " They are looking for me ! They are looking for me, Tonino, Stringhella, Bollo Rosso, and

Spugna. You know his whistle, don't you? He will whistle three times, but will not enter."

The poor lady again gave expression to her feelings by a gesture of despair.

"Let us understand each other," continued Gigi. "You must save her, even at the cost of carrying her on your shoulders if she is too weak to walk. As a last resource, throw her in some ditch. If you make a mistake, there will be some one to settle accounts with you. Take this money; it amounts to some two hundred lire. It will be sufficient until Giulia is again able to work. Let us understand each other. I will not remain in prison for ever, and I will find you even after ten or fifteen years. I will learn what has happened to Giulia, and if she should be in trouble, I myself shall settle your case."

She wrung her hands until they crackled. "Understand," he continued, "that it does not matter whether or not Giulia thinks that I am at my country-seat—say it was for political reasons. Tell her of the many misfortunes I have suffered. Moreover, this is not the first time I have had to steal to maintain her respectably. You can, if necessary, even tell her that—but one more word. The police are searching for all of us. Some one will surely escape. If not Spugna, Stringhella will come to give you warning. Remember this: if three whistles are heard, you must take her away, even if it be on your shoulders. If it is one long whistle, it will mean that you are in no immediate danger but that I am caught. Now I will go and bid her farewell."

"And what then?" interrupted the old lady. "Do you expect to be arrested?"

Gigi answered this query by a shrug of the shoulders.

"But tell me what has happened," insisted the old lady. "Is it a thing of great importance?"

In answer, he stretched his right hand in the air and then suddenly clenched his fingers.

"Strangling!" shouted the old lady.

"Keep still, you fool!" said Gigi, seizing her roughly. "I did not commit the crime, and I can prove it if necessary. Bollo Rosso is the culprit, and he has ruined us all. Besides, it is unnecessary. I knew that Bollo was not one of our kind, but the others insisted on taking him into our company."

Stopping short, he faced about and hastened up the ladder.

Giulia had evidently found some relief. She had undone her blond hair to diminish the pressure upon her head. She looked intently at her brother, and then said softly, " Are you going to stay ? "

" No, I must go," he answered brusquely ; " they are waiting for me."

" Are you coming back ? "

" To-night, or perhaps to-morrow morning. You are to take these powders ; do you understand ? "

" Yes."

Then both became silent and looked at each other affectionately. The young girl had apparently improved, for the feverish glow had disappeared from her forehead. Her youthful comeliness returned in measure as the fever loosened its hold.

" If perchance I should not return," Gigi blurted out unexpectedly, " see to it that I am kept informed of all that you do."

" Why, do you not intend to come back ? " asked the poor girl, trembling.

The man drew on his coat, which was still quite wet, and tossed his hat on his head.

" Good-bye," he said.

Giulia, long since accustomed not to ask questions a second time, gently stretched out her arms as if to embrace her brother, but he, who had never kissed his sister, feigned not to see and turned toward the door.

When about to descend the ladder, he turned about suddenly and approached the bed. Again that tender expression of sympathy illumed the hard and pallid face.

" Take the powders ! " he said, in explanation of his strange conduct.

He moved toward the door and went down the ladder without turning, but before going, he again reminded the woman : " Three whistles, take her on your shoulders. If only one, I am arrested. See that the doors are well locked."

Outside, the rain was falling in torrents.

The trial of the Merry Company had aroused an interest in Milan which was not usual for such common crimes as those of which these men were accused.

Gigi Cavalieri was the first to fall into the hands of the police. He tried to avoid arrest by shooting at the face of one of the police ; and the shot took effect, almost destroying the man's countenance. Gigi's arrest was followed by that of Antonio Stucci, generally called Tonino, then Stringhella. Spugna was captured while enjoying a dance with some ladies on a field outside of the Porta Tenaglia.

It was a year before Bollo Rosso was captured. The police were on the point of giving up all hope of getting him, when one evening he captured a pickpocket in the Scala and took him triumphantly to the nearest station in the district. The inspector on duty was not a little surprised to see before him the notorious leader of the Merry Company, and naturally the petty thief and Bollo, who was charged with murder and highway robbery, were both held.

Bollo Rosso, in bringing to justice this petty thief, whom he had caught stealing a gold chain from a merchant who was listening to the music in the park, had intended to play a practical joke, but the trick surely had not resulted to his advantage. Nevertheless, he explained to the inspector that this act of honesty was the beginning of his reforms, and that if he were set free, he would promise to bring to justice at least ten thieves a day.

The inspector smiled and sent him to prison.

The distinguishing characteristic of this company was its joviality. Bollo Rosso had infused into them a real love for jests and pleasantries. To be sure, his associates assaulted passers-by and broke into jewellery shops, but it was all done with grace, celerity, and humour.

For this reason, they had received the name, "The Merry Company."

The most famous joke had been played on Carlo Matirotti, a rich old druggist. This miser, for such he was, dressed always in rags, ate but sparingly and was never known to have a light at night, for candles were too expensive a luxury. He led a life of constant fear and suspicion.

One night, Bollo Rosso, Gigi, and Stringhella succeeded in forcing an entrance into his house and completely sacked it. Well satisfied with their expedition, they were about to leave, when Bollo expressed a desire to see old Matirotti. To satisfy this caprice, he made his way to the miser's bedroom, carrying a lighted candle.

Carlo Matirotti was sleeping soundly with his mouth open. That black and toothless mouth naturally attracted the attention of the thief. He looked around to see whether he could not find something with which that repulsive aperture could be filled and, seeing nothing more suitable, decided to make use of the candle. No joke could have been more original. The old man, awakened with a start, sprang to a sitting posture and bit the candle between his toothless jaws. Frightened by the scene, he was on the point of crying out, when Bollo, to save the vicinity from such a disturbance, extinguished both the candle and the man.

With the exception of this very unsavoury incident, which really brought an end to that gay company, these five companions were capable of only repeated attacks on property. They were sober, humble, and well-behaved.

Gigi Cavalieri had lived apart from the others and pretended to be an electrician employed by a small establishment that no one knew. His friends often offered him participation in their adventures, and he usually chose those of little risk even though less lucrative. His sister was a seamstress and earned about three lire a day. From time to time Gigi would bring home a bag of money. He had been one of the jolliest of the company, although he had always been grave and taciturn at home. Then, gradually, he became grave even in the company of his associates and at times he seemed melancholy and restless. In the meantime Giulia was becoming prettier, and her form was assuming more graceful contours. With all her cleverness she had never suspected that her brother was anything but an electrician. She loved Gigi blindly, and he, who had never given his sister much thought since her childhood, finally began to consider what the outcome would be, now that every one looked at her as she walked along the street.

His first prison sentence had separated them for several months, and she, in order not to live alone, had asked her old aunt to come and live with her. During the time of his imprisonment the police had watched her closely and investigated the nature of her occupation. Convinced that she made an honest living, they left her in peace, but when Gigi was released he was alarmed at discovering that his sister had been under surveillance, and from that day his manner changed. On account of a harmless jest, he gave Bollo a severe beating, and had he had a knife, probably would have killed him. Bollo, on the other hand, did have a dagger, but as his right hand was pinned beneath him, he had to content himself with the beating. Then both went and drank together.

Giulia had been accustomed to seeing her brother in trouble with the authorities, for he boasted of Socialistic principles, and the government often suppressed this nonsense. Furthermore, Giulia, fearing him at least as much as she loved him, never questioned Gigi. She obeyed him implicitly and was very happy when he came home to sup with her.

She had neither protested nor attempted to discuss with Gigi the idea of secluding her and her old aunt in the hut outside the Porta Romana. It was absolute folly, to be sure, for it made her work much more difficult. To return it to her customers, the old woman had to wait until some cart passed in front of the house, then pay carriage to the point of destination. Besides this expense it consumed a whole day. Ultimately Gigi was seized with the grave suspicion that some one might take his sister away. He literally tortured her with incessant questions. He would sometimes hide behind the window blinds and watch suspicious-looking passers to see whether they glanced at Giulia's room. He asked her not to sing, so that the neighbours might not hear her. As to going out for a walk, that was out of the question, but Giulia became accustomed even to this.

The transport to Milan and back cost so much that her earnings were cut in half and, naturally, life became more burdensome, but Gigi would not hear of returning to the city. Rather than bring his sister back amongst rough men and corrupt women, he had accepted the offer of Bollo, who had his eyes on Matirotti. This was an opportunity for a grand stroke! The time had drawn near. The miser had withdrawn his money from the bank, and it was necessary to strike while he still had it. Then, having received his share, Gigi, free from care, would be able to be near his sick sister for a long time.

But Bollo Rosso's joke frustrated all these plans. The newspapers were full of stories concerning the crime, and in many the particulars were absurd and exaggerated. As for Bollo, he was absolutely disgusted with the reports in the papers, for he was unable to find a true and exact reproduction of one of his simple crimes. A short time before he fell into the hands of the police, he had expressed a desire to send to the papers the true story of his little joke. Had he not feared that his tale would have been inserted in a chronicle, he would have done so.

A year and a half passed before the five thieves were brought before the judge. The hardened and sinister features of these malefactors made a deep impression on the public. Pivione attracted attention not only by his height and leanness, but still more by his brilliant eyes, which seemed to be illumined by some sad thought. Bollo Rosso, small and withered and with features typical of a toper beyond redemption, stood on his right. His eyes never rested for more than a single moment on any one object, but nothing that occurred around him escaped his notice.

The latter declared before the most illustrious judge of this noble court and the renowned members of that jury that he had reformed, and had decided upon an honest and laborious life. But the judge interrupted him and warned him that the court was no place for idle jokes.

"But permit me to remind you, most honourable sir, that I have arrested a thief," added Bollo, as he was resuming his seat.

At this the visitors burst out laughing, and even Bollo joined in the merriment.

"No use, the populace is fond of me," he said to Spugna in an undertone; "I am attractive."

Spugna had to laugh. He was twenty-two years old. The livid colour of the knife scar that ran across his cheek from his right ear to his chin reinforced the ugly appearance of his greenish-yellow skin. Happy because he had had no hand in the murder, he considered himself a victim of the judge's pedantry, who continually asked him questions concerning his history.

"What has all this to do with the murder? On that night, I——"

They were trying to convict him of two assaults and four cases of robbery. But he was obstinate in asserting that he took no part in the murder, the other accusations seeming of very little importance.

Stringhella, who, with Bollo Rosso and Pivione, was accused of the murder, stood next to Spugna. He became so enraged at the latter's attitude toward the affair that he stuck his elbow in the young man's ribs with a force that rendered him breathless for several minutes.

The fifth. Antonio Stucci, called Tonino, caused a great deal of merriment by his squeaky voice and by the curious expressions he assumed by the aid of his crooked back. He, too, was very happy because he was not on trial for murder. Sitting with his hands in his pockets and with a broad smile always on his lips, he seemed more a spectator than a man on trial for robbery. By nodding his head, he approved or disapproved of the judge's statements. As for the rest, he knew nothing, because in his youth, as he said, he had suffered from a disease of the brain.

Then the judge settled his eyes on Pivione, who was gloomy to distraction. He had made a weak defence against the accusation that he had been an accomplice in the murder of Matirotti. During his cross-examination he continually cast his eyes over the spectators as if expecting to see a familiar face.

When the judge learned from a witness that Pivione had a sister, he expressed his surprise at not seeing her in the cage with him.

"What does your sister do?" he asked Pivione.

"She works," answered Pivione, at the same time jumping to his feet as if he wished to leap out of the cage.

"Ah! she works—pursues the same trade that you do?"

"She is a tailor—she earns an honest living."

"Did you live with her?"

"Yes, sir."

"Had she any idea of what you did?"

"No, sir; she thought I was an electrician."

"And how did you deceive her for so long a time?" asked the judge incredulously. "Did she not finally see what you really did? You have been sentenced three times; how did you keep the true cause of your imprisonment from her?"

Tonino looked furtively at his companion, wondering what answer he could give to such an argument.

"The first time," answered Pivione, "I told her I was condemned for political reasons."

The audience laughed.

"The second time I told her that I had to go to a foreign province to do some professional work," continued the thief, casting a look of hatred at the spectators, "and the third time I again gave political reasons."

"Did your sister always believe you?"

"Always."

"She must have been strangely innocent, that sister of yours," added the judge. "But all this is not clear to me. Be seated."

Gigi surveyed the audience, then surlily sat down.

"Do you know her?" asked the judge of a witness, who was an inhabitant of the Porta Garibaldi quarter.

"Yes, your honour."

"What does she do?"

"At one time she worked, but that was before Pivione was accused of murder."

At that instant, Bollo Rosso, who had been watching carefully a spot where the audience was very crowded, rose to his feet and shouted:

"Look! Look! Look!"

"What is the trouble?" the judge asked angrily.

"Most illustrious sir, I see among the spectators my little thief! There he is! He is at this moment making faces at me! It is the young man I arrested almost two years ago!"

In fact, a young man did escape from the crowd and run down the hall.

"He came to see me, your honour," continued Bollo, "which proves the truth of what I have said. I had already started out upon an honest life; I arrested a thief——"

"If you do not stop your chattering," exclaimed the judge, not a little annoyed, "I shall have you sent back to your cell."

At this Bollo sat down.

"That was really the fellow," he whispered to Pivione. "I am glad I saw him after so long a time."

But Gigi did not hear, for he had fixed his eyes on the witness, and was even bending forward a little the better to learn what he had to say.

"Then she worked," continued the judge; "the girl used to work. What does she do now?"

The witness, casting a glance in the direction of Gigi, hesitated.

"You understand, your excellency, that I do not know whether I should say——" he murmured.

"But you must speak. Do you fear the truth?"

"Well, if I must—after her brother was arrested, Giulia, that is her name, worked no longer. I have seen her all dressed up, going to the theatre with a wealthy man."

"What is the matter?" Bollo asked Pivione, seeing that the latter was viciously beating on the bars of his cage.

"I understand," said the judge; "but as long as the prisoner remained, did his sister conduct herself properly?"

"The very best! She worked as a seamstress and earned considerable money. He was very fond of her and treated her with the greatest consideration. Whether she really loved or rather feared him, I do not know. They lived near the Porta Garibaldi for a long time, but later they disappeared, and I found out that they had moved outside the Porta Romana."

" Just one moment," the judge interrupted. " Prisoner, why did you move ? "

Pivione acted as if deaf. He stood with his arms hanging loosely at his sides and his head sunk deep on his chest.

" Answer, you fool ! " put in Tonino.

" It is not true ! " almost shouted Pivione. " It is impossible that my sister should go to the theatre and dress stylishly ! The witness is slandering her."

" That is not the point," added the judge. " I desire to know what manner of life you led after you left Porta Garibaldi. Why did you suddenly disappear with your sister ? "

" Because I had perceived that some young men frequently passed under her window and tried to attract her attention," Pivione answered intensely.

" Was that the only motive ? "

" Yes, sir ; I did not wish them to see her."

" Well said ! " whispered Tonino.

Then Gigi exclaimed very firmly, " I did not want them to see her. I did not want her to have a lover. I did not want to see her life ruined ! "

" All this is very strange," the judge said to the juryman at his right.

The latter made an incredulous gesture as if to say, " Bah ! "

" So that is the reason you took her away from the city."

" Yes, sir ; ten kilometres from the Porta Romana. There she would see no one. Do you understand ? "

" But how did you live ? "

" She continued to work, although she earned less, and I——"

" You kept on stealing," interrupted the judge. " Did you think that you could keep her honest, with such an example ? "

" She did not know. She believed everything I said. Besides, I intended to change my mode of life, but I met Bollo Rosso one day and forgot all my good resolutions. My sister was sick at the time, and I did not have a cent even to buy medicine. I bought some for her as soon as I got the money."

" And Giulia knew nothing of your thefts, of your assaults ? " insisted the judge.

" No."

" And you," the judge asked the witness, " do you believe that the girl knew nothing of her brother's acts ? "

"Yes, sir; I am sure that she did not suspect."

"All this is not very clear to me," said the judge.

As the day was well advanced, the hearing was adjourned.

Giulia Cavalieri, who lived in a six-room apartment on the Corso Venezia, was summoned for next day.

And thus the public saw this dramatic episode resulting from a comedy presented by the Merry Company.

On the following day all the newspapers told how Gigi, so affected by what he had heard concerning his sister, suffered frequent fits, and how, before the guard became aware of his intentions, he had twice attempted to commit suicide.

Some amateur journalist, in pursuit of notoriety, succeeded in finding Giulia's aunt, and told her the complete story. She, in defence of her nephew and his actions, related how fond he had always been of his sister, and with what tender care he regarded her. Why, he had never embraced nor kissed his sister for fear that he might mar her tender beauty! Frequently he would bring her flowers to cheer the gloomy aspect of the dark room; the blinds were always closed, winter and summer, by the express orders of her brother.

When questioned as to Giulia's life since Gigi's arrest, the old lady told, with no little pride, that her niece was betrothed to a rich gentleman. The latter, she added, had very chivalrously undertaken to maintain her, until the date set for the ceremony, in a manner befitting her beauty, if not her humble origin.

Giulia's picture, resplendent with jewellery, appeared in all the daily papers, and in the short interval of twenty-four hours she became famous. But this hardly pleased her fiancé. Such notoriety reflected on that gentleman's good name and family. Still he loved her, and the discovery of her true family connections—for she had often made covert denials of her humble origin—was to him a disagreeable surprise. But the thought of those long tresses of golden hair made prudence impossible.

The stories that were told and retold in the public resorts, all very interesting but none very truthful, acted as charms on the fickle Milanese populace. Heretofore, no ladies had taken enough interest in the doings of the Merry Company to witness that most extraordinary trial. But the announcement that Giulia was to be one of the witnesses brought them out in great numbers.

The public paid but little attention to the cross-examination of witnesses concerning the past life and deeds of Tonino and Bollo Rosso; nay, at times they gave vent to their impatience by continued stamping. But in the afternoon, when the clerk summoned Giulia to the stand, the court-room became as silent as a graveyard at midnight; the nervous movement of Gigi's chair was plainly audible.

Giulia entered. She was dressed all in black. A veil fell from her large plumed picture-hat, but it did not effectively conceal her pallor and her swollen eyes.

"You are Giulia Cavalieri, nineteen years of age, living on the Corso Venezia, Milan, and the sister of Gigi Cavalieri, who stands before you?" the judge asked as an opening question. "Be seated!"

She obeyed meekly, but before assuming her seat, attempted to move her chair so that it would face away from the jury. This evoked a hearty laugh from the audience, for it was known that the chair was nailed fast in that position. The unlooked-for mirth frightened Giulia, and she shivered from head to foot.

"Do you know of what your brother stands accused?" continued the judge.

She answered in the affirmative by a slight nod of the head.

"Your brother is accused of thefts, assaults, robberies, and complicity in murder," continued the judge in a rather condescending tone. "Is it not true?"

He stopped, but only for an instant, then suddenly began again:

"And how do you know all this? How was it made known to you? Did he confide in you all his schemes, all his fears, his innumerable attempts? Naturally, you knew all that concerned him whom you loved so well."

Giulia murmured some unintelligible objection.

"Speak louder, if you please."

"I received all my information from my aunt," answered Giulia in a steady voice, "and I read a great deal in the newspapers. Gigi never confided in me."

The judge was decidedly sceptical both by nature and by profession. He scrutinised carefully the expression on Giulia's face, but was unable to find anything indicative of trickery or falsehood.

"Is it true that there existed a great love between you two, and that Gigi was as jealous of you as a tiger of its cubs?"

Giulia turned scarlet in the twinkling of an eye, and made a gesture as if about to answer, but did not utter a word.

"He himself boasts," continued the judge, "of having always watched and spied on you—yes, of having held you a prisoner. Listening to him, one would come to the conclusion that you were his sweetheart and not his sister."

He stopped and cast a knowing glance at the juryman on his left to see whether his cynicism met with approval, but the latter shrugged his shoulders with indifference.

From the general exclamations and gestures it was plainly evident that the judge had expressed the opinion of the court, for it was highly improbable, nay impossible, that such fraternal love could exist in such an abandoned soul. And Giulia's appearance confirmed this belief. How could such a golden-haired and delicately formed girl be the sister of that lean and squalid criminal!

But the prosecutor, with all his legal experience, was meeting with little success. The girl had a vague feeling that all the questions asked were not in her brother's favour, and with this in mind, refused to answer whenever she had the faintest suspicion that she would incriminate Gigi. The judge was angered by her taciturnity.

"Yes, I loved him; I seldom saw him. No, it was my aunt that kept guard over me." Thus she answered most of the questions.

The last unfair question finally caused a rupture between the prosecutor and the lawyer for the defence. And the recorder, contrary to all traditions and time-honoured customs of the court, openly decided in favour of Gigi's lawyers and brought the examination to a close.

Bollo Rosso was so pleased by the quarrel between the lawyers that it was only by painful efforts that he kept from laughing aloud. Finally he lost control of himself—perhaps intentionally—and sent forth such a peal that the whole court turned its attention to him, to the evident displeasure of the judge. He first threatened to adjourn the session, but on second thought had Bollo led back to his cage, and again turned his attention to Giulia.

After a few moments' hesitation, he said:

"The court has no further questions to ask. You may leave the stand."

She arose and cast a furtive glance towards the prisoners' cage. She recognised her brother, who was standing with his face against the bars. She moved in his direction with the intention of offering her hand.

But he, angered by her changed appearance and delicate bearing, shouted savagely at the top of his voice :

" Go away ! Away ! Keep at a distance or I'll choke you ! " And he extended his lean arms far out through the bars, opening and clenching his hand as if strangling the victim.

This show of malignant anger brought forth from the court-room a tempest of hoots intermingled with curses and threats. In a twinkling of an eye, Gigi's brothers in crime were on their feet and striking furiously at the bars of their cages as if wishing to get out among the throng and avenge the hisses directed against their comrade in sorrow, and instantaneously the Merry Company, which hitherto, in harmony with its name, had been so playful and light-hearted, was transformed into a pack of wolves, threatening murder by every move.

" Down with justice ! " Tonino shouted.

" You pack of curs ! " hissed Bollo Rosso, scrambling up the bars of his cage like an ape.

" To the cells ! Send them to the cells ! " retorted the public

Pandemonium reigned both within and without the cages when the carbineers rushed into the cages and forced the prisoners back into their seats Then, by the judge's order, the court-room was cleared and the session adjourned. While the prisoners were being led back to their cells, Gigi's voice, crying, " I have sworn it ! I shall strangle her ! She cannot escape me ! " rose high above the confusion.

This scene had its effect on Giulia. She had seen her brother's gesture, heard the hisses of the audience, and seen the actions of Gigi's companions. Fear had rendered the poor girl well-nigh helpless, but her brother's threat to strangle her took away what little strength remained. For a moment she supported herself by grasping the corridor rail, then her strength failed her completely, her knees collapsed and she would have fallen had not a bystander caught her in time.

Giulia's fiancé, Ugo Feletti, was confined to his bed for several days.

An ecclesiastical journal published beneath Giulia's photograph a sketch representing her as standing with bowed head before the court of assizes. From a church in the distance there issued bolts of lightning, travelling directly towards her head. On these was the inscription, " Equal justice to all ! "

Ugo Feletti read eagerly the daily reports of the trial, which made slow progress on account of the bickerings between the lawyers for the defence and prosecution. As soon as he had recovered from his excitement he paid Giulia a visit.

It gave him great pain to see her, all dressed in black and with tear-stained eyes.

" Come," he said, " cheer up! you have been unfortunate in having such relatives, but they are not of your choice; the fates have imposed them on you. Rest assured I do not blame you in the least. All will end well."

" Yes," said Giulia, " but will everything indeed end well?"

" Do not have the least anxiety. If your brother is fortunate, he will escape with a sentence of some thirty years at hard labour!"

The young lady, who during the conversation had been reclining on a divan, leaped to her feet.

" And you dare tell me!" she screamed, " and you dare tell me that with a smile! How can you have the courage to speak thus when the life of my brother is at stake?"

Ugo was rather surprised by this outburst.

" Do I understand," he said calmly, " that you wish him to be set at liberty and again come to live with you?"

" And does that seem strange to you?" said Giulia with biting sarcasm.

The young man looked petulantly out of the window opening over the garden, took a few deep breaths of the perfumed air and then turned to Giulia.

" Let us reason; let us reason without anger," he said. " Did he not threaten to kill you? And if reports do him justice, he is capable of carrying out the threat. Is it not possible that he will kill both of us?"

Giulia merely shrugged her shoulders and resumed her place on the divan. Then an expression of cold indifference spread over her face, the expression that the lover feared more than Gigi's dagger. Therefore, in an attempt to pacify Giulia, he continued in a more respectful and humble strain.

" You cannot deny that he is of a fiery and rash temperament. Of course, it is not his fault, but rather that of the times—nay, any other man placed in his circumstances might have done worse."

" I beg of you not to speak of family affairs," interrupted the girl.

It was in this fashion that she often silenced her friend, but for this once she did not succeed.

" God forbid ! " answered Ugo. " I have the greatest respect for your family. Nevertheless, I would rather not see your brother return home immediately. It is a fancy of mine ; perhaps a mistaken one, but still worthy of consideration."

" Yes, altogether so," said Giulia, somewhat angrily. " Do you realise your duty towards me ? You ought to exert every possible means to secure the freedom of my brother ! You ought to approach the lawyers, the jury, even the judge, and make them all feel that there is some rich and powerful man interested in my poor brother's fate. That is your duty, and if you really love me, you will do it ! "

Ugo did not seem pleased at this suggestion, and turned as though intending to go, then glanced at Giulia, and the question was decided. Seizing both her hands in his, he said, passionately :

" You may consider the thing as done ! I will set myself at work immediately. Surely it is a simple matter, a few threats on one hand and a little flattery on the other, and all will be favourable."

" Quite right," said the girl, not understanding the irony of his words. " Perhaps we can save him. I do not believe what the papers say, nor do I believe that my brother was capable of committing the crimes for which he is being tried. It is impossible that my brother should be a thief."

" I shall go now and get to work at once. I shall come to dine with you this evening and perhaps bring some welcome news."

She smiled sweetly and extended her hand. She was as happy as if her brother were already at liberty. Even thoughts of what sort of position Ugo could secure for Gigi were flitting through her mind.

" You are very kind ! " said she to Ugo, as they reached the door. " God be with you until this evening. I shall expect you."

Poor Giulia ! Daily she became more confident in her belief that her brother would be liberated. Nay, she was so positive of this that she decided to be present on the last day of the trial and see him exonerated.

To keep her in good spirits, her fiancé had often invited her to have personal interviews with the lawyers, judge, and jury. And, sad to relate, by lavish use of money, some members of the jury had been won over, but the general opinion was that the members of the Merry

Company would all be condemned, and the penalty would be especially heavy for Gigi, Bollo Rosso, and Stringhella, the accomplices in the murder of Matirotti.

Giulia had great difficulty in gaining entrance to the last session of the trial, for an unruly mob thronged the court-room. She was dressed in black, as usual, and her sole companion was a maid.

A lawyer for the prosecution was speaking when Giulia entered, but as she thought the attorneys on both sides were equally disposed in her favour, she turned an attentive ear to his speech. It was a very short time before she caught the import of his animated words. He was denouncing Gigi's mode of life in a furious tirade.

The five thieves sat quiet and sullen behind the bars, their eyes following the gestures of the prosecutor. Gigi alone, at intervals, forced an ironical smile to his lips ; but it was a vain effort to appear unconcerned.

Giulia turned to a bystander, and nodding in the direction of the lawyer, asked in a whisper :

" Who is he ? "

The tall, lean, and emaciated man looked at her gallantly, but did not utter a word. Giulia did not dare to repeat the question, for suddenly she became aware that the man beside her resembled those in the prisoners' cage, in carriage, dress, and facial expression. She turned to her left, and there, too, her gaze fell upon scraggy and hardened faces. Instinctively she looked behind her, and noticed that the majority of the men were meanly dressed. They chewed tobacco, expectorated on the floor, and watched the proceedings with such ease that they must have been accustomed to similar scenes. Disgusted and frightened by her surroundings, Giulia felt a strong desire to leave the room.

" I think we had better go," she whispered to her maid. In obedience to her lady's wish, the latter had already started toward the door when a renewed outburst of oratory from the prosecutor held Giulia rooted to the spot.

The lawyer, flushed and scowling and with his arm outstretched directly toward the prisoners, was saying :

" Thus, your defence, your sacrilegious falsehoods, have fallen and been destroyed like chaff before the clear light of truth ! Yes, you, Pietro Carenzio, and you, Carlo Pumelli, and you, Gigi Cavalieri, you robbed and murdered the good old Matirotti ! Why ? Because he was too old to defend his wealth, accumulated by years of saving, and which he was using for the relief of the poor. And while you, Gigi Cavalieri, were collecting the plunder, your vile companions were forever extinguishing the precious breath of this life! And the deed, O members of the jury, was not a result of circumstances, but the outcropping of the wicked brutality that lies within those hearts! And you, Gigi Cavalieri, having finished your search for gold, administered the death-wound to the innocent victim!"

"Damnation!" murmured the lean individual near Giulia, moving his quid of tobacco from one cheek to the other. "He is giving it to them straight from the shoulder!"

This harangue was followed by others equally strong and damaging to the prisoners' case. Poor Giulia, terrified by the turn that affairs were taking and frightened by the looks and gestures of these about her, again felt the weakness that had made her faint on that former day. Hope for her brother, however, buoyed her spirits.

At last the judge instructed the jury and the session was temporarily suspended. Various were the opinions of the spectators as to what the verdict of the jury would be. Fear had paralysed Giulia to the extent of rendering her incapable of thought.

A consumptive-looking young man said to her in a hollow voice:

"You have seen little that is worth while. There is nothing interesting. You ought to be present when divorce cases are tried. Then the court-room is better than a theatre. Now there is nothing to be seen but those poor fools behind the bars, who let themselves be caught!" He stopped and cast a disdainful glance in the direction of the cages.

As it was growing dark a few jets of gas were lighted, and they threw a dismal light over the gloomy scene. Soon, however, the jury re-entered amid solemn silence and the foreman read the verdict to the judge.

Giulia was totally ignorant of what was passing, but the consumptive young man came to her assistance.

"What are they going to do now?" she asked.

"Now?" queried the youth, who had witnessed many such cases. "The judge will now fix the penalty. It will only be a matter of a few minutes and then we shall be free to go."

Only a few moments had elapsed before the judge entered and assumed his place. Then he read the sentence.

"Gigi Cavalieri, better known as Pivione, Pietro Carenzio, *alias*

Bollo Rosso, and Carlo Pumelli, *alias* Stringhella, are condemned for life ! "

" Damnation ! " murmured the tall and lean individual near Giulia.

" What does all that mean ? " she asked him in a tone of suppressed excitement. He did not answer.

" Antonio Stucci and Luigi Mordoni are condemned to serve thirty-two years at hard labour."

" What does all that mean ? " again asked Giulia, this time turning in the direction of the consumptive youth.

" What does it mean ? " answered he. " Merely that your brother was given the maximum penalty and must serve for life ! "

" But when will they be set free ? " persisted Giulia, becoming very pale.

" For life ! For life ! " reiterated the young man. " They will never get out ! "

She stood as if rooted to the spot, and fixedly watched the now empty cage. Giulia had not understood in time to bid her brother good-bye, nor even to give him a parting glance. He had gone with the others, never to return.

" Come, let us go," begged the frightened maid.

Giulia left the court-room and descended the stairs mechanically. When she had reached the door to the street, she saw Ugo's private carriage and her fiancé himself beckoning to her.

Her maid assisted her into the vehicle and as soon as it had started, Ugo embraced her and said tenderly :

" I know all. It is an unfortunate calamity."

" I will never see him ! I will never see him again ! " she interrupted, crying bitterly.

" Yes, an unfortunate calamity," repeated the banker.

Giulia's heartrending sighs affected him painfully and he felt tears rising to his eyes. He could restrain himself no longer. Ugo also was now bewailing Gigi's fate, although he knew in his innermost soul that his grief was really joy. But the moans issuing from the heart of the one he loved so dearly caused him sincere sorrow.

" For ever, for ever ! " she moaned. " And I did not even bid him adieu for the last time ! Oh, what could the poor boy have done ? "

Even the maid, although unacquainted with the causes of her lady's grief, was moved to tears.

"Ah, what bad company will do!" exclaimed Ugo, drying his tears. But he dared say nothing more, for it was with great difficulty that he kept from laughing.

"Are you sure that nothing can be done for him?" continued Giulia.

He did not answer. He was no longer willing to raise her hopes by falsehoods. But to reassure her of his undying affections, he pressed her head closer to his breast with one hand and stroked her hair gently with the other.

When the carriage had halted before her door and all three had alighted, she said to Ugo:

"I was happier then!"

"Then? When?" asked the banker as he escorted her to the door.

"Then, when I lived with my aunt, in that hut outside the Porta Romana. Yes, I was poor, but I worked and knew nothing of the world's wickedness. Then Gigi used to bring me flowers."

"But he used to steal," added Ugo.

"I knew nothing of that. I was happy, yes, truly happy."